henry's
daughter

JOY DETTMAN

PAN
Pan Macmillan Australia

For my support team, Ross and Rae, computer wizards,
and for Karli, Shani and Donna, my early readers
and trusted critics.

First published 2003 in Macmillan by Pan Macmillan Australia Pty Limited
This Pan edition published 2004 by Pan Macmillan Australia Pty Limited
St Martins Tower, 31 Market Street, Sydney

National Library of Australia
cataloguing-in-publication data:

Dettman, Joy.
Henry's daughter.

0 330 364 5 7 X.

1. Brothers and sisters – Fiction. 2. Family – Fiction. I. Title.

A823.3

Typeset in Times by Midland Typesetters
Printed in Australia by McPherson's Printing Group

Papers used by Pan Macmillan Australia Pty Ltd are natural, recyclable products
made from wood grown in sustainable forests. The manufacturing processes
conform to the environmental regulations of the country of origin.

chain of events

It's hard to know how some bad ideas get started. This one sort of bubbled and boiled around in Lori's brain this morning until it seemed sensible. It wasn't sensible. It's not even twelve o'clock yet and she's already eaten her Vegemite sandwich and all she's got left is a muesli bar and an apple and she's wishing she was at school instead of wandering around looking at footpaths.

It's all Greg and Vinnie's fault. They started it. They were half killing each other instead of going to bed that night last week, and Mavis, who is Lori's mother, got herself all riled up trying to make them stop, then the next thing you know she's yelling, 'Someone grab me a clean towel. Quick!'

She's pretty cool about having babies, due to oodles of practice; there is none of this pushing and sweating and blowing that you see on television. Anyway, Matthew Charles sort of slipped out about ten seconds later, even though he wasn't due to slip out until March. He was supposed to be a girl too, but he turned out another boy. Mavis wasn't too happy about that.

Lori wasn't happy that he came in February, because it's a pure rotten month to get born in, it's too close to Christmas when everyone is still sick of buying presents. She's already had eleven Februaries to learn about that, and now she has to share her month with Matthew Charles.

But, even if she doesn't get good presents, Henry, Lori's father, never, ever forgets her birthday.

He never forgets anything, like paying bills, like writing to the twins every single month – you'd think it was written on the calendar with invisible ink. That first Sunday of every month, out comes Henry's writing pad, out comes his envelope. The last one he wrote, he was putting a stamp on when Mavis said, 'Did you tell them they've got a new brother?'

Henry looked up, sort of startled, then he shook his head, so Mavis snatched the letter and added her own bit to the bottom, like, 'tell your Aunty Eva that if she'd like to extend her happy family, we have another one up for auction. Only one week old, full new warranty, reserve price fifty thousand'. The words all squeezed in before Henry's 'Love from your Dad'.

Henry wouldn't post it, of course, so Mavis gave Greg a whole five dollars and he posted it. Which isn't fair. He's spoilt rotten. He's always getting money.

Anyway, Matthew Charles never stopped bawling and Greg and Vinnie never stopped fighting, and Martin, who is nineteen and the oldest brother, said at the dinner table last night that he'd had enough of living in a madhouse and that he was moving in with Karen, his girlfriend. Mavis told him he was not moving in with Karen, his girl-friend, because he was too bloody young. They were having one of their blazing rows that can go on all night when Greg and Vinnie started killing each other again, in the bedroom, and one of them broke the top window.

So that was Thursday night and today is Friday, Lori's eleventh birthday.

And not Henry, not one single solitary person, said happy birthday when she got out of bed this morning. And no one, not even Henry, gave her one single solitary present.

So Lori got this mad idea to give herself a birthday present, wag school and spend the entire day searching the streets for dropped money and maybe find enough to buy a bike from the op shop.

She lives in Willama. It used to be a farmers' town with a butter factory and a cannery, sawmills everywhere and a clothing factory

– heaps of places where people could work. These days most people work in shops and motels, due to Willama has turned into a tourist town. In summer the main street is stuffed full of tourists who have heaps of money to waste. Sometimes they drop a bit. One day Lori found five dollars.

Not today, though. It's been a long morning of walking around staring at footpaths and all she's found so far is five cents. She's thinking bigger now. She's at the ATM, in front of the Commonwealth Bank where Henry gets Mavis's money – which the government gives her because of all her kids – and she's watching the tourists hit a few buttons and make the notes roll out. Her fingers are crossed and she's hoping that someone might drop a fifty-dollar note and not notice they dropped it, when Nelly, her neighbour from over the road, grabs her arm.

'You're wagging it, Smithy,' she says. 'I'll tell your father on you.'

'It's my birthday, Nelly, and everyone forgot it.' Lori has known Nelly forever and she knows she probably won't dob, due to she's cool – not young-cool, pretty-cool; she's actually old and skinny and grey and she reminds you of one of those cats that look as if they've been hit in the face with a working boot that has left its tread marks behind. She hasn't got a husband, never had one and never wanted one, she says, which might be sour grapes but it mightn't be.

Her house, which is opposite Henry's vacant block, is always getting a coat of paint, and her garden has always got flowers. She spends her life up ladders with a paintbrush or digging in her garden, hiding under her big hat so she can be as cheeky as she likes to everybody and no one can see her face. Like, most of the neighbours call Henry Mr Smyth-Owen, which is probably because he's not a really neighbourly sort of man, but Nelly calls him, and all of his kids, Smithy. Also, she can swear as good as the high school kids if something riles her up. Lori loves Nelly. She's her best friend.

Mavis can't stand her and Nelly can't stand Mavis either. They are from two different planets, Nelly all wrinkled up like a deflated balloon and Mavis like one of those giant balloons, blown up so tight that if you tried to make a wrinkle in it, it would burst.

'Your pants are falling off you,' Nelly says. 'It's time you learned to sew and started doing a few things for yourself, Smithy.'

'They were Mick's. His brace wears out that leg.' Lori looks at her jeans. The seam is flapping from knee to ankle. 'They're air-conditioned, Nelly.'

'Bring them over after school and you can run them up on the machine,' Nelly says. She's always doing stuff for Henry, like sewing up splits in pants, and she's always trying to make Lori learn to do girl stuff, like use the machine or learn to knit. Nelly makes all her own dresses and knits her own cardigans. She even makes Mavis's tent dresses. She does it for Henry. He gives her eggs every week, and vegetables, and they have long talks at the fence. It's a pity Henry didn't marry Nelly, then they both could have grown their flowers and lived happily ever after, because except for her bad language and Henry's posh pommy voice, they are like the same, the same age, fifty-seven, and they've probably got a matching amount of wrinkles.

Nelly walks two steps into the bank, sees the queue and walks out again. She's got no patience with banks. Lori is poking at the buttons of the ATM and nothing is happening.

'You like that thing,' Nelly says.

'They press a few buttons then wait for the money to come out. Can you do it?'

Nelly takes a card from her purse, and a slip of paper. 'Looks like I'll have to do it today. Every man and his dog is in Willama and the bank has got two bloody tellers open – and if they were moving any slower they'd be flyblown.' She's looking through the door, then back to the machine, she's tapping her foot, looking in her purse as if there might be some money hiding in there. There isn't, so she fronts up to the machine as if it's one of Spud Murphy's dogs, snarling and dragging his chain, and she offers it her plastic card, then changes her mind, digs in her purse again. 'Last time

I tried to use the bloody thing it swallowed my card, so make yourself useful, Smithy. Read those numbers for me.' She hands Lori a slip of paper.

'Is that, like, your secret code number?'

'Yeah. Now read it slow when I tell you or the mongrel will pinch my card again,' Nelly says, changing her glasses for reading glasses.

Lori reads the numbers while Nelly prods them in. At first it won't give her any money, just starts beeping like it's calling for the cops, then it spits out her card, but on the second try, two twenty-dollar notes roll out.

'How come it knows how to give you the right money?'

'Computers.' She says it like it's a dirty word. 'The whole world is run by their bloody computers, Smithy.' Nelly pokes the money, her card and pin number in her purse and swaps over her glasses. 'Come on, and I'll buy you an ice-cream for your birthday.'

'You don't have to. I didn't tell you it was my birthday so you'd – '

'I didn't ask if I had to, Smithy.'

Lori follows her neighbour into a restaurant-cum-takeaway, right in the centre of town. The lady behind the counter knows her, and knows she should be at school. Everybody knows her. When you grow up in a town and your mother is sort of notorious for obesity and having kids, then you get born notorious – which isn't fair. Rotten Wendy Johnson from school has got a gorgeous mother who wears tight jeans and dangly earrings and works at the school canteen and gives Wendy a lunch order every single day. Also, Wendy got a new bike for Christmas.

'Chin up, Smithy. Spit in the eye of the world and tell it you're as good as the next one,' Nelly says, handing her a double-header cone of vanilla and chocolate.

'Ta. You're cool, Nelly, but you didn't have to buy me a big one.'

'Think big and you'll grow big.' Nelly mustn't have learned about thinking big until she finished growing, because she sure didn't grow big. Lori is almost as tall as her, and she's not super tall for eleven.

'Have a lick.' She offers the ice-cream. Nelly shakes her head. 'Thanks heaps. So, where are we going now?'

'I'm going shopping, and you're going to school. It'll be lunchtime. They won't have noticed you're missing.'

'Yes they will, and anyway, Kelly Waters and her gang said they'd get me after school today. That's half why I'm wagging it.'

'Tell your teacher on the little buggers.'

'Tell her! I told you before about her! That teacher hates my guts, Nelly. Anyway, it's not cool to dob on them.'

'What did you do to them?'

'Nothing . . . much.' Lori looks away, stares at a dark-skinned woman. She's got a brand-new baby and it's bawling. This one gets picked up and patted on the back. Matthew Charles just keeps bawling until someone sticks a dummy in his mouth. 'I wonder if she got stolen,' Lori whispers.

'Who?' Nelly doesn't know how to whisper.

'That lady with the baby. You know. You know about how all the Aborigine babies got stolen by the white people in the old days. Did your family steal any?'

'They had enough trouble feeding their own. I reckon I might have grown a bit bigger if some bugger had stolen me and fed me on something other than bread and dripping and stewed quinces. Now, that's enough talk out of you. You get yourself back to school or I'll be telling your father tonight.'

'I'm going.' Lori walks off in the right direction, licking ice-cream and not allowing one drip to escape, but she keeps checking over her shoulder until Nelly disappears into a shop, then she turns and wanders back the way she came.

The main street is long and most of the buildings are pretty old, but if you keep walking down past the shops and a few posh houses, you get to the really old part of town, which is the reason why all the tourists come here, so it's an excellent place to find dropped

6

money, due to tourists queue up here and pay heaps just to walk through old houses and jails and blacksmiths' shops full of old junk.

Most weekends and holidays the caravan parks and motels are full of tourists and at Christmas time Henry says the main street gets like Bourke Street, Melbourne. Lori doesn't know Bourke Street, but she knows Spencer Street Station from when Mavis and Henry took her and Mick and Jamesy to Melbourne one day so they could bring the twins back home, but couldn't get them. Since that day, when Henry says the town is like Bourke Street, Lori changes the picture to Spencer Street Station, which is what her rotten school-teacher says, like if you write that something is the same as something else, then it has to be a thing everybody knows, or it's wasting words. Such as, when Wendy Johnson says that Mavis is a hump-back whale, well, everyone knows what a humpback whale looks like, but if Kelly Waters calls Mavis a fat white gubba, no one, except the Aborigines, have got a clue what a *gubba* looks like.

The old coach and horses are working today. They are beautiful horses but they have a boring life, just clip-clop down to the bridge, turn around and clip-clop back and all the tourists get so excited to be riding in a coach and seeing a few old buildings, a few grey trees and a lot of dirty river that Lori can see any old day of the week. She leans against a wall, licking all the sweetness from her fingers when the last of the cone is gone and watching the tourists queue so they can get the next ride when the coach comes back.

And she sees it. A dollar coin lying in the dirt as if no one wants it. She pounces, snatches it as a tall tourist lady, dressed up like a fashion model advertising anorexia, is about to step back on it. She's with two boys and a rangy old dame who looks more like a guy except she's got boobs. Anyway, they give Lori a look they'd give a used condom, then the old grey one snarls something that shows all of her giant yellow teeth while the younger one sucks her mouth into a shrivelled tut-tut. She steps away, lets the old dame and two boys keep her place in the queue.

Lori is staring at those two tourist boys – twin boys. She's got the dollar gripped in her hand but she's standing there, mouth open, staring.

It's them! What the hell are they doing up here?

ifs and effs and stuff

She's not game to go home. She's got to tell Mavis and Henry who she saw down at the tourist centre but she can't tell them because she shouldn't have been where she was when she saw who she saw, so she's hiding down at the river in her yowie nest, watching speedboats and the people at the caravan park on the opposite bank.

They've got a whole state forest behind them but they're all crowded in close together, like they've lived in the city for so long that they're plain scared of being free. If she had a caravan she wouldn't just park it some place and stop; she'd take it all the way to Western Australia and she'd take Henry with her, and when she got there, she'd put her caravan on a boat and take him home to his England. If she was big enough to drive a car and if she had a million dollars in the bank.

If. That word shouldn't have ever got invented. *If* I hadn't wagged school then I wouldn't have seen them. *If* someone had remembered my birthday then I wouldn't have wagged school. *If* Matty had come out when he was supposed to come out, he would have got born in March and someone would have remembered my birthday. *If. If. If. If If.* It probably wasn't invented, probably someone just started saying 'eff' one day because they weren't game to say the proper F-word or they'd get thumped, so 'eff' just got turned into 'if'.

She's starving hungry. She ate her sandwich too early, ate her wormy apple from Bert Matthews's tree, ate her muesli bar and she wants to go home and have dinner. But if she goes now she'll cop it for coming home late, so it's better if she goes home really late, then Mavis won't have so much time to get stuck into her.

Her hands cupping her mouth, she lets loose a yodelling scream and on the opposite side of the river faces turn. No one can see her. Her yowie nest is behind a mass of exposed gum tree roots. It's a good place to hide. Again her war cry goes out across the water and this time it really sounds like a huge, hairy yowie howl.

The river alters sounds. Even the birds sound different down here. She just loves this place, loves this time of day when the dark is getting ready to come down and all the birds are niggly because they want the best branch to roost on, like Greg and Vinnie fighting over who gets to sleep in the top bunk.

By the clock, it's way past the birds' bedtime, but the sun won't leave Australia's sky tonight and go off to Henry's England; it's stuck up there, melted into the blue like a blob of orange bubble gum stuck on the sole of her school shoe.

She's not wearing her shoes now. They are in her school bag. Bare feet are free. Bare feet run faster, climb trees, write words in the dust, then rub them out again. She writes the F word in the dust then adds 'birthday'. Writes 'Lorraine's' up the top so it reads, 'Eff Lorraine's birthday'.

Lorraine. It's a horrible old-fashioned name and she hates it. Who else in the whole world is called Lorraine? No one else at school is, or even in the newspapers – except one television lady. She likes Smithy better than Lorraine, likes Lori best of all, because it sounds like a boy's name. She looks like a boy; most people think she is a boy.

The dust is thick and grey down here. Everything is a bit grey, trees, river, clay, due to Australia is worn out. That's what Henry says. The tall clay banks of the river are hard as rock and interwoven with tree roots from, like, a million years ago. They've probably got dinosaur bones mixed up in those roots because the river banks sure look old enough. Nothing much will grow in them, except gum trees, but their leaves are grey too. The river is pure filthy grey, but that doesn't stop tourists coming here and messing it up even more with their speedboats. Everyone in town says that those boats are messing up the river but no one stops them doing it.

It's not safe for swimming, Henry says. He's wrong about that one; this spot is especially good for swimming, because the water sort of bends around and once you climb down the clay banks, there's no more dust, just clean sand. Lori's brothers have always swum at this bend. It's close to home – just over the road, really, and down a clay track that wanders through the bush for a while. Lori isn't allowed to come here by herself, but she comes anyway, all the time. It's her favourite place for thinking and talking to the trees, like Henry talks to his flowers.

He's not the same as other people's fathers, he knows pretty much everything. Actually, he probably does know everything, which is because he's read nearly every book in the Willama library and probably in the Melbourne library as well, and even all the books in the London library, which made his shoulders hunch over through sitting and turning the pages. He's old enough to be a grandfather, and he's a pom – or he was until Aunty Eva went over there and brought him back to Australia like a trophy. Mavis says that. She's only thirty-seven, and Aunty Eva is her sister, and they hate each other like rat poison because Mavis pinched Eva's husband so Eva pinched Mavis's twins.

Across the river three tourist kids are paddling a canoe. Lori lets loose a howling yowie yodel, and this time she backs it up with a rain of clods, spraying them over the water, though she can't make them go right across to the other side; the river is wide here. The kids start looking for her, then when they can't find her, they row their canoe back to the bank.

Willama has got plenty of water. That's why the town was first built, and that's why it grew. Towns don't grow big unless they've got plenty of water and this river has so much that it has to pour some out into a little creek just east of town, then when that little creek has had enough of wandering around the farms behind Willama West and getting itself extra filthy, it finds its way back to the mother river ten kilometres south of the town. Lori has been out to that junction where you can see two different sorts of water moving along, trying hard to stay separate. It's interesting the way those waters pure refuse to join into one, which is like Eva and Mavis, when you come to think of it.

Lori tosses a few more clods but she can't scare those tourists into packing up and going home, so she may as well go home and get it over and done with. Except . . . except that this is the beautiful time in the bush when other colours start teasing the grey. She just loves this time, because way up at the top of the trees the sun is already touching them, and it's got them glowing, like there is red fire in their leaves. Even the water doesn't look so dirty now, and across the water there are little tourist fires starting up for barbecues and little gas camping lights that look magic amongst the trees. She crawls out of her hide and jumps down to the sand, squinting now to see the tourists.

There is a movement in the patch of water reeds. She steps back, looks at her bare legs and feet. It could be a snake, a black snake, or a tiger snake, which is the worst kind. They love the river and those reed beds; she often sees snakes down here, or sees their tracks in the dust – funny ripply, wriggly lines, like they're trying to write snake messages to their friends.

She hates snakes. Henry doesn't. 'Leave them alone and they'll leave you alone,' he says. He's into leaving things alone, probably because he wants the world to leave him alone. Like even ants and redback spiders, Henry won't kill. They are all God's creatures – so he says.

The sun is hanging on tight to those tree tops tonight; it just hates leaving the peace and freedom of this place. Lori understands exactly how that sun feels, but sooner or later it's going to go and she's got to go too.

She lives in Willama East, not far from the old cannery, which is not far from the railway line, or the bridge, not too far from the main street or anywhere else really. Willama isn't like a huge city where you have to catch buses and trams and things. She can walk or run anywhere she wants to go, and she has to run or walk everywhere because she hasn't got a bike. She thought she might get a bike for Christmas – thought she might get one for her birthday.

'*Eff* Lorraine's birthday,' she says and she runs for home up the darkening track, pretending she's Cathy Freeman and she's going to win the Olympic Games.

The railway line cuts Willama in half. The East got started on the wrong side of the tracks so it never had a chance to grow proud, Henry says. Tin rooftops get hotter in the East, so hot they almost sizzle some days. Most of the East houses have got tin roofs because most of the houses are old. Most of the dogs are old, and mean too, like Spud Murphy's dogs that live over the road, right next door to Nelly's place; they are tied up, all day, every day, and they bark, all day, every day, like they want to get off their chains and eat the whole world alive.

And who'd blame them? Lori wouldn't – not if they ate Spud Murphy first. He's a lazy bugger who made his wife do all the hard work, like mow the lawns and take out the green bins, because he had a bad heart, but she died and he didn't. Now he hasn't got any wife to torment so he torments his dogs. That's what Mavis says.

Henry won't let Mavis get another dog, due to his fence is falling down and he says a new dog will just wander off and get run over like the last two got run over. He used to close the old gate and prop up the fence a bit, but the pickets are mostly rotten and falling over so the gate just stays open now.

Henry's house got built about a hundred years ago and it was probably an almost posh house back then with its tall roof and its lacy wooden bits between the tops of fancy verandah posts. It had a lattice along the side of the west verandah once too, but the lattice is mostly falling over, like the fence, and the house sort of stands lonely at the end of Dawson Street, sort of ashamed of itself. The verandah boards are pretty much worn out and some of the windows won't open, the guttering is rusted and the downpipes are mainly down, so when it rains the verandah makes waterfalls all the way around. Poor old house, it looks as if it wants to hide in the bush too, but it just can't get across that road.

On the other side of the house is Henry's vacant block where he's got his chook-pen and his potting shed. That block is worth good money these days and Henry should sell it, Mavis says, and bugger his chooks and his flowers.

When he bought the house, Martin was about seven, which was twelve and a bit years ago. Martin can remember heaps of things, like how Henry and Mavis were going to fix up the roof and paint it, get a new fence to keep the kids and the dog off the street, sell the vacant block and play hell with a broomstick, Martin says. Henry got around to buying a giant bucket of blue paint and putting it in the outside laundry – and it's still in there. He got around to paying a man to put in a new bathroom and a new stove and hot water system, he got around to fixing up the roof by putting bricks on the loose bits of tin, and that's about all he got around to, because of Mick getting himself born with a crippled leg that looks like it's made out of rubber. Mick is number five brother.

Lori has got a pile of brothers – eleven, if you count the twins, who she never counts because they went to live with Aunty Eva when they were two, due to germs and stuff and a long story. Until they were five, Mavis tried all the time to get them back, but she can't do much about anything nowadays. She can't even get in a car, can't even have her babies at the hospital. She'd break the hospital bed.

It's stupid how Henry keeps letting her have more babies, because every one she has makes her bigger and makes him smaller. It's true. Every time that milky new-baby smell comes into the house, Mavis needs bigger tent dresses and Henry's face grows older, his hair goes greyer, he shrinks shorter and his shoulders stoop a bit more.

He wasn't ever a big man, but he's got a really huge secret. Lori knows what it is too, but she's not allowed to tell because Henry said so and Martin said he'd murder her if she told. And what's the use of having a secret if you can't tell anyone? The kids at school are always whispering secrets, and Henry's isn't a bad one. It's just about . . . well, it's partly about him being Australian but growing up in England and going to a posh school so he grew up talking with a plum in his mouth, like Prince Charles, which sounds a bit funny in Willama – unless you've got a posh house and about a million dollars in the bank. Henry hasn't got anything in the bank.

He would have stayed in England if Aunty Eva hadn't got there just after Henry's mother died. He was a bit old even then and so was she, so he ended up buying her an engagement ring. It was when he was getting a passport so he could come to Australia and have a big wedding that he found out he was actually born in Australia.

All the way across the oceans, it felt like he was being drawn back to his roots, Henry says. Except adoptions were secret things in those days, so when he got to Melbourne there weren't any roots for him to find. He found a heap of trouble instead. He found Aunty Alice living in her bungalow out the back of Eva's place. And he found Mavis. After a bit, Martin accidentally got started, so Mavis and Henry ran off together. They nearly ran off to England, but Mavis got pregnant again and had Donny, then after the first five brothers, they stopped moving around Australia and ended up in Willama.

About two years ago, Henry got an office job at an estate agent's so he's finally got superannuation and he says that when he's sixty-five and retires he's going to go for a trip and see his homeland one last time, see the age and the green of it, feel the rain of it, see the daffodils and the trees and the softness of a land not ruled by the sun. That's what he says, and usually at Christmas time. He always gets the wound-up talks at Christmas and no one can shut him up.

He's got his flowers from England, or from some place that's not Australia, begonias and orchids and really weird things, and he's got his songs from England. Nearly every night he sings to his flowers, sings songs no one has ever heard of, like 'I'll Take You Home Again, Kathleen', and 'My Precious Son', and 'Autumn Leaves'. Hundreds of old songs he knows, which have words that tell stories about people dying, and he knows all the words too. He just wanders, waters, fertilises and sings, and his voice sounds truly excellent, and too big to come out of such a skinny, grey little man. His voice is like the only strong part of him that is left.

He's in the potting shed now, singing his lungs out. Lori is a bit scared to go in there tonight. She's sort of creeping in slow, while his back is turned, sort of hiding behind that first shelf of pots then sneaking along to the next. He knows she's there. His head turns, and he smiles his little dry-mouth smile then he licks his lips and sings on.

If he knew she'd wagged it, he wouldn't be smiling. If he knew who was in Willama tonight he wouldn't be smiling either. And if Mavis knew, then God help him.

He doesn't ask why she missed dinner. He probably didn't notice she missed dinner, which means that Donny didn't bring a birthday cake home from the supermarket. He doesn't say happy birthday, doesn't say anything. If she didn't love him so much, she'd almost hate him a bit for that.

He's singing 'Danny Boy' and it's making her feel stuff she doesn't understand. His voice is as good as those three tenors who get paid millions of dollars to sing at the Opera House, it just hits some special quiver place in her brain that makes shivers of pure ecstasy in her head. He probably would be famous and make heaps of money if he didn't look so old and if he didn't only sing in the shed when he watered his flowers.

If.

'You should get a job singing on the television, Henry,' Lori says when the song is done. He smiles, sort of shy, which looks funny when the face smiling shy is all wrinkled up. The hose moves on to another pot and he finds a new rhythm as Lori steps nearer.

The shed smells of green things and wet wood and earth. Lori loves that smell, breathes it in deep. It's a big shed, long and narrow, built by the last owner out of corrugated iron. Before Lori was born Henry paid a man to take the iron off that shed, except the part that's against Bert Matthews's fence, then he took the roof off and put on a new one of fibreglass and he made the walls of fibreglass and shade cloth so it's like a glasshouse. But not glass.

The light is fading and Henry, in his faded shirt and rusty old working trousers, is blending into the shadows now so you can barely see him. You can sure hear him. Probably all the neighbours are out watering their gardens so they can get a free concert.

'Or why don't you join the music group, like old Clarrie's daughter asked you to, Henry?'

For a moment his lips try to find an answer, then he shrugs, turns his face to a flower, cups it in his hands and again his voice flows free and strong. 'I'll take you home again, Kathleen.'

The sound is even better when you are down the bottom of the shed with the empty pots and junk from the last owner, because it gets trapped, like it's got no place to get out. Lori walks by him and perches on an upturned pot, listening and looking at an old oval picture frame that's been here forever. It gets her thinking of other photographs, like the ones of Henry's English parents. Their names were Daniel and Kathleen Smyth-Owen. He sings all of his songs to them – there is one called 'Mumma' and one called 'Oh, My Papa'. That one has got such beautiful words they make Lori's heart cry. If she could sing like Henry, she would sing 'Oh, My Papa' to him and maybe make him . . . make him be less grey, less small, less sad.

As *if*. She can't sing. She's dumb – she's dumber than dumb. She can't even learn her spelling for school, can't even remember how to spell disappointed.

There is no more light to see the flowers so there is no more singing. Henry rolls up the hose, hangs it on a hook, then together they walk from the shed.

Hum of voices from that house. Baby crying in that house. Slam, bang, whiz of television in that house. The noise cowers Henry. He stops midway across the vacant block and looks towards the dying sunset. England is sort of west, sort of northwest; he's probably wanting to be there and not standing on a vacant block with Lori.

'There's a mozzie eating you,' she says, slapping at his arm, and maybe there was a mosquito and maybe there wasn't, but that slap reclaims his attention. He pats her head, smiles a small smile but doesn't look at her, doesn't say happy birthday.

That western sky is like another land tonight, like all the colour has faded now except for this golden highway that is leading away over the cloud-mountain horizon.

'There is more than this, little lost Lorraine,' he says.

'What more, Henry?' She draws her eyes away from the west, squints to see his face.

'I don't quite know. You'll have to find it for me, little one.'

He looks older, more sad tonight with wanting more, and she understands that sad, wanting feeling. She wants more, wants a bike, wants a lot of things.

'That's like playing Pin the Tail on the Donkey, Henry,' she says. 'I mean, if I don't know what you want me to find for you then it's like . . . like I'll be searching in a blindfold, like feeling for the right place with my hands, but even if I find the right place, I won't know that I've found it.' She slaps at his hand. It's too dark now to see if there is a mosquito there or not, but it's reason enough to touch him.

He pats her head and for a moment his long chin lifts, just a little bit.

'Henry! Henry! You said you were going to cut the kids' hair tonight. They're tripping over it,' Mavis yells from the back verandah, and Henry sighs, shrugs, his chin and shoulders low as his feet move him along the track they have worn through the brittle grass. His eyes, Lori's eyes, watch those traitor feet. They are walking him to Mavis.

18

Lori stands on alone listening to the night sounds, and to the old house tut-tutting and sighing, like the poor old roof is taking a breather after a hard day's work, grateful for the shade of night and soaking it up, gaining strength for tomorrow. It's a tall roof with silly little gables – a roof on a roof. It looks good now the light has gone. It looks taller, stronger, like it might stand up for another day.

'Eleven. I'm eleven.'

It's a weird feeling, being eleven, a bit like this time of day, sort of balancing on the edge of the dark time before tomorrow. Or . . . or like when she walks along the top of old Mrs Roddie's brick fence, which is next door to Bert Matthews's place. That fence is too narrow to walk on, but Lori walks it anyway, every day, on her way to school. There's a concrete footpath one side and prickly rose bushes on the other, so she has to keep moving fast to keep her balance. Sometimes she falls off before she gets to the end.

A long shuddering sigh shakes her, and it almost sounds like Henry's sigh.

Yesterday, when she was ten, the world was bigger. Tonight even the horizon looks as if it's moved closer, like there's not so much space between her and what is out there waiting. Yesterday there wasn't much to worry about, really, except if she'd get a bike for her birthday – and about her rotten teacher. She always worries about her.

Today has been a long, worrisome kind of day and now she's got another worry. One day she has to ride that sunset highway until she finds Henry's *more*, because somewhere out there, somewhere beyond the river, beyond the roads, and way over that horizon, far, far away from Willama, there is . . . *more*.

Henry said so, and he knows everything – almost everything.

the brothers

Matthew Charles is going to be another redhead but he's not going to need a haircut for a long time; all of the redheads start out bald and this one hasn't got a hair on his head. Mavis calls him Number Twelve. Henry has to think of all the names and he sure comes up with some weird ones – like Lorraine Louise, Michael James, Vincent Andrew. None of those posh names last long. Matthew Charles has already been turned into Matty – and he's bawling again.

Lori is inside now, hiding behind the dusty brown curtain Henry hung when he took the kitchen door off, due to it took up too much space. Making space is important in this house.

The kitchen is packed wall to wall with brothers. They stand, lean, sit, crowded into this kitchen like drinking straws jammed into the straw-holder at McDonald's. Lucky the room is nearly big enough to hold everybody, which it wasn't until last year when Martin and the builder he works for knocked out the back wall and window then made half of the back verandah into part of the kitchen. They put down a new bit of chipboard floor, filled in the verandah part with boards and louvre windows, then Martin and Henry painted the kitchen and got new vinyl for the floor. It's the biggest and best room in the house now. It also gets a breeze from three sides, from the old west window, the south wall that is mainly louvres, and also the back door which faces east. Everyone lives in the kitchen. They have to. It's the only room not full up with beds. It stinks, though, due to too many brothers with too many smelly feet.

The quiz show is on and everyone is watching it, so Lori lifts the curtain and walks by the stove, which is pretty much beside the brown curtain. Henry hasn't totally forgotten about Lori; her dinner is being kept hot over a saucepan of water, the saucepan lid covering the plate. She juggles the plate to the sink, which is on the west wall, not far from the stove, where she grabs a fork before reaching into the cupboard up top for Henry's jar of Vicks VapoRub. The investigators, before they examined that dead body in *Silence of the Lambs*, dabbed a smear of something strong into each nostril, and it works too. Lori smears Vicks up her nostrils and the stink of dead feet and diseased sneakers disappears like magic while she forks up mushy potatoes, silverbeet and stew, which tastes like all of Henry's stews – pretty rotten.

Mavis is feeding the baby and Henry's scissors are snip-snip-snipping at Jamesy's hair. Neither of them look at Lori, and if Jamesy had dobbed on her about wagging it, Mavis would be yelling and Henry would be looking disappointed. He's just cutting carefully around Jamesy's ears.

Jamesy turned eight in July and he's the image of Lori, so everyone says. He's one of the dark-curly-haired ones with the brown eyes and suntanned skin and no freckles. His nose is pointy and his chin is pointy and he spends a lot of time grinning with one side of his mouth, even when there is nothing much to grin about.

Henry cuts a lot of hair. Lori runs her fingers through her crewcut. Last week she nagged and nagged Henry to keep cutting it shorter, for swimming, she said, but half of the wanting it shorter came from wanting to be close to him. While he's cutting and combing, his gentle hands touch her head and her face, and she gets huge jolts of his life force running through her.

Her fingers creep to the new swellings on her chest. She first noticed them yesterday and she hoped she'd wake up this morning and find they'd gone away. They haven't gone. She doesn't want to turn into a girl and be stuck in the middle of all of these brothers. Different.

If that new baby had been a girl . . . *If*.

'Big *eff*,' she whispers.

'What did you say, Lorraine?' Mavis sort of yells and the baby jumps and loses his grip, starts his bellowing again.

'If. Big *if* is all I said.'

'I'll give you big *if*. I know what you were thinking, and where have you been to this hour?'

'Wendy Johnson and her mother took me to McDonald's and shouted me some chips and an ice-cream for my birthday,' Lori says, and wishes it was true, and wishes that her hair would grow faster so Henry could cut it more often.

The mention of her birthday shuts everyone up, though. They all look at her, like, oh my God, what's the date today?

'Pass me the paper,' Mavis says. She wants proof of today's date.

The paper always gets put on top of the fridge. Lori reaches for it, passes it to Donny, who swaps it with Mavis for Matty, who is refusing to drink any more. He probably got full in the first two gulps, anyway. Donny puts him in the pram and stands rocking it while Mavis buttons the shoulder of her tent.

Lori stares at her, allowing her eyes to slip out of focus, until all she can see is the round face and the cloud of red hair, which Henry cuts so all the curls stand up tall. She has a pretty face and not one wrinkle, except where the corners of her mouth get dragged down around her nubby little chin.

'I thought it was tomorrow. We'll have a cake tomorrow,' Mavis says, glancing at the top of the paper.

Everyone looks sort of relieved and goes back to whatever they were doing. Except Martin. He reaches out a hand, brushes Lori's spiky curls. 'Sorry, Splint. Blame the new bawler. He went and upset the apple cart.'

Martin and Donny are pretty much grown up, like they've got jobs so they pay for their own haircuts. Martin has got medium dark curly hair and a lot of it; he's almost getting to be good looking. He's nineteen and a quarter, and a qualified bricklayer; he's got an old Ford ute that spends its life driving backwards and forwards to where Karen lives, which is about forty kilometres away, on a posh farm, in a mansion – so Martin says. He's ironing his shirts and jeans tonight because he's going out to spend the weekend with her and her parents. He's never once brought her to this place; she'd run a mile if she saw this madhouse. That's what he said to Donny.

Donny will turn eighteen in June. He's good with babies and he's got the bawler quiet but he's getting impatient to use that iron. He works at the biggest supermarket, which means he has to iron a shirt every day. It's worth it, though. He gets a discount on food and this house goes through an awful lot of food. He's half a head taller than Martin, but skinny, and he's not even nearly good looking, just a blotch of pale skin and freckles, pale eyes, stubby eyelashes and stubby red hair. He's never had a girlfriend and the way he looks he probably won't ever get one, like his hair is about half a centimetre long and it shows all the bumps on his head so he looks ridiculous.

The next three brothers are at high school. They get Henry haircuts and two of them don't like it. Greg was fifteen in December, Vinnie will be fourteen in April and Mick turns thirteen in June. Those three must have come out of Mavis like bullets, sort of bang, bang, bang – probably she was getting desperate to have a girl.

Anyway, it's pretty easy for people to remember which of the middle-sized brothers is which. Greg has always been Mavis's pet because he was her Christmas present and he used to be cute. He's medium sized with medium dark brown hair and he's spoilt rotten. However, since he turned fifteen, that spoilt rotten inside him is working its way to the outside, because lately he's looking pure pimply putrid. He's a thief and he'd kill you for a stick of chewed-up chewing gum.

Vinnie you have to feel a bit sorry for. Mavis says he was hiding behind the door when brains were handed out, and she could be right. He's the dead spit of Mavis's father – curly carrot-red hair, hands and feet twice as big as everyone else's, and a year ago he started growing into his hands and feet and he hasn't stopped since. He's huge for nearly fourteen, like giant huge. Already he's nearly taller that Donny. He can be pretty rotten; like he'd pinch the last chip off your plate, though he hasn't got enough brains to be as devious rotten as Greg.

Mick? Well, some people are rotten and some are beautiful and that's all there is to it. Mick is pure beautiful, even though he has got a crippled leg. He speaks soft, like Henry, and he's gentle, like Henry; Mick should have been the girl. He's even got a beautiful face, sort of freckled but neat sprinkled freckles, not blotchy, and he's got these gorgeous big blue-grey eyes and one of those mouths that always look as if they are going to say something nice about someone, which is not common in this house.

Lori is Number Six, like she's the comma that you put in the halfway mark of a sentence then forget why you put it in there. Probably she only got put in so people could take a breath between reading the names of all the brothers.

Thirteen months after Lori, the twins turned up with messed-up hearts. They spent most of their time sick and seeing doctors or living at the hospital, so when they were two Henry did that deal with Aunty Eva, then spent most weekends going backwards and forwards to Melbourne. He was happier then, younger then; he hasn't been to Melbourne for years now, so everybody has pretty much forgotten about those twins, except Henry. They've sort of become his other family, kept safe from the mess of people he's made in Willama.

The next three brothers are Jamesy, Neil and Timmy. They are pretty easy to remember too. Everyone calls Jamesy Gnome Face; he's always been Gnome Face since he turned up a year and four months after the twins. He got born old, got born knowing that no one was going to pick him up if he cried so he didn't bother crying, and due to all the talk in the house still being about if the twins were going to live or die, Jamesy pretty much grew himself up until one day he climbed out of the pram and squatted under the kitchen table. That's where he stayed too, sort of grinning at the stupid world with his lopsided mouth.

Something must have happened then, though Lori can't remember what it was – maybe Mavis had a dog or something – anyway, there is a huge space of no babies between Jamesy, who is eight, and Neil, who is four, and a pure little redheaded, face-pulling bugger of a kid. Timmy came next, he'll be two in June. He's not a redhead and he's not dark yet, but he will be. And now there's the new one, the bald-headed bawler who hasn't shut up for more than five minutes since he stuck his head out and saw Mavis, and who'd blame him? That's what Martin said.

'When are you going to learn to iron, Splint?'

'Oh, yeah, cool,' Lori replies. She's found a space between the television and the fridge, where she's leaning, smearing more Vicks up her nose, watching the iron work hard. Martin is better at laying bricks. He and Donny always call her Splint or Splinter, like, chip off the old block. And she's not like Mavis. She's not a bit like her.

The television is on an angle, positioned for Mavis's couch, which is against the east wall. She's smoking and answering the quiz questions before the contestant. Mostly she gets them right too, and when she does, she wriggles, and each wriggle makes her couch dig a deeper hole through the plaster wall, like it's trying to burrow its way into Martin and Donny's bedroom. It's a double-seater couch that seats only one, and lucky for it, its frame is all metal. It used to have a brown and green pattern on the material, which you can still see in places though it's mostly worn away.

'Get some more wood, please, Vincent,' Henry says.

'Can't you let the stove go out tonight, Henry?' Vinnie moans, sort of slow. He does everything slow – except pinch your food; he does that fast. He and Greg and Mick sleep in the west bedroom, and the kitchen chimney, a double one, has its other half in their room, which might be good in winter but it's not good in summer because the heat from the stove goes through that chimney and turns the middle-sized boys' room into a sweatbox.

No one listens to Vinnie – just looking at him is sort of over-powering lately. Henry is pretty much scared to look at him, in case he's grown out of his shoes or his trousers again. Anyway, that stove never goes out, due to it being one of those combustion things you can close up so they just keep licking at wood and heating up water that crawls through pipes from the stove to the hot water service in the roof. This house needs plenty of hot water.

Vinnie gets the wood then takes the hair-cutting chair. Greg, who went out with him to help get wood, doesn't come back. He's not going to get an old-fashioned Henry haircut; Mavis will end up giving him money to have a proper one like she did the last time, which isn't fair.

Nothing is really fair in this house. Like, Henry works all day then comes home and works half the night. Mavis can't do any-thing except have babies. She used to be a good cook but he's a rotten cook. He boils rice to a gluey glug, turns green cabbage into grey rag, boils beans watery, and mince stews greasy; they all taste the same, of onions and carrots and curry, and he forgets to put salt in it half the time. He uses a lot of onions and carrots because he grows his own. He grows pumpkins too, and broad beans that taste like chaff and look like kidneys that died of some terrible disease. His silverbeet is pure poison, due to his eyes aren't good enough to get the bugs off before he cooks it, so half the time he cooks them too.

Martin calls silverbeet 'bug stew' since he found a cooked earwig on his plate one night. He might look a bit like Henry on the outside but he's more like Mavis on the inside; he can be funny, and also he can be tough. Like on Mavis's birthday, like, he can remember her before she got fat, he said, 'Knowing what a gorgeous chick you used to be a few years back, how could you eat your way to *that*?' Then he offered to buy her a Jenny Craig diet.

'Buy me a box of chocolates,' she said.

Anyway, the next day Martin cut out this newspaper advertise-ment that is a cartoon man, made out of tractor, truck and car tyres, then he drew frizzy red hair on it with a biro and he stuck it on the fridge. Mavis thumped him a good one for that.

She's getting meaner with her thumps lately, and she's also getting bigger, or maybe her thumps are getting meaner because she's getting bigger. She never stops eating, even when she's smoking. She's always got a packet of lollies in her pocket and every time she lights a cigarette she pops a lolly in her mouth. Maybe she doesn't like the taste of cigarettes.

Through slitted eyes Lori stares at her, making the image unclear, just the chewing chin which gets lost in the swallowing throat, except for a little round bulge where her chin used to be. It's like that chin is so determined it refuses to give up and roll down. Everything else has rolled down – until you get to her wrists and her ankles. Mavis's feet aren't fat, or her hands. She's got pretty hands, with nice nails. If you could cut her off at the chin then halfway down her shins and around her wrists and just look at those bits, you could get an idea of what Martin can remember.

Vinnie's red curls are all on the floor and Henry is looking for another head. Mick isn't around. He's never in the kitchen, except when he's eating, so Henry starts on Neil.

Then Mavis gets up and everyone flattens against wall, table and cupboards, making space. She gets the custard powder, goes to the fridge, which is in the southwest corner, between the louvres and the west window, and she takes out three eggs, and the milk; she gets her favourite saucepan from beneath the sink, pushes between the brothers to the stove where the milk goes into the saucepan, then she stands cracking eggs, spilling their golden brains into a basin and bashing them to death with a fork. She gets a cup, mixes custard powder with a pile of sugar and a dribble of milk, adds vanilla, but all the while she's watching that saucepan, waiting for the milk to boil, sort of impatient.

And just as the milk is ready to go over the top, she pours in the custard powder stuff and stirs, stirs until it boils again, then sort of lovingly she pours what's in the saucepan over her eggs, stirring slow, stirring lovingly. Her custard tastes of love and Lori's mouth is watering for a bit of it. She won't get any. Mavis takes her bowl and spoon back to her couch and she flops down without spilling a drop. The poor old couch thumps back against the wall, making a deeper hole through the plaster.

One day that wall will fall down on top of her, but she'll just reach a hand out of the rubble, push the wall off and keep on eating her custard.

aunty eva

'Stop your staring at me,' Mavis says. 'Every time I look up, you're staring at me.'

'I'm not. I'm just . . . looking at the wall, thinking. Aren't people allowed to think in this house nowadays?' Lori replies.

Henry is in the shower and Donny's waiting to use it next. He looks more like Mavis than Henry, but he doesn't act it. He goes off to work every day, never forgets to bring the shopping home and never says much to anyone, just leans, waiting to use something.

Mavis is spooning up the last of her custard, and the scrape of that spoon is sort of tantalising. Lori's tongue escapes, does a circle of her lips.

'You're getting to be a cheeky little bugger lately, Lorraine. And who said you could go to McDonald's with your friend, anyway? You've been told to get yourself straight home from school. I've told you. Your father has told you a thousand times. We were damn near ready to send a search party out after you. You could have been kidnapped for all we knew.'

'Who'd want her? She can't even iron,' Martin says, walking through one doorway and out the other. The loo is an outside one, down the back behind the old laundry, and as the back door is also the kitchen door, there is a lot of coming and going through this room.

Lori is thinking about McDonald's, thinking that her lie about going there might be a good way to mention those tourist ladies and those boys, like maybe they were at McDonald's too and that's how she saw them. She's trying to make another lie come out, but Mavis has lost interest. She's watching Timmy, who is watching that new baby sleep, and maybe considering stealing his dummy; Mavis stole his only a few months back.

'Timmy, come here,' she says and her chin bump wobbles. 'Come to Mummy and get some custard.'

Timmy used to be a tub of lard but he sat up at five months, crawled at six and by twelve months he'd started leaving home. He's doing everything fast, though he walks slow to Mavis. He doesn't trust her since she got that new baby, but he gets a spoonful of custard.

Lori doesn't, and it's her birthday.

Timmy gets to crawl up on the couch, gets his face kissed, gets a cuddle.

Lori doesn't.

And Mavis has got the nerve to keep saying she wants another girl. What for? She doesn't want the one she's got. She doesn't even know that Lori hasn't got any friends to go to McDonald's with, doesn't care that she's had the most rottenest, stinkiest, longest day of her entire life. She can't even see those pink boils growing under Lori's T-shirt that are probably going to explode into giant boobs tomorrow.

The custard bowl now on the couch beside her, Timmy on her lap, Mavis flicks the remote, trying every television channel. It's all commercials, except the ABC; she settles for that. There is nothing worth watching until the movie starts, so she flicks down the volume and does her own show, like putting her own words into the mouths of the interviewer and the woman he's interviewing.

Lori giggles. You can't help but giggle, though Mavis keeps checking that brown curtain, making sure Henry isn't coming through; she's not game to do her comedian act when he's around. He never laughs at her, just looks startled, due to she's not too fussy about her language and being politically correct – actually, she prefers to be politically incorrect.

Then someone starts knocking at the front door.

Jamesy and Neil run to see who it is. Timmy wriggles down to the floor and goes after them while Lori looks at the back door, thinking maybe it's nicking-off time.

'Henry. How *lovely* to see you. So *pleased* to find you *in*. Just thought I'd pop around on the *off-chance.*'

'You're looking well, Eva,' Henry says. 'Come through.'

And the wire door slams shut and Mavis's jaw drops open. She thinks about standing, changes her mind, pushes the custard bowl beneath her couch, runs her fingers through her hair and pulls her tent dress down to cover her giant knees as that anorexic tourist lady comes stepping slow into the kitchen, stepping high, as if the whole house is full of used condoms. Henry is behind her wearing his old tartan dressing gown, which makes him look about eighty years old. He turns the television off.

There is a rare silence for a second or two, then Mavis says, 'Well, look what the cat dragged in. If it's not the little mother herself.'

'Goodness *me*, darling.' The tourist lady's eyes bulge, nearly pop out of their sockets. A lot of people stare like that when they see Mavis.

Martin comes back from the loo. 'How's life, Aunty Eva?' he says. 'Long time, no see.'

Eva has stopped her staring. She's stretching her lips in a fake smile, offering her hand to Martin but not wanting him to take it, while Henry starts listing names – as if she's going to remember who is who. As if she's interested, even. He says Lorraine, and Lori gets pushed in almost close enough to shake Eva's hand. She's wearing a huge diamond ring that is probably the one Henry bought in England. It probably cost as much as a new roof and a new fence, and even someone to paint the house.

Eva's eyes fix on Lori's face; she frowns. She's going to dob. Now. She's going to say, 'Didn't I see you down at the *tourist* centre?'

Lori steps back fast, behind Martin, steps back again and keeps going until she's outside the back door. She's learned a lot from listening at open doors. That's how she knows Mavis and Henry ran away together and that's the reason Mavis got written out of the will. Eva got everything when her mother died. That's how she knows that when the twins needed an operation and needed a place to stay between hospital visits, Henry went to see Eva and ended up making peace with her and making a deal. Eva said she'd look after the twins until the doctors had fixed up their hearts and then she'd give them back.

Only one problem with that plan. Eva married Henry so she could be a respectable married lady and have his baby, so now she had two of them. She reneged on the deal, and since about two years ago, when she sent money to soften Mavis up, she's been begging to adopt those twins, which, due to her and Henry never getting divorced, would only be a formality – or that's what Eva's solicitor wrote in the letter that came with the cheque.

As if Mavis would ever agree to that!

'Put the little ones to bed, boys, then go outside,' Henry says, wanting some privacy now that the small talk is over. That's funny. As if anything is private around this place.

Lori, already outside, gets the best listening spot, below the open window on the west side, close to the table. When Donny and Martin come, they crouch down low behind her. Greg hasn't come back since he went out to get the wood, but Vinnie, the moron, tries listening at the louvres, which aren't even close to the action. He won't learn much over there.

'What's she doing up here?' Martin whispers.

'It's about the twins again,' Lori says. 'She's talking about her solicitor. Shush.'

Then Mavis shocks everyone. 'Of course Henry and I have no desire to disrupt the twins' lives. What do you think we are, Eva? Thanks to you, we're strangers to our own sons.'

'Christ,' Donny says. 'She's going to sign.' Now Martin shushes him.

'You'll allow me to *adopt* the boys? You'll *sign* the papers, darling?'

'Did you bring them with you?'

'The twins?' Eva says. 'No. No. No.'

Liar. She did so. Not that Lori can tell anyone. She was supposed to be at school.

'I'm talking about the adoption papers, Eva.'

'You'll sign, darling?'

'What's the alternative? We've got nothing to offer them up here. You got all the old bitch's money.'

'Oh, darling, darling, darling. *Thank you.* How can I ever *thank* you?'

'Oh, I could think of a few thousand ways – if I put my head to it.'

Eva ignores that one, but she pats Mavis's hand. 'You don't *know* what this means to me. You'll *never* know, darling.'

'I've got a fair idea. However,' Mavis says. She likes howevers, and everyone in this house knows that when she gets started into her howevers, some good fiction is getting ready to come out of her mouth. Henry should know it too but he's sitting there, nodding, smiling, letting his wives talk. 'However, Henry and I both feel it could be detrimental to the twins' future wellbeing for them to grow to adulthood not knowing that they have brothers. We want them to know their family, don't we, Henry?'

Then Vinnie sneezes, and when he sneezes, half of Willama knows it. The listeners skedaddle down behind the old laundry where they wait a while before creeping back. But it's all over bar the shouting. Eva is mock-crying, like dabbing at her eyes with a proper handkerchief and saying a lot of junk about how many years have been lost.

Then Mavis does it again. 'However,' she says. 'The papers will have to be signed up here, Eva. As you can no doubt see, there's no way I can get to a solicitor's office.'

'Yes, darling.' Eva nods, attempts to look concerned. 'Mr Watts *could* drive up in the morning and *bring* the papers,' she says, dabbing her eyes again, just so no one will see what is going on behind those eyes.

'Get him to bring the twins with him, Eva, and bring them around for dinner tomorrow. We're having a birthday party for Lorraine. It would be the ideal opportunity for them to meet everyone in a social situation.'

Eva pushes her cup of tea back, stands. 'It's such a *long* trip for them, darling. You *know* that they are still not well boys.'

'Those two are going to know they've got brothers. It's our one stipulation, isn't it, Henry?'

'Certainly better for them, Eva,' Henry says.

'Then I dare say we will have to *arrange* it.'

Arrange what? Those twins are already in Willama. She's a cool liar.

She's got a mobile phone in her purse. She uses it to call a taxi. Mavis's eyes want that mobile. She can't have it. Henry won't let her have the phone reconnected; he won't even let Martin and Donny have mobile phones – for various reasons, such as pizza shops that do home deliveries and taxi drivers who will buy takeaway then taxi it to the house. Anyway, eventually Eva drives off and Mavis turns on the television and starts looking in the fridge. Lori and Jamesy walk in and lie on the floor to watch the movie.

'You kids get to bed now,' she says. They don't move. 'Henry! Henry!'

'I'm in bed.'

She's getting niggly. There is nothing much in that fridge except green stuff; there are eggs but no more milk to make custard. 'You're like a bloody old chook,' she yells, slamming the fridge door. 'You stick your head under your wing and snore. I want to talk to you.'

'Keep your voice down. You'll wake the baby.'

'Wake the baby? He'll be awake again in five minutes, the bawling little bugger. Greg!' She walks to the back door, sticks her head out. 'Greg, love. Greggie! Where are you?' She's not going to find him, and maybe she knows it. Her tone alters when she calls Vinnie's name. 'Vinnie. Where the bloody hell are you?'

'He's gone to find Greg, and Martin went to Nelly's to call Karen and tell her he can't come out tonight because something came up,' Lori says. 'Me and Jamesy will go to the shop for you.'

'It's too late for you to be wandering around, and I told you to get to bed. Get your shower and go. Now!' She walks off to her bedroom to talk to Henry.

Lori and Jamesy have got the television to themselves until the bawler starts bawling and Mavis comes back, unbuttoning her tent, just at the most interesting part of the movie. The girl has got naked and the man's head is –

'What are you doing watching that thing, you disobedient pair of little buggers?' She reaches for a long electrical cord that has been hanging on a nail behind the back door for all of Lori's life. Mavis can crack that cord like a whip when anyone gives her big strife, and if she doesn't hit the one she's aiming at, she gets close. Someone yells. A calendar also hangs behind the door. It is beautiful. Blue water, yellow sand, sailboats gliding, seabirds soaring. Cool. It makes the room hotter, and the whip harder.

Jamesy dives under the table and out, he's through the brown curtain door. Lori goes the other way. She's on the back verandah. They've got a pact, these two; divide and conquer.

The two big globes in the kitchen are bright enough to cast their light on the verandah where Mick is building a bike. He's been out there all the time, sitting on a box, surrounded by bits of bike, his bad leg with its brace stuck out in front. When he takes the brace off his leg is rubbery, so Greg and Vinnie call him Pullit, as in 'pull the other one, it's made of rubber'. His arms and his right leg are strong, which make up a bit for his left leg; he can swim okay, but he usually only swims at night so people can't stare when he takes that brace off. He's one of the redheads, but not carrot red, sort of dark and quiet, like the inside of his head is quiet, like his eyes are quiet.

35

No one is allowed to thump Mick, due to he's got no balance. Not even spoilt-rotten Greg thumps Mick, which might be the reason why Mick got to be so lovable. Also, he never does anything to get thumped for, so it's like this circle of good just keeps wrapping around and around him. Summer and winter he stays close to the house, except when he's at school. He fixes things, just loves screws and nuts and nails and he collects them, picks them up from everywhere. All the bikes and bits of bikes the brothers bring home are treasures to Mick – bikes being his favourite things to fix, even if he can't ride them. It's like he enjoys the freedom they give his brothers, so maybe fixing them gives him a bit of borrowed freedom.

'Lorraine. I said, Get. To. Bed. And you too, Mickey.' He doesn't like being called Mickey and he doesn't want to go to bed, but he packs up his spanners and takes them with him, leaves the bike bits there. 'You'd better move it, Lorraine.'

She doesn't move. When she was ten, she was afraid of Mavis's whip, but now she is eleven she's not afraid at all. She walks back to the open door as soon as she hears that couch groan and the wall moan.

'Mick hates being called *Mickey* and I hate being called *Lorraine*. I said for everyone to call me Lori.' She thrusts out her chest. There are no brothers around to see her twin boils. 'I'm eleven now, and it's Friday night, and me and Mick shouldn't have to go to bed with the chooks.'

'If you make me get up from this chair then you won't live to see twelve, you cheeky little skin-head bugger. And if you ask your father to cut your hair again, I'll shave the lot off.'

Lori shrugs and gets.

The lounge room is big, which is lucky. It's got three beds and a cot in it, also a chest of drawers and huge old-fashioned wardrobe. Matty's bassinette will probably be moved in soon. All the babies get put in this room because its door is just across the passage from Mavis and Henry's door. Lori's bed is the one nearest to the door so she can hear Mavis and Henry talking some nights when the heat is too bad to sleep. She has learned a lot in that bed, like why Henry never got a divorce from Eva, which isn't due to divorces costing heaps of money but to Mavis finding out something about her father which put her off wanting to marry Henry. Some nights Lori hears Henry saying, 'For the boys. It would be better for the boys.' He never says, 'Better for the girl.' He's probably forgotten he's got a girl. He used to know. Mavis used to know too. She used to buy pretty dresses and dolls and girls' things.

Lori yawns, rubs the sore spots on her chest, scratches her head and hopes she hasn't got nits. Henry hates nits. They are definitely not God's creatures. Lori had long hair until she was five and Mavis would curl it, but the first year she was at school she got nits, so Henry gave her a boy's haircut. She can still remember her curls, remember Mavis fussing with her, dressing her like a girl, almost remember Mavis when she used to wear a tickly maroon cardigan with a pattern on the bottom. Almost. Almost remember Henry's twins living in this house too, or remember the blur of one of them nearly dying one day and Mavis having to give it mouth-to-mouth.

There's lots of stuff she can remember from when she was little, like the day Mavis and Henry took her and Mick and Jamesy to Melbourne so they could bring the twins home. It was about four or five years ago, but to Lori, that memory is as clear as if it were yesterday, like it was something so precious, it just got embedded in her brain so even a lobotomy could never get it out.

She can remember the long bus ride, and busy Spencer Street Station, and the tram that wasn't quite a train. And she can remember the colour of the ocean, and the house where Mavis used to live when she was a girl. It was big, made of red brick, sort of cool, and quiet and posh behind its tall fence. She can remember the garden too, and the trees, and the magic green moss on the footpath and the stillness that swallowed her up as the heavy gate closed. Everyone stopped talking then because that gate had locked them into another world.

Lori must have been around six, the twins about five, and Mick seven; he was in the old pusher – due to his bad leg and not being able to walk far. He hated it too. And Mavis, she wasn't so gigantic big then, and she'd been happy, laughing and mucking around, excited to be in Melbourne again and finally getting those twins back home where they belonged.

Aunty Eva refused to give them back. She said they were not at home, and she wouldn't even open the security door and let everyone in to wait. Mavis said she was going for the police, and then Aunty Alice, who isn't really an aunty, went driving off with the twins in the back seat of a posh white car.

Except for the photographs Henry used to bring home from Melbourne, that was the only time Lori saw those twins as real living boys. Alice had to get out of the car to open the gates and Mavis started running so Lori had run after her. Mavis couldn't get the car door open but Lori saw those twins. They were identical, straight, dark auburn hair, big wide blue eyes and twin navy and white shirts. She had felt a sad pulling feeling in her stomach that day as the car had driven off, like there was a bit of elastic tied around her insides, sort of joining her to those brothers like it went right through that door, and as the car had driven further up the road, that elastic got pulled so tight, it hurt. But that elastic must have got broken, because down at the tourist centre today, she had been close enough for those twins to almost fall over her and she hadn't even felt a tug.

She rolls onto her side, hears a mosquito, hopes it flies off to suck on one of the little ones. They're asleep. They won't feel the sting. Then it lands, right near her ear. She slaps it, squishes it, and her head starts thinking again of elastic. That's probably what is wrong with Henry, like his life-force elastic got cut from his real people when he was only one year old so the elastic sprang back and got all curled up inside him, and it has been rolling around inside him ever since.

It's pure awful when you come to think about it. It's so awful it makes that hurting, pulling feeling in the pit of her stomach come back hard, like that elastic is stretching out, like it's searching all the motels in Willama, looking for the end bits that broke off.

Or maybe it's just a bellyache from Henry's stew. Probably there was a poisonous bug on his silverbeet tonight.

the birthday party

Mavis is looking pleased with herself today. She fed Matty until he was tiptop, overflow full and now she's helping Henry cook the birthday dinner, or sort of supervising and tasting, adding a bit of this, and a bit of that.

'Henry, get me the ground ginger and crush me a bit of garlic,' she says.

Garlic and ginger taste awful, except when Mavis uses them, then you can't taste them, just their flavours. There was a time when she could make the most super fantastic stews and gravies and she still makes the best roast potatoes; she's made a baking dish full up with her crispy roast potatoes today, and Lori counted them, counted them when they went into the oven and again when Henry turned them over, and there are enough for her to get two pieces. She hopes she'll get two.

Mavis smells of baby powder and deodorant, due to Henry helped her have a shower after he finished stuffing the two chickens. The shower is over the bath and Mavis can't step into it any more, so Henry bought her a shower spray thing he connects to the two taps, then he sits Mavis on a special stool with two short legs and two long ones which he stands half in and half out of the bath. Water goes everywhere so Henry and the floor get as wet as Mavis.

He helps her get dressed too. Today she's wearing her best tent dress, light material, sort of pink and yellow and white swirls. It's pretty. She looks pretty. Her hair has dried all high and fluffy and she's wearing lipstick and blue eye shadow which makes her eyes look big and sad. Lori keeps stepping close to her as she passes, keeps walking around her so she can smell the sweet lost smell of *Mummy*.

The kitchen looks good too; everyone had to put their junk away and Martin mopped the floor and doused the room with air-freshener, then tucked the tartan blanket over Mavis's couch. All the brothers are home, except Donny. He had to work. Even Greg is staying around the house; cooking like this only ever gets done on Christmas Day and he's not going to miss those roasted chickens and potatoes.

Then a posh car is in the drive and Aunty Eva is getting out of the back seat and that rangy greyhound lady and a fussy little ferret man are getting out of the front. Lori watches from a distance. The little ones aren't into watching from a distance, they are swarming around Henry's feet, staring at the visitors, who look scared to move far from their car.

The twins don't want to get out, and who'd blame them? Eva has got them dressed up like they are going to a funeral, and their faces look as if they're going to a funeral too. They are staring at Henry's house, sort of cringing back from it, rubbing against the car, probably scared stiff that house will fall down before the funeral is over.

Until one of them sees Lori leaning against her favourite verandah post. He whispers and they both stare at her, so she does to those twins what she does to the schoolkids when they whisper – gives them a look at her middle finger. It isn't as if they are really her brothers, or they won't be after today. They'll just be posh cousins, and she doesn't have to like cousins who get every single thing they ever want.

Henry likes them. He's smiling and treating them like lost treasures dug up from Egypt, sort of touching their heads, patting their shoulders. Then he kisses them!

He doesn't kiss anyone, not even Mavis, or not when anyone can see. Lori's eyes narrow. She's just discovered something and she doesn't like what she's discovered. She's just found out exactly who Henry is singing about when he sings that 'My Precious Son' song in the potting shed. She's going to hate that song now for ever and ever more. Like, whose sons does he think the rest of the brothers are – Spud Murphy's?

After a bit of posh talking to Eva, Henry walks her around to the back door, which is safer than walking her through the front door, unless you know which of the verandah's broken floorboards you have to dodge. Lori knows which ones to dodge; she races through the house, down the passage to the kitchen where she stands with Mavis, watching the visitors walk by the louvred windows.

The ferret with the bottle-top glasses is stepping close to Eva's heels. He's got a briefcase with him, and he's hanging on to it tight and taking stupid prissy little steps like he's about to enter a rabbit burrow, full of killer rabbits.

The greyhound lady, who is Aunty Alice, hasn't got much hair left and what she's got looks mangy. She's old. She used to be Eva's high school teacher and she was about thirty-five when Eva was sixteen – that's what Mavis says. Her name is Miss Blunt, which is absolutely the wrong name for her, due to her nose and teeth are chisel sharp. She probably taught science, probably cut up frogs and rats and her nose got pinched extra long through wearing a peg on it when she had to cut up smelly things. And she probably sharpened her teeth every night with a file so she could bite the heads off dead rats then spit them at the students and that's how her teeth got stained yellow – by rat juice. She's dressed like a man, drill trousers, check shirt, but she's sure making the front of that shirt stick out.

'I see she brought her chauffeur,' Mavis whispers, putting on a posh voice and smarmy expression. Lori giggles, pictures old Alice in a chauffeur's uniform.

That's what she's supposed to be. She went to live in the bungalow behind Grandmother Hilda's house when Mavis's father died, because she could drive the car and Grandmother and Eva couldn't. That's their story, though Mavis says something entirely different at night when she's talking to Henry in the bedroom. She says heaps of things that Lori can't quite work out – like about her father, who died of a stroke when Mavis was only twelve. She loved him, and she's got a wedding photograph of him, with the bit showing her mother ripped off. If he hadn't died of a stroke before Grandmother Hilda died of her heart, then Mavis might have got all the money instead of Eva.

Henry is such a well-mannered man usually, but he's totally ignoring Alice, who looks as if she's been blackmailed into coming here. She's walking slow behind the ferret, lighting a cigarette, blowing twin streams of smoke and showing all of her snarling teeth. Lori shows her teeth to Mavis, snarls, and Mavis smiles, gives her a wink, then draws her away from the louvres because Eva and the ferret are coming inside.

'You'd remember Mr Watts, our solicitor, darling?'

'Not a face you're likely to forget in a hurry, Eva,' Mavis says. She's more interested in the twins, sort of gives them a big smile. 'Okay, which of you is which? And no trying to trick me.' The twins take one look at her then shrink back behind Eva, so Mavis stops smiling and walks to the stove where she tastes the gravy, adds pepper, tastes it again, a big spoonful taste which doesn't even smear her lipstick.

Alice has got rid of her cigarette. She comes in last. Mavis ignores her too. Henry is still fussing around his twins. They are not talking to him either and his face is starting to get that tight grey worried look. He gives up, takes the gravy spoon from Mavis's hand while there is still some gravy left in the pan, then he checks on his roasting chickens.

The solicitor sits down, chooses a chair as far away from the stove as he can get. He doesn't know it, but he's got the chair next to Mavis's. No one ever wants to sit on that chair because Mavis pinches your food, like when they have fish and chips, she eats half your chips – so does Vinnie. No one wants to sit next to him either.

The briefcase gets put on the floor, and Lori giggles, because it disappears under the table. Neil has got it and he's trying to open it. The solicitor reclaims it, places it under his chair, guards it with his feet and keeps on talking about the weather and stuff. Henry knows Mr Watts; when he first married Eva, he used to do office work for him.

Mavis sits, so Eva sits on the other side of her solicitor. She's smiling, trying to carry on as if she's pleased to be here, like saying happy birthday, and saying what a *tall* girl Lorraine has grown into and how *wonderful* it is for them to be together again.

Alice coughs, sounds like one of Murphy's dogs, and that's what smoking does to your lungs; she's going to do more of it, though, because she's seen Mavis's ashtray, a tall metal thing; it's been emptied, wiped clean, so it's gasping for a butt. Alice sits on the couch and doesn't use all of it – doesn't use much of it. God, she's skinny. So is Eva, only Eva is fluffy skinny, like her dress is sort of gorgeous and she's got almost shoulder-length blonde hair and make-up plastered like mortar on brick. She's soaked herself in perfume too, which smells better than Vicks.

Everyone is dodging around the twins, who don't know where to go. No one is telling them, so they stand near the couch, their heads swivelling on skinny necks. They are truly identical, not like the Morris twins at school, one fat, one skinny. These two are like the same person. If one stares at something, so does the other, as if their eyes are connected up to the same brain. They stare at Henry. They stare at Lori, stare at the sea of brothers. They frown at Matty, still sleeping in his pram beneath the louvres. They stare at Timmy. He's standing beside the pram watching the inter-loper sleep. That pram belonged to him until two weeks ago.

Neil, who is the image of Mavis with his mop of frizzy red curls, gives up on getting that briefcase and goes after the twins. A while back he discovered he could wriggle his ears while poking out his tongue and crossing his eyes. It's nothing personal, but he does it now, and the twins back away, in step. They even move together; they must only have one brain between the two of them.

Mavis gives Neil a toe in the backside and he dives under the table while Henry adds bean water to the gravy, adds a bit more then has to stir in more Gravox to thicken it again while Lori studies those twins.

'Sit down, boys,' Alice says. 'You're underfoot.' Eva hasn't spoken to them yet. 'Sit,' Alice repeats, and the twin heads swivel again, like where are they supposed to sit? They're looking at the couch, at the chairs, then they back along the wall, to the open door and sit side by side on the floor, their backs against that door, making sure it doesn't blow shut and lock them in. They are pretty much Lori's size, except they look well fed. They've got round faces and their old-fashioned funeral pants are sort of tight around the tops of their legs. They sure look out of place in this kitchen.

Martin squats in front of them, and in one action four round knees get tucked beneath two round chins. 'G'day,' Martin says. 'So who's who?' They don't answer him. Maybe they can't talk. 'I reckon you're Alan, the mollydooker, and you're Eddy. Am I right?' They cringe, don't know what a 'mollydooker' is. He keeps it up for a while but he can't get a word out of them.

Mavis is staring at them now. She's eyeing Eva too, sort of like a cat eyeing a rat, sort of disdainful, like the cat isn't hungry at the moment, thank you, but she's got that rat right where she wants it.

And the rat knows it too, it's getting flittery, jittery. Like Eva can't sit still for a second. She's fiddling with her hair, her sleeve, glancing at the twins, at Henry, who is getting more meat off those two roast chickens with his knife than Mavis could get off them with her teeth. She's done the weather bit and now she forces her mouth fast into a fake smile and asks Henry when he learned to cook. She hasn't tasted his cabbage yet or she wouldn't ask. Then the smile gets sucked back fast into wrinkles and her cheeks look like one of Bert Matthews's wormy apples that's been off the tree too long. She looks at Mr Watts, at his briefcase. It's probably got the adoption papers in it and maybe some money for Mavis. Eva gave her

45

money before when she thought she might get the twins; that's how Henry had enough to pay for getting the kitchen extended.

'Are those two brain damaged?' Mavis says.

Eva flinches, looks where Mavis is looking. '*Very* bright. Both *exceptional* students, darling. And your boys?' No one mentions girl. No one sees girl.

From her chair at the head of the table Mavis has a good view of the room. She's got her back to the louvres and she's the closest to the back door, so she's feeling any breeze that might stir. She's eyeing the bread now and wanting a slice or six. Can't do that today so she lights a cigarette instead. It's a contagious disease, because Greg goes outside to have a stolen smoke and old Alice takes out her packet, lights up. Eva doesn't like the smoke. She stands, walks to the pram where Matty is pig-grunting and getting ready to bawl again.

'You *dear* little pet,' she says. 'He is *gorgeous*, Henry.' He's not gorgeous. He's probably the fattest, ugliest, baldest baby in Willama. 'What did you name him?'

'We give them numbers up here,' Mavis says. 'He's Number Twelve.'

Eva reaches out a finger to touch Matty's fat little leg. He bawls. She steps back but he keeps on bawling.

'I can smell him from here. Change his napkin, and put him on our bed,' Mavis says. She's talking to Martin but Eva flinches, moves back to her chair fast, looks at the hand that might actually have touched the shitty baby, looks at the sink, purses her lips, then takes a handkerchief from between her boobs – which are pretty much not there – pretends to wipe her nose, rubs the perfumed hanky across her palms while stretching her mouth and cheek wrinkles flat. She glances at Alice, her eyes talking a secret, silent language. They are like Greg's eyes, pale blue and glinting greedy.

The twins haven't moved; they've got to be retarded. Or maybe Alice is a mad scientist who's got a laboratory where she does lobotomies. Lori watches a lot of television and videos. Once Martin hired *One Flew Over the Cuckoo's Nest* and by the time everyone got to see it it was nearly worn out, but by then Lori knew all about nuthouses and lobotomies and she was only about seven.

Mick walks in and Eva stares at his rubber leg in its metal contraption. Her mouth and cheeks screw into their puckered pout as she watches his throwing walk.

Then the twins stand. Together. Walk to her chair. Together. 'How much longer do we have to stay here?' one says, and the other one adds, 'When are we going to the party?' No wonder Henry wanted to kiss them. They talk like posh poms.

Eva aims a single kiss between the two clean heads. 'Be good, darlings.' She's not real. She's a television actress mother who always wears beautiful clothes and never gets them sweaty.

Lori is feeling sweaty. Mavis made her put on her best T-shirt, but underneath it she's wearing a singlet that belongs to Neil. It's skin tight and cutting into her armpits, but flattening those pink bumps. She's standing in her favourite spot beside the fridge, looking down at those bumps and thinking maybe she should stick a pin in them and let the infection out. That's what Greg does to his pimples, except for every one he squeezes, he gets two more.

Henry wipes sweat from his forehead with a tea towel as he counts plates, counts chairs. 'Get the old stool from the verandah, boys, and the little chair from our bedroom, then set the table.'

It's an extension table, metal legs and wood-coloured laminex on top. It's long enough. Martin and Vinnie organise knives and forks while Henry scrapes saucepans, scraping out every bit to the mess of plates all lined up on the sink and bench, and when they are packed with vegetables and chicken, the boys pass them around the table.

Lori takes her position on the old stool, which is against the west wall. She likes to sit with her back to a wall. Vinnie hands her a plate of chicken scraps and cabbage, a mound of orange pumpkin, watery beans, watery gravy – and only one quarter of a roast potato!

She looks at the other plates. The solicitor has got two big bits of potato. He got the extra one that was supposed to be for her birthday, and she knows it, and she hates his stupid little moustache and his stupid glasses that make his eyes look like cheap chipped marbles. All the little ones only got one quarter of a potato. Even Mick only got one quarter, yet he's going on thirteen. It's a big quarter though, bigger than Lori's.

Bloody solicitor. Mavis always says that they are thieves, and this one is a roast potato thief. She watches him pick up his fork, stab her potato, cut her potato, tuck it underneath his moustache. And she hopes he chokes on it, hopes it burns all the way down to his ferret belly. She eats her beans while counting potatoes and bits of chicken, working out exactly what bits are not on this table.

Mavis hasn't got a lot of food on her plate, only a quarter of a potato, a small piece of chicken breast and beans, no pumpkin, no cabbage. She won't eat vegetables. She's already told Eva that the doctor said her weight is glandular so she has to prove it by not eating too much. There are three pieces of potato missing, and a whole chicken thigh and drumstick. They'll be on a plate in the fridge, all covered with foil and ready to go back in the oven to get heated up as soon as Eva has gone.

'Is there nothing the doctors can *do* for you, *darling*?' Eva says, taken in by what is on Mavis's plate.

'Not a thing, *dear*.' Watch it. Mavis is getting plain sick of hearing that fake 'darling'.

Lori glances from sister to sister as she makes a puddle out of her cabbage, pumpkin and gravy then swallows the mess down fast. The meat goes down next; she saves the potato for last because she loves roast potato, loves it next best to crisp chips from the takeaway, loves it, loves it, and hates the solicitor, who is staring glassy-eyed at Mavis, like he's never seen anyone as big as her. No one has, except on television, and so what? That's her funeral. And it might be soon if she doesn't lose some weight, or that's what the doctor said after Matty got born.

'Have you seen a *doctor* recently, darling?' Eva asks.

'I've got a two-week-old baby, *dear*.' There's that 'dear' again.

'What did he say?'

'He can't talk yet. As you know, my kids are all smart but they're not that smart.' She's winding up. You can tell by her eyes. They are getting that excited look.

'He said that her heart will give out, that she'll be dead before she's forty,' Martin says.

'Unless she has her stomach clamped,' Lori adds, mouth full.

Martin nudges her. She elbows him back. They are elbow to elbow, sharing the outdoor stool from the verandah.

Mavis's eyes narrow; she places a sliver of chicken in her mouth and her throat muscles try to get it, toss it down but she forces herself to chew, keep chewing. 'It's a genetic condition, passed down the male line – as you well know, *dear*.'

Eva looks down at her plate, cuts a lump of potato and puts it in her mouth. It's scalding hot and she can't spit it out onto her plate, which Henry says is bad manners, so she swallows it, gasps, swallows hard again, helps herself to a slice of bread, eats it dry, breathes deeply, letting in some air which is almost as hot as the potato. At least that changed the subject away from stapled stomachs. The doctor also said tubes tied, and Valium tablets for sleeplessness, because Henry dobbed. He told about how Mavis does most of her eating at night.

The plates are emptied fast, except Eva's plate. It's still half full, and that's wasted chicken, and wasted potato. Then Henry puts a supermarket apple pie on the table, with one candle stuck in its middle, and everyone sings 'Happy Birthday' – except the twins. They look at each other, cover their mouths and start laughing. Eva tries to hush them with her eyes and when she can't, she takes two envelopes from her purse, hands one each to the boys. They hand them to Lori, but the little mongrels are still laughing.

She doesn't even say 'Ta,' just gives those two a dirty look. Maybe those envelopes have got money in them, not just cards, and she'd like to open them and look but she's not going to give those laughing little mongrels the satisfaction of seeing her accept their money.

Anyway, Henry is cutting the pie into wedges, then cutting a second one, serving it with ice-cream. Nelly from over the road always has ice-cream in the freezer and cones in her cupboard, but Mavis can polish off four litres while she watches *Play School*, so Henry only ever buys it when he's going to serve it all out. He doesn't even leave a lick for later and Mavis's big eyes threaten to murder him because he's only given her a tiny wedge of pie and a baby dollop of ice-cream.

Lori eats her giant serve slow, dipping from the outside, working in, licking the spoon clean between each dipping while she watches Mavis sling her serve down; she can't pretend to chew ice-cream.

Tea is poured into a mess of cups and mugs. Martin passes Eva a chipped cup, notices the chip, snatches it back and replaces it with an unchipped mug. He hands the chipped cup to the solicitor, who sees chip, thinks germs, turns the cup, holds it in his left hand and drinks from the unchipped side. Alice pushes her chair back, lights a cigarette just to keep Mavis company, then she's puffing smoke and drinking her tea, not caring about the crack in her mug one bit, due to her being used to biting heads off dead rats.

The ferret glances at Eva. He's in shock, shocked silent. It's plain obvious he just wants to get those papers signed and get the hell out of this place. Henry offers him more tea. No, thank you. He eases his chair back.

Eva glances at her watch. That solicitor is probably charging her by the hour. 'Well, goodness me. Just *look* at the *time*,' she says. 'If you could get the *papers* out now, Mr Watts.'

'You're still gullible, Eva, still greedy. Gullibility and greed don't mix well.'

'I beg your pardon?'

'Thanks for bringing them home. You can go now,' Mavis says, helping herself to one of Lori's envelopes, ripping it open. There's a five-dollar note in it. Lori rips the other one open, finds another five, but Eva's chair is squealing back from the table, her eyes darting to Alice, to the solicitor; their eyes are sort of saying 'we told you so'.

'We agreed last night, Mavis.' Eva lowers her voice. 'The divorce, and the adoption papers. You said you wanted – ' She turns to Henry, who is standing behind his chair, swallowing spit. 'You said you wanted – '

'Spit it out. We've got no secrets in this house – unlike some.'

And Henry finds his voice. 'Go outside now, boys. All of you, outside. You can finish the dishes later. Take Alan and Edward with you.'

'They're staying right where they are, Henry!' Mavis stamps her foot and the rafters shake and any termites who might have been thinking of moving in for a quick chew pack their bags and run. The brothers stay and the twins stay.

'I don't *understand*. You said . . . you *said*, Mavis, you *said* you'd *sign*, that you have no *desire* to disrupt – '

Lori scoffs the last spoonful of ice-cream, wipes the rim of her plate clean with her finger, her eyes watching the play.

'I'd be up for child abuse signing those poor little buggers over to you.'

'She will sign, Eva. You will, Mavis. I've got nothing here to offer those boys.'

'You've got me,' Mavis says. 'And I'm a lot more than "nothing", Henry.'

'They'll visit us twice a year, Mavis. That's what we agreed last night. We'll still watch them grow.'

'Ah, go outside and sing your bloody love songs to your chooks. You can't see what's right in front of your own eyes, for Christ's sake.'

Mr Watts reaches for his briefcase but Mavis is fast when she wants to be. She pounces on it, tosses it out to the verandah. He and Neil follow his case.

'We can do a lot for those boys,' Alice finally breaks her silence, and Mavis turns to her. Almost, but not quite, looks at her.

'I know exactly what you can do, you bloody old bull dyke. Exactly. And I know how you do it too. You weren't invited to my house, now get out of it, and take your girlfriend with you. I wouldn't trust you pair to raise a Rottweiler with rabies.'

Voices are running together. The brothers move away from the sink, take up positions on the safe side of doors. The twins, who don't know a thing about survival, have got a chair and they are sticking to it. They look bored, lean heads on hands at the table, see Alice walk away, pleased to walk away. Lori hears the car motor, then the car horn. Beep-beep-beeeep-beep.

'I'll pay you fifty thousand. Fifty thousand dollars, Mavis. That will make a lot of difference to your lives. Think of it. Think of your children.' She's talking fast now. She's sounding more normal.

'It's too little, too late, you cold-eyed, lying bitch. And I am thinking of my bloody kids. Now get out of my house before I have to throw you out.'

Eva ups the price. It's like when the house down the street got sold at auction. 'I'll give you a cheque in your hand now, Mavis. Sixty-five thousand.'

'I'm not too sure of the going price of child's flesh these days, *dear*. Have you had an appraisal recently?'

Henry is standing there with a saucepan full of hot water, and by the look on his face, he's thinking of letting Mavis have it. 'They don't know us,' he wails.

'Then it's past bloody time they got to know us, isn't it?' Mavis roars. She's getting mad. She's on her feet and looking for a weapon. 'And if it hadn't been for that screwed-up bitch, they would have known us five years ago when we went down there to bring them home. Get her out of here, Henry, before I have to do it myself.'

Eva starts towards the twins. Mavis blocks her with her bulk and Eva backs off.

'We're booked into the motel for the night, Henry. We'll discuss this again in the morning. Come, boys.'

'They're staying where they belong. It's you who is leaving.'

'Oh, you know me better than that, darling.' That 'darling'

sounded like a curse word, but every word coming out of the sisters' mouths is a curse. 'You certainly know me better than that.'

Then Mavis is a combine harvester coming to mow Eva down. 'I know you too bloody well, don't I? And that's the trouble. I know you and that old bitch were too money hungry to leave that house and find a bit of bloody pride. I know you hated my guts from the day I was born, too. I know a lot about you, Eva.' The harvester has picked up a slashing blade from the bench. 'Get! Before I shove this through the bloody bankbook you call a heart.'

Eva is at the brown curtain. Through it she can see the passage leading to the open front door, but she's not going anywhere until her possessions are out, and those twins are on the far side of Mavis and her carving knife.

'You have the audacity to call this hovel a house. Do you really think you can take those boys away from me now, bring them back to *this*, let them rot here with the rest of you? Dear God. You don't know me at all, Mave.'

'Do you want me to tell the kids what I do know?'

'You're repulsive. You're an insult to womanhood. If Mother could see what you've come down to, she'd roll over in her grave.'

'And if it had been up to me, she wouldn't have had a bloody grave to roll over in. I would have left her to fossilise on the garbage dump like the hard old piece of pill-popping shit she always was. Get out!'

Words are flying backwards and forwards now, words dredged from the past Lori can no longer follow, though she's trying hard. The twins, fingers jammed into their ears, are looking from Eva to Mavis, from Mavis to Henry. Then the harvester heads for them and they've got enough sense to get out of the way. They go under the kitchen table with Neil and Timmy.

It's a bomb shelter with strong metal legs, a house within a house. It's spare, unused floor. Lori has done her share of time beneath that table and today looks like a good time to see if she's still small enough to fit.

Eva's high-heeled shoes make ground back to the table. They are almost toe to toe with the flattened scuffs. Then they head them off at the pass, giving the twins a clear pathway out the back door.

'Out to Alice, boys!' Eva yells. 'Run for your lives!'

Those twins have been well trained. They make their break for freedom from either side of a table leg. And they're through the door and running, until one falls over Mick's bike parts and sprawls on the verandah, lies there and bellows.

'Help me, someone,' Mavis yells. She slams Eva against the table, beats her to the door. No one is helping her, so she's helping herself. She's slow moving, but if she's going through a doorway, there is no room for anyone else to get by. And she's on the verandah, dragging the bawling twin up by his arm; he's probably split his head open, but she gets his head and his shoulders captured beneath her arm while Eva screams for Alice and the chooks cackle and squawk and Murphy's dogs over the road want to eat meat but can't get off their chains to party.

Eva is running down the drive, looking for her reinforcements while the captured twin screams and his other half is bundled head first into the rear seat of the car.

'Get the other one!' Mavis yells. All Henry is doing is trying to remove the captured twin from Mavis's armpit. He might get the body, but he won't get the head.

'You can't do this, Mavis,' Martin says, goes to assist Henry. She thumps him with her free elbow, curses him and Henry for a pair of blind fools, then heads for the bathroom, dragging the twin with her. It's got the only door with a key, and she's in, throwing her weight against that door, she's turning that key.

Martin and Henry have a go at twin retrieval by trying to go in through the bathroom window. She slams it down, almost takes the first knuckle off Martin's thumb. He probably won't be doing any bricklaying for the next week.

Eva is in the drive and she's bawling but there's no help to be gained from Alice and the solicitor. They're in the car and it's moving, one twin safe in the back seat.

'Get in, lass. Get in,' Alice urges.

Is a bird in the hand worth two in the bush? Eva looks at the house, sees, hears bedlam. She cuts her losses and runs after the moving car.

It looks as if one of Henry's twins has come home.

the freedom fighter

No one has cooked any stew. It's after six o'clock and that twin is still screaming. He's doing it in the kitchen now because two hours ago Henry and Martin went around to the motel to talk to Eva, so Mavis came out of the bathroom to heat up her chicken and roast potatoes while standing guard over that twin and not letting anyone else in the kitchen. She's armed with her whip now. No one wants a dose of that so they're giving her plenty of space.

The twin is under the table again and he's going to sit there and scream until Eva comes back. He'll be ten in a few weeks time but you'd think he was about three because he's wet his funeral pants. No one knows which one he is, either; Mavis couldn't get his pants off to see if his mole is on the right or left side of his bum. All of the kids are outside, even the little ones. Most of the neighbours are out too, watering their gardens so they can get an earful.

Donny comes home from work around half past six and doesn't know what's been going on, but he says that the cops will be coming around here in a minute. He could hear that kid screaming from up at the corner. He's not treating Mavis as if she's got the plague, though, so they sort of get their heads together, get her Valium down from the top cupboard over the sink and crush a tablet between two spoons, mix the powder in condensed milk, then Donny grabs the twin from behind, drags him free of table legs and Mavis forces the spoon into his mouth, which isn't hard to do because it's sort of

56

open in a never-ending scream. He gags and chokes, but he swallows some of the concoction and ten minutes later he's zapped. Donny picks him up and they put him into Neil's bed.

The silence is so good, until Henry and Martin come home and Mavis has to go in and sit guard on the bed while she feeds Matty. She's not modest about breast-feeding, but Martin is, because it is a seriously awesome sight – Nelly makes those tents with buttons on the shoulders instead of down the front. Martin waits until she's buttoned before he tries kidnap. A lot of cruel stuff is being said, but the twin isn't hearing it; nor is Henry, who is outside rounding up the rest of the kids, except for Greg and Vinnie, who are long gone. He finds Timmy asleep on Nelly's front lawn and he puts him to bed down one end of the lounge room while Mavis and Martin are still going at it at the other end.

Donny, who has been back to the supermarket for bread and cold meat and stuff, starts making a pile of sandwiches, and saying he's going to murder Martin if he gets that twin screaming again. He's been at work all bloody day and he's come home to bedlam and nothing to eat. And it's bloody Sunday tomorrow, and Martin might be able to piss off out to his girlfriend's place but Donny has to work again, so everybody just shut up their yelling and come out and get a sandwich.

'One way or another I'm taking that poor little bugger around to that motel, and that's the bloody end of it,' Martin yells. 'She can't do this to a little kid. You can't do it, Mavis.'

'I've done it, and you as much as touch him, then I'll do something to you too, you treacherous little swine,' Mavis yells back. 'Why didn't you help me get the other one instead of turning on me, and crawling around that twisted bitch?'

They are screaming across that bed now, but the twin keeps snoring. He's probably in a drug-induced coma, and it's a pity someone doesn't give Mavis a dose of her Valium and put her in a coma for a while. It's not good for her to get riled up like this, and Martin knows it. Maybe that's why he gives up, slams the front door and takes off in his ute, screaming the tyres, roaring the guts out of the motor. He's going out to Karen and the farm to find some bloody sanity. That's what he yells.

'And you better stay out there too,' Mavis screeches after him. 'We're going to need your bloody bed.' Then she goes into her bedroom and actually goes to bed and it's not even eight o'clock. She doesn't even have a sandwich. She must be worn out.

Donny makes good sandwiches. The kids eat, they drink their mugs of half milk and half tea then, without being told, they go to bed. Lori zaps her two five-dollar notes under her pillow. She's dreaming a gorgeous dream about a beautiful house when something wakes her up right in the middle of the best bit of the dream.

The world is almost cool and it's silent and she doesn't know what woke her. She listens. The baby isn't bawling and it's still dark outside, like it's the time-space between when the sun falls down in England and rises in Australia, an unreal, sweet-smelling time. The front door is always left open on hot nights, and the windows. She can smell the mint growing wild in Nelly's garden, and even the roses and the red geranium. Sweet smells are so delicious.

Then she sees what woke her. It's a tiny flame, just on, then off. It's a cigarette lighter. She freezes in her bed. It's not Mavis, because if she was up she'd have all the lights on. It's mangy old Alice and she's pulling Lori's sheet back. She's either half blind, or dark red hair and dark brown looked the same by a cigarette lighter's small flame. It's out now but she's found the right-sized arm and she's pulling on it. 'Up you get, boy,' she whispers, trying to drag Lori from her bed. 'On your feet now. Hop to it.'

'I'm the wrong one, Aunty Alice,' Lori whispers back.

Alice drops the arm, and she's gone. Lori yawns, hears a car door close soft, hears the car creep away, then she rolls over, yawns again and wonders why she ruined her chance of being kidnapped to television land where nobody sweats and you get to live in a house like the one in her dream.

If Alice had dropped in an hour later, she would have found the right body with no trouble at all. It's barely daylight when the Valium wears off and the twin goes off like a mad alarm clock. Henry is up, giving the baby a bottle. He always gets the dawn shift with babies.

No more sleeping is going to get done in this house. Soon everyone is up, scratching ribs, yawning and going about the business of trying to find something for breakfast. There's no milk left and the milk bar doesn't open for an hour. No one except Henry ever gets up this early on Sunday anyway. Donny doesn't start work until eight-thirty.

'Use some of the condensed milk in the shed. It's under my begonias, behind a packet of potting mix,' Henry says. He gives the baby weak condensed milk when Mavis is asleep, hides emergency rations in his potting shed with his strange flowers because Mavis really likes condensed milk. She can open a tin and sit there eating it with a spoon as if it's yoghurt.

'I want my mother,' the twin wails. He won't eat his breakfast. He stands in the kitchen bellowing. 'I want to go home. I want Eddy.'

And they finally know which one he is. They all start calling him Alan. Like, come and see the new baby chickens, Alan, or come and play under the sprinkler, Alan. He sure needs that sprinkler. He's hot as fire, but he won't move from the kitchen. He's red in the face and sort of panting, but he won't even sit down.

'He's Alan,' Henry tells Mavis when she gets out of bed, due to Matty is also throwing a screamer and Timmy, who never bawls, is bawling with him. Neil isn't, he's sitting under the table with Alan, making demon faces at him. Jamesy has left home. He's sitting on Nelly's front fence. Lori wanders over the road and sits with him, smells mint, smells roses and waits, waits for the waiting to end.

It doesn't. By lunchtime, more sandwiches, Henry is looking pasty grey and exhausted. He didn't take the twin to the motel while Mavis was asleep. He could have. He knows he should have, but he knows life wouldn't have been worth living if he had, though he's not too sure this morning that it's worth living anyway.

The little kids are still howling in sympathy with Alan, and Henry is trying to plug Matty's wail with a dummy, but Matty keeps spitting it out. Henry gives him to Mavis then he walks out back, walks in circles like a little grey shadow.

'I want to go home. I want my mother. I want Eddy,' Alan screams, and won't eat his sandwich. 'I want my Eddy,' he wails while the sun moves across the iron roof and Matty bawls and won't drink from Mavis. She's howling too. She sort of tosses the baby at Lori, then goes outside to walk in circles.

Lori plugs one bawl with a dummy, holds it in so Matty can't spit it out while she stares at that twin, wishing she could plug his mouth with a dummy.

'I want to go home.' Alan's voice grows husky as the day wears into night. He's done so much screaming there's barely a croak left in his throat.

Donny comes in from work, he's got a pile of shopping, even ice-cream, which Alan won't look at – he's got to be retarded. Anyway, Donny and Mavis try the old Valium in condensed milk trick but Alan's stomach isn't up to it. He gags, vomits on the kitchen floor.

He's burning hot, dry retching between croaks, and Henry is worried. They fight Alan's funeral clothes off, get him into a cool bath and find out he's Eddy, due to the mole being on the left cheek of his backside instead of the right. Stupid Eva has gone and got them mixed up. It's too late now. While they're talking about it, Alan fights his way out of the bath and runs for the space beneath the kitchen table and he's stark wet naked, and no one runs around naked in this house after they're about three years old.

Henry is trying to get some underdaks on him, but that twin is slippery when wet, and he's kicking back now. No one is going to save him so he has to save himself.

'We'll have to get the doctor to you, Alan,' Henry says. That threat works well on the rest of the brothers, it's usually enough for them to shake off appendicitis or even pneumonia, but it just makes

Alan scream with new hope, makes him dart backwards like a yabby, get his borrowed underdaks on, pull on his borrowed yellow shirt. He's getting ready for the doctor. God, give him a score of doctors. God, give him a brain transplant, just transplant him out of this place. He wants trousers. They haven't given him trousers. He wants his expensive shoes. Jamesy is wearing them.

Mavis has had enough of Henry's eyes accusing her every time they meet head on. The fridge is a gold mine and she keeps digging into it. She gets out the ice-cream, starts looking for a spoon and not worrying about a bowl. Henry tries to take it from her, but she snatches up her whip. One way or another, she's going to clear her kitchen and eat that ice-cream.

'Will you stop your gluttony! Can't you see what you've done here? Can't you see what you've done to this boy?'

'You did it, not me. You let them stay there when I begged you to bring them home. Two years ago I begged you and Martin to go down there and get them for me, but you wanted them to stay with the queer bitch, didn't you? You wanted something better for them than me, didn't you? I'm just a vile-mouthed, obese, eating bitch, aren't I? You wanted something better for yourself than me too, didn't you? Why don't you go back to the bitch and try it three in a bed? I don't need you. I don't need any man. You're all per-verted bastards anyway. Get! Get out of my sight. Go and sing your love songs to her, like you used to, and give her "Mumma" while you're about it.'

Henry walks outside and the twin screams louder.

'For God's sake, will you shut up,' Mavis moans. He wouldn't know how, even if he could hear her. 'Have some ice-cream,' she says. 'Here. Look.' She offers him a spoonful.

He won't accept it and won't shut up and Mavis is sweating and pale and sort of shaking, but she's eating ice-cream, shovelling it in fast. She tries a different tack. 'One more peep out of you and you'll get the whip around your bum,' she warns. 'Do you under-stand me, Alan? You're home, where you should have been five years ago, and you're going to stay home with your family. Do you understand me? We are your family.'

'I want my mother.' He's staring at her, screaming at her.

'I am your mother, not that lying, money-hungry bitch. This is your home. All of these kids are your brothers, for Christ's sake.' She thinks she's explaining things but he hasn't got a clue what she's talking about.

'I want my own brother,' Alan screams.

Lori watches, listens from the doorway, seeing this twin as a hostage in some mad old war that has been going on since Eva and Grandmother Hilda first set eyes on Mavis. Maybe she was supposed to be a boy and she turned out a girl. Lori doesn't know why that war got started but now some poor innocent little country has gone and got itself caught up in it and it's going to get bombed; it's going to get wiped off the planet.

That peculiar feeling has come back, that weird eleven year old, lonely knowing feeling – like she's a girl whether she wants to be or not. Like those twin boils under her T-shirt are going to turn into great Mavis boobs one day and she can't stop them doing it no matter how much she flattens them with Neil's singlets. And it's like, this is a female war, and only females can fight in it, so she has to fight for that little country's freedom or he's going to be dead. She's just got no choice . . . except her legs won't move her to do anything. Her head is running wild with making mad pictures which she can't keep in a straight line. They are all curving around things, curving into something different while her skin gets cold and goosebumpy, and the inside of her head sort of swells up like it will explode with doing nothing.

Then Mavis has had enough of Alan screaming for Eva and not her. Her whip flicks at Alan's round bare legs. It probably doesn't hurt that much, but his scream is cruel, his air-intake scream more awesome than his air-out scream while his bare feet stamp the floor, running, running, running to nowhere.

'For Christ's sake, leave that poor little bugger alone, Mavis,'

Donny yells and he grabs at the whip. Mavis is out of control now. She's bawling, shaking, screaming crazy stuff. She aims the whip at Donny and gets him a beauty around the ears. He grabs the end, pulls on it; he might be taller than her, but he's a nine-stone weakling trying to pull a tractor.

Henry tries to hold her whipping arm. Mavis shakes him off. She's so powerful when she goes into her bad, mad, eating-mood place. All you can do is run from her when she's in that place.

Lori doesn't think about what happens next. It's as if her thinking has stopped stone dead. Just her feet are thinking. They move her forward, closer to the action.

Then she's 007 racing into a war zone, she's grasping an arm, and Alan's feet, already running on the spot, keep moving behind her. They are out the back door, over the fallen lattice, up the west verandah, out on the road while Mavis bulldozes through the front door with Donny and Henry behind her.

The neighbours are watering their gardens again, glad of a bit of entertainment; there hasn't been a thing worth watching on television since before Christmas. Lori looks at the shapes hiding behind shrubs, behind gates. With Alan still half naked, there is nowhere to go except bush. She swerves, heads across the road and towards the river, dragging him behind her. She could climb up a tree and Mavis would never get her, but Alan probably doesn't know what a tree is. Lori keeps dragging him down the hard clay track.

Henry hasn't followed them, or Donny; those two won't bring this fight out of the house. Mavis is following, slow but dogged. She's still yelling too.

They hide behind a gum tree, but when they see that she's still coming, Alan starts forward again, dragging Lori by the hand. The river is before them, Willama West and the caravan park full of tourists on the other side, and suddenly those tourists are no longer the enemy, but safe territory. Lori waits. Mavis will give up soon.

No way. Not today. Eva might have won the battle of their

mother's money but she's not going to win the war of the twins. Mavis fought hard to get him and she's not losing him now.

Lori leads Alan down to the water's edge and he's more than willing; he drags her in, thigh deep, then deeper still because Mavis's bellow is hitting the river, sort of bouncing around, coming from all sides. It sounds as if there are six yowies pursuing them when one is more than plenty. Alan, too scared to look behind, keeps pulling on Lori's hand until her feet lose their grip on the sandy floor. He goes under, and comes up spitting water, his arms wrapped around her.

'Swim,' she says. He's not swimming. His hands are grasping at her hair. Nothing there to grasp. He grasps her ears. 'Swim, you moron!' Her last word becomes lost in bubbles because they are both under, and suddenly the familiar old river becomes an alien, dragging thing.

She cancels out Willama West, fights her way up, looks back at the home bank. Got to get him back to it. She's been swimming since she was three; the only thing she wins at school is the swimming, but his weight is too much, and his grip is stopping her arms from moving. She's dragged under again, dragged deep. This time she lashes out with a foot, connecting with the softness of his stomach. That breaks his grip. But the current snatches him, takes him.

Fear driving her, her arms reach, her fingers reach, and her feet. One brushes the smoothness of bare leg, and her ankle hooks on while her hands grasp. She surfaces. He comes up bum first, and when she rights him with a hand in his hair, he bellows, gags on water while she searches the bank, hoping Mavis is still coming after them. She might float, might make a raft.

Gripping the collar of his borrowed shirt, holding his head high, she shakes him, slaps him, and all the while the current is carrying them downstream. He bellows and gags and his hands grasp what they can while his legs lock up her own.

She is tiring, and when they go down for the third time she knows they're in trouble; the current has taken them too far from the bank.

She hammers Alan's head with a clenched fist, hammers until her air is gone and her lungs are bursting.

Short war. Freedom fighter massacred. Little country wiped out. No bombs necessary.

But this is Henry's twin, his hidden treasure. She can't let him drown. She drags one foot high. Kicks. It catches Alan in the throat. Beyond caring, she kicks him below the belt, just for good measure. And he stops fighting her. Rolling onto her back then, she exchanges her hold for a headlock. He is limp, easy to control. Almost floating.

Dead men float. On television they call them floaters. Maybe she's drowned him already. She's thinking of Henry as they float towards the bridge. He'll never forgive her. She took Alan into the river when she should have just kept running, gone bush, introduced him to a tree. The stupid moron, she thought he'd be able to swim. Everyone can swim.

Got to trust the river now, not fight its current. That's what Martin tells all the little kids. Never try to fight the current. Never panic if you think you're in trouble, just go with the flow and keep your cool. Let the river carry you.

Using one arm only and kicking slow, she goes with the current; it supports her, carries her down to the bridge where it sweeps her into the shallows. She's surprised when her feet touch bottom, though they are useless, tired, scared feet. Her legs tremble as she drags Alan ashore and he's a dead weight once landed. On her knees, panting, she gets most of him out of the water and calls it good enough, rolls him onto his stomach.

'Wake up.' She sits on his back, hoping to squeeze the water from his lungs. Her heart is racing like crazy. She's trying to think, and she's sucking air while her jelly limbs cry out for help.

'Wake up, you idiot.' The school showed everyone how you give people the kiss of life. She probably knows how. She might have listened, and maybe she'll try it – for Henry. But she doesn't have to because the last thump down on his back did the trick. He bucks her off then vomits and splutters out half the river, which at least got some water into him, because when he takes up his wail again, it's strong, like he'd never even been dehydrated.

'I want my brother.'

Lori rolls onto her stomach, shaking her head in disgust. 'Can you say any bloody thing else at all? You nearly drowned both of us, you moron.'

'I want my mother,' he screams.

'Mavis *is* your mother, so shut up or you'll get what you want.' Grasping a handful of his wet hair she points his nose first towards the river and the dark trees beyond, then towards the town lights. 'Which way do you want to go?'

'I want my – ' he starts. He's sitting up now, his head swivelling, then one hand points to the lights. 'I want . . . that way.' Any way that doesn't lead back to that giant lady and her whip has got to be the better way.

Lori helps him to his feet when her own legs feel strong enough and for once she understands exactly how Mick's bad leg must feel. Hers are as wobbly as jelly snakes.

'Where was Aunty Eva and Alice staying?' she says, taking hold of his hand and leading him towards the town.

'Where *were* they staying.' He stresses the *were*, like he's correcting her! The bloody smartarse, posh-talking, howling, useless little mongrel! She should have let him drown for laughing at her birthday cake. Should have. She hates people laughing at her and hates it more if people correct her speech. She knows what's correct. Henry always says things the correct way, just everyone else doesn't, so why bother?

She drops his hand. 'Find them yourself then, you laughing, bawling smartarse.'

He takes her hand again and holds on tight. 'I don't know where. It's a motel and it's got a swimming pool.'

'They've all got swimming pools.'

'No, they haven't, because my mother asked on the phone.'

'You're a pure smartarse, that's what you are. And they nearly all have got swimming pools. What's its name? Is it in the town or out of the town?'

'It's . . . it's . . . down the road to home, but after you drive off the freeway.'

'Willama doesn't have freeways. We've got roads. Come on. And you whinge one more time, or try and be a smartarse once more, and I'll take you back to Mavis.'

Two hours later Martin and Donny find them heading over the bridge to check the Budget Motel in Willama West. They are exhausted, but still holding hands, and even Alan is pleased to get into Martin's ute. Donny buys them a bucket of chips each and a bottle of Coke to share and no one has to talk Alan into eating. He eats every chip and drinks most of the bottle of Coke too while Martin drives to the motel where he and Henry last saw Eva. She's checked out. There are many motels in Willama, and one over the bridge. None is giving shelter to Eva or her car tonight.

'They must have gone home. Quit while they were ahead,' Donny says.

'Drive him to Melbourne. She might give us the fifty thousand for a reward,' Lori says around a yawn.

It's too late and too far and Martin hasn't got enough petrol or maybe he would. He's still mad enough to do it. He doesn't want to take the poor little bugger back to Mavis. That's what he says, but Donny says, what's the alternative? So back they go, over the railway lines, back to the madhouse.

They can hear Mavis going at Henry in the kitchen, but Alan is half asleep so they lead him in through the front door to the lounge bedroom where Neil is in his own bed. There are no spares so they put him in Lori's bed.

'Climb in with him, Splint. Look after him. I think he's taken to you,' Martin says.

She climbs in and snuggles down, yawns, thinks Alan takes up too much room, but at least he smells good. Even after the river and the walking, his hair still smells good, like expensive shampoo. She sniffs his hair and it cancels out the smell of socks. She sniffs, puts her arm over him as she fits herself into the limited space.

She sleeps.

a best friend

Mavis's bad, mad eating moods are pretty awesome to live around, but they're old news to Lori and the brothers. Not to Alan. Each day is an eye-opener, and each day his wide baby-blue eyes grow wider as he watches her stuff her face with chocolates and biscuits, potato cakes and fish and chips, custard, pancakes and tins of condensed milk. He doesn't want to eat, doesn't want to go to school, just wants to go home to Eddy.

Willama is a fire-breathing dragon, stalking him from sunrise to sunset, burning him with its breath and dazzling his eyes with its fire, eyes that won't stop crying, though he's doing it soft now, doing it outside, where the sheets on the clothesline reflect the dragon's white-hot heat, and there are sheets on the clothesline every day because Alan wets the bed every night. Lori kicked him out of her bed that first night because no normal person over three ever wets beds in this house.

Henry buys a new set of bunk beds and the next weekend he and Martin wallpaper the west room with tough vinyl stripey stuff before setting up the new bunks opposite the old. Mick's single bed is moved into the lounge room, then everyone gets to play musical beds – nearly everyone.

Greg and Vinnie now own a top bunk each, which will stop a bit of fighting. Mick gets the bunk under Greg, and Jamesy is moved in to sleep under Vinnie, due to he'll survive Greg and Vinnie better than Alan would. Neil moves into Mick's old bed, Alan into Neil's, with the rubber mattress cover. Timmy, who still wears disposable napkins at night so doesn't need a mattress cover, gets moved out of the cot and into Jamesy's old bed and Matty goes into the cot, even though he's sort of lost in it.

Lori doesn't get moved. She's the girl so she has to sleep closest to Mavis's door – and why she can't sleep in the bunk room instead of Jamesy, she doesn't know. She's the next biggest to Mick and she's heaps bigger than Jamesy, and it's not fair that she's got to be stuck in the lounge room with the little ones, and bawling Matty too. It's just not fair.

All day the house stands in the sun, windows open, collecting the heat, storing it up so it can roast people in their beds at night while mosquitoes suck blood and bodies toss and turn like oily sardines packed into a tin. All day Mavis rants and eats and smokes while Henry and the kids wait for her bad mood to pass. It will pass. Her eating moods always pass after a bit – though this one is lasting longer than most. And that's Alan's fault, because he won't stop howling, and he won't talk to her either; he runs away if she comes within two metres of him.

'I'm your bloody mother,' she yells. 'You grew inside me, not her.' He looks at that massive jelly mound of her stomach and has another fit of the screams. And who'd blame him? It would be better if she'd just leave him alone. And leave Henry alone too. He's copping it every night, she's keeping him awake every night and when he goes to work after getting no sleep, she goes to bed and sleeps most of the day while Matty bellows and Alan howls.

People can't cry forever. They run out of tears after a while. People can't eat forever, either. They run out of food in the cupboards and fridge and out of money; Henry is refusing to get Mavis's child allowance money from the bank. Things settle down a bit and Alan starts acting like that last retarded Labrador pup Mavis adopted, except Alan is on Lori's heels all day instead of Mavis's. Every time she turns around, he's behind her. He sits close to her each night at the table, though he still won't look at a plate full of pumpkin, cabbage, grey broad beans and Henry's stew. He looks at Mavis's roast potatoes she cooks for herself. He doesn't get them because if Henry cooks him roast potatoes, all the other kids will want them too.

This seems to be the year for forgetting birthdays. Alan's tenth birthday gets lost sometime in mid March. No one remembers it, except Eva, who sends him fifty dollars which Mavis accepts gratefully. By the time Henry remembers, it's too late for the usual bought cake and candles, and by March's end, Alan's eyes look bigger due to his face looking smaller and his hair being shorter – it and his feet smell like everyone else's now, but he's stopped most of his crying and as Mavis has no intention of ever sending him back to Eva, Henry gets him enrolled at school. He is put in grade five, two years ahead of Jamesy when he seems like two years younger.

Lori's teacher still hates her, and some days Alan gets pushed through the school gate then Lori nicks off, goes home to find Matty bawling and Mavis sleeping. She plugs the bawl with a bottle of weak condensed milk or, if Mavis is out of bed and eating, Lori nicks off to town to watch the tourists and look for money, or just to prowl the supermarkets, pinching grapes and nuts. You can eat a lot of grapes and nuts without being noticed. Everyone tries them before they buy – it's not really stealing. She'd like to test a banana too but she's not game. She never gets a whole banana at home.

It's really weird about Alan and school, though; like, it's totally weird. He might be a bawling, bed-wetting two year old at home, but he knows everything at school – even when Captain Cook landed. Lori knows too much about many things, and not enough about Captain Cook, who she has to do an assignment on for homework, and because she can't get away from Alan, he does most of it, even draws a picture of a sailing boat for her. He's like a pup on a leash, but a useful and a nice enough pup. You can understand his writing too. She gets to almost like having him dogging her footsteps, maybe gets to even like him a bit, which is pretty easy to do with pups, because they make it plain obvious that they just love you.

There's no more wandering around the river by herself, though, no more scaring the tourists by herself, and no more free thinking time either. If she goes to the river, Alan follows her, but it's good having someone to swim with. She teaches him about the current, and how you never try to swim upstream, and how you never swim out to the middle if the speedboats are out. They'd cut you in half as quick as look at you. She shows him how, if you want to swim across the river, you have to start way upstream, and let the current help you across. He could already swim but now he's an excellent river swimmer, which is different to being an excellent swimming pool swimmer.

So the weeks keep on going and the solicitor's letters stop coming as regularly and Alan stops bed-wetting, which is around the time Lori discovers he is truly as mad as a rabbit because he actually loves his schoolteacher. No one, but no one, even likes schoolteachers. And he doesn't just know about Captain Cook and that sort of stuff. He can spell! And he's truly excellent at maths; also, he knows things like where Turkey is on the map. His head must have been crammed full of school stuff by old Alice.

Anyway, Mavis finally comes out of her mad bad mood; she's back to feeding Matty regularly and Matty is glad to be getting fed so he's smiling and not quite as ugly as he was, or quite as fat, though he still hasn't got any hair. She's back to cuddling Timmy at night and watching the quiz shows. It's a huge relief. Everyone is laughing again and so happy, and Martin isn't talking about leaving home.

Alan has been in Willama for two months when Greg borrows *Basic Instinct* from the video shop. When Henry gets finished with the washing and the mopping and goes to bed to read, and when everyone under Greg has been sent to bed, Lori shows Alan how to creep out, how to stand with Vinnie behind the curtain in the passage and watch the video without being seen by Mavis.

He doesn't know what those actors are supposed to be doing against the wall, though; he's like a newborn baby about sex so Lori has to tell him heaps. Like where Matty came from, even, and how he got inside Mavis in the first place – how all the kids got inside her.

'Eddy and I didn't,' Alan says.

'You did so.'

'We did not.'

'You did so.'

It's a bit like having a friend to talk to and argue with, having Alan at home. She hasn't had a friend since about first grade, and she knows she shouldn't do it, due to Henry said so, and Martin, who said he'd murder her if she ever told one single person about it. But in books, best friends tell all their secrets, and anyhow, Alan is more than a best friend, he's a brother, so one Saturday afternoon she tells him Henry's BIG secret, because what use is a secret if you can't tell it to people?

'Well, you're not allowed to tell anyone. Ever. Spit your death and hope to die. And you're not allowed to tell Henry or Martin that I told you, and you're not allowed to tell the little ones – or anyone at school, ever, in a million years, even.'

'Okay.'

'Well, spit.' He spits and looks over his shoulder just to make sure Alice isn't still watching him. 'We've got Aboriginal blood in us,' Lori says.

'Who?'

'Us. All of us . . . except Mavis, and nobody knew until about a year ago because Henry got adopted, but his real grandmother was a light complexion Aboriginal, and his grandfather was a Indian man called Woden – '

'Didn't he have a mother?'

'Of course he did. Whose stomach do you think he grew in, moron?' Lori says.

Growing in stomachs still has a way of turning Alan's. His

shoulders sort of hunch up, then he shakes his head. 'You're telling lies. Show me your tongue.'

'I am not. And I will not. His mother's name was Lily.' The papers didn't say much about Lily, but Lori's imagination fills in the gaps. 'She was actually an Aboriginal princess and she had long black hair, and she used to wear jeans and long diamond and ruby earrings from the West Australia diamond and ruby mine, because our tribe owned it first. She died when Henry got stolen. Actually, she tried to stow away on the plane that took him to England and she suffocated in the luggage compartment – '

'If you tell lies, your tongue turns blue and yours is blue. How could his mother be a princess if his grandfather was Indian and his grandmother was only part Aborigine?'

'You don't have to be black to be an Aborigine.'

'I mean about being a princess.'

'Well.' Lori scratches at the dust with her foot. 'Well, I don't know, really, not about that, but she was. She probably got elected or something.'

'Was Henry's father Aboriginal?'

She squints at the sun, tries to remember what Mavis said when she got that brown envelope about the adoption last year – or maybe the year before. 'I think the letter said he was a white boy. I think he was Henry someone – probably Prince Henry, and that's how Lily came to be a princess.' It sounds logical. 'So, do you feel different now?'

'About what?'

'Like about Aboriginal culture and Captain Cook pinching Australia from you?'

'He discovered Australia, he didn't pinch it. Anyway, that's stupid. How could I feel Aboriginal culture now if I didn't feel it before?'

'I do, and I hate Captain Cook like rat poison, and when I grow up I'm going to claim land rights in that diamond mine in West Australia and be as rich as Eva.'

Alan shrugs, walks off to the kitchen and comes back with Henry's vegetable knife and four apples, which the kids collect by the bucketful, due to Bert Matthews's two huge apple trees that lean over the vacant block fence and drop apples by the thousand unless the kids get to them first. Anyway, Alan sits down and starts cutting one into slices which he offers to Lori. 'That's about how much of an Aborigine you are – if it's true.'

She eats the apple. 'It's true, and anyway, I hate fractions. Us Aborigines don't think in fractions. If we want to be black we just say that we are – like Kelly Waters. She used to be white and then one day her grandfather said that his grandmother had black blood so now they've all gone black – Martin says it's so Kelly's oldest sister can go to university for free.'

He stares at her with his big blue eyes, sort of shrugs as he selects another apple. It's seriously wormy, but good enough for what he wants it for. He cuts four quarters, calls one Henry's grandmother and he sets her on the verandah, cuts a quarter in half and calls one bit Lily, places her down too. Another cut, Henry is a sixteenth, and one more makes Lori into a paper-thin slice. 'You'd be about a thirty-second,' he says.

She's learning something here, though she's not going to let him know that.

'What about thirds and sixths? Say if Henry's grandmother was a third?'

You can't cut thirds into thirty-seconds but you *can* make a quarter and a third into twelfths. Fractions start to make sense. Lori watches each cut. She watches Henry's grandfather, a full apple, placed down on a verandah board. And Lily, she gets to be half an apple this time. Henry, the quarter, joins them, then Lori, the eighth, is placed directly below Lori the thirty-second – and makes her look very small.

'You're more Indian – if what you said is true. Why don't you say you're Indian if you want to be someone different to who you are?'

She starts eating apple pieces, even the thirty-second, which isn't a very big bite of an apple and not much of a claim on land rights in that diamond mine either. She's got heaps more Indian blood, but who wants to claim land rights in India and die of starvation or get sold for sex?

They share the apples, squash the worms, then she shows Alan how to peel and eat apple seeds, which he has never done in his life; like, he didn't know you could even eat them. Lori sticks a black apple seed on her forehead with spit. 'Do I look like an Indian princess?' she says.

'You look like a skin-head Australian girl with an apple seed stuck on your face. Anyway, in Melbourne, it's not what you look like, it's how you talk. In Melbourne everyone comes from everywhere and you don't even think about where they come from first, not if they talk Australian,' Alan says, killing that plan too and peeling another apple seed. He likes them, says they taste like almonds.

What with his fractions and stuff he gives her a lot to think about; also, having him home has stopped the kids, white and black, from picking on her. Alan is a wide-eyed wimp, but he's a tall wimp, and Jamesy, who isn't tall, isn't a wimp. It's like Alan has filled up the gap in the family, like eleven and eight have got themselves welded together by Alan's ten. Mavis did a good thing getting him home. She says she's going to get the other one too, though Eva sure won't be gullible enough to bring him up here again.

Alan is a bit soft in the head, due to all the schoolwork stuffed in there; he likes doing weird stuff, like getting Jamesy and Neil to help build a cubbyhouse from the pile of bricks which Martin always reckoned he was going to use one day to build himself a bungalow. Everyone knows that his one day will never come now, because of Karen, so they can use his bricks if they want to.

They build the cubby under the peppercorn tree, which is behind the chook-pens at the back corner of Henry's vacant block where the fences and the low branches make it private. Lori starts carting bricks too. She's just doing it to keep Alan happy. That's what she says to

Mick, which isn't the truth, because she's having fun doing it, building it big, building lines of bricks for walls with gaps for doors. It's like Alan knows how to make magic in his head as well as fractions, and his magic is rubbing off on Lori.

They make brick chairs and tables with the old palings the fence man tossed onto the junk heap when he built the new fence at the back. They get some old sheets from Henry's rag-bag for tablecloths, and plastic knives and forks from Mavis's Chinese takeaway, and they pick a few flowers and put them in a jar of water and sit it on their table. It's like they've got their own house to go to. For the first time in her life, Lori plays tea-parties, fills Coke bottles with water and eats wormy apples. The magic gets so good sometimes that the water really tastes like Coke.

Maybe Alan is helping to turn Lori into a girl. But her chest bumps aren't getting any bigger and she hasn't got any hair under her arms and she still makes Henry cut her hair like the boys, so on the outside she still looks like a boy.

Then May is finished and overnight the rains come to turn dust into mud. To get to the loo or to the cubbyhouse they walk though mud, and Henry's floors are covered in it. He mops a lot and the rain keeps on falling, like it's been storing it up for months. The sides of the roads turn into lakes and getting from one footpath to the next is slippery.

Some days when they walk to school in the rain, Alan talks about Eddy and home, but it's funny, because it's not people things he seems to miss; what he misses most is being driven to school, and going to the cinema with Eddy, and flying in aeroplanes to Queensland for the holidays, and even to America once. And he really misses his drawer full of soft socks. The missing is getting less, though. He loves little Matty, tickles him and makes him gurgle, and Timmy, who used to spend half his life staring at Matty or wandering over the road to squat in Nelly's garden, now follows Alan around like a pup.

Also, Alan has discovered Henry – not the house Henry, but the singing, potting shed Henry. He tells Lori that he can remember Henry being his father before, even remember him singing before when he used to fly over from London to visit them.

'He never did fly over from London,' Lori says.

'He did so,' Alan says. 'He did fly over, heaps of times, because I can remember him singing.'

'He didn't ever live in London since you got born. He lived here and he used to always be going to Melbourne on the bus until after you were five. Mavis even went sometimes if you were in hospital.'

'He lived in London. He wrote to us from there, all the time.'

'He wrote to you from Willama and I saw him do it, every month. Like on the first Sunday of every month. I even posted some of the letters. Him and Mavis have been here in this house since Mick was born. You were even born here, in this house – or one of you came out in this house. The other one came out at the hospital.'

'We did not come out of her.'

'You did so, and you're not even Alan anyway. You're Edward, because everyone could only ever tell you apart by the moles on your bums and your mole was on the other side, so you're Edward.'

'You're making it all up . . . like you did when you said Henry's mother was Princess Lily and she owned a diamond and ruby mine.'

'I didn't make up about you getting born here.'

'You did. Henry always lived in London, because my mother said so.'

'Eva is a liar, and she's not your mother. She pinched you from us because Henry was her husband first, but Mavis pinched him from her. And they lived all over the place, like gypsies, until Mick got born with his crippled leg,' Lori says. She wants Alan to believe her, but he's still shaking his head. He can't believe her because if he does, then that makes his mother not his mother, and if Eva isn't his mother then Mavis might be.

'He lived in London,' he says, his eyes staring at his muddy shoes. 'He lived in London, because he wasn't ever happy in Australia, and he used to get on the plane and fly over the ocean to see us. And Eddy and I got born in London, and we lived with Henry until we got bad hearts and Henry brought us to Australia because the weather was better and we needed a caring mother to make us well. And I heard Eva say that to Mrs Howard from school. So there.'

'What a bloody lie that is! You got born right here, and your hearts were messed up from the day you got born and you lived here in this house for two years – when you weren't in the hospital half dying. And Eva hasn't got any right to get you back and she hasn't got any right to keep Eddy either – and that's why she keeps writing letters and trying to buy you off Mavis. And Mavis is keeping all of her letters too, and she's going to show them to a judge one day for evidence and he'll make Eva give Eddy back. And you go and ask Henry if you don't believe me, because I'm not wasting my breath any more on talking to idiots who believe in lies.'

Alan goes with her each night now to listen to Henry's potting shed songs. They are watching him re-pot some lumpy looking bulb thing when Alan asks about London and how many times Henry flew over from London.

Henry, being a totally good person, couldn't tell a lie to save his life. He tells Alan the truth, while making excuses for Eva instead of rubbing in what a liar she really is.

Lori rubs it in later.

tonsillitis

June can get bitter, killer cold in Willama so the tourists stay away, which is good, but the old house isn't so good; it's sort of damp and freezing cold. It's got two open fireplaces, one in the middle boys' bunk room and one behind a big old wardrobe in the lounge-room bedroom. Henry says it's too dangerous to light open fires, which might burn the house down, so the brothers crowd into the kitchen at night, where the breeze seeping through the louvres is no longer called a breeze, but a draught. Alan sits in the draught one night and he gets sick.

'Uncle Henry,' he says. He can't call him just Henry, and no one else calls him Dad, so he has found his own special name. 'Uncle Henry, my throat is very sore this morning. I think it's my tonsillitis. Eddy and I always get it in the winter.'

Henry looks at the diseased strawberry tonsils blocking Alan's throat. 'Give him a Panadol, Martin, and keep him inside today. Make him a salt and water gargle every four hours or so,' he says, and he washes his hands of the matter and goes back to cutting a thousand Vegemite sandwiches. Mavis doesn't like Vegemite so all the kids get Vegemite sandwiches for school lunches.

Henry looks sick too. He's got a terrible cough and it's making him greyer and smaller every day but he still goes to work. Martin is a bricklayer and brickies never work when it's raining. He was planning to go out to see Karen and now he's going to be stuck at home all day with Mavis. He's not happy.

Donny rides off to the supermarket; Greg and Vinnie ride off towards the high school, though they probably won't get that far. Henry drops Mick off before he goes to work and Lori and Jamesy walk to school in the rain.

Alan's sore throat is only the start of a bad winter, because every homeless germ in Willama comes looking for him; they chase him until they catch him. He's always sick, always in bed, and Lori misses arguing with him. Henry just gets him better with his salt and water gargle and his Panadol and Alan goes out and soaks up some more germs. They live on him, and slowly he starts sharing them with the rest of the family.

Henry is worried about Alan's old heart thing – there is a huge scar right down the middle of his chest. He doesn't worry about the other kids. Like Lori, they got born tough, got born into tough. He gets the boys to help clean up the house and he gets the doctor to come. Alan's heart is okay, it's his tonsils; they may have to come out, the old doctor says. He gives Henry a prescription for antibiotics, which work fast, and Alan goes back to school. A week later some flu germs track him down and he brings them home to share with Mavis.

When she gets sick, she gets sick, and there is a lot of her to get sick. She's hacking and coughing and smoking and she can't even eat. It's killing her. She's sick as a dog and madder than a hornet on heat and maybe she even loses a bit of weight, but by the time July is over, she's making up for lost time. Her bad, mad, eating, no-sleeping mood has come back, like in triplicate.

The doctor comes again to Alan, but he's more worried about Mavis. He says she has to diet or her heart will give up, so Henry tries to make her diet, like he's serving her steamed fish and vegetables at night and he's keeping his fridge and pantry bare, and when Greg gets bribed to buy her a huge mess of fish and chips one night, Henry takes them, wastes them, puts them in the stove and lets them burn.

Mavis throws a screamer. It's a bit later when she puts her best tent on, puts on her make-up and walks off to the hotel for a counter meal. It's not far away, just around the corner and down a bit from the milk bar.

Every night then she's walking off to the hotel as soon as Henry gets home from work. She drinks wine there too, because one night she comes home laughing, not average laughing, but over the top laughing. For a while Lori thinks that her mad eating mood is over, but it's not – it's just a different type of mad mood. Anyway, that night she gets out Henry's typewriter and writes to Eva, says that they want to go through with the deal. Two ten year olds for one hundred thousand dollars and ten per cent of the shares Eva inherited. Bargain rates, never again to be repeated. Mavis reads her letter to everyone. She doesn't sign it with her MSO squiggle, though, she signs Henry's name and tries to do his long skinny signature, and she's laughing so much that the kids can't help laughing with her. Henry is not laughing and he's not going to post that letter.

Greg does, though, and gets five dollars to do it.

Poor Henry, he coughs and pleads, shrugs and coughs, cooks and coughs.

Then two days later Mr Watts writes back in one of those yellow Express Post envelopes. Henry opens it, his hands shaking and sweating because he thinks there is going to be a court case over selling the twins, but all the letter says is that Eva and Alice have rented out the St Kilda property and have gone to London for twelve months. Henry let Eva get passports for the twins so they could go to Disneyland when they were seven, so Eva has flown away and stuck Mavis with a kid who can't take her without antibiotics.

She starts getting into Henry for not bringing those twins home five years ago, gets into him for letting Eva get passports, gets into Henry by writing another mad letter. She writes truly excellent letters. All the kids laugh when she reads them out. They'd make a cat laugh. She writes to Lori's teacher one day and that teacher is not laughing – neither is Henry, because her name is Mrs Cripps and Mavis spelt it with an 'A'.

'You're behaving like a fool,' he says. 'And worse than that, you've made a fool of that child.' He coughs and cleans, coughs and shrinks a little more each day.

Mr Watts sends another Express Post envelope. He says Eva is prepared to pay seventy-five thousand dollars and five per cent of the shares; however, the house has been leased until May of next year. Eva will not be back in Australia until then, whatsoever and how-for-so-ever, or whatever, if Mavis is prepared to sign the papers, Eva is prepared to pay Alan and Henry's airfares to London where the final signatures can be added to the document.

And Henry has had enough of Mavis. He's going to London whether she signs or not. He applies for renewal of his passport, rings Mr Watts about Alan's passport, gets the doctor around again. It's that doctor who throws a spanner in the works, says that at the moment Alan is not up to a twenty-four hour flight to London, nor is Henry. Alan has got a middle ear infection and Henry can't shake his bronchitis, which isn't bronchitis, it's emphysema, due to growing up in wet England or to Mavis's smoking like a chimney. The doctor prescribes a heap of antibiotics for him and a week off work. Alan gets more antibiotics and eardrops and Mavis gets more Valium and some new antidepressant tablets because she's probably got post-natal depression or whatever.

Henry takes his pills and he pleads with Mavis to take hers. That's exactly what she wants, because when he looks worried about her, she knows her eating is doing some good, so she eats more. Eats anything. When there's only flour and eggs in the house, she makes pancakes and stands in front of Henry eating them, even if she's got no jam to put on them. He hides condensed milk in the old trunk in the laundry. She finds it, and follows him around, eating it with a spoon and telling him what he can do with the antidepressant pills, which doesn't sound comfortable. She sends Greg to the bank for withdrawal forms, then sends him back to get the money out – and gives him ten whole dollars for doing it. Then she walks off to the milk bar and comes back with half a dozen blocks of chocolate and she stuffs the lot, her big eyes sort of flirting with Henry while she's stuffing chocolate into her mouth, hurting him, making him care – trying to make him care. You can see her getting bigger with each block. You can see Henry caring less.

All the chocolate comes through her milk, into Matty, and straight out the other end. His nappies are terrible. Martin tells her she is making Matty sick with her stuffing, but he may as well tell her she's won the lottery, so he and Donny buy a tin of baby formula and Henry gets a doctor's certificate for another week off work. He feeds Matty formula, won't let Mavis near him.

Mavis doesn't care. She didn't want another boy.

By mid August her tents are too tight and Henry looks as if he's taking diet pills. He's hanging on, just hanging in there. He's doing what he can; he's back at work and he's coughing, sucking on an inhaler and coughing and trying to make Greg and Vinnie go to school. He can't sing, he's got no breath. He's looking after Alan, and he's mopping the floors and sweeping up Mavis's butts and making up Matty's formula each night, lining the bottles up in the fridge. He's trying to keep things together, hanging in there by his teeth and toenails, but the rest of him is a floppy, grey, coughing rag.

Then Greg gets expelled from school. He's been pinching stuff out of the other kids' lockers. Everyone in the house, except Henry and Mavis, have always known that Greg is a spoilt-rotten thief, so now it's official.

Greg starts sleeping all day and roaming all night, or some days he just roams all day and all night until Martin or Henry track him down some place and bring him home fighting. Then one night the police bring him home. Seeing a policeman at the door breaks up the last of Henry's heart. He cries. He's the only glue holding this mad-house together, but Greg and Mavis are doing their level-best to rip that glue apart.

Martin comes up with an idea. He tells Greg he'll pay him ten dollars a week to stay at home, rip up the back verandah floorboards and dig the foundations for the room Martin has been planning to build on the back. Martin, bricklaying since before he was sixteen, has been hoarding leftover bricks for that room since he started work.

Greg thinks about it. He's also thinking about nicking off to Melbourne so he can get a special allowance for abused kids, because Martin and Donny are abusing him when he tries to sneak out at night. Donny says he'll give Greg five dollars a week – that's fifteen – that's a fortune.

'But you're going to work for it,' Martin says. 'And you're not going near the town unless you're with Vinnie or Mick.'

'That fucking pair of morons? Who'd want to be seen dead with them?' Greg sneers.

Mick is no moron, though Vinnie might be. Stick a ring through his nose and you can lead him anywhere, get him to do anything. Like, Henry can even get him to help do the washing on Saturdays, can get him to mix Matty's bottles, cook sausages, boil rice.

Martin starts wrecking floorboards, showing Greg how to do it while he stands back leaning but not learning much. He gets a few boards up that first week and gets paid, then he nicks off. And good riddance to bad rubbish.

That back verandah roof propped, the floor half wrecked, little kids running out the kitchen door and disappearing down the gap – well, there's no stopping now. Vinnie says he'll work for five dollars a week. He's only fourteen but he towers over Martin, is taller than Donny, and heavier. He's going to be a giant, and every inch he grows, Mavis hates him more – and Matty is getting to look a bit like him too, which might be why Mavis prefers Timmy. The fact that she's showing some interest in Timmy could mean she's coming out of her mad mood, though.

The boys should get a permit from the council, Henry says, but Martin reckons that the back yard is a junk heap anyway, so a bit more junk won't be noticed. And they own the block next door, don't they, so who is going to complain? Henry hasn't got the energy to argue. It's like he's done with trying to do the right thing. He shrugs, coughs. He shrugs and coughs so much and so often his shoulders are sort of growing forward, crowding his ears.

The digging out for the slab is something new to talk about. It makes a hell of a mess but it takes over the kitchen talk. Martin tells everyone that the new room will be for Splinter, because she's growing up and they'll need to get her out of the lounge room soon. Because he's sleeping with Karen, he probably knows about girl stuff, and he's sort of in awe of the changes going on in Lori. She's got two hairs under her left arm now and the boils on her chest have got lumps under them, which might be breast cancers.

'Don't cut her hair, Henry. Let it grow a bit,' Martin says one night when Lori pushes in for a trim. She misses out on Henry's gentle touch and she hates Martin for a while. Martin and Donny are always staring at her lately, like it's a shock to them, like they really forgot there were girl parts under the shorts and jeans.

She is looking different, and it's not just because her hair is growing frizzy, and it's not just because of her little green apple boobs either. She's heaps taller and she's getting hips and a waist and her bum is getting a girl shape. All the brothers hammer on the bathroom door now when she's in the shower, instead of barging in like they used to, so she gets the idea that she ought to lock that door.

Greg being kicked out of school was what Lori's rotten school-teacher calls a catalyst, which is like one thing making something else happen. It's made a chain of things happen, actually – like, it's got Mavis out of her mood, it's getting the brick room built, and it's turned Greg into a druggie.

Vinnie said so. He said he saw him down the town with a girl who is on drugs and so is her mother, and he said that Greg and the girl did their block because Vinnie wouldn't do something. Vinnie won't say what it was they wanted him to do, just that he got attacked by them and another girl, and in the main street, because he wouldn't do it. Anyway, once Henry finds out where Greg is living, he gets the police to bring him home and scare him into staying there.

It doesn't work. He's never home, except when Henry is home, and who cares? And maybe Mavis has finally woken up to what a rotten mongrel he really is. She's sort of ignoring him, but she's good again, back to her normal eating – which isn't really normal.

The kitchen extension stole less than half of the back verandah, and it was a big verandah. The cement truck comes early, drives onto the vacant block and all the boys are shovelling cement, putting down a cement slab floor on the second half of the verandah, right from the kitchen wall to the corner then up the side of the east verandah. It's going to be a big room, and they'll need more bricks, Martin says.

Then a few bricks that don't get bought start finding their way home and no one knows where they came from. From Greg, of course. He's pinching Henry's old car at night and he's bringing it home full of bricks. He gets away with it half a dozen times before Henry finds a brick under his seat and works out how all the different coloured grit is getting into his car, and also the girl's bra.

'I'll have no thieves living beneath my roof. Take those bricks back,' he says.

'You take 'em back, you geriatric old bastard,' Greg says. It's not the first time he's called Henry that, but it's the first time he's said it in front of Martin, so Martin hits him for it, not for the bricks. He's a bit pleased about the bricks, even if he won't admit it. Greg comes back fighting, kickboxing, so Martin hauls off and punches him, really punches him, like a prize fighter punch, right in the face. He's got good muscles, due to his brick lifting. Greg goes down.

'No more,' Henry sort of cries. 'No more of this violence, boys.' He picks up his car keys; he's got two sets, and he holds a set in each hand, and he's walking away, shaking his head. He takes his car keys to bed and he probably cries.

Greg's got a bloody nose and his thick lips are thicker, but he's wiping at his nose, wiping at a mouth that's saying worse than geriatric old bastard, and his eyes above the bloody mouth are threatening to murder Martin. Lori is holding one of the stolen bricks and she wants to hit Greg in the face with it, belt him so hard he goes into a coma for ten years until he gets some sense.

'Thieving, spoilt-rotten, nicking mongrel,' she yells.

Greg eyes her up and down. He's standing there, his nose running blood. There is stuff out there he wants. He's got used to getting what he wants. He uses about fifty F words on Lori, then he walks off, slinging more F words and even the C one over his shoulder.

Mrs Roddie's tall brick fence is one house down from Bert Matthews; Lori has been walking it for years, and it's been cracked and leaning for years. Greg gets rid of some of his frustration on it, and Mrs Roddie gets a few C and F words too, which get her so riled up she comes down and belts on the front door, all hyped up to get into Henry.

Martin talks to her. He walks her home, offers to repair the fence. He's apologising all over the place and she ends up saying she's been wanting to get a new fence and a gate she can lock for years. She won't report Greg if the boys will wreck the rest of her old fence and cart the bricks away for her.

'Not a problem,' Martin says.

They wreck it in a day and bring the bricks home in the wheelbarrow. They don't match, but none of the bricks match anyway, and who cares? There are thousands of them now, and a new job cleaning old mortar off bricks with flat shovels.

Mick lost his back verandah bike shop and had to move it to the east side. Stuck around the corner in the wind, he's been feeling a bit lonely, so he leaves his bike building and starts cleaning bricks. He's truly excellent with his hands. He's sitting on a drum, bad leg stuck out front, cleaning bricks by the dozen and stacking them instead of just tossing them down like everyone else.

It's peaceful again for a week with Greg gone missing, but he eventually gets hungry and turns up at the high school one lunchtime, begs Mick's Vegemite sandwiches. Mick gives them to him, and that night he's waiting with Mick when Henry drives down to pick him up. Of course, Henry brings him home. Of course, Henry sits him down at the kitchen table and does his old lecture, talks for hours and hours, trying to teach him some sense of values.

Some chance. He's valueless. He's got a syringe under his mattress. Mick saw it. He sleeps under Greg.

There is a sort of hush in the house when he walks in, quiet as a disease-carrying rat. Vinnie has been working hard on the brick cleaning, he's been going to school too, keeping out of trouble; it's like he's got no will of his own, like he becomes whoever he's spending time with. He's spending time with the two big boys now, so he's acting like them, sort of ostracising Greg, so Greg starts sticking close to Mick, trying to get him onside. If he wants to go over the town he says to Mick that he'll dink him around to talk to his bike shop friend. Mick loves going out, loves that bike shop and the old bloke who runs it and gives Mick free nuts and bolts and things as well as advice. He calls Mick 'the professor'. Anyway, Greg mustn't have been able to get what he wanted. He comes home in a pure rotten mood, calling Mick Professor Pullit. Mick doesn't care. He had a good day.

It's funny, really, what starts to happen. It's like a seed has to get planted in Henry's garden before it can grow, and that Professor Pullit name has somehow got itself planted deep in Mick's head where it can get its roots well down into virgin soil. He starts growing like a weed and his face starts changing, like his nose is growing and his chin is getting longer, and he starts practising his spelling!

Everyone is at the dinner table, eating Henry's stew and grey cabbage and half raw carrots, when Mick says he's going to be a trade schoolteacher when he grows up. Of course, everyone, except Henry, nearly kills themselves laughing. All Henry says is, 'We're going to have to think about a new brace for that leg, Michael.'

Mick looks scared, rubs his head. He's had enough of doctors and hospitals and new braces to last him a lifetime. 'It's all right,' he says.

Poor Mick, as if he could ever be a schoolteacher. His writing is worse than Lori's. He's a reader, but due to his crippled leg, he learned to read too young, so his eyes got used to reading great lumps of words instead of single words, sort of racing ahead to get the important bits out. When you read that way it doesn't matter how the words are spelt, the brain just skips over spelling, just ignores it totally while it scoops the good stuff off the top. Lori is a pretty rotten speller, but Mick is worse, and that's because they are the best readers, except Alan, who doesn't count; he's best at everything. Anyhow, unless you need to write a word down, who needs spelling?

Teachers do, even trade teachers. That's what Henry says . . . or not exactly, but he says a teacher has to finish high school then go to university. 'But you can do it if you have the dream, Michael.'

Who'd want to be a rotten teacher anyway?

Mick would. He's got his one good heel dug in deep and he's not proud either. He borrows Jamesy's spelling list and Alan's and Lori's and he studies them, then gets Alan to listen to his spelling at night in the bedroom, and later, when the Willama germs start leaving Alan alone, those two boys sit on the verandah building a bike and practising spelling. Nobody bothers them out there except Henry, who takes sweaters and coats out for Alan, and worries about his tonsils and his heart and calls him 'my boy'.

'Threatened.'

'T-h-r-e-t-e-n-d,' Mick says, tightening up a nut.

'It's got an a in it, Mick,' Alan says. He's holding the bit that Mick has got the bolt through. Lori is a window away, standing on the edge of the bath, listening to them going though her spelling list.

She uses the word in a school essay and it's about the only word more than four letters long that she gets right.

'Spell ancient,' Alan says one afternoon.

'A-i-n-sh-a-n-t,' Mick tries hard.

'A-n-c-i-e-n-t,' Alan corrects.

Lori is green jealous that Alan is spending so much time with Mick and she's double green jealous that Mick is making him a bike – and she just knows that he's wrong about ancient. It's got an s-h in it for sure, and she's caught him out wrong for once. She walks around to Mick's bike shop and tells him so.

Alan shakes his head, sort of gentle. Sometimes she wishes he'd be a smartarse again so she could really give it to him. She gets Henry's dictionary down from the top of the bookcase and looks for ancient with an s-h, which she can't find. She could ask Henry but he's sort of lost interest in everything except work and keeping Greg away from that nest of druggies. If anyone asks Henry anything at all, he just looks at them like he can't see them properly, or maybe he can't believe he's responsible for this mess of people. He shrugs, shrugs a lot, shrugs his shoulders until they get transplanted up to his ears.

'Greg! Gregory! Where are you?'

In the end Lori finds ancient, spelt like Alan said it was. How can a ten-and-a-half year-old head remember how to spell every word that's ever been written when she can't remember from one day to the next how to spell d-i-s-s-a-p-p-o-i-n-t-e-d?

She uses ancient when she has to write an apology to Kelly Waters for eating her banana. She uses something else too that she found in the dictionary, due to she doesn't deserve to have to write a stinking apology anyway. She was searching that dictionary for Gubba or Gubber when she came on Gueber, which gave her an excellent idea for her apology letter. She writes heaps too, writes almost two pages and gives them to her teacher.

GUEBER means fire wereshiper or follower of some ancient relligon from Persia which is now called Iran and isn't too far from India which isn't far from australia. About fourty-thousand years ago before there was any Jesus Christ or anything else much so no one remembers anything about it the Aborigines came from another country over near India and they got marooned here when australia got dissconnected from the rest of the ancient world and they brought their old langwhich with them from werever.

I think probably when the aborigines saw Captain Cook's

91

gun shooting at them or at kangaroos they must have thought
he was an ancient fire-wereshiper from Persia and after a bit of
calling all white people Guebers it got changed to Gubba.

And that is why Kelly Waters called my mother a fat white
gubba yesterday for about the hundredth time due to she hasn't
got a gun but she smokes worse than a chimny. And that is why
I called Kelly a skinny white gubba for the first time due to
she's whiter than me and she's skinnier. Then she threw my sand-
which in the dirt and stomped on it so I took her banana and
ate it and that's the truth. if teachers are even interested in the
truth. And I am not appologising to her until she appologises to
me because I was the one that got sent out to stand in the passage
and if I deserved that then so did Kelly Waters for insulting my
mother who can't help being fat due to its glandula.

That rotten teacher doesn't care. She sends Lori out of the room
again, and she's not standing in the passage like an idiot so she
goes home because it's too wet to go walking and there are no tourists
around anyway.

Martin is at home again. His boss never makes him work in
the rain but he's working in it. He's laying a row of bricks around
the outside of the cement slab, leaving just enough room between
where the kitchen ends and where his bricks start, making a narrow
passage from the back door to the back yard so people can still get
out to the loo and laundry. He's also leaving enough room between
the side brick wall and the vacant block fence so Mick can get his
bike bits through.

'What are you doing at home, Splint?'

'I hate school, and I'm telling that teacher I'm black, because
it's not fair.'

'And I'll murder you if you do. That won't be fair either.'

'I hate you too. And I hate Kelly Waters. I hate everyone.'

'Right. Now get back to school or I'll dob to Henry. And you
know I will. Run.'

She goes, but she doesn't run.

The next day it's still raining and one of Martin's brickie mates comes around and they both work in the rain. Those walls go up like magic. When Lori gets home the next afternoon she finds a new room with three and a quarter multicoloured brick walls. The quarter bit is the bit that used to be the east verandah, so the bricks stop when they hit the outside weatherboard wall of the big boys' bedroom. Martin and his mate have sort of tied that quarter brick wall to the wooden one with strips of twisted metal, then filled in the space between bricks and boards with mortar and a bit of timber. It's nearly finished, and thank God for that much! Mavis is sick of the mess and the boys are sick of spending their money.

Then Vinnie comes home from school one night with a green loo on his shoulder. The new owners are renovating some old house over the railway line and they threw that old loo in the dump bin. He goes back for the seat and the bit that holds the water and everything, and there is nothing wrong with it. Rich people must have to worry their brains out trying to find stuff to spend money on.

'We'll put it in the bathroom,' Martin sighs. Queuing up for that outside loo in the mornings is a major problem.

'There's always someone showering in there,' Donny says. 'What if you build a brick loo on the back of Splinter's room?'

'I thought we could just put it in the far corner of Splint's room,' Vinnie says.

'It's illegal,' Henry mutters. No one hears him. 'Gregory! Greg! Where are you?'

September gets finished and daylight saving will be starting up again soon and Lori's new room gets a ceiling but still needs a window and door. The green loo has been tossed out the back with the rest of the junk – until Vinnie comes home from school one afternoon with its matching hand basin. It's got a few chips but it isn't cracked.

'What if we put the loo behind the door and the basin opposite, then build a bit of wall between it and Splint's bit? The room's long enough,' he says.

The big boys look at him. It's not a bad idea. They look at his basin, which has got the taps and pipes still connected. They walk the brick room again. It's sure long enough. Narrow, though. For two days they talk interior wall, but Karen is talking of breaking it off so that wall gets tossed into the too-hard basket and the boys' talk changes to finding a plumber who will connect it all up to the sewer pipes and not rave on about the legalities of a loo and washbasin in a bedroom.

Martin talks to an apprentice he knows, then Vinnie is into digging a sewerage trench from the eastern corner of the room, down the back of the outside laundry to the existing loo.

The plumber kid, Jeff, comes one Saturday and joins up the sewerage pipes to the old loo pipes, then he joins in a piece of copper pipe to take the hot and cold water down to the basin and Lori's brick room is turning into a self-contained flat. She'll be able to lock herself in there and only come out to eat.

'Incredible,' Alan says, getting a cup of hot water from the brick room tap so he can mix his salt and water gargle. He doesn't want to go to the hospital to get his tonsils out, and it's that salty water gargling twice a day that has got him fit.

'I-n-c-r-e-d-a-b-l-e,' Mick spells.

'It's i-b-l-e, not a,' Alan says.

Natural disasters are incredible and do incredible damage to people and places, Lori writes in her essay about natural disasters. *However, all of australia's volcanos are exstinct due to the country is worn out. We still have a few hurrycans up the top of australia, which are caused by hot and cold air mixing or something. We also have a few earthquakes which are caused by two bits of the earths foundation which has got a falt in it so it doesn't join up properly. that's why you have to poor all of you house foundation in one day so you dont get a falt line.*

Schools are also natural disasters and I hope there is a earth falt or a foundation falt right under this one and one day while everyone except me and my family is in it the school falls down.

That teacher hates her guts, but who cares? Home is the best place. Home is like a magic place. Daylight saving starts up again and the boys move Lori's bed into her new room. It's a whole huge space and it's all hers. She's got her own chest of drawers which Henry got from the op shop and he's going to get her a wardrobe too when the op shop gets one in. She's in heaven.

For two weeks she folds her jeans and shirts and even her pyjamas and she puts them in the drawers and she makes her bed, and the room looks like a room, not much light for reading, and not much air for breathing, but she can get dressed without people walking through. She's got a dangling electric light bulb which Martin fixed up by joining a new wire to the light wire in the big boys' bedroom then poking it through the brick room ceiling. It's a bit of a madman's light, and illegal, so Henry says, if Lori wants to turn it on, she has to use the switch in the big boys' bedroom, which also works backwards, like if the big boys want light, Lori gets it whether she wants it or not. Martin and Donny come home at all hours so she gets a lot of light she doesn't want.

Also, at night everyone in the world wants to use her loo instead of walking in the dark all the way down behind the laundry, which is darker now since the brick room cut off the light from the kitchen. No one takes a scrap of notice when she slides her bolt at night, or if she hangs a 'do not disturb' sign on the outside, if she yells at people to nick off. They just belt on that door until she gives up and opens it.

'The whole idea was to get Splinter away from all the boys,' Martin says. 'She's growing up, Henry.' He, Donny and Henry never use her loo.

Anyway, after those first few weeks Lori's room loses its wet brick smell and takes on the stink of a public loo, and then, on one hot as hell night, Greg comes home around daylight. Lori's door is open to let some air in, and she's sound asleep and he . . . well . . . Greg does something worse than bad and she's only wearing a T-shirt and knickers. But he's drugged or drunk and she isn't, and he gets a wild horse kick in a place that nearly cripples him, and while he's nearly crippled, he gets his eyes nearly gouged out too, so he won't be trying that again in a hurry, but just in case he does, Lori runs in and dobs to Martin, who gets Donny out of bed to help finish off what Lori started.

After they toss Greg into the back yard with the rest of the junk, they drag Lori's mattress back to the lounge room, where she sleeps on the floor, close to Mavis and Henry's door, sort of safe – with the stink of stiff socks and Vicks VapoRub up her nose. Maybe she knows now why she always had to sleep beside Mavis and Henry's door.

Martin and Donny move her bed out the next day and move their beds in, which is a bit crowded. When Henry wants to know why they are doing it, they say it's because of the loo and everybody using it. No one is allowed to use it any more, except Martin and Donny. Martin buys a big sliding bolt for the outside of that old green door, and puts it up high so the little ones can't reach it. He puts a stronger one on the inside too, so no one can get in while he and Donny are in bed. They buy disinfectant and air-freshener and the room smells better than okay for a day or two.

It's a waste of time, though. Mavis prefers their loo and she can reach the bolt. Not only has that room got a light globe, but it's got a higher loo seat and it backs up to the far corner so she's got more room. She's never been modest, and she likes to smoke while she's sitting. The floor gets covered in ash and butts, so Martin and Donny give up.

Something else is happening too, which probably helps make them give up. Since two months back, Henry has been going to the chemist to buy packets of those women's things for Mavis because he's too embarrassed to ask Donny to buy them at the supermarket.

She's so happy, so really honest to God happy, like cuddling little kids happy, like laughing happy, like even playing cards with the kids at night instead of watching television, like playing chess with Henry

– and she's looking at him with her beautiful big sad eyes measuring him up, wondering if she can squeeze that baby girl out of him.

It's embarrassing, sleeping beside that door now and having good ears that hear everything, even if sometimes they don't want to hear anything.

It's safer, though, due to Martin and Donny have both left home.

christmas tinsel

It's a pity that brick room ever got built, really, because it stole a perfectly good back verandah with no broken boards; it killed a cool place where you could always get a bit of shade, find a bit of breeze and also find Mick working on his bikes. Now there is just a big ugly multicoloured mound of bricks with an old green door, and it's there, in your face, every time you step outside the kitchen door, and due to Greg spending his days sleeping in there on an old mattress, it smells like a wolf's stinking den.

Henry has given up on Greg. He and Vinnie moved the big boys' beds back to their empty bedroom and now Vinnie sleeps there on his own; he won't share with Greg, won't talk to Greg. He knows what Greg did. Henry and Mavis don't know, but even Mavis is now saying, 'Give him enough rope and he'll hang himself.'

For a few weeks after Martin and Donny moved into their flat, there seemed to be so much more room in the house, but it's interesting, really, like when Lori had that baby European carp in a jam jar one year and it only grew as long as her little finger, but when she filled up an old baby bath with water and tipped the fish in there, well, it started suddenly exploding, like every day it grew bigger – until a bird got it.

That's what is happening to Mavis. She's filling up the space the boys leaving made. She's so happy, though. She's looking after her hair and putting her make-up on every day and not going to the milk bar. She's going to bed early instead of making her custards and pancakes, though Vinnie reckons he caught her washing up a pile of dishes and stuff one day when he nicked off from school early.

Henry wouldn't notice if food was missing. He's not noticing much at all. Christmas is coming to get him. He's the one who needs Valium and antidepressant pills now. He's the one who's not sleeping.

He always gets this way at Christmas time, all wound up with sad talk about England and his English parents and about going home to visit their graves before he dies. He's not that old, and who cares about dead people's graves? Mavis says she's never been near her father's grave, but once Henry gets going on England, he can't shut up. He's like an old-fashioned record player with one record, and the arm of the player is broken so it keeps on playing the same old boring stuff, over and over and over again – he never tells anything interesting, like what he did with his friends, just castles, and old villages.

Every night he's sitting in the kitchen instead of going to bed, and maybe that's just sort of self-preservation – except he's talking, talking, talking to Mavis and she's pretending to listen while she's beating him at chess or baking him apple pies.

He'll get over it. He always does. The kids have learned to live around the moods in this house.

So school finishes, and on the last day everyone is giving that rotten old teacher Christmas cards and presents so Lori gives her the wormiest old Bert Matthews apple she can find, and who cares, next year she'll be at high school. And thank God she didn't get failed.

Poor old Vinnie did. He has to repeat year eight so next year he'll be in the same group as Mick, which is killing him, due to he's now six foot one and not skinny and already shaving. He looks about eighteen and exactly like the old wedding photograph of Mavis's father. It's pure reincarnation. Lori has never seen a photograph of Grandmother Hilda. There is not even one in the photo box.

Lori didn't know it, but that bike Mick and Alan have been working on isn't for Alan. It's a girl's bike, and they tricked Lori by hiding the girl's frame down behind Nelly's place. They get up with the birds on Christmas morning and go over to Nelly's to finish putting the bike together, then they bring it back to the east verandah and cover it over with an old sheet. As soon as Lori wakes up, they blindfold her with a tea towel and take her out to the verandah.

And like super cool wow! Mavis even gave them money to buy brand-new tyres for it, and Mick has painted it bright red and painted LORI on the bar, like a brand name. And Henry bought a carry seat to put on the back so she can dink Mick to and from school each day, which will mean he won't have to hang around waiting for Henry.

She loves it, and she loves Mick and Alan too, loves how their faces sort of look nearly happier than her face when she pulls the old sheet off the bike and sees it. This is the best day ever. This is the best day ever in her whole entire lifetime. The Christmas chickens are roasting and the pudding is bubbling in the biggest pot, and the table looks like a picture in a magazine with flowers in a jar and paper Christmas serviettes from Kmart.

Mavis is overdue, and boy, is she happy today. Henry helped her have a shower and wash her hair, which has just been cut. All of her curls are standing up tall and she's wandering around smiling, waiting for the food, and peering into the oven, checking on her potatoes.

Henry isn't smiling. He's staring at her back as she walks out to the brick-room loo, like he's hoping against hope that she's not pregnant, just late. She probably is pregnant because today Henry looks more grey, like she's finally got the last of him – even his fingernails look like grey rags. He picks at them as he watches Mavis walk back to the table and he can tell by her smile that it's no use hoping.

'Six days now,' she says. 'And it better be a girl this time or I'll drown it at birth.'

He nods, walks to the door, looks at that lump of brick room, looks as if he's thinking of throwing himself at it, ramming his head into it, or bricking up the door and window, building himself in while he sings 'Land of Hope and Glory', forcing that final brick in to silence his song.

The television is on and some mob are singing Christmas carols. Henry sighs, leans against the door. 'The date might be the same, the songs might be the same as I sang in England when I was a boy, but the shift, the mental switch to acceptances of southern hemispheric Christmases won't happen in my head. A pine branch, draped with tinsel, does not a Christmas tree make.'

Southern hemispheric Christmases? Henry's off again.

'I was born here. I was born in this land, but my roots are in England,' he says as he turns glazed eyes away from brick, to the window, then down to the bunch of red geraniums in a jam jar. Apricot jam, Mavis's favourite. He starts laughing, but it's not like happy laughter, more like howling.

The table looks good and the jam jar doesn't look too bad, though Lori couldn't get all the label off it. The flowers look good.

Henry can't see the good. This kitchen, maybe the whole world, looks as bad as it can get, worse than yesterday when Mavis was only five days overdue, and it will keep on getting worse. He's got holidays. Four weeks of watching that new baby grow in her belly. Four weeks of thinking of a new baby, thinking of more napkins, more bottles, hiding more tins of condensed milk, thinking of little Matty, who can't even walk yet, and he's thinking, when will it end?

Lori looks at Henry, then by him to the plaster walls. It's time they were painted again, or wallpapered. Martin helped him wallpaper the middle-sized boys' bedroom walls when they bought the new bunk beds and those walls still look clean and strong. Back then, those two were always doing something, painting, mopping, sweeping up, keeping the rooms looking okay.

But Martin has gone and Henry has stopped doing things. Maybe it happened when the big boys left home, or maybe it was sooner, when Greg got kicked out of school . . . or maybe when the brick room turned into a hot white elephant and Henry realised that there was no *more*, that the most fantastic of dreams all end up stinking like a public loo.

He used to help Mavis shower most days. He used to get Nelly to make new tents when Mavis grew out of the old ones. He stopped that too, like he stopped nagging the brothers to hang their clothes, like he stopped reading library books, stopped watering his strange flowers in the shed, stopped his singing. He just stopped. Lori waters his flowers now, but half of them look sick from too much water or not enough and she doesn't know which, so she just keeps on adding water.

Today Henry has got that wanting look in his eye, that reaching for things he knows he can't have look, like life in this house is a cruel joke someone played on him.

'Snowmen peeping in the windows, calling children from their beds,' Henry sings to the window. The sun is hard on him, hurting his eyes, making them wet, making water run from them, trickle down his wrinkles. It's hurting his head too; he's rubbing it, rubbing it, shrugging his shoulders up to his ears, trying to think of the words. 'Dar dar dar the sleigh bells ring, dar dar dar dar – '

Greg looks at him as if he's gone crazy. The closest he's ever come to a snowman is the supplier of the stuff he shoots up his arms when he can get it. He sniggers, sniffs the air like a diseased hyena.

Lori moves closer to Henry. She's standing beside him, wanting him to sing of his snow, wanting him to remember that better place and not be so bloody sad. It's Christmas Day and she got a bike, which she's been riding up and down the road all morning. And Martin and Donny are coming home for Christmas dinner. They'll bring a heap more presents.

But Henry has stopped his singing. He mops at his face, wipes his eyes with a crumpled handkerchief, keeps staring west. Then he says something weird – for Henry. 'Had someone told me thirty years ago that I was born to this heat, I would have named him a liar. I had no idea,' he says. 'No idea. I thought I was an Englishman.

My parents allowed me to grow to adulthood believing I was their natural son. Adopted? Me? Henry Smyth-Owen's first Christmas spent in an Aboriginal camp? I would have named him a liar, my little lost Lorraine.'

For a second Lori feels lost, sees a man she doesn't know. Maybe a man who doesn't know her, or himself. She's staring at a wrinkled old stranger and it's making her afraid of what she is, of who she is.

Who is she, anyway? She's half of Mavis and the English and German people of the old photographs before Mavis. Okay. But she's half . . . like, who is her other half made of? It's not made of Henry's Kathleen and Daniel photographs, like she used to think it was. It's like there's a gap now, a gaping greedy gap hidden behind Henry and she's never going to be allowed to see into it. So she *is* lost. Half of her is lost.

Lori gets scared, moves in even closer. She's almost standing on top of him, breathing his air, when Donny comes in. He's got his presents stuffed into three supermarket bags. He stands in the doorway listening to Henry, who is still going on about Aboriginal camps.

'Ever think about trying to trace your natural parents? They'd only be in their seventies,' Donny says, putting his bags on the floor, sits down.

Henry tries to smile. Can't make it. His face is too thin, like he's been eroded, like time has dug deep gullies from his eyes to his mouth. No more Henry smile. He looks about seventy, more Indian than pom. Maybe he's like his grandfather, old Woden, eyes sunk into pits of shadow, looking today like two lost and lonely beetles, trying to find a way out. They search past Lori, search for Alan. He coughs, shakes his head. 'My parents gave me a wonderful childhood, a wonderful life. I could not have asked for better.'

'Lucky you,' Mavis says.

'Everyone is into searching for their roots these days. It's the in thing. There are a heap of people in Willama finding out they've got Aboriginal ancestors . . . or just admitting that they had them,' Donny says.

Henry looks at him, then at Mavis. 'The thread has been broken, my boy. A late knot would only be another obstacle for me to climb over at this stage.'

'It could be interesting, though. We've probably got a heap of relatives out there. You've probably got half-brothers and sisters, people who look like us. Ever think of that, Henry?' Donny is trying to make him feel better but Henry doesn't want to.

'Not like you, my boy. You and Vincent lean towards the Irish, the Scottish, the German on your grandfather's side.'

'And double so,' Mavis says.

'As you say, and doubly so, my dear.'

Mavis slams the oven door, a baked potato impaled on a fork. She's blowing smoke, biting at the hot potato. She's not going to be dieting today. 'There's all sorts of help out there these days for people wanting to trace their families. You were one of the stolen generation. Instead of talking about it, why don't you do something, find your roots and – '

'And demand compensation for the medical treatment I received, for the education, the love of gentle parents, my dear?'

'That's not what I said, and you know it.'

Henry looks at her, smiles again. 'Dwelling on the past cripples us. We hobble into our future instead of walking forward, head high.'

'Yeah, I noticed that,' she says. 'Your head is always held high, Henry. Ha ha ha. You've been crawling around this house for days with your tail between your legs and your chin dragging on the bloody ground, and I'm getting sick of it.'

He coughs, has a suck on his inhaler. 'And how would you describe your own posture, my dear?'

Lori's neck is beginning to crawl. If he keeps this up he's going to spoil a perfectly good day.

'I don't know. You tell me how you'd describe it.'

'Ah, you are siren, the earth mother, the huntress.'

Greg starts laughing, and Vinnie, the moron, joins in.

Mavis stares at them, then turns to Henry. 'Yes, I remember that siren. I can also remember a poor, mixed-up, drowning bastard clutching at straws – '

'That's enough!'

'You started it. You've got a great habit of starting what you can't finish, Henry. Have the guts to finish what you start or don't start it.'

He coughs and checks the oven, silent now. The room is too quiet. Only the sizzle of chicken, the quiet rattle of the kettle lid and Alan's voice from the verandah. 'Disappointed has got a double p, not a double s, Mick.'

Henry lifts his head, smiles, and Lori almost cries with wishing he might smile like that when he hears her voice. 'That boy has a brilliant mind.'

'Brilliant, my arse.'

'A bad choice of words, my dear, though it is looking excessively brilliant today.'

He's gone mad! What the hell is he trying to do? This is *so* not good. Mavis hates people laughing at her, loathes people making fun of her weight, and Greg's laughing again.

Donny gets up from the table, gives him a filthy look. 'So, what did you get for Christmas, Mavis?' he says.

'Oh, fuck off,' she says. 'And stop trying to change the subject. He started this. I didn't start it, but he knows that I can finish it, don't you, Henry?'

'You started something you can't finish with Alan. I'll be flying with him to London while I'm off work. I've been in touch with Watts. He's looking after the details.'

'I'd like to see you try that,' Mavis says.

'What can we offer him here?' he says.

'His mother, his family, that's what. And as soon as that other one is back on Australian soil, I'll get him home too. That queer bitch

105

doesn't give a shit about those kids. She's never given a shit about anyone other than herself – and you know it better than most. And after what she did to me, you think I'd let her raise my kids? Now you shut up with your maudlin bullshit, and get some dinner on the table.'

'Martin isn't here yet,' Henry says.

'That's his funeral. He knows what time we eat.'

But Henry is not doing as he is told today. He's going to wait for Martin. He's losing his onions – or something.

Lori watches Mavis spilling over the table. She's not happy now and her useless, plump, pretty little hands with their long strong fingernails touch the bread plate. They polish her knife on the white tablecloth which Alan found down the bottom of the sheet cupboard. He and Lori set the table and it was like bringing their cubbyhouse play inside and making it real. Martin will get a surprise when he walks in and sees this table.

They hear the old ute rattle into the drive and Lori and Alan stand together, wait together beside their table, eager for Martin to see what they've done, wanting his approval. They miss him. All of the little ones miss him.

'So what are you waiting for now, you miserable old bugger?' Mavis says.

'Have a slice of bread while you're waiting. Have two. Eat the entire loaf, my dear. I bought three.'

Donny's eyes widen and Lori turns to Henry, wanting to kick him in the shins and wake him up. This was going to be a good day, like a party with Donny and Martin home and Mavis over the moon about being pregnant. Just because he's feeling miserable, he doesn't have to make everyone else feel miserable.

Donny wants him to shut up too. He gets a bottle of beer from one of his bags he's put in the freezer, then he fills four glasses. Henry hands one to Mavis, touches his glass to hers. 'Merry Christmas, my dear.' It sounds like a curse.

Mavis eyes him, drinks her beer, doesn't like it much. She

snatches a slice of bread, spreads it thick with margarine, pushes it into her mouth, washes it down with more beer. She's going to fix his bad mood by getting a better one of her own. She spreads another slice, punishing Henry, her eyes wanting him to comment. He won't look at her. It's like a play without words until Martin stops looking at Lori's new bike and finally walks in, loaded up with presents.

'Jesus,' he says. 'Am I in the right house? I must have gone to Nelly's place.' He's looking at the tablecloth. 'Better take my presents and go, eh?' He says this to Alan, and Alan giggles. Then he starts handing out colourful parcels. He gives Mavis a big box wrapped in Christmas paper and Lori knows it's chocolates, which she also knows he bought on special at Donny's supermarket then hid in the bottom of his wardrobe. They'll be past their use-by date and probably smell of dead socks, and it's the worst thing he could do today, just the worst, but he's been mad at Mavis since he offered to pay for a Jenny Craig diet for her birthday and she told him to buy her some chocolates.

Everyone is opening their presents, but when Martin gives Lori her parcel, he ruffles her hair, which, thanks to him and Mavis, Henry won't cut short. Her head is covered by a nest of curls. 'I wouldn't open it in here, Splint,' he whispers, winks.

She picks a hole in one end, feels her face begin to burn, and she's out in the brick room, the bolt rammed home, before she rips the paper off. It's two training bras and two pairs of matching knickers and a book on 'growing up' – as if she needs that around this place, as if she hasn't known about that stuff since she was six. She waits in the brick room until Martin knocks on the door.

'Do they fit?' he says. 'Karen's mother picked them out for you.'

'Shut up.'

'Dinner's on, and Mavis is looking at your roast potatoes. You got two.'

Lori opens the door and Martin ruffles her hair again; he likes doing that now that there's some hair to ruffle.

'Quit that, and ta,' she says. 'I need the knickers,' and she takes her present to her room, places it in her drawer then takes her place at the table, at Martin's side. He elbows her, and she elbows him back. It's good having him home, hearing his laugh and feeling sort of safe at his side. Henry has shut up picking on Mavis, so it's going to be a good Christmas after all.

Glasses fill and empty. All the kids are giggly and having fun. Donny bought a box of crackers, and he pulls one with Jamesy, who gets a purple hat; he puts it on and looks more like an old gnome than usual. Martin gave Mick a handyman book, and some electronic stuff to put together and Mick is sitting there jiggling his good foot; he can't wait to get to his electronics. Alan got *Jurassic Park*. He's smiling a lot, as if he sort of belongs now. Maybe he won't want to fly to London with Henry. Lori doesn't want him to go. He's turned into a brother, like equal favourite brother with Mick and Martin and Jamesy.

He's funny with Mavis, though. He still doesn't talk to her much, doesn't call her anything. It's like she's not his mother, though Henry is his father. He's sitting beside Matty, who is in the highchair, happy and playing with a squeaking toy he got from Martin and sucking hard on his dummy, having a great time.

Alan looks at Henry, keeps looking at him like he's got a special present hidden under the table and he's waiting for the right time to give it to him, waiting for a silence. He's eating slow, watching, chewing.

There aren't going to be any silences here today, so he coughs, makes a silence, says, 'Can you pass the salt, please, Dad.'

Henry sort of half jumps up from his chair, spills his beer. There is an expression in his eyes no one has seen before and that *Dad* word put it there. It's too rare. It's a baby word that dies fast in this house. Tears fill up Henry's eyes and one falls onto his chicken leg as he passes the salt without looking up from his plate.

Dad. That word has silenced the room. Everyone is looking at Henry, watching his face sort of get tight with holding in pain, like he's holding all of that pain in his mouth so he can't eat. He glances at Mavis and his face gets tighter. The plates on the table are still half full but Mavis's plate is empty and she's ripping the cellophane from her stale chocolates.

Then Greg says, 'Can I have a beer, Daddy?'

When that Dad word came out of Alan's mouth, it sounded like diamond, like begonia, like 'Oh, My Papa', something precious and . . . Greg makes it dirty, though Mavis doesn't see the dirt. She lets loose with a laugh, like Greg is her favourite again. Then they are both laughing, both saying Daddy this and Daddy that, making the word hurt worse than a whip around the legs.

Vinnie has been sitting at sniggering Greg's side, just eating, eating slow but steady. He's an awful slow mover, like thunder grumbling in the clouds, moving around slow and getting nowhere due to the bit that makes the action happen being so high up; he probably needs a second brain in his hip to move his lower bits.

Then something happens, like bang! And Vinnie is greased lightning striking, and it's striking Greg. He gets elbow jabbed in the soft part of his belly and when he gasps forward, Vinnie gives him a better elbow jab right under the jaw – knocks him clean off his chair. Then the slow washes over Vinnie, he turns back to his plate slow, goes back to eating slow – as if he hasn't done a thing.

Henry's not eating. He's up. He's looking at Greg's mouth, which is bleeding. Everyone is looking at Greg, then sort of darting-eyed to Henry, who is standing there swallowing spit. Greg is probably swallowing blood, but he's up and he's picking up his chair. He's going to kill Vinnie, who sort of smiles, gets his feet under him. If there's any killing done here today, he's big enough to do it.

'Try it, you piece of dog shit,' he says, sort of slow.

Greg tosses his chair at the stove, walks, and Mavis starts laughing. 'Oh, Merry Christmas, Daddy,' she says, and she stuffs another chocolate into her mouth. 'Merry Christmas, Daddy dear, and a ho, ho, ho.'

Henry stand there. He cries.

'Haven't you stuffed enough of his guts down your throat already, you thoughtless bitch?' Martin says. He doesn't know what has been going on here today. Why couldn't he just keep his big mouth shut? Why couldn't he just –

'What bloody guts?' Mavis says, watching Henry's soft brown eyes leak silent tears. 'Fuck your tears,' she says. 'I've seen too many of your bloody tears. What about the tears I've cried? You had it all, and what did I have? Do you want me to tell the kids what I had, Daddy, what I've got, Daddy?' Then her hand reaches for the nearest plate and she tosses it at the wall, tosses a second plate after the first. Food and china spray everywhere.

She's screaming that 'Daddy' word now, she's looking for more ammunition. Jamesy is hanging onto his plate; little Neil lost his, and he's crying instead of pulling faces. Donny reaches for him, plucks him away from danger. It's too late. It's just terrible. It's the end of something or the beginning of something worse than Lori has ever known.

Mavis is up. 'Wipe that bloody stupid grin off your face,' she yells and she slugs Jamesy with a backhand, sends him toppling off his chair, then she's got her whip and she's moving in on Martin, who is trapped behind the table, Lori on one side, Jamesy and his fallen chair on the other.

Lori dives under the table, clearing a pathway as Martin snatches the whip, jerks it from Mavis's hand like it is so easy, like why didn't he do it before?

'You cruel bitch,' he says, and he whacks her around the thighs with her whip. She picks up the box of chocolates, throws them at him. She's not backing off.

Neil, all the little ones are crying. And Alan. He knows he started this with his 'Dad'. He started everyone wanting Henry's *more*. That's what he did. 'I'm sorry, I'm sorry. I'm sorry. I'm sorry.' He's shaking, a forkful of beans poised halfway to his mouth. It's shaking too. Matty is screaming around his dummy. 'Get out!' Mavis is screaming. 'Get out of my house and don't you ever come back. Don't you set foot inside that door again. Get out. Get out, all of you.' Her face is red, her chin nub white, chocolate saliva drizzling from the corner of her mouth, framing that little circle of her chin.

'Look at yourself. Take a good look at yourself in a mirror, why don't you, Mavis? You look like something a bloody dinosaur might have regurgitated. You disgust me,' Martin yells, and Henry is gone.

Mavis screams, grabs the tablecloth, sends the plates to the floor.

Jamesy, now under the table and still grinning his twisted grin, is picking up spilled chocolates, putting them into Donny's supermarket bag. Vinnie picks up an empty beer bottle. Lori grabs the cordial bottle before it all spills out as Jamesy starts scooping up roast potatoes and chicken and dropping them into another plastic bag. Vinnie grabs a loaf of bread and the margarine, then they have to run because Martin and Donny are heading out the door and Mavis is going to be ready to get into someone else.

Lori follows the brothers to the river. Alan has got Matty on his back and Matty is hanging on, sucking hard on his dummy and squeaking his toy.

They have Christmas dinner by the river. They pour cordial into Vinnie's empty beer bottle and fill it with river water, share sips. They eat roast potato and spit out the china chips. They make chicken sandwiches for the little ones, using fingers for knives, they gnaw on chicken bones, suck on melted chocolates, make them last for a very long time. And they stay away from that madhouse for a longer time swimming in the clothes they wear.

The vacant block is full of neighbours when they get home, and the chooks are all squawking like crazy.

Henry is hanging by a length of clothesline wire in his chook-pen. There is a piece of silver tinsel dangling from his shoe, stuck there by chook dung.

survival

There is a new red mound in the cemetery and it doesn't even have a name. Henry has gone to heaven and Willama has gone to hell.

In the vegetable garden the weeds grow taller than the onions. No one can weed like Henry. No one cooks stews and cabbage, no one helps Mavis wash her hair and it's greasy, daggy, dirty. Everyone throws junk on the floors that no one sweeps. Greg is with the druggies, Vinnie sits and stares while Mick limps around and around the house instead of fixing bikes. It's like everybody has been struck dumb. Except the little kids. They just cry. All day they cry.

No more Henry to make their world a not too bad place.

How did he do so much? How come no one saw what he did and how he did it? It just got done. Lori misses him. Misses following him around. Misses his songs. Misses his stews. Misses seeing him and his rusty old working clothes.

Mavis is howling crazy with missing Henry, she's so crying-crazy she tries to cook stuff, but instead of a big stew and vegetables, she tries to make a light sponge cake like she used to make for Henry. She burns it, then gets so screaming-crazy with missing Henry that she throws the cake and the tin at the west window and breaks it. There's nothing to eat for tea and no glass in the window to keep the flies out either.

Donny brings food around after work. He gets the broken glass out and sticks some cardboard over the gap with sticky tape before he starts cooking sausages and potatoes. Mavis knows she's mostly to blame for Henry but all the time she's trying to push the guilt onto Martin, so she yells at Donny, tells him to get out, to go home to his bloody flat and to bloody Martin, who might just as well have cut the clothesline wire and got the drum for Henry to stand on. 'Get out. Get out!'

Donny walks off howling again, leaves Mavis howling, leaves the little kids and Alan howling. And when is that howling going to end?

Vinnie finishes cooking the sausages, and he doesn't burn them either; he mashes the potatoes, mashes them fluffy, but the kids can't sit down and eat them at the table because Mavis is at it again. She's making pastry this time and using the good butter. She's making an apple pie and making a mess. She's standing at the table, shaking and bawling and rolling pastry, salting it with her tears, she's swollen eyed and half blind with bawling but she's decorating her pie with perfect curly strips of pastry; it looks and smells so good when it's cooked, but it's not big enough to go around. It wasn't for the kids, anyway. She made it for Henry. He used to love her apple pies

She tries to get stuff in the washing machine one day but she can't bend over to pick things up and she's never used the new washing machine. Doesn't know what buttons to push so it's better for the washing machine if she doesn't try, better if she doesn't cook, better if she just sits and smokes and bawls.

And that's how it goes for the week after Henry's funeral, which Mavis couldn't go to because she can't get in and out of cars. She's feeling guilty too because she couldn't go, and she's feeling a fool because she actually thought she was going to go.

She talked to Nelly and got her to make a new dark tent, and she forgot her pride and asked the undertaker man to hire a disabled taxi with a special lifting thing for wheelchairs. She couldn't sit in the wheelchair, and couldn't heave herself into the van. Couldn't stand on the lifting thing with Vinnie and Donny and some of the undertaker men trying to balance her. She tried, though, while the neighbours stared; then she got bright red in the face, bawled and walked inside, walked in circles, looking terrible in her new dark green tent. Nelly bought the material and it looks like a camping tent.

Henry always called Lori little lost Lorraine. Now she's truly lost. She went to that funeral, but it wasn't like it was real – just play-acting while everyone is sort of waiting, holding time still, until Henry comes back and gets things right again.

She knows he's dead. She saw him hanging there. In her head she knows he's not coming home. She watched the big boys carry him from that church; saw him go down into that hole.

But she still sees him. All the time she sees him – in the shadows near his potting shed, and she hears his car coming, and she sees the passage curtain move like he's going to come through and he'll be wearing his old tartan dressing gown.

He can't come through because he's dead.

No more haircuts, no pats on the head, no more clean knickers folded in the drawer. Just a house without Henry, and Lori can't stand to be in that full-up empty crying place so each morning she gets some flowers from Nelly's garden, rides out to the cemetery on her new bike and sits on the cool grey marble of 'Barbara, beloved wife of Howard,' and she stares at that raw mound. Sits for hours some days, letting the hot sun burn her, watching the flowers wilt.

She is sitting there the day an Aboriginal family come to bury a son. It was in the papers. He went to Melbourne and died of a drug overdose.

The Aborigines used to bury their dead in the sand dunes but this family is using the cemetery, having the same old words spoken for him as were spoken for Henry. Lori stares at the family and the minister, stares as the coffin goes down, down that hole. Forever and ever and ever amen.

Henry used to say, 'The urban Aborigine claims his mother's culture but he buys his food at the supermarket, buries his dead in the white man's cemeteries.'

Cold, dead place, the white man's cemetery. Better if Henry were buried high on some sand dune in Western Australia where the wind could blow clean. Better not to be locked in a cheap wooden box, beneath a ton of dirt. He shouldn't be here in this dead place.

That Aboriginal family are bawling their eyes out. And what's the use of bawling? Tears won't make dead people come back to life, will they? She watches the family leave, arms around each other, holding each other as they walk by Henry's mound and she recognises one lady. She's the one who had a baby girl when Mavis had Matty. And those girls – she knows two of them from school. They stare at her, give her a dirty look because she's staring at them, then they whisper, and their mother turns her head, stops walking. She's dark, and her face is shiny with crying; she's not slim and not fat either – just a mother with red eyes.

'Go home, love,' she says. 'No good sitting here. They're not coming back.' Then she says the words that Lori has been thinking. 'This is a dead place.'

Go home? What for? Too many strangers at that house these days, and they keep on coming. It's better sitting in a dead place than being at home.

No school to go to, even. January has just come and there is the whole of January before school goes back. Nothing to do except ride her bike all over the place, and end up out at the cemetery or down at the river.

Then two men come to the house one day and one buys Henry's car for five hundred dollars. Donny wanted to buy it for four hundred because that's all he's got left in the bank since the funeral. Mavis wouldn't let him have it, so the old car drives away with a stranger in Henry's worn-out seat.

It looks so bad, cruel, sad. Henry's gone. Now his car has gone.

That crying January is almost over when Mavis gets on a disability pension. She can't believe her first payment. The kids can't believe it. She's got nine dependent children, if you include one out-of-work sly-eyed druggie who has come home again, because

115

Mavis is going to be making more money than Henry could ever make, more money even than the Prime Minister – almost. That pension sure stops her crying but it starts her eating. Every day for that first week, Greg or Vinnie get takeaway for lunch, takeaway for dinner, piles of chips and potato cakes, dim-sims and pizzas. Everyone loves junk food. The little ones think it's picnics twice a day.

Then school is due to start again and Vinnie is not going to go and that's that. He say this to Martin and Donny when they come around on the Saturday with a few books and pens and stuff – and a ridiculous high school dress and new shoes for Lori. They buy a pile of stuff to make the school lunches too. Except Mavis eats most of it, so after that the boys keep what they buy at the flat, and on school mornings Donny brings the lunches around before he goes to work. He always did make the best sandwiches, like meat and salad and even mayonnaise.

Lori's school uniform is ridiculous; the skirt keeps trying to get caught in the bike chain. She hates dresses. Hates the leather shoes that burn her feet. Hates high school worse than she hated sixth grade. Now there are a dozen teachers to hate her instead of just one. It's like she's in some crazy nightmare and she can't wake up. She hasn't got the right school books, the ones she has got were Mick's and Vinnie's and probably Greg's, and they are past their use-by date. She's always in trouble for not having the new edition, and she's lost all the time because she has to change rooms all day. Can't concentrate on anything. Can't keep her mind in the classroom even when she finds the right one. Keeps looking out the window, wanting the day to be over so she can go to the cemetery, which is not far from the high school.

Mick hates going there; he tells her it's no use going there every day, but he can't fight for what he wants so he sits on the back of her bike and goes where she takes him, then he waits with her bike, his face pale, his freckles looking like coffee granules scattered over pale paper.

'It's no use, Lori,' he says.

Nothing is any use, is it? Even the flowers. One day she brings Henry one of his own flowers from the potting shed, a beautiful orange thing, almost as big as a saucer, but it gets crushed in her school bag and it's nearly dead by the time school is over. She still waters his pots most nights, and Alan still waters them but they don't do it together.

Lori can't stand being anywhere near Alan. Like, if he hadn't said, 'Pass the salt, Dad,' then Mavis and Greg wouldn't have started laughing and Martin wouldn't have –

A c-a-t-a-s-t-r-o-p-h-i-c chain got started by that *effing* word and it killed Henry, and if Lori goes anywhere near Alan, then she's going to scream that at him, so she's staying away from him. And Mavis too. She was old enough to know better. And mongrel Greg too, who is always looking at Lori with his druggie eyes, like looking at her stupid boobs in their stupid bra that make them even more obvious because they are getting more obvious. She looks like an *effing* girl in that *effing* dress.

She's got Henry's smallest vegetable knife, though. She takes it to bed with her, puts it under her pillow. She'll get Greg if he comes near her. She'll cut his eyes out, cut something off so he won't go looking for any girls. Ever. She takes that knife with her when she goes to the river, just in case he follows her. It's not a big knife. The handle is wood and it fits down the inside of her shoe and the blade stays hidden beneath her sock, but it means she can't go barefoot any more.

The pension gets paid into the bank each fortnight, so if they run out then they know exactly when there will be more coming. Mavis signs withdrawal forms which Greg takes to the bank and they give him the money, like they used to give her child allowance money to Henry, except Greg keeps some of it. Mavis doesn't care. Actually, she doesn't seem to care about anything. Like, she always used to nag the kids about going near the busy road up at the corner, and now she sends little Neil to the milk bar for chocolate and bags of lollies and even cigarettes, and he has to cross over that road. Mick and Vinnie tell him not to go or he'll get run over, but Neil likes going because he always gets his own bag of lollies. Mavis is going to turn him into another Greg if she's not careful.

Anyway, because of Vinnie not going to school, the people start coming after Mavis again, official people in posh cars, who sort of high-step over the mess. A counselling lady from some church or something comes to talk to Mavis about bereavement and the normal cycle of grief and she arranges for another lady to come one day a week to help clean the house, just until Mavis is able to cope with her situation. That cleaning lady, who is almost twice as old as Mavis, takes one look at the kitchen, which is the best room, and decides to retire, leave Willama, maybe leave Australia even.

The whole house is starting to look like a dog's sicked-up breakfast, and who cares? Not Lori, she's never there except to sleep. Due to having to stay away from Alan and Mavis and Greg, it's easier if she stays away from everyone, pretends she can't see or hear them if they talk to her, like she's dead, except she's one of the bike-riding, walking dead, a modern-day zombie.

She starts doing it with the teachers, and when Crank Tank, who is her English and her social science teacher, asks her why she still hasn't got the right book, Lori just looks straight through her. And when she gets sent to the vice principal, she looks through her too, then instead of going to her next class, she goes to the cemetery and comes back later to dink Mick home.

There is a new lady with Mavis and her counsellor today. She's a dietitian and she's going to get Mavis on a diet. Mavis is doing her glandular thing, as if she thinks people can't see the lolly papers on the floor and the block of chocolate in her tent pocket with her Minties – as if she thinks she's fooling anyone.

Maybe she is. Those ladies sit at the table working out a diet plan full of fruit and celery and carrots, the stuff Mavis calls rabbit food, and Mavis nods, looks at the clock, nods, walks them to the door, watches them leave in two cars, then she's off, walking up to the hotel for a counter meal or two. She goes there a lot since she got the pension.

Martin and Donny are still bringing food around, but it's not fair that they have to pay for it seeing as Mavis is now filthy rich. That's what Martin says. He can't get anywhere near inside the house, but he stands at the back door, trying to talk sense.

'For Christ's sake, will you let us help you, Mavis? Let us cook the kids a decent meal and clean this bloody house up for you. You can smell it from halfway up the street. And Vinnie has to go to school. And you've got to keep those two little kids off the bloody street. One of them is going to get run over.'

Mavis does the usual, tells them to get out, but she eats their food, eats Weet-Bix and keeps on eating them until the milk is all gone. She roasts their potatoes at midnight and Lori can smell them roasting in her dreams, in which Henry is cooking them. Then the dream turns into a terrible nightmare because he's not in the kitchen, he's in that hole and he's turned all green and she's in there with him. She wakes up screaming, and she's out of bed, and she's never going to sleep again in case that dream comes back.

She creeps out to Mavis, needing to cry so bad her whole body is shaking with it, needing to hold on to someone who is warm and alive. And she tries, creeps close, touches Mavis's arm.

'Get back to your bed and get out of my bloody sight,' Mavis says.

Lori gets out of everyone's sight, gets out of her own sight. She rides down to the river and she stays there. She's sitting on the clay bank when the sun comes back to Australia and she's still sitting there when it starts packing its bags for England. She's just sitting there, watching the grey water flow.

Alan finds her. She's not going to talk to him, never, ever again. He howls and runs off, and a bit later Nelly comes walking down that track, catches Lori playing with her vegetable knife, sees her hide it beneath her sock. She sits down on the dirt like she's a kid, doesn't mention the knife.

Lori stares at the grey water, letting the sun-flecked ripples blind her eyes and silence the world – but nothing can silence Nelly. She doesn't care if she's talking to a zombie, she keeps doing it, keeps sitting there until the sun gets so low it starts painting the tops of the trees red. She's saying anything that comes into her head, like it doesn't matter if Lori is listening or not. She's saying stuff about how the world is full of grief and always has been. She's saying that in the olden days, people talked it out, talked to the butcher, and the grocer, the postman, and their neighbours, so they didn't need grief counsellors filling their heads with airy-fairy shit that screws them up worse than ever. Then she starts talking about Henry's singing, and how she always used to go out and weed her garden when he was singing in the shed, just so she could listen to his song.

She says she knows that Lori loved Henry, knows how much she's missing him. 'But like it or not, he's gone, Smithy, and he's not coming back. All the kids are missing him and they are getting worried about you. You've got to eat to live, and you need to walk past twice to cast a shadow these days. You're going to end up getting sick.'

She just talks and talks until the sun is gone and the mosquitoes start biting, and the European carp are plopping around in the river. Lori hits a mosquito, feels the satisfying wet squash, grinds it into her shoulder, and zombies probably don't feel mosquitoes biting, and zombies probably don't feel so full up with raging anger that they want to scream sixteen F words at Nelly, one after the other after the other.

'You're breaking young Alan's heart, Smithy, and you're not being fair to any of those boys. They've got to deal with losing their dad – '

'Don't you say that fucking word to me,' Lori yells. It makes Nelly flinch, like maybe a snake bit her. She shuts up for a second.

It sort of makes Lori flinch too, but inside. She's never said that F word, not out loud, but it sort of felt like it came out by itself, like it was the only word strong enough to let out some of the chewed-up hurting that's eating her insides. Anyway, who cares? Nothing is the same as it was before. The whole world has changed and that F word is coiled up ready on her tongue and waiting its chance to strike again. 'No fucking thing in this whole fucking world is fucking rotten fucking fair, Nelly.'

'Too true, Smithy. It's a fucked-up unfair fuck of a world, and once we learn that then we're halfway to growing up.' She pats Lori's shoulder, leaves her arm sort of loose around her shoulder for a long time, then she gets up and walks off home. Lori sits on, saying F words to the stars, and the moon, to the river of water rustling by, to the mosquitoes she murders, until Mick comes limping down the track.

'Full moon,' he says, standing there on his good leg. It's a hard walk for him even when he can see where he's walking, and it's a harder walk back due to the rise. He needs a new brace. Mavis has received letters about it, which she's got no interest in, like she's got no interest in the bill letters with the windows.

'Why did you walk all the way down here for?'

'I felt like it,' Mick says.

'You did not. You can hardly walk with that stupid fucking thing. You're just checking up on me, that's all. Nelly told you where I was and you thought I was going to drown my fucking self, didn't you?'

'Alan couldn't drown you that night. Good swimmers can't drown, and stop saying that. You sound stupid.'

'Get on my fucking bike,' she says and she dinks him home.

Home? That's a fucking joke.

leaving home

Mavis doesn't go to bed at night. She makes custards and pancakes while the television goes on and on, then when the kids get up and start whingeing for breakfast, she goes to bed to get away from them. Vinnie looks after the little ones during the day, mostly.

Not on Thursday. Lori and Mick ride around the corner into Dawson Street and see Timmy and Neil being hunted home by Bert Matthews, who is holding bawling Matty under the armpits, holding him at arm's length due to he smells. Lori tries to take him, but Bert doesn't want to give him up. Anyway, what happens next isn't good; Mavis has to get out of bed to take delivery of Matty at the front door.

. He hasn't got any clean nappies. Lori finds a cot sheet and Mavis is trying to pin it on but Matty won't lie still. His poor little bum is red raw from crawling around in that shitty nappy all day and he's only a baby, and the safety pin Mavis is trying to use isn't big enough. She's yelling, maybe embarrassed about Bert Matthews bringing him home, or maybe because of the terrible smell, then she starts slapping into his poor little sore bum, just holding one of his legs up and slapping so hard, like she's loving it.

She's always looked like a monster. Well, she's turning into one now. That's what she's doing.

'You leave him alone.' Lori snatches Matty's top half, slides him across the table. 'You leave him alone. It's not his fault that Henry's dead.' Mavis throws the cot sheet at her, and the pin, then she goes back to bed.

It's Matty who makes Lori stay around that rotten house, not Mick or Alan. It's poor little bawling Matty, who is still bald and still can't walk. He traps her. She takes him over to Nelly's and borrows some antiseptic cream, uses half the tube on his poor sore bum, then she sends Jamesy to the supermarket to get Donny to buy a big pack of cheap disposable nappies and some cream for a sore bum.

Jamesy is such a weird sort of kid; he's lost Henry too but he's never said one word about it. He always spent a lot of his life sitting on Nelly's fence, and that's where he's living these days, when he's not at school. He just sits there quiet and smiling his twisted grin, watching the house over the road, like he's waiting for it to fall down.

And it's falling. It's falling. It's caving in fast. Someone has dropped a bomb on their little country. No proper meals at night, no clean clothes for school, no clean beds to sleep in, unless Martin and Donny take the washing to the laundrette. Everything that was isn't any more.

Donny gives up first. He's got himself a job at a supermarket in Albury. 'I'm sorry, kids. I'm sorry,' he's saying. They're all standing at the front fence, except Greg, except Martin. 'I can't do anything, can't watch this any more and not be able to do anything. It's killing me. No one can do anything with her, and it's killing me, and killing Martin too. I'm sorry.' He gives Mick some money then he turns and walks away. Lori knows he's howling. He's hardly stopped howling since Henry died.

Martin goes a month later. Everyone has known for ages that he wanted to move in with Karen. It's like getting that flat was a halfway station and now he's moving on, thinner, weaker since Henry died. Smaller, pale, he never smiles.

'Don't go leaving yet. She'll come out of it after a bit. She always comes out of her mad moods after a bit,' Vinnie says.

'I can't afford to keep paying the rent and paying her bills too. I can't do it. And if me and Donny aren't around, then the welfare might have to step in and do something with her. I can't, kids. She's off the planet.' He takes the electricity bill so he can pay it before he goes. The electricity people are threatening to cut off the power. Martin doesn't know about the woodman's bill because he just knocks at the door and asks for his money.

It's about two weeks later when the cops come knocking on the door. They've got Greg with them because he got caught in a stolen car. The lady cop wants to speak to his mother, who has walked up to the hotel. Vinnie tells the cop where to find her, and Mavis comes panting home, not worrying about Greg's stolen car, just looking for some lollies she hid on top of the cupboard over the sink. Vinnie ate them. He's the only one tall enough to see up there. She goes crazy, like they are the last lollies left in the world and she's got to have them.

'Give me some money and I'll get you some more,' Vinnie says. She doesn't want other lollies, she wants the ones he ate and she's going to claw them out of him. She gets a grip on his face and she rakes it with her nails, from his brow to his cheek.

'I should have scratched your eyes out instead of combing your bloody hair, you bastard,' she screams.

'You've gone crackers. You never combed my hair in your life. You were too busy combing little Greggie's hair. You've gone around the twist, Mavis.' He's backing off, though, fending her off. He gets out to the front verandah but she's still after him, screaming crazy stuff about redheaded bastards, like she pure hates his guts.

Spud Murphy is out at his gate, watching, listening. Bert Matthews is watering his nature strip. Nelly is weeding her lawn.

Poor Henry. He would have hated this. Proud Henry.

Not too proud to hang himself, to let all the neighbours and his kids see him hanging there. Not too proud for that.

'Where am I supposed to go?' Vinnie yells, one hand holding his eye in – probably.

'Get out of my sight, you perverted bastard, before I scratch the other one out.'

Night comes before Vinnie creeps inside, his face white except for her claw marks and his eye. Mick lifts the closed eyelid and what is behind it looks like a blob of blood. She's probably cut his eye with her beautiful long fingernails. He'll probably go blind in that eye.

The little kids are in bed, Mavis is staring at the television, Mick is leaning against the bedroom door, pale and silent. 'She'll forget about it in the morning,' he says.

'She won't bloody be here to forget about it. She'll be dead in the morning. They mightn't be able to do anything with her, but I will,' Vinnie says, still holding his eye in. 'I'll do her. Knock her bloody crazy head off, Mick. That will cure her.'

Then Greg comes to the door, stands behind Mick. He's supposed to go to court in a couple of weeks and Mavis is supposed to go with him, which she won't be able to do unless she hires a furniture van and a forklift to get her into it. 'Want to fuck off out of this shit hole,' he says. 'I got a car but it needs fucking petrol.'

Vinnie looks at him. 'The bank's shut.'

'Won't be tomorrow, moron.' They are talking another language. They are talking about something the kids don't understand. 'We got enough in it to get over the border.'

'I'm coming.' Vinnie is hurting, he's shaking and he can't find his other boot to leave home in. It's probably under one of the beds, but he's gone way past the stage of thinking straight as well as seeing straight.

'You ought to go up to the hospital and see if your eye is all right,' Mick says.

'I'll cut her bloody mad eating head off if I hang around here, Mick. I know I will. I'll get the axe and cut her bloody head off.'

Greg is grabbing stuff, tossing it into the back seat and boot of Mrs Roddie's little Datsun, which he's backed up against the verandah. She always leaves that car on the street since she got her new fence and gates, due to she can't be bothered opening her new gates. He's got her keys too. Maybe she left them in her car, or maybe he pinched them from her house. She's old and goes to bed with the chooks and it's after midnight.

'Move it, you fucking moron,' Greg says, grabbing a pillow and blanket.

Vinnie finds a pair of worn-out sneakers, grabs his own pillow and blanket, his old school bag and he's out, in the car. He's going, and he's not even old enough to leave school.

They drive east, Lori and Mick standing at the gate, watching until the tail-lights disappear into the dark. Gone off to someplace, just as far away from Mavis as Mrs Roddie's old Datsun will take them.

Half of the beds are empty. The brick room is empty. Henry's world is disintegrating.

D-i-s-i-n-t-e-g-r-a-t-i-n-g.

Lori takes the vegetable knife from her sock and puts it back in the cutlery drawer.

ridiculous

Foggy mornings, misty days and the year just keeps on getting older, colder. The house is cold, school is cold, life is cold. It's ridiculous.

Lori likes that word, uses it a lot. She tells Crank Tank she's ridiculous. Tells Mick he's ridiculous wanting to go to school, because Mavis has gone mad and the whole world has gone mad and he's pretending it's normal – like hiding condensed milk in the potting shed is normal, like it's quite normal hiding the bread Martin buys in Nelly's freezer.

And Alan, he's ridiculous too; he's spending half his life crying and saying it's his fault about Henry. And how can Lori agree that it is? He'll probably go out and hang himself too, or he'll die of coughing; Willama germs are attacking him again so Lori can't start attacking him. She gets him a Panadol, makes him gargle with salty water.

He's given his germs to Matty already, and now he's trying to share them with everyone else, like coughing them all over the school lunches Mick is trying to make with frozen-solid bread, which they should have got out of Nelly's freezer last night but forgot to do.

That's the trouble with kids trying to run a house; they don't know how to do stuff, and they don't understand that fixing one problem makes two more worse things happen. Like Jamesy, he let the half-starved chooks out of their pen so they could eat grass and rotten apples on the vacant block, but they preferred Henry's garden,

127

ate everything above the ground then they headed for the laundry and pecked holes in two big plastic bags of rice Henry had stored in there, which no one knew he'd stored there until they started treading in it when they tried to do some washing.

Rice doesn't seem to agree with chooks. A few of them die from overeating it, but a few start laying eggs again. The kids find them in the laundry, on the east verandah, in the potting shed. Mavis uses them for her custard, when she's got milk. She uses the kids' condensed milk one night because she knew all the time where Henry used to hide it, so there is no condensed milk to put on the porridge and the kids don't like it much even with milk; Mick's porridge is either burned or half cooked.

He and Lori go together to get Mavis's money from the bank now and they do the shopping together, and always buy heaps of porridge, not that anyone ever liked it much, but Mavis hates it. There is not much she hates, except baked beans and vegetables. They buy heaps of home brand baked beans. Anyway, after the condensed milk disappears from the shed, they have to start leaving it at Nelly's place with the bread and margarine. Mavis calls them thieves. Maybe they are thieves. They feel like thieves, ridiculous ones, hauling stuff backwards and forwards over that road.

Lori gets the whip around her ears one night when she tells Mavis that she's acting like a nutcase who should be locked up in a nuthouse. That whip hurts like hell and leaves a mark, like she's been branded from her ear across to her nose, which is a good enough reason for not going to school. What's the use, anyway? She's an alien at that high school, wandering some lost planet, ten trillion miles from the sun.

Of course, then Mick can't go to school either so they end up stuck in the house all day, and it stinks of Mavis and Matty, who is now sicking up every time he coughs. It's Friday when he ends up in hospital. He's really sick, and no one knows it until Lori carries him over to Nelly early in the morning when she is freezing cold but he is red-hot burning up and can't breathe. Bert Matthews drives him and Nelly up to the hospital, which needs Henry's Medicare card but no one can find it.

Martin comes to the fence that night; he still brings food and money on Fridays, and what's the use of bloody Fridays? 'Matty could have died,' Lori says, accusing Martin for nicking off to rotten Karen and her posh house. 'He's got pneumonia and he could have died. And we can't find the Medicare card and living like this is ridiculous.'

He comes back on Saturday and he's got more food and two mobile phones, which he got on some cheap deal, two for the price of one. He gives one to Mick so he can get in touch if there's an emergency.

'Hide it,' he says.

That's another case of fixing one problem and making it double. Henry had the phone cut off when the pizza place started doing home deliveries. Henry knew what he was doing, because Mavis is like a dinosaur dog that knows there's a brontosaurus bone buried some-place and she wants to party. She upends the house searching for that phone but she can't find it – until Alan, silly, trusting, coughing Alan, gets the phone from inside a boot, from under a sock, from under Mick's bed, and he gives it to her so she can ring the hospital and check on Matty.

She checks on Matty, then she checks if the pizza place still does home deliveries, then the phone goes into her pocket and no one is going to get it back. Which sort of proves that she's not really nuts, just insane.

It starts in for real then. She rings a taxi to buy her a carton of cigarettes, and she always smokes more when she has a whole carton. She rings up the bank and asks about chequebook accounts. A man comes to bring her the forms. The kids have seen him before at the bank.

'In your housebound situation it will be more convenient for paying the bills,' he says.

Paying what bills? The rates haven't been paid since before Henry died, and if Martin hadn't paid the electricity, they wouldn't have any lights.

Martin picks Matty up from the hospital a few days later, with his bottle of antibiotic medicine, so Mick tells him about the phone.

'Shit. Shit, shit, shit, shit. What am I going to do, Mick? What can I bloody well do?' He pushes Matty into Lori's arms. 'Keep him warm, Splint. Give him that eye-dropper full four times a day,' he says and he walks back to his ute saying 'shit'.

The postman delivers Mavis's book of cheques, plus a bank card and a heap of other stuff in a black wallet. The letter says that the bank is delighted to open up its vault for their rich friend Mrs Mavis Smyth-Owen – not in those exact words, but that's what they've done, because the Willama taxi drivers start making a fortune. Mavis is ringing them and talking to drivers at the front door every night; they are delivering stuff and driving away with her cheques.

Martin doesn't come the next Friday so Mick asks Mavis if she could please write out a cheque for the supermarket so he can get some food. She won't. She won't even write a cheque for Henry's woodman when he drops off a final load then comes to lean a while at the back door. Mavis owes him a heap of money, because for months he's been taking pity on her. That's what he says. And he says that he's not into subsidising those who have got the money to waste on cigarettes, so until he gets paid what he's owed, there won't be any more wood delivered. She tells him what he can do with his pity and his wood. It sounds splintery.

No baked beans left at Nelly's, the porridge is all gone but there is plain flour and Jamesy finds two eggs in Henry's potting shed. Mick makes pancakes and the kids eat them with tomato sauce, but by Saturday night the tomato sauce is gone and they're sick of pancakes so they go out to the laundry and half fill a saucepan with rice, which has almost as many black bits in it as white. There were always mice in that laundry and now the rotten chooks have opened up holes in the bags and the bloody mice have got in.

Then it's Sunday. They ring Martin on Nelly's phone and find out why he didn't come on Friday. He's on his way home from Melbourne. He took Karen down to see a show and to buy her an engagement ring.

'Put Nelly on,' Martin says, and he sort of sighs.

Nelly talks for a long time, and it must be costing her a fortune to talk so long to a mobile phone, but later, when she hangs up, it probably costs her even more because she makes toasted sandwiches and packet soup and syrup dumplings, which they eat with ice-cream. Her food tastes so good and there is so much of it but Lori and Mick feel bad. They are beggars now. They are bludgers. Henry hated bludgers.

And that's life. And the weather keeps getting colder and there's not even any hot water because there's no wood for the stove. Alan can't live without hot water; he takes Matty's pram over the road to the bush and picks up enough wet wood to get the fire going. Then it's every day. It's finding wood, it's finding food, and it's waiting for Mavis to use up all her cheques so she has to send Lori and Mick to the bank again.

Except that doesn't happen. The stupid bank sends her a new chequebook before the old one is even finished.

Tuesday. Long way to Friday. Mavis is smoking, staring at the television and her green tent is filthy. She doesn't see Mick when he limps into the kitchen, tries to rub the frown lines from his brow, tries to rub the ache from his back.

'We need money for food,' he says, waits, his good foot on the floor, one hip high, the other low. He's grown so tall. If he doesn't get a new brace soon, his hip and back bones are going to grow so crooked he won't be able to walk at all. He moves, blocks her view of the television.

'Get out of my way, you twisted bloody little thief,' she says, and she stuffs two mints in her mouth, moves her head so she can see around him.

He moves too. He's going to make her look at him. 'You're the thief,' he says. 'You're getting money from the government so you can look after your children and you're not looking after them. How much money do you think you'll get when they put us all in homes?'

He turns to walk away, and Mavis puts out a foot and trips him. Oh sure, she tries to grab his arm when he starts to fall, but it's too late for that. Mick's got no balance, he never did have any balance and she knows it. Everybody knows it and that's why no one is allowed to thump him. His braced leg goes one way and he goes the other, goes down hard. There is a sort of non-Mick-like moan, a sort of surprised turn of his head and then he's flat out on his stomach and he's not moving.

Jamesy picks up the broom. It's not much good for sweeping, most of its hair is gone, but it's good enough for what he wants it for. He's smiling and belting at Mavis with it, belting at her shoulders and trying to get her head, belting her fat thighs while Alan runs for Nelly.

She calls the ambulance then comes running into the kitchen, finds Mick sort of fainted, still on the floor, finds Jamesy with his weapon and he's not retreating, finds Mavis, standing back, wild eyed and staring at the floor where Lori is kneeling, trying to put Mick's braced leg back in a straight position and he isn't helping; he's ghost white and floppy, his eyes sort of opening, then closing again. Nelly tries to wake him up with a wet tea towel, and when she can't, she tries to lift him, but it's like he's dead.

Lori just holds him, both arms around him. She's heart-jumping, head-crawling, sick scared. This is Mick. This is pure good person lovable Mick who never hurt anyone in his whole life. This is Mick and he's hurt bad.

The little ones are howling, Matty is coughing and howling. Nelly ignores them, turns on Mavis and goes at her like a sardine with a dirty mouth attacking a humpback whale. She's still going at it when the ambulance men walk into the shambles of Henry's kitchen.

They get Mick's brace off, get him on a stretcher, start asking questions.

Mick fell over. Mavis didn't see it. His boot must have slipped.

Nelly is saying something different and peppering what she's saying in her usual way.

Nelly is a lying, troublemaking old bitch, Mavis says. Always has been.

The ambulance men don't know who to believe, due to what Nelly is yelling sounds like she might be a pure troublemaking old bitch. The men look from one to the other, look at Lori.

She has to sleep in this house tonight. Where will she sleep if she tells that Mavis tripped Mick? Where will the little ones sleep?

The ambulance men will call the cops and the cops will take the kids away and put them in homes so Mavis doesn't abuse them. That's what police do on television. Lori has seen too much television, read too many newspapers, stood outside too many doors. And she's heard Martin and Nelly talking about kids' homes. If she dobs now, that's it, so she stands, her back against the door, stands dumb, stands shaking her head.

Jamesy is staring at her. Alan is coughing and staring at her. The little kids are crying and staring at her as the ambulance men take Mick away.

One by one they have left her. It started at Christmas with Henry. One by one until all of the big ones are gone. Now Lori is the biggest; she's twelve and three months and all the kids are staring at her as if she's really the biggest.

Big happened too fast. She's not big enough.

Her ears are ringing and her head feels as if someone put a bike pump in her ear and blew her head up so it's twice its size. She's hot and she's cold and a thousand thoughts are darting backwards and forwards between her ringing ears and she can't make one darting thought join up with the next. She's got to ride up to the hospital. Stay with Mick. Can't leave the little ones. Should have said something. Should have told on Mavis.

Henry! Henry! Henry!

Matty is crying, pulling himself up on her jeans, reaching his little arms up. She looks at him, lifts him, walks outside with him.

Henry!

Late. Winter, after five o'clock late. Cold. Ice coming up from the cold earth. Smell of winter's wind cold. Too cold for Matty, but she's walking off to the river with him on her back, his little hands choking her, his little bum wetting her. She's walking, head down, not seeing, not feeling, not thinking.

Alan and the other kids follow her, so she turns up another track, runs from them, but you can't be Cathy Freeman when you're wearing a Matty backpack. The kids keep running after her, all the way to the bridge.

Someone must have been fishing up there because a European carp has been tossed up on the bank. They're like pest fish, those carp, no good for anything except messing up the river. It's a big one, though. Lori stands, watching it flap, gasp for air, try not to die. A lot of carp get tossed on the bank and Henry used to say it was cruel to let them flap themselves to death. She always kicks them back in the water; the poor things want to live so much.

Not Henry. He wanted to die, so let it die. Mick's going to die, so let everything die. Who cares?

Alan is coughing and looking at the fish. 'Henry said they're no good to eat. Are they poison?'

She slides Matty to the ground and stares at that fish. It's coughing too, or trying to suck in air to live.

'They're not poison,' Jamesy says. 'Some people eat them.' He picks up a stick, moves the fish further away from the water.

Maybe the time comes when there is no such thing as Henry, no such thing as Henry's *more*. There is just less, and less, and less until there is nothing.

Lori watches the fish grow weaker. She's going to stand there and watch it die, just to see how long it takes for it to give up, for it to just lie still and be nothing.

Jamesy is looking at her. 'They're not poisonous, Lori.'

134

No air to reply. She stands looking that fish in the eye, wanting it to stop gasping.

Jamesy goes running off through the trees, but he's back in minutes and he's got Henry's big stew saucepan, one of Mavis's lighters, the sharp vegetable knife, an onion, some silverbeet that's gone to seed and an empty condensed milk tin full of rice that is half mouse dung.

The fish has stopped its gasping but Jamesy finishes it off while Alan pours the rice into the saucepan and picks out the black bits. Jamesy hacks the fish's head off, guts it, pulls its skin off then hacks it to bits, hacks at the bones while Alan builds a fire, burns his fingers with Mavis's lighter. Lori is not saying a word, just watches Jamesy drop his hunks of fish on top of the rice, watches him cover the mess with silverbeet leaves and hunks of onion, pour in a condensed milk tin of water and put the saucepan on the fire, which is more smoke than flame. She's standing, trying to be dead, until the mess starts to warm up and it stinks worse than stiff dead socks.

'You can't eat that, you morons. It will kill you.'

'They're not poison. It will be fish stew.'

The stink is like . . . like something terrible. 'You can't eat it, I said.' She puts Matty on her back and walks away from the stink, leaves them stirring it.

No one eats the stewed fish. Maybe the birds will. It gets poured onto the mud.

'We should have roasted it in mud,' Alan coughs. 'It looked like proper fish.' He coughs, sounds as if he's trying to cough his heart out through his diseased tonsils.

'If we had some oil we could have fried it,' Jamesy says.

'I don't like that stinky rice,' Neil says. 'I only like Vinnie's rice with milk.'

Lori carries Matty home and he's asleep on her shoulder before they get there. She pours the last of the baby Panadol into him, pins a cot sheet on for a napkin, finds his spare sweater on the floor and tucks him into his filthy blankets, then crawls into her own bed, thinks

135

of Mick, thinks the kids didn't have any dinner – instead of thinking of Henry, stuck in that hole.

Maybe she's hungry, because she dreams of Nelly's sultana cake and Jamesy is cooking it beside the river but the sultanas are fish eyes.

european carp

The next day Mavis gets a phone call to say that Mick is being sent to Melbourne. His crippled leg has been dislocated and the doctor wants a specialist to look at it.

People come around in packs, cops, the old doctor, a guy with verandah eyebrows, heaps of people, because Mick might have been dislocated but he's still trying to fix up Mavis from his hospital bed. He's been dobbing and though Mavis might be stark raving crazy, she's sane enough to realise she's in trouble. She starts bawling for Henry.

'You poor woman,' the doctor says. He's going to organise some help for her in the house, get the counsellor to call again. He's going to get her on some new pills. He's writing his prescriptions again. He's going to play hell with a broomstick, and it is a pity Jamesy didn't knock her bloody mad head off with his broomstick last night.

'The older boys left me when their father died,' she sobs. 'I've never been able to do anything with Michael. His father gave in to his every demand. He's always at me, always wanting money.'

Lori's mouth gets jammed full of dobbing words, until the police lady and the doctor start talking about emergency care for the children – just for a while. And it's pure blackmail, that's what it is. It's like on the television when people are blackmailed into keeping their mouths shut. There is no way out of this.

'Gregory will be home tomorrow. He is the only one I can lean on.'

'Where is he, Mrs Smyth-Owen?'

'He took off,' Jamesy says.

'He's staying with my sister in Melbourne.'

'He took old Roddie's car and he took Vinnie with him too,' Neil says.

The lady cop looks at Neil, believes him. She knows all about Gregory Smyth-Owen, who didn't turn up for his court appearance. She also knows about Mrs Roddie's missing Datsun. Mavis probably knows that she's opened her mouth and put her foot right in it so she grasps her stomach, sits down hard on the couch. 'It's the baby,' she says. 'I'm losing it.'

The doctor didn't know there was going to be another baby. He looks at the kids, sort of counts them. He's old, his face worn, his glasses thick. He sighs, doesn't want to know about this baby, but he checks Mavis's blood pressure, tries to find a heartbeat.

The lady cop is tough; she doesn't give a damn about new babies. She wants Eva's address and gets it too before she leaves. She and the doctor walk outside for some fresh air and Lori follows them, watches the lady leave, watches the doctor step on a broken floorboard which jumps up, tries to get his shin. He dodges in time. He's not blind – just can't see anything he doesn't want to see.

'Matty and Alan are sick,' she says. She's standing half in and half out the door.

He turns, looks down at that floorboard then directly at her, and as their eyes make contact, for a split second she sees deep behind his glasses, reads what's there. That doctor knows exactly what happened to Mick, knows that Matty and Alan are sick too, and the rest of the kids neglected. He can't fix it, so he'd prefer not to see it, but he follows her back into chaos, looks at Alan's throat, listens to Matty's chest, writes two more prescriptions, then leaves, taking note of that broken board, stepping high.

Lori gets the medicine from the chemist. She hands Alan

his bottle, doses Matty with a double dose then puts both bottles safe on top of the kitchen cupboard with Mavis's Valium and Aropax.

There are two packets of Aropax and six of Valium with only a few tablets missing from each packet. Lori packs them, one on top of the other, thinks of crushing them all up, mixing them with condensed milk and leaving it on the table for Mavis to eat from the tin or use in her custard – or maybe crush them and put them in the custard powder, which is yellow, about the same colour as Valium – like, only leave enough custard powder in the packet for one last serve.

But things get a bit better that week. The district nurse and two cleaning ladies come and everyone is busy and tripping over kids and when Mavis is all pink and glowing clean, her hair long and fluffy, the nurse cleans up the little kids and the cleaning ladies go out to the laundry where they have a great time looking disgusted while cleaning up a mountain of mouldy clothes.

Alan doesn't go to school, due to his tonsils and cough, and Jamesy doesn't come home from school. Lori thinks he's left home too, but he turns up late and he's got three European carp in his school bag. One of the cleaning ladies tells Jamesy to take the fish outside but the other one tells her that a small European carp is okay to eat.

'You have to bleed them while they are fresh, though, cut their tails off and let them hang, then freeze them for a few days.'

Jamesy is listening. 'Why?' he asks.

'I dunno, really. Someone told me to, love. Then I thaw them, give them a good soak in salty water, stick a few slices of lemon and onions inside them, pour over a bit of oil and salt and pepper and a few herbs, wrap them in foil and cook them in the oven. You wouldn't even know you were eating carp.'

Jamesy borrows the wood axe from the Salvation Army bloke who is out there cutting up old boards and stuff from the junk heap, and he tops and tails his fish, doesn't try to cook them because someone has done a heap of food shopping for Mavis and she's up and boiling a packet of spaghetti and she's got a jar of sauce and even grated cheese to put on it so Jamesy puts his carp in the freezer, wrapped up in supermarket bags.

Nearly every day he adds a fish to the freezer, because Mavis has been shocked into action, scared she'll lose her kids and her pension; every night she's heating up pies or something, because that social worker man is checking on her and shopping for her.

It lasts for two weeks then the police lady gives up looking for Greg, and the social worker man stops knocking at the door, and the district nurse stops coming to help Mavis shower because a man has been working in the bathroom and he's put metal handles on the tiles so Mavis has got something to hang on to. Only one young cleaning lady comes now, twice a week.

She's there one day when Lori rides home from school mid afternoon; she got sent to the vice principal again and decided not to go. It's mid winter and wet. The house is freezing because there is no wood for the stove, and maybe that's why Mavis is still in bed. Anyway, the home-help lady finds the three little kids running around half naked, coughing and runny nosed. She's sick of this mess, anyway, so she starts doing her block as she works her way towards Mavis's door, where she stops picking things up, leans, looks at the hump of quilt and pillows.

'If you'd get off your fat backside and do a bit of work, you'd be better off, Mrs Smyth-Owen,' she says, starting slow. 'And so would those poor bloody little kids. You're like a bloody queen bee, you are, laying around in your hive, laying eggs and letting the poor bloody workers run around after you. Yeah, well, I just stopped running, Mrs Smyth-Owen. Find yourself another fool.'

No more clean kitchen. No more frozen pies and spaghetti, due to the social worker man fixed it up with the supermarket so Mavis can phone in her order then give the delivery man a cheque when he delivers. Mavis isn't phoning the supermarket, or not often, but she's back to phoning her taxi friends.

It's Jamesy who gets the stove going, then he takes two frozen-stiff carp from the freezer, sticks them in a cold oven. After an hour or so those fish sort of boil in their juices and they taste like that one smelt down at the river.

waiting for friday

The less and the less keeps on getting less but it won't end. School is just a place Lori goes to wait for the day to be over so she can go to bed, hoping the next day will forget to come, but a new day comes, and it starts all over again. It's like there is an old clock somewhere that has to work its way down to the end. She can almost hear it tick-tock-ticking in her head.

Martin still comes on Friday nights with his food, and money for Nelly, so she can get stuff to cut the school lunches. She makes really good sandwiches, even puts a whole banana in Lori's bag sometimes, and that might be enough to keep kids alive. It's not enough to keep kids wanting to stay alive – like seeing Martin on Fridays isn't enough. Fridays are useless.

Lori's bike is useless too. Something has gone wrong with the bit that drives the chain and she can't fix it, and Vinnie's old bike has got a puncture, so on Friday she walks to school in the rain, which is better than staying at home. Weeks back she lost her parka or some other kid pinched it. And the hem Nelly took up on her uniform has come down and it's not too long, even with the hem down. Her bones don't know that it's no use growing – or her boobs.

Alan sounds as if he's dying of consumption. He's in bed, coughing a duet with Matty in a bottom bunk, the other two little ones sound asleep on the other bottom bunk, only the tops of their heads visible beneath a mound of blankets.

So tired, she wants to go to bed too, get this day done. All the time, she's tired. Tired and cold, and tired of waiting for Martin on Fridays. Tired of him coming around and beeping his horn out front and expecting her to run out through the rain, listen to him. Tired of him thinking Friday is enough. Tired of his voice sounding like it always used to sound, like, we've set the date for our wedding, Splint. Cool. Like, look what I've got you tonight, Splint, chicken and chips. Super cool.

'Mick's okay, Splint. He'll be down there for a while yet, though. They let me talk to him today, and he said they are fitting him with a new brace. He's needed a new brace for ages.' She stares at the dashboard, and at the rip in the vinyl. It looks like an eye staring back at her. 'Talk to me, Splinter.'

She looks at him, shakes her head, thinks how she always wanted to be one of the big kids. So she's the biggest. What is she supposed to do about it? What does he expect her to say? Alan's sick? That's old news. Who wants to read last week's newspaper? The news isn't going to change. She's sitting, smelling that chicken and chips, and in some stupid kid place inside her head she's thinking, yummy, chicken and chips for tea, but there is a new place in her head that is thinking other things, like writing tomorrow's news in big black headlines: MURDER BY VALIUM AND CONDENSED MILK. MURDER BY CUSTARD.

'Is it so bad, Splint?'

'Is it so bad, Splint? Has getting engaged to that fucking stuck-up rotten idiot turned your brain into bug stew or something?'

He sort of sits back, shocked, like she's slapped his face. Then he slaps her face, so she thumps him with her closed fists, and she starts yelling stuff and she can't stop yelling and she can't stop thumping him either. She's yelling about cooking European carp and Henry's rotten onions, and she's yelling about school books and her parka and about the letters that keep coming from the bank because they gave Mavis too many cheques, and she writes out too much money on her cheques. And she's yelling about how the bank doesn't like it when Mavis writes out more cheques than they can pay, so they charge her more fees. She's thumping Martin, thumping his head, his shoulders, any place she can make contact. 'And there's no wood for the fucking fire, and we're fucking freezing, and Mick wrote, and he's living in a hostel, not at the fucking hospital, and he won't ever come home again, because who'd want to come home to this fucking place? And you come here on Fridays and you say is it so bad, Splint? You're as fucking mad as Mavis. You've both gone round the fucking twist.'

He tries to grab her wrists to stop her thumping, and it's raining outside the ute, but it's wetter inside because Martin is making it wetter. He's bawling now, and she didn't know that he still knew how to bawl, so she stops thumping him.

'What's the use?' she says. 'What's the use of your fucking Fridays?'

'No use, Splint,' he says, wiping his nose with his wrist, wiping his eyes with his thumbs, sniffing, sort of sobbing breaths. Then he picks up his parcel of chips and chicken which has steamed up all the windows and he gets out of the ute and walks towards the house. He never goes inside. Hasn't been inside for weeks. 'I'll keep her busy while you get some food into the kids.'

He keeps her busy, all right. If the rain wasn't so heavy, all the neighbours would be out on the street watering their gardens tonight, listening to just how busy he's keeping her. But it is raining, cats and dogs. It's flooding Willama. The verandahs are pouring waterfalls down to the mud while chicken and chips are pouring into sleepy little bellies. They have their dinner in the bunk room with Alan, who even stops coughing long enough to eat some chicken, so maybe he's not dying yet. They stay in the bunk room until Martin drives away, then Lori gets scared and she drags the chest of drawers across the room, pushes it against the door so Mavis can't get in and kill them for eating all the chicken and chips.

But Martin comes back and Lori has to move the barricade and let him in. He's got cough medicine, and Panadol, disposable napkins, cornflakes and milk for breakfast. Alan takes a Panadol then drinks cough medicine from the bottle. He goes straight to sleep, and when Matty coughs, Martin gives him half a Panadol crushed up in cough medicine. He stops coughing and starts snoring. Neil coughs, because he wants some, then Timmy. They get half a Panadol and a suck on the medicine bottle and they are all druggies and who cares, because the sound of no coughing is so bloody good.

Almost like a proper family, all together in the bunk room, Lori in one bottom bunk with Timmy; Jamesy and Neil up top, Alan and Matty curled up together and Martin sleeping alone. It's warm in that room. It's almost safe in that room.

The next morning it's not safe.

They go to Nelly's, and Martin phones the bank manager, who he knows well because he helped build his house. It's Mrs Smyth-Owen's account. Privacy laws and that crap. That was a waste of time. Nelly tells Martin to cut out the middle man, go direct to the taxi people, tell them not to answer Mavis's phone calls.

And he's off, his ute roaring up the street. He goes to the pizza place, goes to the fish and chips place, goes to the hotel on the corner and it takes him the whole day almost, and he's supposed to be taking Karen to a friend's place for dinner but he doesn't even ring her. He eats dinner with the kids at Nelly's before he gets around to ringing Karen.

She tells him it's all off. She's taken his ring off. She'll post it to him. She's packed his bags too and they are standing out in the rain ready for him to take home to his family, who he obviously loves more than he loves her.

He's breaking up. He's the last of the past and sanity, and he's going insane. He's sitting at the window. 'I love her, Nelly,' he's saying. 'I love the way her family live and I want it. I want to go back there and never see this fucking street again.' That's what he says. He never uses that word. Maybe he learned it from Lori last night because he's sure using it now. He's parked his ute in the street, and he's looking out from Nelly's window, looking at the rain so the kids can't see his eyes. 'I love the kids too, Nelly, but there's nothing more I can do for them. They'd be better off in a home.'

Then Nelly sends the kids back to the kitchen so she and Martin can start plotting. Lori can hear them. Martin is going to call the social worker on Monday morning, first thing Monday morning.

Lori opens the door, stares at them, until Martin looks at her eyes.

'It will be better than that, Splinter.' He points at the house over the road, wipes his eyes with his thumbs.

Lori doesn't say yes, doesn't say no, just thinks of little Matty getting adopted by some stranger and carted off to England, thinks of Jamesy someplace where they'll try to treat him like a little kid when he's always been an old man since the day he was born, just an old man laughing at the world with his lopsided grin. She thinks of Mick, who will have no place to come home to, if they ever let him come home. How can getting split up be better? But doesn't she want someone to look after her? Isn't that what she wants? Doesn't she want her head to stop feeling blown up and thinking mad thoughts?

No. Not if it means getting put in a home.

Then Mavis is out front looking around for Martin. She's got the wood axe but she's not thinking about chopping wood. And when she can't find Martin to kill, she starts killing his ute's headlights. She must have tried to call a taxi and got an earful instead. Martin is out the door running. He gets in the ute and backs away, his head outside in the rain, taunting Mavis, telling her to have a go. He's keeping enough distance between her axe and his ute, though. She's yelling and he's yelling louder, taking that war out to the street, up the street, due to she's following him, and maybe he wants her to follow him and drop dead or something.

The house is empty.

No time to think about it. Lori is out in the rain and across the road, she's in Mavis's room, looking for the chequebook. It's the big, bad bogyman, it's the monster that came into this house and finished things off. It's in a black wallet thing; she knows what it looks like but she can't find it. She's looking in the wardrobe, feeling along the top of the wardrobe. It's not there. She's looking in all the sensible places, then she stops, stops thinking sensible, thinks Mavis. She looks under Mavis's pillows and it's there, and it's got all sorts of stuff in it and even a little pen.

She runs with it through the kitchen, grabs the telephone charger. Runs into the brick room and bolts the door, then she rips the cheques out of the book and flushes them one after the other down the loo.

She's using that F word again. She's putting it in front of banks. She's shredding cheques with Mavis L Smyth-Owen printed on them and she's using the F word in front of Mavis L Smyth-Owen and she's using it in front of state-run homes, then in front of the F word and then there is a long stream of F words, and she doesn't care, because there is more noise coming from the street.

Someone must have called the cops because they come with their wailing sirens; Lori can see the reflection of their blue lights on the rain. By the sound of it, half the neighbours are out the front. Half of Willama, even. Lori stays where she is. She's shaking and she's stopped saying the F word, she's singing 'Oh, My Papa' to the beat of the rain on the roof. She's teeth-chattering, freezing cold but she keeps on singing loud, hitting her head against the brick wall and singing 'Oh, My Papa'. And she knows all the words and she didn't know she knew all the words.

And she's crying, or hot rain is running out of her eyes and pouring down her face, but she keeps singing that song, over and over again, singing and pumping out hot rain until everything goes quiet. Stays quiet. Even the rain. Even her tears.

They must have got Mavis. They must have stuck chains around her and dragged her up onto a tow truck.

But they haven't got her because Lori hears her coming. She hears the puffing and blowing and it's coming closer. And if she truly had a bad heart, then it would have stopped for sure by now, wouldn't it? She was swinging that axe like she could have cut up a ton of wood and Lori expects that axe to start cutting through the old green door.

Mavis is pushing at it. She's gasping words, hasn't got enough wind left to roar. She's thumping against the door and Lori is watching it strain in against the slide bolt.

Good old green door. Be strong, old ancient door.

Silently Lori winds the window open. The gap is small because of the chain, but she'll get through, or maybe she'll just break the window and go through the frame. She pulls the old chest of drawers nearer, climbs up on it. Waits. Maybe the door hinges will hold. She waits.

Her lungs wheezing for air, Mavis gives up and flip-flaps off through the mud to the outside loo. Minutes later she huffs and puffs back. Lori hears the thunk of the couch digging a deeper hole through the wall into the big boys' bedroom where nobody sleeps, and she hears Mavis yelling into her phone.

No taxi driver comes knocking at the door.

The chest of drawers is wobbly and Lori's head and stomach are wobbly too, but she listens. Mavis is still yelling at someone on the phone, but no taxi beeps out front. Maybe Martin has fixed up the taxi people.

No sound of kids in that kitchen. They must still be at Nelly's. Lori is shivering, teeth-chattering cold, but she's not opening that door to find out what's happened to the little kids. She's got Mavis's bank stuff and her battery charger, and she knows that mobile phone doesn't hold a charge for long. It will run out of power, sooner or later it will run out of power.

She looks at the charger, then slides from her perch to the floor. Holding on to it by the electrical cord, she dips it in the loo water, like she's fishing; she dips it deep, almost loses it around the S bend. For an hour she sits there fishing, drowning the charger, killing it while in the kitchen the phone calls go on, and on, and the cement floor keeps getting colder. She sits on the loo seat, props her feet against the chest of drawers and hangs on to the charger.

They're back. Martin and Mavis are going at it again. And Jamesy is there too. She listens. And Alan, she can hear his cough. No little ones, though. It's way past their bedtime and Nelly hasn't got enough beds to put them in. Lori knows what has happened to them, knows that they've been taken away. She's letting tears drip again on the concrete. She's bone-aching cold but her tears are hot. Big, fat, scalding, splatty tears.

The doctor and some strangers' voices are out there. Maybe the lady cop. It's late, like it might even be midnight, but those people get things quiet.

'Lori,' Jamesy calls out back.

'Splint! Where are you?' Martin tries the door. 'Splinter. Answer me.'

Lori is on the other side of that good old green door. She's still got the charger and the bank stuff she's been holding in her hand for hours. She tucks them down the front of her sweater, pokes them under her bra, and they look like misshapen boobs, but she slides the bolt, folds her arms across her square boobs.

Martin takes her, holds her while she cries out the last of being one of the little kids. She cries for Henry and for the home he used to make. She cries and she shakes and Martin is warm and he keeps holding her, letting her cry. Alan puts his arms around her too, and he coughs and cries with her.

It's later when she finds out why he's crying, and it's for a different reason. Eva is back in St Kilda. The police lady has been in touch with her about Greg, and Martin has bought Alan a bus ticket home.

'It's what Henry wanted,' Martin says. 'Alan is sick, Splint. He's not as strong as you and Jamesy and he needs a decent place to live. I've just done what Henry would have wanted me to do,' Martin says while Mavis sleeps.

The doctor came with three helpers and he hit Mavis with an elephant dart, Jamesy says. 'Knocked her out in seconds. Pow.' Jamesy is grinning, not crying. He mimes the injection, mimes the extended-arm, stiff-legged walk to her bedroom, the collapse. Lori watches him as she sniffs her final sobs away.

'The little kids are in emergency care,' Martin says. Lori looks at him as if he's a kid thief. She looks at Alan, the traitor. 'It's better for them,' Martin says. 'They are together, they'll keep them together until – '

Until it all gets broken up for good, and they'll grow up strangers, and who cares? She'll have brothers everywhere and she won't know them, like she doesn't know Alan's twin, who he's going back to. They'll all end up like Henry, who didn't know any of his blood family.

Getting adopted must run in families. Being taken away from your mother must run in families. Being deserted by your father must run in families. It's interesting – almost. She never thought it would happen to her. A year ago she thought she'd grow up in Willama, leave school and get a job at the supermarket or McDonald's, but the clock has nearly run down.

Too tired to fight any more. She leaves Martin and the other boys in the kitchen and goes to bed in the clothes she's wearing. The battery charger digs in. The chequebook wallet is sharp. She puts them under her pillow and shivers herself warm.

alan's gone

Alan leaves at eight the next morning, his antibiotics in his hand. It's not easy waving him goodbye, but it is what Henry wanted, and better for Alan to go back to a rich home and his twin than to die of Willama germs. Lori walks him to the depot, waves to him as the bus drives away. He came, and now he's gone. She knew him, and now she won't know him any more. She stands there and bawls. Just bawls her eyes out. Can't stop doing it, either. She's been doing it half the night.

The doctor keeps coming back, keeps injecting Mavis, due to she won't take pills. Martin has moved back home because Karen still won't talk to him and Mavis has been tamed by that doctor and, also, he's got no other place to go.

Willama is pretty big for a country town but it's not big enough for secrets. Everyone knows about that street war and the little kids being taken away, and if they haven't heard about that, then they know a taxi driver or one of the people in the takeaway shops, or even the cleaning lady. Everyone knows someone, so just going to school is pure gruesome embarrassing. All the kids look at Lori, whisper behind their hands. Lori gives them a look at her middle finger.

Martin has taken three weeks holiday from bricklaying, which is not much of a holiday, but since that crying night when Karen dumped him, he's tough, like his word is law. Mavis signs the withdrawal forms, she lets the doctor give her injections, lets the nurse shower her. Her blood pressure has gone through the roof, the doctor tells Martin. Her system has taken too much abuse, she has to diet or she won't live long enough for the baby to be born.

It's like Henry killed himself, so she's now killing herself. It's like she hates her kids and wants to get away from them. That's probably why Henry did it – hated looking after all of those kids and when he found out there was going to be another one, he got away the only way he could.

It's in the second week that Mavis starts spending a lot of time sitting on the verandah. She's probably watching for the postman, hoping the bank might send her another chequebook. Lori watches for him too, because if that chequebook comes, she's going to get it first and rip it up, flush it too.

Anyway, after a bit, because of Mavis now taking her pills and Martin being home and the house back to clean, the little kids get brought home from emergency care. They are all over their colds and they've got nice clean clothes and shoes on, and they don't look the same – they look better. The social worker man brings them and while he's lifting those eyebrows and having a good look around, Martin takes the opportunity to get Mavis to sign a withdrawal form.

For a while it's almost back to normal, like vegetables and sausages and frozen fish and supermarket chips, but Mavis isn't normal, and Martin isn't Henry. Though he's cooking and cleaning all day, he's spending his nights phoning Karen's parents or just sitting, playing with his mobile and waiting for Karen to forgive him and call. And he's hating Mavis more every day.

Then about a week after his holiday is over, Karen forgives him, and he starts driving out to the farm after the kids are in bed and coming home in time to make breakfast, or not coming home at night to cook dinner. Matty is bawling again because Mavis tossed his dummy out. And she's not taking her pills. She's hardly taken any of her pills. Lori knows exactly how many have gone from those packets.

She climbs on a chair, looks on top of the kitchen cupboard for money. Henry sometimes put coins up high. No coins, but she pinches a packet of Valium then goes over to Nelly, borrows two dollars and buys Matty a new dummy from Kmart, which she threads on string then pins to his sweater.

'Stay away from Mavis, or she'll take this one too. Run over to Nelly's if she tries to get you.' The packet of Valium still in her pocket, her fingers play over the little bubble-covered pills. Mavis is in the loo, so Lori pops one small yellow pill free and crushes it between two spoons, like Mavis and Donny did the night they zapped Alan. It's easy. It turns into powder. She tastes a bit on her finger. It's sort of tasteless. A bit sweetish. A bit bitter.

One day before the clock runs down again and they take her away to put in a home, she'll hammer all the pills to powder and mix them with condensed milk and she'll stick a funnel in Mavis's mouth while she's asleep and she'll pour in the lot. Mavis will just think she's having a lovely sweet dream. She'll swallow it, and then Martin will come home for good and Donny will come back, and Mick, and they'll all live happily. Lori washes the powder down the sink, washes the spoons, watching the water circle as it finds its way down the plughole. She's never noticed how that water circles before.

She washes the dishes, wipes the bench, the table, like Martin wipes it. She takes a bag full of rubbish out to the green bin, looks at Henry's potting shed and wonders if his flowers are all dead. She hasn't given them any water since Alan left, and too bad. She has to sweep the floor so Martin won't have to do it when he gets home and his eyes won't get that trapped, hopeless expression.

She never swept the floor for Henry. She never washed dishes, never washed anything. When Henry was alive, she was like a baby caterpillar, woven into a soft cocoon so it didn't have to see anything, and even if she did see it, she didn't have to understand. Like Henry's eyes that last day. His eyes were already dead and she didn't even know it.

She walks into the bathroom, turns on the two taps, stands watching the hot and cold streams join, making that same circle. How come they make a circle? Henry would know. Alan might know. But they're gone. She shrugs, glances up at the shaving mirror where her face is sort of hiding behind the foggy cocoon. Quick as a flash, she wipes away the fog, wanting to see into her eyes before they start looking at themselves.

And for a second she does. It's, like, dark in there, like it's a horror show on a stormy night playing behind her eyes. She wipes the mirror again, and stares into those dark eyes. The storm is gone and they just look big and dark and sad.

No more baby caterpillar. She's been ripped out of her soft cocoon too early, so she didn't have time to grow wings. She's turned into a wingless moth with two big eyes that can see the whole world is waiting out there to stomp on her because she has to crawl along the gutter instead of flying in the sky.

the last straw

Martin hasn't been home since last night and there's no bread, no milk, no nothing, plus Mavis has been out of cigarettes all day due to Martin forgot to get them. Maybe he forgot on purpose. She's stomping mad and the kids are staying out of her way. They are watching her, though, when she starts washing her green tent in the sink, when she gets the iron and starts steaming up the kitchen trying to iron that tent dry.

It didn't come clean and it's not big enough any more. She's massive, like twice as massive as she was when Henry was alive. She gets it on, then goes to her bedroom, gets a giant's jacket from her wardrobe and tries to put her arm in, and when it won't go in, she screams and pitches the jacket, tries to kick it, and lucky the bed is there. It saves her from falling.

It's strange, really, the way Lori's eyes are seeing things so clearly today. They're seeing that red hair hanging around those humpy, bumpy shoulders. They're seeing that awful sagging mouth she's painting with lipstick – seeing the hands that paint it. They look fat, not beautiful. Seeing those bare fat feet. Mavis always had okay feet and ankles. Today they won't go into those old flattened scuffs.

It's raining, not much, just a steady drizzle, and she's got no jacket, she's got no shoes, but she sways out to the verandah, stands there a while, then she's walking out to the road.

Lori watches from the lounge-room window, sees Mavis stop,

wipe rain from her eyes as she looks forward, looks back, looks at Nelly's house. She won't go to Nelly's house to beg, so back wins, though she has to heave herself, like each footstep through the mud is pushing a mountain uphill. She can't make the step up to the verandah, and she has to hold on to a verandah post to make that step; the spouting over that verandah post is all rusty so there's a waterfall and it's wetting her, soaking her.

'Bastard,' she says, and the post shudders, but she gets one foot up, then the other, gets herself back to the kitchen and flops down onto her couch, sits there, dripping water and gasping for air.

'Get down . . . to the bank. Get . . . forms. Withdrawal forms. Chequebook forms. That bastard . . . that bastard better not . . . come near me. He better . . . stay away . . . from me. They'd all . . . better . . . stay away from me.' She'd be better off saving her air to pump blood, because she's looking blue.

Lori doesn't say a word, but she tosses her a dry towel; she's feeling guilty-sad, like, she's the one who flushed the cheques down the loo, and that battery charger she chucked into a green bin at school. Didn't chuck the other bank stuff. She hid it where Greg used to hide his stolen cigarettes. Maybe she should give it back.

Martin has been looking for it. Lori didn't tell him she hid it, which is thieving. Henry hated thieves.

The kids wait until five, then Nelly comes over with her big black umbrella.

'His ute has blown a head gasket,' she says. 'Come on. Get your coats.'

She's been plotting with Martin again and Lori knows it by the way Nelly isn't meeting her eyes, but they eat her good dinner gladly, eat thick soup and toast, then bread and butter pudding and ice-cream. They are still eating it when the phone rings.

'It's got to be better for them,' Nelly says soft in the next room. 'This is doing none of them no good at all, Smithy.'

And Lori is up, her pudding forgotten. She snatches the phone. 'You're not splitting us up, Martin.'

'I can't do anything else, Splint. And you know I can't. She's gone around the twist. There's nothing anyone can do with her – not long term.'

Gone around the twist might be one of his expressions but *long term* isn't. And it doesn't sound like his voice either; it sounds tired, sounds as if maybe his head gasket isn't even blown, he's just sick of looking after kids.

Then Lori hears Karen's voice coaching him in the background. She's given him an u-l-t-i-m-a-t-u-m. That's what's happened. Like, you do as I say, Martin, get rid of them or the engagement is off again. She's probably listening in to the phone call too.

'You tell that stuck-up bitch from me that she can fuck off while I'm talking to you, Martin, and tell her from me that she can keep her nose out of our family's business.' She hangs up before he can say anything and she goes to Nelly's front window and stares at that falling-down house over the road.

Mavis is on the verandah looking around for someone. She's probably starving. It's like a family who got themselves a new pup for Christmas and didn't know it was going to grow into a giant man-eating killer dog, and now that it has, they don't even bother to feed it, which just makes the man-eater even more determined to eat everyone.

Lori watches her walk to the road again, where she stops, looks back but moves forward. It's the cruellest, saddest walk Lori has ever seen. She bites hard on her hand trying to stop her eyes from dripping those big scalding tears as Mavis plods barefoot through the mud, sort of stopping and starting, but heaving herself forward, one plodding step at a time.

'Smithy. Come and finish your pudding before the plagues of Egypt eat it.'

'That's what we are, just pests. Why don't you and Martin spray us with pest killer?' Lori says. Shouldn't have said that, but her stomach is feeling all churned up with something she doesn't understand, maybe with wanting that pudding. She's wanting something,

157

a little bit of something – maybe a tiny taste of Henry's *more*. She doesn't move, just keeps dripping tears and watching that street, watching Mavis plod on to the corner, then turn that corner and disappear.

She comes back too, and there is the glow of a cigarette moving to her mouth. Lori is still sitting there, her eyes still dripping, her shoulders heaving and she can't stop them doing it. It's not that she's bawling, not out loud.

Nelly comes to stand beside her and have a bit of a stare. 'She's all right, Smithy.'

'She hasn't got any money. Martin told that hotel not to give her stuff.' The words don't come out right, they sort of heave themselves out in shaky sobs.

'They know her, Smithy. They'll look after her.'

'Henry made us all into beggars, Nelly.'

Nelly wipes tears from Lori's cheek, brushes her hair back from her face, kisses her while she's holding Lori's face between warm hands. 'We're flogging a dead horse here, love, and it's time we all admitted it. This is screwing up the little ones, and it's not doing you any good. You're my best mate, Smithy. The best one I ever had, and we've got to start thinking of what's best for everyone now.'

'It will be better for you and Martin if we get put in homes.'

Nelly doesn't deny that. 'It will force somebody's hand – make them do something about her. And it won't be as bad as it sounds for you kids, either. Homes aren't like they used to be in the old days. You'll have three good meals a day and warm beds to sleep in. You're missing too much school and this is the only time you've got to set yourself up for some sort of future. You're a smart kid, Smithy. You can't just drop out of school the day you turn fifteen, end up wasting your life.'

'It runs in the family, Nelly.'

'You poor little bugger,' Nelly says.

They stand together, Nelly's arm around her as they watch Mavis try to heave herself up to the verandah. She can't do it. Her tents always creep up at the back when she walks and that green one has crept up high tonight. The people at the hotel would have seen what Lori is seeing. They probably laughed at her. She doesn't look real, she's like one of those blow-up advertising toys that shops tie onto their roofs, like she's got a valve in her navel and someone connected a tractor tyre pump to it and inflated her.

That baby inside her must be a monster thing. It was supposed to come out in August. That's what the doctor said, late August, and now it's September, time for the seasons to do their changeover, but the year is sort of jammed like it's got no place to go.

'She can't get in, Nelly.'

'We might have to get someone to help her up, Smithy.'

For half an hour Lori and Nelly stand at the window watching Mavis cling to that verandah post. Then the rain starts falling again and Lori sees Jamesy running across the road. She goes after him.

'He left me without cigarettes, the bastard,' Mavis says, drips from the spouting turning to trickles, falling on her hair, running down her back. 'He made me walk up there and beg for one lousy packet of cigarettes.'

'Nelly said she'd buy your smokes,' Lori says.

'That old bitch can shove her charity.' The trickle of water is a running tap now. Soon it will be a waterfall. 'Bloody interfering old bitch, she knows exactly what she can do with her charity.'

'I don't get it,' Jamesy says, and it's like he's so far away from getting it that he's forgotten you need to give her plenty of space. He's standing on the verandah, right up close, staring at her, his lopsided grin fixed to his face with superglue.

Mavis never did like being stared at and she just hates being laughed at. Lori is backing off and she wants Jamesy to back off too. He's not backing, and it's like that grin doesn't even want to be stuck to his face tonight, though he couldn't move it even if a bus came down Dawson Street, knocked the last of Henry's fence flying, ran right up on the verandah and squashed Jamesy flat as a pancake against the front door; his smile would just get squashed flat too.

Then he says, sort of quiet, 'Who do you think fed us tonight, Mavis? That's taking Nelly's charity, isn't it, seeing as you're the one who gets the pension money for all of us kids? Or do you think you're getting all that pay to be the local freak show?'

Mavis makes a superhuman effort. She gets one foot onto the verandah and Lori grabs Jamesy's arm, drags him by that arm back over the road.

'Where do you think we're going to sleep tonight, you moron?'

'I got her inside, didn't I?' Jamesy grins.

They creep home late, Matty asleep in Lori's arms, and they tiptoe into the bunk room, close the door and slide the chest of drawers hard against it. Little ones in the lower bunks, Jamesy and Lori in the upper, opposite, their two heads close to the window where the wind, leaking between plastic and broken glass, is whistling a cheeky tune.

child henry

The kids are woken early by her banging around. She's wrecking the house, searching again for her chequebook and her telephone charger. She's tossing all of Henry's books and papers and photos around, leaving junk where it falls. She can't find her chequebook but she finds an old withdrawal form and takes it out to the kitchen.

Lori picks up some of the junk, mainly the photographs. Henry's photograph is there. It was taken before he left England. There's also one of his parents, Daniel and Kathleen, and a really nice one of a girl, probably one of Henry's old girlfriends. She puts them back in their box, back safe on top of Henry's wardrobe.

In the kitchen, Jamesy is looking at two typewritten pages he has slipped from a brown envelope and Lori knows what it is.

'You're not allowed to read that,' she says, claiming one page.

Jamesy shrugs, grins. 'He didn't have to be dead. He didn't die of old age, did he?' he says, like, so why shouldn't I look at his stupid secret papers if I want to?

She shrugs, glances at the typewritten words that give up Henry's BIG secret.

Who was he, anyway? Who was he really? He could sing. He could cut hair. He could spell every word in the world, but was he anyone real?

Male child [Henry] of European appearance. Pneumonia, severe ear infection. Possible hearing loss. Approximately one year old. Underweight [eleven pounds]. Deserted by his mother, Lily [fourteen/fifteen], whereabouts unknown.

Child's father. European. [Henry. No surname.] Worked for Mr Howie. Left the area before the child was born.

Mary. Grandmother. Pregnant. [Quarter cast Aborigine. Light complexion.]

Grandfather. Woden. [Afghan /Indian.] Sixty plus. Twelve children counted. Camp squalid.

That's who Henry was. That's all Henry had behind him. A Mary, a Woden – no surname. A Lily, whereabouts unknown, and a boy called Henry who worked for Mr Howie. Poor little boy baby with Matty's pneumonia and Alan's ear infection. Poor little lost Henry no-name.

Lori puts the papers in the stove. Henry had no use for these papers, and as sure as Bert Matthews grows wormy little apples, Martin doesn't want them. And Mavis is not going to have them. Lori lights one corner with a cigarette lighter, watches it flare.

Child [Henry] sort of glows red for a moment then turns to ash. And Henry is gone.

'Goodbye, Daddy,' she whispers, and she rounds up the kids, herds them over the road for breakfast, and this morning she pure hates doing it. Hates eating Nelly's Weet-Bix, eats one fast, then she and Jamesy go to school and leave the little ones watching Nelly's television.

School is useless; the high school teachers might just as well be talking Chinese for all that gets through. Lori is thinking of *Child Henry*, which leads her to thinking of his funeral and the boys carrying him from the church. Vinnie and Donny up front and crying, Martin and Greg down the back, stone faced. That makes her sad, so she forces herself to think about Mavis's coffin. Who will carry it from the church? Not the boys. They'll have to hire a forklift and drive it down the church aisle.

She giggles, sees a forklift trundling down the aisle and giggles more. The teacher tells her to stop or to leave the room. She nearly gets control, until she pictures the forklift crying big drips of black oil, then doing a back-flip and turning its wheels up. It cracks her up, like totally.

Old Crank Tank can get madder than most of the teachers, and she gets so mad, she sends Lori to the vice principal again, who is sick of the sight of Lorraine Smyth-Owen. Lori decides to give her a break and go home early.

It's raining again and before she's left the school grounds she looks like a drowned rat, her long hair dripping around her face and down her neck. She walks up back streets, forgoing the shelter of shop verandahs so she can dodge the stares in the main street. Everyone stares. Everyone knows her, thinks, she's one of *them*. She considers going to the supermarket where Donny used to work. It's on the next corner and it would be warm in there – but too many people would stare, or feel sorry for her, so she keeps walking, turns down another back street.

Her socks are soaking wet, due to there are holes worn right through the soles of her shoes so they squelch with every step. Her head down, she's looking at those squelching shoes – and she sees it!

She wasn't even looking for money. She nearly stepped right over it. It's like fate turned her shoes down this street. She never comes down this way because no tourist would be seen dead down here, but she snatches that coin not caring who dropped it. No one is staring at her. No one around. Nothing much in this street – except the op shop.

It's Henry! He made her come this way, and that two dollars is a sign from him because it was practically out front of the op shop where he used to do heaps of shopping. She used to come here with him sometimes and find hidden treasures.

No one is in the op shop except the saleslady, so Lori walks in, wanders around a bit, then sort of casually asks if they might have an old parka for two dollars, please.

The saleslady is one of those white permed hair grandmothers. She looks at Lori's sweater that's halfway up her back, and at her wet dress hobbling her knees, then she goes to a bin and she takes out a navy parka with a hood, and she says, 'Do you think this might fit you, love?'

'Is it two dollars?'

'Twenty cents is near enough,' the lady says.

Lori takes off her wet sweater and tries the parka. It's big but it's warm. She stands looking at a smaller parka in the same bin. 'Are all those . . . are all of those items twenty cents?'

The lady nods. 'Take whatever you need, love.'

'What about shoes?'

'Twenty cents.'

Most of the shoes are dressy ladies' shoes. Lori isn't game to take off her own shoes to try any of them but she finds a pair that look as if they'd fit. They've got little heels and buckles instead of laces and they are brown instead of black. They'll do. She finds a pair of sneakers that should fit Jamesy and some tracksuit pants for him, and it's like the old treasure hunt with Henry, and she keeps finding treasures until she's spent the whole two dollars. Two other ladies walk into the shop then, so Lori has to go. She offers the bundle she's been holding in her arms, and the coin, hot from her hand. The grandmother lady smiles, stuffs everything into two plastic bags. She doesn't want to take the coin. 'Have you got a winter uniform, love?'

'No. Yes. But . . . but it's at the dry-cleaner's at the moment,' Lori lies. She pushes the coin across the counter, runs. Pity is hard to take and lying isn't good when someone is being nice to you.

That lady must know all about fake pride, and she must have known who Lori was too, because she comes to the front door of the house about two hours later and she's got a cardboard box of stuff that looks good enough to sell, but she says the shop boss was going to throw it out and she thought that maybe Lori would be able to use some of it. There's a high school winter skirt and sweater, and they look almost new and they are going to fit Lori whether they want to or not. There is a pair of sandals and a heap of old-fashioned underwear, three bras even, and shirts, and socks.

Lori piles the treasure into her drawers then she takes the cardboard box to the kitchen, rips it to bits and gets some chips from the wood heap, gets the fire going just in case Martin comes tonight. Jamesy brings in a few rotten pickets from the front fence and half a fence-post they can just wriggle into the firebox. It's soaking wet and it juts out a bit so they can't close the firebox door, but they feed their fire with junk mail, keep it hissing.

It's funny watching that fire come alive on the wood. It starts small, a tiny little flame that just keeps going, just keeps smouldering blue around that hissing fence-post, until it catches one side, gets a bit of colour, then wood starts to glow and the fence-post stops hissing. You can feel the heat. She picks up a cigarette box, tosses it in and watches it burn. Her face is getting warm. She thinks of the uniform and those brown buckle shoes, she thinks of the two-dollar coin, thinks of giggling at school.

Maybe that giggle started up a chain of . . . of hope. Like she saw the funny side of things, and if you can see the funny side and laugh at it, it doesn't hurt so much. Jamesy has always known that. He probably even knew that the first day of his life when he decided to slip out of Mavis while she was in the old loo and he nearly got drowned.

The fire grows and Martin doesn't come. They watch for him on the verandah. It's Nelly's bingo night and Martin knows it, and it's six o'clock and why doesn't he come?

Because rotten Karen won't let him, that's why.

Lori goes out to the laundry, scoops up rice from the least ripped plastic bag and stands a long time, picking out the black bits, stands for a longer time washing the rice, which makes the black bits rise to the top so she can rinse them away, and when she thinks it's clean enough she puts it on the stove.

'Run over to Nelly and say Martin said to borrow a tin of

condensed milk and some sultanas, Jamesy. Don't say we want to borrow it or she won't go to bingo.'

Mavis smells that food when it's ready and comes from her bed. There are six plates and spoons ready on the table, but she goes for the saucepan.

'Don't you dare!' Lori yells, runs at Mavis, bumps her so she has to grab the wall instead of the saucepan. And Lori has got the rice.

'Run,' she yells.

The kids are well trained since they came home from emergency care. They run while Lori faces Mavis across the table, spoons one dollop of the mixture into one plate, then dodges left, but runs right, right out to the brick room, gets half the kids in and bolts the door. Jamesy goes after Matty, who ran too far; he lifts him in through the window then comes in behind him while Mavis belts on the door.

She won't get in. Lori knows just how strong that green door is. That's not Mavis banging on the door anyway. That's a bogyman who hates everyone's guts.

They've only got the big stirring spoon between five so they sit in a circle on Greg's old mattress and take turns at passing that spoon, dipping it into the saucepan, eating rice and sultanas and sweet, sweet milk. It's a spooky game in the dark while outside the rain pelts down and the bogyman belts on the door. The little kids love it, and the rice fills everyone up, tiptop full. They couldn't stuff in any more if they tried, but Jamesy and Neil are trying hard. Those two are not going to leave one scrape for the bogyman in that saucepan. Not one scrape.

She's on her couch when they come out, and she doesn't say a word, but behind her eyes a serial killer show is playing. There is hot water in the pipes, though; that stove heats the hot water service fast if you give it decent wood to burn. Lori pushes the fence-post in deeper, then she runs a bath and puts the three little ones in with some dish-washing detergent and all of their dirty clothes.

Little kids are funny things. It doesn't take much to make them happy. A tummy full of rice and a warm bath are enough. They are laughing and stomping and flopping down, blowing bubbles and making noises like washing machines, having a really good time, and they come out shiny and pink and the washing even comes out a bit cleaner. Lori hangs it over chairs in front of the stove.

She's keeping well clear of Mavis, keeping the table between them, when she sees the withdrawal form on the table.

It's been made out for two hundred dollars. And it's signed with that MSO squiggle.

grand larceny

They sleep late, stay warm in bed until Mavis starts thumping at their door, yelling about that withdrawal. Then they dress fast, in shoes and socks and parkas too, and they all go out the window, Lori first to take the little ones, Jamesy last so he can lift them over the sill. Lori won't let them go to Nelly. She takes them to Henry's potting shed and instead of flowers, she finds an old hen there, sitting on nine eggs. Silly old hen doesn't know it's not the old days. She's trying to hatch chickens, just as if Henry is still around to feed them.

It's got to be about ten o'clock and the little kids are grizzling. They still expect such things as breakfast at breakfast time.

'Shut up.' Lori is watering Henry's pots because some have green shoots poking up from dry dirt.

'Nelly has got a big new box of Weet-Bix,' Neil says.

'We're not beggars. Shut up and just wait a minute, will you?'

She's not sure what she's waiting for. Maybe a sign from Henry. Maybe those green shoots are his sign. Maybe she's just waiting until she's hungry enough. Her stomach isn't hungry. It's rolling, paining. She's got that withdrawal slip in her parka pocket, but that's not what she wants to do. Can't get the nerve to do what she wants to do. It's not legal.

Legal is part of the old world, Henry's world. In his world, Greg might have pinched Mrs Roddie's car but Vinnie wouldn't have gone off with him. In the old world, Martin might have got engaged to Karen, but Donny wouldn't have gone to Albury and Mick wouldn't have been sent to a hostel. This is a new world so everyone has to make different rules . . . like, even the Prime Minister understands about that.

Her stomach gives in. She has to make a dash for the outside loo, and it's like fate gave her that pain, like when she found the money for a new parka, because just as she flushes the loo, the sun comes out from beneath a cloud and there is this twinkling star of light coming through a nail hole in the roof and shining down on that black wallet.

Henry is watching her, his eye to a peephole in heaven. Maybe burning those Child Henry papers sort of released him from that mound at the cemetery and now he's up there keeping his eye on things again, and this morning he's saying to her, it's all right, you do what you have to do, little lost Lorraine. It's time.

She's crying again, but she's up and standing on the toilet seat, reaching into the rafters to where she hid that wallet that contains Mavis's bank things. She's going to go to the bank for Mavis, but not to get two hundred dollars so Mavis can go down the pub and get someone to get her a new telephone charger. That's not what she's going to do.

The sun stays out and it's even hot, and the mud on the sides of the road sort of starts steaming, trying to dry out fast, like finally the season is turning, finally it's time to move on into the new world.

She walks fast, walks all the kids fast to the main street, tells them to wait on the other side of the road while she runs across. 'If I don't come back, then go to Nelly and get her to ring Martin, okay?'

'Okay.' Jamesy is looking at her hard. He knows Mavis has been searching for weeks for that black wallet full of bank stuff. He's looking at the hand and the wallet, knowing Lori knew where it was all the time. There is not a sign of his twisted grin, he's looking big eyed and worried as Lori crosses the road and walks up to the ATM.

She always liked that thing, the way people push a few buttons and make the money come rolling out, but she's shaking, inside and out, as she reads the instructions about umpteen times. Mavis kept a piece of paper with a number on it, which is probably her secret pin number. Lori is holding it in one shaking hand while the other one is too slow at keying it in. The machine gives up, starts beeping for help, then it spits out her card.

There is a lady waiting, staring, so Lori snatches the card and steps away, watches the lady press buttons fast, watches two fifties come out. Lori steps up to the machine again, her heart beating so loud all of Willama can hear it, and all of Willama knows exactly what she's going to do. The cops will come and stop her before she can do it, or the bank will swallow her card this time like Nelly said it does sometimes.

Her stomach is rolling; she's going to have to run for the public toilets in a minute, so she pops the card in and the machine starts working again, asking for instructions. She takes each step carefully, willing her hand to stop its shaking, doesn't know if she should press the savings or cheque account button so makes a guess.

And the cops don't come and the bank doesn't swallow the card. It works. The machine gives up twenty dollars. It's red and crisp and new and Lori's stomach stops hurting. She looks around. No one waiting, so she does the whole thing all over again, gets another twenty, then she's over the road with the little kids.

'Come on.' She's pale. Her hands are shaking. 'Come on, will you? Hurry up.'

They run behind her, away from the busy part of the street, and they go to Mavis's favourite takeaway where they order a pile of chips and potato cakes and dim-sims. They wait for, like, a million minutes while people stare.

Two cops walk past the door and they sort of look in, look at Lori. Someone has dobbed on her. Her heart is going to jump out of her mouth and land in the fish and chip oil, get fried.

The cops walk on.

Then the lady is wrapping the food, and one twenty-dollar note gets swapped for some change and a huge parcel, and they are out on the street and there is no sign of the cops. Jamesy takes the food and Lori picks Matty up, walks with him on her hip, crosses the road to the little park near the post office where they eat the lot, every chip, every dim-sim. They pig out on delectable hot greasy potato cakes, and Matty wants a drink, so she sends Jamesy to get milk. He comes back with a huge bottle and they drink the lot.

It's early and though the sun is out, a wind is blowing, trying to help the sun dry out the mud. They go to the supermarket, get a trolley for Matty and Timmy to sit in while they look at all the food and socks and stuff, look at the books. Lori picks up a twin pack of dummies for Matty because he's chewed through his old one. She tosses them in the trolley. They look at fruit and vegetables and at chocolate biscuits, then they pay for the dummies and push the three little ones in the trolley to the other supermarket.

Neil wants a lollypop. Lori picks up six, walks to the checkout, but there is a mob of people in front of her with trolleys full of meat and vegetables and food, and one of them is a teacher from the primary school. Lori backs off, gives her space to another lady.

She's got an idea. She puts the lollypops back and Neil howls and kicks the trolley; she lets him howl and kick while she takes five dollars from her pocket and hands it to Jamesy, sends him back to the takeaway for three dollars of chips and the rest in potato cakes. 'We'll meet you at the railway crossing,' she says.

Minced steak is, like, only four dollars for a lump. She tosses a lump in her trolley. Picks up half a cabbage from the bargain bin for 50 cents. Picks up a whole big bag of potatoes for two dollars twenty. She takes one giant carrot, one huge brown onion, two lots of home brand bread, cheap soap and a packet of home brand laundry detergent, all the while keeping the total in her head.

The whole lot only costs a bit over fifteen dollars. The chips and dim-sims and stuff cost twelve dollars and were gone before you could say fish-'n-chips.

Jamesy is waiting for them at the crossing. He's hugging his parcel of chips and pinching chips through a hole. Lori pinches one for herself and one each for the kids, then she takes charge of the parcel. She's not feeling guilty at all. She's feeling new-world powerful. She's got Matty on her back and nearly eight dollars in her pocket, which is not stolen. It's pension money from the government so Mavis can feed her kids, and she's going to feed her kids whether she likes it or not. They share the supermarket bags and walk home, just as school is coming out.

Mavis is asleep on the couch; she looks like stale bread soaked in water. The smell of chips and potato cakes wakes her up, though. She takes the parcel, doesn't say anything, just starts stuffing chips while the little kids watch, their tongues hanging out for one.

Jamesy gets the fire going with pickets, then he runs over to Nelly to tell her that they've got some food. He rips off more pickets on the way back, hacks at them with the axe until they break, and soon that stove is going well. He gets the vegetable knife and starts hacking up carrot. He can remember what this stuff is for. It's for one of Henry's stews and he wants some.

The meat starts spitting and Mavis never did like that smell. She tosses the chip paper onto the floor, sort of rolls, gets her feet under her. The little ones scatter, but she's not interested in them; she's heading out the back door, holding on to what she can hold on to.

'The chips must have gone straight through her,' Jamesy says, watching Neil dive on the white paper, unroll it. There isn't a chip left. His finger wipes at the leftover smear of oil, and he licks. Lori takes the paper, puts it in the stove, then peels seven potatoes.

She's trying to conjure up the picture of how Henry cooked his stew. The little ones are watching her, watching Jamesy hacking cabbage, watching that knife work hard. Then the potato saucepan is over the hotplate and Lori is tripping over little ones as she scoops Jamesy's cabbage into a big saucepan, places it beside the stew.

She cuts up the onion, tosses it in with the meat, tosses in the carrot, stirs, stirs and adds water. She's still stirring when they hear the scream.

'What's got into her now?' Jamesy says.

Lori shrugs, puts the saucepan lid on, thinks maybe it's baby-slipping time. Someone always used to ring the doctor when they started slipping, but the baby was always out before he got here.

The stew is starting to boil. Jamesy is poking in more fence picket when they hear Mavis again. She's bawling. He goes to the green door, opens it slow. Mavis is standing back against the loo and there's something on the floor.

'Lori! Lori!'

She walks out to the brick room, the little ones at her heels, and she stands with Jamesy at the door, staring at the floor and at what is on the floor.

It's like an alien baby. Its head is not right. The little kids start trying to get in but Lori pushes them back.

'Get over to Nelly. Now.' She's shaking worse than she shook at the ATM.

Jamesy herds them over the road and Nelly rings Martin, then the doctor, who rings for reinforcements, and all the time Mavis stands staring at what's on the floor.

The doctor and his helpers get Mavis into bed, hit her with an elephant dart; they take the poor dead baby away as Martin's ute drives in. He's still in his work clothes, like he dropped tools and ran.

The stew has boiled over. The kitchen smells of burned fat. Lori lifts the saucepan, and her hand trembles so hard she needs her other hand to help lift it. She moves the potatoes to the side, watching her hands, feeling her knees shaking in sympathy. Salt, pepper and she stirs the stew with a long spoon. No burned bits stuck to the bottom. She tries to taste what is left on the spoon, but it won't find her mouth. Today has been a shaky, achy sort of day.

Jamesy takes the spoon from her hand. He tastes the stew. 'It's not burned. Probably too much water in it anyway.' He sniffs the steam then gets the Worcestershire sauce. Lori drips some in. Then a bit more. The doctor, who is finished with Mavis, is trying to talk to Lori but she can't talk, she's got to cook Henry's stew. That's all she's thinking about. Won't think of that alien, new-world baby. Won't. She turns her back, looks through the cupboards for Henry's curry. Can't find it. She's doing things, just finishing what she started.

The doctor gives Martin a prescription for more Valium and a heap of other stuff. Lori takes the prescription and puts it on top of the cupboard and she finds Henry's curry up there. What's it doing up there? Who put it up there? It doesn't matter. Got to concentrate on doing, not thinking, let that picture of that baby go away. Got to let it go away.

She adds a teaspoonful of curry to the meat, stirs it. Sees the baby's head in the mince steak and carrot. Sees the rest of that poor baby in the steam.

It was going to be a girl. A poor mixed-up little baby girl. It was trying to be a little sister for her, until Henry killed himself, then it turned into a monster, like life in this house turned into a monster.

The doctor leaves and Martin looks in the brick room, closes the door and walks back to the kitchen.

'It didn't breathe,' he says.

How could it breathe? It didn't have a proper nose to breathe with.

He stirs the stew. 'Have you got any rice, Splinter? It makes the meat go further,' he says. He doesn't care about the little sister. He didn't see that head that looked as if it was trying to be two heads and ended up as –

Martin goes off in his ute and comes back with two big bags of rice, a huge bottle of tomato sauce, ice-cream, cornflakes, two bottles of milk and some floor-washing stuff, then he goes out to the brick room while Lori tosses a handful of rice into the stew. Jamesy chucks in a bit more. Lori shakes in a heap of tomato sauce, Jamesy adds a bit more curry and more salt. Lori stirs the cabbage. Jamesy looks at the potatoes, now boiled to a pulp. They've soaked up all the water and almost mashed themselves.

It's starting to smell familiar, though. The smell is seeping into Lori's brain. That baby is dead and it wasn't a baby anyway. It stopped trying to be a baby when Henry died and the old world ended.

She moves the stew pot over the centre hotplate, gets it boiling again, and she stirs. Stirs. Shadows play out her movements. Arm shadows, head shadows, shaky shadows. Too much rice, she thinks. It's soaking up all the meat juice and looking thicker than Henry's stews. She stirs it, adds a spurt of water from the kettle.

'It smells like Henry's stew. Can you remember what we put in it?' Jamesy says.

She shakes her head.

Martin walks in smelling of disinfectant. He sniffs, lifts the lid on the stew, tests to see if the rice is soft.

No Mavis in this room. No television with its canned laughter. No more babies.

Nelly turns up with the little kids, but Lori isn't talking. She pats Lori's shoulder then leaves, and the little kids sit quiet around the table, wanting to go to sleep but wanting some of Henry's stew more.

'Get some plates out,' Lori says.

Martin eats with them. He doesn't talk about the baby. He says that he knows he's deserted Lori and the kids, that he should have been here for them. He eats while he talks and he talks as bad as Henry talked at Christmas time. The little ones eat every rag of cabbage, wipe up the stew juice with bread. They eat ice-cream, eat until they start falling asleep, ice-cream melting on their plates.

Martin helps wash small faces and hands, carry little ones to bed. He talks to Lori while she gets a load of washing in the machine. 'I wish I hadn't taken her on that day. If I could go back and undo that day, I would, Splint, but I can't go back, so I have to find a way to go forward.'

Lori is working on automatic and so is the washing machine. Press a few buttons and it does the lot. She's sorting the underwear and the light clothes from the dark clothes, like Henry did – not touching the socks, though, just kicking them over to wait until last. Not thinking about socks. She's thinking of the bank stuff, and thinking should she tell Martin about it.

But he said it, didn't he? He said you can't go back, so you have to go forward – and she's not going to go forward into a home for unwanted kids. She's not.

She's still seeing the baby's head too. Can't kill that picture. Can't kill the image of its perfect little legs and girl parts; it was perfect from the chest down.

Jamesy saw it, but he hasn't said a word. He saw Lori get the money from the ATM and he hasn't said a word about that either. It's like he was born knowing about life, and that's why he never dobbed when she used to wag school in the good old Henry days.

'I've tried, Splint. I've done all I can with her and I can't do it any more.' Martin is still doing a Henry, talking, talking, wanting words to make it all right, and she wishes he'd shut up with his words and let her just . . . just . . . do the washing.

She sighs, pours some washing detergent in, and it doesn't look enough so she adds a bit more. 'I know you tried, Martin. I know Nelly tried,' she says, just to shut him up and make him go home to rotten Karen. That's what she wants. Then she can keep the bank stuff, keep getting the money out and keep making stews. And she'll feed Mavis too, even if she is a monster man-eater, and she'll get Nelly to buy her tons of cigarettes and . . . and . . . and if Mavis gets cigarettes and food, and everyone gets food and shoes and stuff, then no one will have any excuse to split the kids up. And . . . and if they ever let Mick come home, then he'll have a place to come home to.

Martin won't go. He's washing the dishes, washing the pile of saucepans. She stands beside him, dries them.

'You're an incredible kid, Splint. Do you know that? That was an incredible meal.'

'I-n-c-r-e-d-i-b-l-e,' she spells the word out loud. 'That baby was incredible. It was probably trying to be twin girls until Henry died, then it gave up trying to be normal – like we all did. Everybody. Not just Mavis. We just gave up. At least you have to try, don't you, and you have to do it the best way that you can, don't you?'

He doesn't say yes, just helps put away the saucepans and the dishes.

Then he is going home to Karen. He even calls it home. 'I've got to go home, Splint,' he says. 'Will you be all right with her tonight?'

She'll be all right. She got born tough, got born into tough. She locks the bunk-room door with the chest of drawers and crawls into the lower bunk with Matty, holds him close, feels his perfect little head, kisses his perfect little head, now covered with reddish fluff; it helps take the image of that other head away. She holds him close, closer. She's never thought much about loving him, didn't know that she loved him. He howled so much when he was little and she'd wanted him to be a sister, but he's sort of grown himself into being loved, lovable. And he's not ugly – not now that he's got some hair.

Sleep wants her. Her mind starts to wander away into a half dream in which Henry is singing 'Danny Boy'. She listens to him, thinks of his stew, thinks of what she put in the stew. Salt and pepper, Worcestershire sauce, curry, and some tomato sauce. Meat and rice and onion and carrot. She can remember, and she'll do it again too. Tomorrow.

> *But should you come, when all the flowers are dying*
> *And I am dead, as dead I well may be.*
> *You'll come and find, the place where I am lying,*
> *And kneel and say an Ave there for me.*
> *And I shall hear, though soft you tread upon me,*
> *And all my grave shall warmer sweeter be.*
> *For you will kneel and tell me that you love me,*
> *And I will sleep in peace until you come to me.*

And so she sleeps and dreams of Alan and the cubbyhouse. They're making fractions with apples.

falling down

Mick came home six weeks before Christmas, which wasn't much of a Christmas, just sad, just like you wanted it to be over so a new year could get started. He's still the same Mick, a bit taller, his freckles not so dark and his new brace lighter, but miracles don't happen in real life; his leg still looks like rubber and he'll grow out of this brace like he grew out of the last.

Having him home has been truly excellent, though. The first thing he did was to fix Lori's bike, then he fixed up Vinnie's for Jamesy. Next, he fixed up Henry's woodman by paying the bill off a bit at a time. That wood is expensive and it needs cutting, so he fixed that too by getting Nelly to ring up the sawmill to deliver a huge truck-load of mill-ends, which are cheap, because they are just bark and leftover bits of wood off the sides of logs, all cut up into foot lengths. They're a bit green, make a lot of ash, but you don't have to chop them and if you mix them with a little bit of the woodman's dry stuff, they burn.

It's working. Most of the time it's working well, but Mavis is dying anyhow. The doctor said so to Mick. He took some of her blood when she had a fall in late January, and he got it tested, and he told Mick that Mavis's system is being poisoned and that her heart isn't pumping well enough to get rid of the fluid. She's gone all puffy, sort of swollen from her feet to her eyes. He gave her a heap of new prescriptions, like she's supposed to take about ten pills a day – not that it matters much; she prefers lollies. The doctor said not to buy her lollies, but the kids still buy them. She yells and throws stuff if they don't, so what else can they do? He also told them not to buy cigarettes. That's a joke. She's still smoking like a chimney. Nelly or Martin used to get them for her until Nelly found out that supermarkets are allowed to home deliver cartons for housebound people, so she wrote a note and Mavis signed it. Lori keeps it in a plastic cover with that old withdrawal slip for two hundred dollars, like they are her licences to buy food and get money out of the ATM. No one has tried to stop her getting the money out yet, due probably to no one usually sees her. She and Mick get it at night now.

It's mid February, and hot again. Lori turned thirteen yesterday. She looks older, or that's what Mick said when he came home. He said she looked heaps older. She sure feels heaps older. She's standing at the sink, peeling potatoes and tossing them into a baking pan when Nelly's hat wanders past the west window. A few seconds later it pops in through the back door, has a look around to see if it's safe to come in, then she steps in and her mouth starts going ten to the dozen.

'I just got a call from young Alan, Smithy. He's coming home.'

'Alan?'

'Yeah. He said he got the morning train to Albury, but there's no bus until tonight, and he wants to know if Donny is still working in Albury. I didn't know which supermarket he was at. Anyway, he said he might call back and if he didn't, then he'd be on tonight's bus, and to tell you to meet him and bring Matty's pram because he's got two cases and they're heavy.'

'What's he think he's coming home to?'

'He didn't say no more, Smithy.' She looks at the potatoes, watches Lori pour oil into the baking pan. 'Christ, you got enough there to feed an army.'

'They're cheap. She loves roast potatoes.'

Nelly nods. Maybe she sees the sense in it. 'Do you want me to ring up Martin for you?'

179

'I suppose so.' Lori hasn't seen Donny since he went to Albury but Martin sees him. Maybe she doesn't blame Donny for staying away. Maybe she does. Martin still comes on Fridays, but he never comes inside. Maybe she doesn't blame him. Maybe she does. She shrugs, places the potatoes in the oven.

But Mavis is up. There is thumping and blowing as she comes slow, sidles slow and sideways through the curtain door. It's after four o'clock and she's just out of bed. She's panting, hanging onto walls, swaying herself along the walls.

'Get out of my house,' she says. She's unwashed, uncombed, wearing one of her petticoat tents, which used to be cream but she's been wearing it for weeks; it's the only thing that nearly fits her, like it's stretchy material, stretched to fit and showing everything, pulling up at the back too; she's a terrible awesome sight and each shuffle she makes on those swollen feet is a painful effort. She's always barefoot now. Lori bought her a huge pair of slip-on slippers but she can't see where she's putting her feet so she never wears them.

They leave her alone and stay out of her way. She's gone nutty as a fruitcake. Even Nelly keeps her mouth shut these days. She gives Mavis a bit of a stare then heads for the back door, which is no longer hanging on its hinges. Mavis finished it off the night she fell over; she tried to grab it and it came down on top of her. The doctor had to ring the ambulance men, who rang for more assistance. They couldn't get her up with the strap beneath her arms like they did the last time, so they got her onto the door, then all of them lifted it until her feet hit the floor.

Mick hasn't bothered to fix that door. It's easier for Mavis to get out to the loo with it off and the doctor might need to use it again anyway. Some of the louvre windows are broken now and a few of the cupboard doors, but what's the use of fixing them? Mavis would just unfix them again. Her hands aren't pretty any more, they're puffy, and so weak. She can't get lids off jars, can't use a tin opener, so she throws stuff if someone isn't around to do things for her. About the only thing she can do is make her custards, which she still cooks in the night, and pancakes. She makes an awesome mess of the kitchen, burns saucepans, leaves junk all over the place.

'You're too skinny for my liking, Smithy. You're feeding the masses, but not feeding yourself properly,' Nelly says. 'Do you eat anything?'

'I eat heaps.' Maybe it's true. She is thin and it's probably like Nelly says, she's taken on too much responsibility too soon and it's showing on her face, like it's pretty bony and her eyes look as if they've sunk in deeper. They were always dark but now they've got smudgy half moons beneath them so they look even darker.

Those eyes are watching Mavis work her way towards the couch, watching her stop to light a cigarette, watching – but she doesn't want to watch any more. Alan is coming home, and God, she's missed seeing him. She walks to the door. 'Mick.' He's down at the bottom garden, checking his silverbeet for snails. 'Mick, Alan's coming home.'

'What for?' Mick replies.

'I don't know.' The kettle boils over and Lori runs to it, lifts it to the side, then makes Mavis a mug of tea, places bread in the toaster, while Nelly stands by, her head through that doorway.

Mavis has made it to her couch. The couch groans, burrows deeper through the wall.

Poor old house, it's falling down around them, like it knows it only has to stand up until Mavis dies, which will happen soon. It's not even a sad thought because Lori won't let herself think of that day. Won't let herself think any further than today. There is no future any more, there is just the now.

She makes six slices of toast, spreads butter and jam on them, then sets them on a folding table-tray at Mavis's knee, and not one word spoken. It's like she's offering sacrifices to some primitive god figure so it doesn't bring destruction down on this family.

Without the Mavis figurehead there would be no pension, no bankcard and no ATM, so without her presence there will be no family. While she lives the house will stand and the kids will stay together. Lori is hoping to continue making these daily sacrifices for two more years when Mick will be going on seventeen and she'll be fifteen, then no one will be able to split up this family. Just two more years. That's all she wants and each day that passes is one day less.

Poor old house, it must have been nice when it was built, like a hundred years ago. It's got good touches, wooden panelling, which has come back into fashion, picture rails, open fireplaces in two rooms. Someone cared about this house once, spent money building it, making it nice. Now it's only fit for the bulldozers, while Nelly's house, which is nearly as old, has smaller rooms and no panelling, still looks like a good home, because it's had ongoing care. Life is about making the things that belong to you better, not worse.

'I'll go now, Smithy, and give Martin a call for you,' Nelly says and her hat disappears.

She pops over most days, just to see how the kids are getting on. She has taught Lori heaps about cooking and sewing up stuff that gets ripped. And since Mick came home, Nelly and Martin have totally stopped plotting about the kids going into homes.

This year there are only two little ones left at home during the day, due to troublemaker Neil has started school and he's giving his teachers hell with his face-pulling. Timmy is a good little kid, he doesn't say much and he'll be four in June, but he's smart enough to work the video player. Lori and Mick leave him in charge of Matty on school mornings. They give them breakfast, cut their lunches, then turn on the television. They've got half a dozen kids' videos from Henry's days, so the little ones watch them over and over until Mavis gets out of bed, then they go to Nelly, watch her television or go shopping with her. She's so good. They'd never cope here without her, but they can pay her now with eggs and vegetables, like Henry did, so they are not bludging any more.

Mick has got Henry's garden growing. He's got tomatoes and some pumpkins that planted themselves, and he planted onion seeds and the silverbeet, carrots, but no broad beans. Everyone still hates broad beans. He bought a book on gardening, picked it up for fifty cents at the Willama West Trash and Treasure market and he loves reading it, loves standing out there watering his vegetables while Jamesy pulls out a few weeds. Mick's bad leg makes it hard for him to get down low enough to pull many weeds.

Henry could squat there for hours. Just squat and pull, toss what he pulled over his shoulder. Henry used to –

Mick got most of the chooks penned up too, and those chickens the old speckled hen hatched in the potting shed are already half grown. Two other hens are now in the potting shed sitting on eggs, so there should be more chickens soon. They'll have too many chooks but heaps of eggs.

Henry used to only let the chooks hatch chickens when – Lori sighs, thinks Alan, thinks he's going to be in for a shock, thinks maybe she'll make Nelly's bread pudding for dinner.

For the next two hours Mavis sits staring at the television, smoking up the kitchen, missing her ashtray most of the time and dropping ash and butts on the floor. She used to wash her hair, shower herself a bit with the hose spray, flood the bathroom but she got herself clean. She doesn't worry about showers any more because that was the first time she fell over and they had to get the men in to get her up. It took them almost an hour. The doctor said he could get the district nurse in to shower her, but as sure as hell is hot, that nurse would order her another chequebook and another phone, which would make the house fall down sooner.

Time, that's what Lori is trying to buy. Just two years of time.

Mavis needs new tents too, which Nelly would make, but Lori is too scared to spend money on material. Mavis costs too much already. And there are so many bills, there is wood and electricity and school stuff. And the council rates, they cost thousands, due to owning two blocks. It's scary to think about the new rates coming when they still owe most of the rates from last year. Since Mick finished paying the woodman's bill, he's been taking a hundred dollars a fortnight to the council to take off the bill, and it's getting smaller, but the next one will come soon and swallow up this little bit of safety they've made for themselves.

Dinner is on the table by six-thirty. Mavis gets hers on her tray. Mick sits with his back to the tray because Mavis's petticoat tent has worked its way up and she's flashing two tons of spread thigh. She eats fast; they eat faster, leave the dishes then go outside to wait for Alan.

It's almost eight when Martin's ute drives up. All the kids are waiting out on the street. They're just dying to see Alan, but when two of him step out of the ute, Lori's head starts seething and buzzing like Henry's electric drill is inside her brain, trying to drill its way through to some sort of sense. It's not getting there. What the hell is *he* doing up here?

'Ah, home sweet home,' Eddy says in his posh pom voice, his eyes laughing at their house, and probably at them. Everyone stares at him, stands back from him, so he walks to them, offers his hand as if he's a grown-up.

Mick takes the hand. Lori doesn't.

'I'm your long-lost brother,' he says.

'I've got enough already, thanks,' she says.

'Yeah, well, up you too, Sticksville. Now you've got another one.'

They are eyeing each other like a pair of young roosters, their hackles up. This is starting out wrong.

Alan takes Lori's arm, draws her away, walks her to the front verandah while she keeps looking over her shoulder at the other one who is following behind, sort of smiling, or sneering. She hopes he falls through a broken floorboard.

'What did you think you were going to find?' she says. 'What does he think – ?'

Martin comes behind them with a case, drops it off in the bunk room and goes back for the other one, then he leans against the passage doorway, sort of peering around the brown curtain, looking for Mavis. She's in the loo, so he steps into the kitchen. 'You crazy pair of little buggers. Eva will have a search party out after you.'

'Eddy gave her a call from Albury. He told her Mavis arrived in a furniture van with a kidnap team and they got us at the tram stop,' Alan explains. 'He's not staying.'

'I'm planning my escape tomorrow or the next day,' Eddy says, and he sounds like Henry with two plums in his mouth.

'What about your cases?' Martin says. 'Did Mavis pack them for you?'

'We packed them weeks back, left them in a luggage locker at the station,' Eddy says. Then there's no time for him to say more. Mavis comes out of the brick room, heaving those giant thighs forward. She stops at the doorway, holds on to the frame, doesn't comment – probably she's used to seeing double – until she sights Martin.

'Get out.' Wasted energy. She'd be better off saving it to heave her foot up that twenty-centimetre step, gain a foothold on the kitchen floor. It's all too much effort. Breathing is too much effort, but one shapeless foot is up, and the floor timbers shake as she bears down, gets her other foot inside the room. It's awful. It's terrible to watch, but they're all watching. She hauls her feet to the couch, flops down, flashes flesh while the couch digs deeper into the plaster.

Eddy, slack jawed and bug eyed, freezes, like, what the hell is that that just walked in? 'Shit!' he says, but it's a long drawn-out, shiiiiiiiit. He's standing close to the couch and he's, like, mesmerised. 'Shiiiiiiiit.'

Jamesy walks by him, pushes him towards the table and out of harm's way while Lori tosses an old sheet over Mavis's lap as if she's a piece of embarrassing furniture. She's staring at Eddy, wondering what his game is. Alan, okay, she can understand him coming home for a visit, but Eddy – he's excess baggage she can do without, as she can do without him and Martin stirring Mavis up.

'Sheeeiiiiiit.' Eddy's still saying it.

They don't know it, but he's been fantasising his welcome home for a month. He's been planning this meeting with his blood mother, had it all worked out, what she might say to him, what he might say to her. She's not saying it and neither is he. He's just standing there staring at the worn-out sheet with its faded yellow roses and finding that same word but expressing it a bit different each time it comes out, like higher, lower, longer.

'Shee-iiiiiit.'

He phoned Eva so she wouldn't have a meltdown, told her he was calling on Mavis's mobile while she was buying petrol. Eva started talking police, so he yelled, 'Don't do anything until I call you. She's talking court case and taking us back permanently, Mum, and she's got one of the Willama policemen with her, leading the SWAT team. He's driving the furniture van.' It's not as if Eddy is planning to stay; give him two days without his computer and his homework and he's in withdrawal, but those two days might just be long enough to gain him some bargaining power.

He and Alan want to go on a school camping trip to Tasmania and Eva won't let them. They want to board at the school too. Old Alice has been pushing for boarding school for months now, ever since Alan came home, and maybe if Eva thinks Mavis kidnapped them, she might change her tune about letting them board; she might even change her mind about a camping trip being too dangerous.

'Sheee – '

'Shut up, you redheaded little bastard,' the flesh factory says, and Eddy jumps back, shuts up, looks around the table, around the room. Lori is making cocoa, like this is just a normal day, like, will you join us for a drink?

'Grab me some biscuits,' she says to Jamesy, who goes out back, returning a minute later with two packets of biscuits which he tosses onto the table.

'How many are left?'

'Only three more in the trunk – unless you put some somewhere else.'

It's like a science fiction novel. It's like lock up the biscuits, here comes the cookie monster. Lori keeps staring at Eddy and every time he catches her eye, that eye says fuck off. He's starting to wonder when the next bus leaves for home. He can remember Mavis from the last visit, but her face had looked okay that day. Fat, but okay. Her dress was big but pretty. Eddy turns his stare again on his birth mother, trying to relate the misty image he'd taken with him to England to the gruesome image on the couch.

It can't be done.

Martin is silent, standing beside the table, shaking his head. He picked the twins up at the bus depot and thought he was seeing double – the silly little buggers. It's just a lark to Eddy, but Alan reckons he hates Melbourne and he's never going back, and it looks like he's found some heels to dig in too. 'I'm never going back,' he kept saying. 'I'm never going near that place again. I'll hang myself like Henry if you try to make me go back to them.' He's still saying it too, though omitting the hanging bit in front of the little ones.

Martin glances at Mavis. No one can cart that tonnage around and expect to live. He's thinking, when she's gone, Alan might be more than pleased to go back to Eva. What's the alternative? They're only kids. If Donny would come home, then between them they might be able to keep this place together, but Donny isn't coming back.

The house is a shambles. Lori has done a good job of feeding the hordes, but the house – there's junk from arsehole to breakfast time and it smells bad. Matty is still a baby, Timmy's not much more.

Karen says she never wants to have kids. Maybe that's why he fell in love with her, and there is no way that she's going to consider having any of these kids living with them when they get married.

She's the greatest thing that ever happened to him. No one has heard of Mavis Smyth-Owen in Bungala, and since he moved there, he's been calling himself Martin Smyth; now he's changing his name by deed poll because he doesn't want to saddle Karen with the Smyth-Owen name. He's not proud of that name, not proud of his roots, and he sure as hell hasn't told her the BIG family secret. That's one of the reasons he's never brought her home – her old man would throw a fit if he ever found out about Henry's touch of the tar brush.

'Christ,' he sighs and he sits down. Eddy has claimed the chair that used to be Mavis's. He looks like being a handful and Lori doesn't need the trouble. 'How long do you reckon on staying?' Martin asks.

'When's the next bus out?' Eddy replies, reaching across the table, helping himself to two biscuits. He doesn't know about Lori's food rationing. She snatches the packet, deals out the remaining biscuits like dealing cards.

Mavis has got her own packet on her tray, chocolate coated mint slices, and Eddy's favourites. He grabs two before she scoffs the lot.

'Give them back,' Lori warns as Mavis tries to get a foot under her. And the sheet falls from her lap.

Eddy starts laughing while the rest of the kids scatter. He's laughing, choking on biscuit crumbs, his eyes running. Like, what the hell is going on here?

Then Mavis screams. It's crippled animal screaming, wild bear caught in a trap screaming. She's screaming at Martin, at Eddy, blaming the world because it's the world that built her that trap.

'Oh, fucking great shit. This is unreal,' Eddy says. He's stopped laughing, though, and home is looking very good. Old Alice is even looking good. He walks slow to the brown curtain, crunching on biscuit, walks through, finds his way out, the animal scream following him.

Most of the kids are grouped under the streetlight, except for Alan; he's heading for the river. That's what he's missed, that's what he wants and that's what he's going to have, and tonight. It's not the Thames he's never seen but was expected to lie about seeing, it's not even the muddy old Yarra, it's his and Lori's river.

Eddy looks at the crowd beneath the streetlight. They don't want anything to do with him, and if they don't want him then he sure as hell doesn't need them, but he's stuck here for the moment, so he takes off, runs after Alan, catches him up.

Jamesy leaves the group beneath the light and he follows the twins, Neil follows him, so Lori chases Neil. Mick starts walking, which is better than listening to Mavis. She's bawling now, and it's worse than her screaming. Martin waits a while, watches a while. He's got Matty on his shoulders, Timmy at his knee.

'Where the hell do you think you're all going?' he yells to the herd, strung out like Brown's cows along a moonlit path.

'Swimming,' Jamesy yells back. He's caught up to Alan and Eddy, and Alan reckons he's going for a swim.

Martin crosses over the road and Matty wriggles down; as soon as his feet hit the dirt, he's off, after Lori. 'Get back here,' Martin yells. 'All of you. It's too late.'

'Too late for what?'

'Oh, shit.' Martin follows them down the track and they all go swimming, in the moonlight, in the clothes they are wearing. Alan duck-dives deep, testing his brand-new underwater watch. Then Eddy tries to outdo Alan and he gets carried downstream because he's only used to swimming pools and the beach, doesn't know about currents. He panics, yells, tries to turn around and swim back. Alan and Martin go in after him, and Martin is a speedboat cutting though the water. He saves him, pulls him ashore two hundred metres downstream.

Those waiting at the bend hear Martin's laughter. Maybe he's only laughing with relief, but it's so good to hear that sound again. It's ages since they've heard that sound.

They sit on the bank later, watching the moon float across an ocean of stars and they slap mosquitoes while Alan tells everyone the story of the night he almost drowned Lori. It wasn't funny that night but it is a bit funny now. Also, it makes Eddy feel less like the smartarsed fool he is. He could have drowned.

Their laughter starts small but it grows until they are choking with it. It's forever since they laughed together; even the sound of it sounds funny, so they laugh at each other's laughter and every time they gain control, someone starts it up again by saying something crazy, something that's not even funny. It just seems funny. It's mad, and it's fun and they haven't felt this good since Henry died.

Then Eddy starts with his posh 'shiiiiit' again. He's looking in his wallet, which was in his pocket, which had his return ticket in it. It's wet. And the wallet is full of money!

'Where did he get that?'

'Eva gives it to him. He just tells her he needs a new CD or something and she gives him a fifty – then gives me one so it's fair.'

'Have you got that much too?' Lori says.

'No, he's got all of it. Just as well it's only Eva's money, or it would have been mush too,' Alan says. It isn't funny, all money is plastic, but it is funny too – or the dry way Alan says it makes it funny, like it's got extra plastic on it because it's Eva's. Anyway, funny or not, they all start laughing again, all take a note or two and wave them in the air to shake the water off.

Eddy is laughing with them now and Lori looks at him, thinks she might get to . . . to almost half tolerate him. He's the one who brought the laughter home.

'I feel like a hamburger,' Eddy says, his notes reclaimed, his return ticket tossed.

'You look like one too,' Jamesy says.

That joke was old when Elvis Presley was a boy, but they're rolling in the sand with laughter, holding their stomachs and trying to slap mosquitoes. The noise is wild. Tourists camping over the river probably think there is some drug orgy going on.

'Where do you buy a hamburger in Sticksville? Have they heard of hamburgers yet in Sticksville?'

Jamesy wants a hamburger. He's never had a proper one from the takeaway, only McDonald's. 'They make better hamburgers here than they do in the city, Twitpill.'

'Prove it, Sticksville.'

'Put your money where your big mouth is, Twitpill.'

They can't go home, don't want to go home where their laughter will die stone dead, so they walk back up the track to the road, and they follow it south, their clothes drying in the night's oven-heat. They go over the railway line and straight up the road to the take-away where Eddy shouts hamburgers, with onions, egg and lettuce, and real meat. He pays with a clean-washed fifty dollar note.

The little ones are falling asleep on their feet. Lori lifts Matty onto her back. He goes to sleep, his head on her shoulder, his hamburger in her hair. Martin puts Timmy on his shoulders, Alan holds Neil's hand and they walk the deserted main street, drunk on food and laughter.

It's half past twelve when they get home. Mavis is snoring on the couch and Alan's new watch is truly water- and shockproof.

12:30 it blinks.

brother stranger

Alan has come back to them in duplicate and his other half has turned into a walking, talking madman with no return ticket. He's like Spud Murphy's dogs, chained up all their lives, but God help the neighbourhood when they get off the chain.

Eddy is off the leash now and there has to be some place for all the years of chained-up energy to go. He's at it day and night. He's their brother-stranger, but that coiled-up life-force elastic is shooting out of him and it's roping them in, one by one, and the weird thing about it is they don't know why – except that he's a posh-talking, big-mouthed maniac with no conscience, and all the kids seem to do these days is laugh.

Like he rings Eva from the post office and tells her that Mavis said she'd buy their ticket home next Friday. 'Good news to report, Mum. She's decided not to keep us after all, so just relax and let Alice enjoy the break.' He says that last bit for Alice's benefit, because he can hear her teeth gnashing on the other end of the line. He's talking posh to Eva while showing his own teeth, his lips sort of snarling like a mangy greyhound. Lori gets the giggles again, has to cover her mouth and run.

They go to the main supermarket after the phone call and Eddy buys four packets of choc-mint biscuits which he presents to Mavis instead of putting them in the tin trunk.

'Sorry we got off on the wrong foot last night,' he says. 'Call it jet lag, Mave.'

She calls it a few other things, calls him a few other things too, but accepts his biscuits. He finds the bald broom and starts sweeping the floor, sweeps around Mavis like he's not even scared of her. He gets on his knees, sweeps under her couch, shooting out butts and lolly papers which have been there since Henry died. He empties her ashtray into the stove, feeds the flames with lolly papers, feeds them with a stiff dead sock too, and a pair of holey underdaks and anything else he finds on the kitchen floor.

That stove is like a new toy to him. He's never seen a wood stove before, never seen a kettle, never seen an axe before, never chopped wood before and he hasn't got a clue how to do it either, but he's a good cleaner. He even cleans the bathroom, pretending he is Eva's cleaning lady, who can hardly speak a word of English.

'You have a . . . a da whoosh, whoosh, whoosh . . . for bath? Yes?' His accent is perfect, his miming of a scrubbing brush a scream. Lori finds Henry's scrubbing brush in the laundry and Eddy uses it on the bath, because he's not having a shower in that bath just to come out of it with legionnaire's disease. That's what he says, with an accent. 'Is germ. Yes. Is everywhere germ. Is nottink but germ in diss pigpen. I getting a vera bed disease from all diss germ. Yes. What you thinkink, ah?'

It's not like the same room when he's finished with his scrubbing brush; everyone had forgotten that the bath and basin were white.

The next day it's not only odd stiff socks that disappear, it's most of the socks and the little kids' sneakers too. They get tossed into the green bin and Eddy comes home from the shops with an assortment of cheap sandals. While he was cleaning the bathroom he found Henry's bottle of Condy's crystals in the shaving cabinet. He mixes the stuff up in a bucket of water and makes all the little kids stand in it for five minutes. They think it's a game, and they come out of that bucket with brown feet and orange toenails. They don't care.

They've got new sandals. Those little kids would damn near sell their souls for something that smells new.

Alan knows what Eddy is doing, and why he's doing it, because Alice did the same delousing routine to his own stinking feet when he first went back to St Kilda. 'She tossed everything I took back. Even my books went in the bin. The orange wears off after a while,' he says. 'It's some sort of chemical that kills foot bacteria, or something.'

Lori's eyes widen. She stares at Eddy and his purple water, then she claims it, and claims the Condy's crystals. For the next week all of the kids, Mick included, have to soak their feet in the purple brew, and each night every shoe in the house gets a spray inside with white vinegar, due to Alan said that's what Alice did to his new shoes.

The stink of dead socks leaves the house like magic. It's gone. Totally. Gone from the bedrooms, even. Lori spends a lot of time sniffing, testing the air. Not a whiff, so no more Vicks VapoRub stuffed up her nose. She'll probably get a cold now.

Eddy is a pure smartarse with a germ fetish, that's true, but it's so interesting watching him, and sort of seeing life new through his eyes. Every night he wants to go walking. He's never walked anywhere, never seen a bush track and walked it by moonlight, he's never stood under a streetlight before and watched the moths commit suicide, never done anything before.

He doesn't go home on Friday. He rings Eva and tells her that Mavis meant the next Friday, then on the Saturday, he shouts the kids a day of playing tourists. They are wasting money but it's only Eva's, so it's not real, not like the pension money; still, it's real enough to get them into seeing stuff they never saw before. Eddy turns them all into fake tourists with his fake money and suddenly they can see a bit of what the tourists see.

Everything is new to him. Even a snake on the river track is new; he's never seen one outside a zoo. For hours he watches that sluggish snake shedding its skin, then he takes the skin, holding it as if he's found a true treasure, and his eyes, which might be the same shape and colour as Alan's eyes, don't look anything like Alan's eyes. They sort of look awestruck.

'You'll get a snake disease,' Lori says.

'Just wait until the kids at school see this,' he says. 'Nobody has ever had anything like this. This is better than camping in Tasmania.'

Even the stars in the Willama sky are newfound treasures he's just dug up from Egypt. He buys mosquito repellent and he soaks everyone with it, and all the kids sprawl on the front lawn, just looking at stars, tracking satellites and planes and not getting eaten alive by mosquitoes. The next day he finds Henry's hand mower in the potting shed and decides to cut the lawn so they can roll on it without rolling in prickles. It hasn't been cut since Henry died but Eddy gets it looking nearly like a lawn instead of a cow paddock. He's got energy to burn. He's one of those electronic toys on the television battery commercial that never go flat.

Then on his last night in Willama he's wearing his snakeskin as a headband; they are all sitting on the verandah watching the stars when he tells them that he could get to love the life they've got; he makes it sound as if their freedom is something so special. They've never thought much about their freedom. They didn't even know they had it.

'Who's free when they've always got a kid stuck around their neck?' Lori says. Matty is stuck to her knee, not her neck at the moment, but he's always stuck to her some place when she's at home.

'You gotta serve time in the pen to know what getting out feels like, babe,' Eddy says. He sounds like Marlon Brando, doing his part in *The Godfather*. They laugh again, look at him, love him a bit – just a bit. Don't want him to go home tomorrow but he's spent all of Eva's money so he's going, and without Alan, who refuses to even consider the possibility.

They walk Eddy to the bus depot and even Lori shakes his hand. He's wearing his city clothes and his snakeskin headband, and maybe old Alice is going to have a fight on her hands if she tries to toss it in the bin. They watch him walk up the steps, then the door closes and they stand a long time, waving him goodbye, waving the bus goodbye, then they walk home, sort of sad, sort of missing him already.

It's lucky he went, really, due to the next night it happens. It's around twelve o'clock and the kids are in bed when Lori hears moaning. The television is never turned off and for a while she thinks the moaning is coming from the television, but it goes on and on and on, sort of getting higher.

It's Mavis. She's flat on her back on the floor again, gasping, dripping sweat and blue-white in the face.

'Someone get Nelly,' Lori yells, and Jamesy is out, running in his underdaks over the road to bang on Nelly's bedroom window until he wakes her. She calls the doctor and after a bit the men come again, six of them, including the doctor. They use the door again, get Mavis up; lucky that Mick didn't put that door back on its hinges.

Mavis doesn't say a word, doesn't say thanks. Maybe she hasn't got air enough to say it, but the doctor is saying she's probably had a heart attack. 'We'll have to see if we can get you to the hospital for tests,' he's saying.

She's standing between two of the men and she's panting air and shaking, all of her is shaking, and it's like a localised earthquake, shaking the men who try to walk her to the passage door, and God knows how they think they're going to get her up to the hospital. And God knows what's going to happen to this place if they do take her.

Mavis can't get her balloon feet moving. She's standing there, looking as if she's dying, then she gasps, 'Get out,' and she heaves an arm free, takes a step back. They can't hold her, can't force her to go forward. They look at her, give up on her as they watch her step back again, then flop down onto her couch.

Lori sees the doctor out. He talks about pills, like, 'Is your mother taking her pills?' Lori shakes her head. The doctor looks at Mick, standing on one leg behind Lori, looks at the others. 'Call me in the morning if she's no better,' he says.

She's no better, but no worse. She's slumped on the couch, covered by the quilt someone tossed over her when the doctor left. Lori puts two fluid tablets, two Valium and an Aropax with a cup of tea and a big glass of water on Mavis's tray. Mavis drinks the tea, ignores the pills, which she bumps to the floor later. Alan picks them up so the little ones won't eat them.

'Watch her. If she can't get up to go to the loo, get Nelly to call the doctor,' Lori says. She's got to go to school because Mick isn't going to miss school just because Mavis is dying.

'I want to go to school too,' Alan says.

'It's no use you getting enrolled. You'll have to go back to Eddy. It's stupid staying in this place. She's going to fall down one night, we won't hear her and she'll die, then what do you think is going to happen to all of us? We're not old enough to stay here by ourselves, and Martin sure as hell won't be coming home. Go over to Nelly today, ring Eva, and go home, Alan.'

'That place isn't home. This is home, I said.'

There is a hopeless feeling in the house now, the kids have tried so hard to hold it together but it's all coming to an end, and they are watching the end come for them, come slow, just waiting for Mavis to fall down again. Every time they hear a noise, they run in, expecting the end. Every time she gets up to go to the loo, they don't think she's going to make it to her feet. Alan doesn't want to be stuck in that house, watching the end come. Every day he nags about going to school.

'You're not going to school. You're going back to Eddy.'

'I'm not. Can't you get that into your thick head? I'll go to whatever place they send you and Mick and Jamesy.'

'You belong in Melbourne, with Eva.'

'Yeah, like a lost dog with a disease belongs there. That's what I was to them when I went back, Lori. They shampooed my hair with special stuff to kill fleas, then they made me take deworming syrup. I couldn't take my shoes off or they'd get this long-suffering look on their faces, and if they weren't around, Eddy would start singing,

"Put your shoes on, Sticksville, cause your stinking feet aren't pretty". Then Alice got that stuff and every day for a week they made me soak my feet in it.'

'You can't blame them for that, Alan!'

'Can't I just? Well, I do.' He looks at his bare feet, then up to her eyes. 'Do you think that Eddy and I are the same person now you've met him?'

'Don't be stupid! Of course you're not. Except in looks – until you get close up.'

'Eva and Alice don't even want to tell us apart. It's always boys, do this; boys, do that. They make us get our hair cut the same, and they buy two of everything so we can dress the same, and if we're going some place and we put on different shirts, one of us gets sent back to change.'

'You're nearly twelve years old. Just refuse to change your shirt.'

'I did, but Eddy always says, go with the flow, Sticksville. He changes his shirt.'

'Well – it's still got to be better than this. Like living in that house, getting new clothes and money thrown at you all day.'

'And getting treated like Eva's matching pair of toys that she keeps in a box and only takes out when she wants to show them off. It seemed all right before, I suppose.' He sighs, looks out the window, sucks in a big breath. 'It's different now. It's like one half of her pair got carried around England in its velvet-lined box for a year and the other half got . . . got picked up by a wild mob of kids who nearly wore it out playing with it all day long and sort of . . . sort of loving it.'

Lori loves him all right. She gets a lump in her throat with loving him, though she's not going to say it, not exactly. 'Only just sort of,' she says, and gives him a punch, turns away fast to hide her eyes. She doesn't want Alan to go back, anyway, never did. Doesn't say one more word about it either.

Two letters come from Mr Watts, Eva's solicitor. Mavis isn't interested in letters so Mick opens them. It's just more threats about court cases and stuff about separation being detrimental to the twins' wellbeing. And who cares what they think?

Then on the Friday, two weeks after he left, Eddy phones, and waits on the phone like he's a millionaire, which he is, until Nelly comes over to get Alan. The twins talk for ages. Eddy rings again on Saturday, then twice on Sunday night.

'I don't care whether we're allowed to go to Tasmania or not, so stop making Nelly run backwards and forwards getting me over here. I am not going back to that *effing* place, and you can tell them that too,' Alan yells and he hangs up the phone.

So it gets to the next Tuesday. Everyone is in bed except Mavis, who hasn't slept in her bedroom since the night she fell, like she's too scared to leave that couch. Somehow she gets herself out to the toilet, but not often, though she's usually got the brains to go out there before the kids go to bed. They watch her, wait for her to heave herself back.

It's got to be after twelve when Lori is dragged from her sleep by the blinding light of a torch directed into her eyes.

'Is she down?' She swings her feet to the floor, still half asleep, doesn't know where the torch came from, but as her eyes evade the light, she thinks she sees Alan behind it.

'She's in the brick bathroom.' Then the torch is off and the lounge-room light switched on and Alan doesn't sound like Alan and he isn't even dressed for bed and he's wearing Eddy's snakeskin headband. 'I've got a plan, Lori,' he says. And maybe she's dreaming this, maybe she's sleepwalking, because that's not Alan standing there.

'Are you both as bloody mad as rabbits?' she says. 'What the hell are you doing back here?'

'I'm not here. I'm on that school camp in Tasmania,' he says, leading the way to the brick room where Mavis is sitting on the loo and sort of slumped against the corner wall, which is the only thing that's stopping her from falling.

'Mick! Mick! She's dead!'

'Stop your yelling. She's not dead.'

Mick comes hopping out, Alan behind him. They stare at Eddy, like, what the hell is going on here? Eddy just leans against the doorframe waiting until they wake up enough for him to explain what he's doing back here.

'Alan told me on the phone that she's dying. Right? You all know that, but you keep stuffing food into her. Right? Now stop and think of what you're doing to her – and to me. You're actually murdering my natural mother, and when she's dead they'll pack all of you off to homes or hostels. Am I right?' They don't argue, just stare at him and scratch heads, yawn and scratch ribs. 'What I'm proposing to do is to put her on a diet. She gets to live, you mob get to stay free and I get to come for a visit from time to time.'

'You moron. As if we haven't tried that. As if Henry didn't try that.'

'Alice and Eva will be up here tomorrow to get both of us now,' Alan says.

'No they won't. I'm on that camp for ten days.'

'How come she changed her mind?'

'I told you that having Mave kidnap us would work, didn't I? Anyway, that's where I am tonight, so we've got ten days before they start chasing me and ten days to try something different.' Lori is staring at him, shaking her head. 'She can't walk as far as the bedroom, Alan told me. She can hardly walk out to the toilet. Right? So what if we lock her in here and she learns to eat what we give – '

'You're even crazier than you look, you moron. The camp people will have told Eva that you're missing. She'll already have a search party out looking for you.'

'No she won't. It's all under control. The school has still got her note saying that we're not allowed to go. I went into fretting for Alan mode again and Alice actually suggested I go to Tasmania. They wrote another letter and gave me a cheque to pay for it – and two hundred dollars for emergencies, so stop worrying about me and them, and listen for a minute. I was looking at that brick room when I was up here before. It's rock solid, it's got a toilet and a wash-basin – '

'You can't lock people up.' Lori is at the door, staring at Mavis, who definitely isn't dead because her head has fallen back and she's started snoring. 'She wouldn't just go to sleep sitting there like that. There's something wrong with her.'

'No there's not, or nothing that is beyond my control.'

'Stop talking like a smartarsed snob. What did you do to her?'

'I've been here since nine . . . I came on the bus . . . I mashed a packet of Mum's Xanax tablets on the way up . . ., then put them in the custard powder . . . as soon as you lot went to bed.' Eddy is looking around, stepping from foot to foot. 'I stirred it well.' He's trying to look confident but he's sounding a lot more confident than he's looking.

And how the hell did he think of doing that? Lori thought of doing that same thing with Valium ages ago. What the hell made him think of doing that?

'What's Xanax?' Jamesy has joined them.

'Tranquillisers. They're similar to Mavis's Valium . . . or so it says on the Internet. She looks tranquil.'

'How much custard powder was left?' Lori yells, loud enough to wake the house. Mavis doesn't move, doesn't interrupt her snore.

'Plenty. She only uses one tablespoon. I watched how she made it when I was here the last time.'

'One heaped tablespoon,' Jamesy says.

'How many tablets?' Alan asks. He's picked up the custard powder packet and he's peering into it.

'A new packet. Fifty.'

Then Jamesy has got the packet. 'There's a ton of custard powder left. She probably only got five tablets worth and the last Valium packet says two tablets three times a day and two at night if she needs them.' He's eyeing the empty couch and liking what he's seeing.

'And who says she only made one lot of custard?' Lori yells.

Mick is back. He's put his brace on. Neil wanders out, pulls a face at Eddy – only because he's pleased to see him.

'It's just another game to you. You go back in ten days and we have to live with her when you're gone,' Lori says.

'I might decide to stay for a while. They can't make me go back.'

Lori is staring at him. Mick is checking the level of two milk bottles in the fridge and he's concerned. 'She's got to have made two lots of custard, Lori. He's overdosed her.'

'I didn't make the custard, Mick. I didn't make her eat it – '

'Yeah, well, someone better go over and get Nelly to ring the doctor, that's all I'm saying. There's too much milk missing for just one lot of custard.'

Lori is leaning against the open door, staring at Mavis, or at her exposed thigh, which is bigger around than most men's stomachs. She's not dead, but she just as easily could have been dead. Lori wouldn't have heard her if she'd fallen in the loo. She probably would have died, due to she can't breathe properly when she's lying flat out.

And how come Eddy thought of the custard powder idea? How come? How did such a crazy idea get planted in two separate brains? It was her original crazy idea – that or mixing the crushed pills in a tin of condensed milk.

'You can't even think about doing it, Lori,' Mick says.

'Just let me think. Just everyone shut up and let me think for a minute.'

They all shut up for a minute, then a minute more as they stand and lean, watching the sleeper. She looks unusually peaceful.

'She's killing herself. What's the difference between her killing herself with food and Henry hanging himself?' Jamesy says.

Lori looks at him. It's true. There is no real difference. If the kids had seen Henry cutting the clothesline wire, they would have stopped him. She picks up the old quilt and walks into the brick room, places it over Mavis, tucks it between her shoulders and the bricks. Mavis doesn't move and Lori returns to the door. It's a strong old door, made of thick, long boards with other boards going across it like a double Z, and it's got huge old-fashioned hinges. She has seen them tested, has been behind that door when those hinges were tested.

'We put her couch in there, give her the television – ' Eddy starts, but Lori pushes by him, walks into the kitchen. The boys follow her, Eddy behind them, his snakeskin now being drawn backwards and forwards between his fingers.

'Okay. I know we're still thinking about it, but think for a minute on this. The doctor gives her Valium for her nerves and antidepressants for her brain and that other stuff for something. She won't take her medicine so we lock her in the brick room and give her the pills in her food. The doctor told Alice to do that with Eva's pills when she was going out of her brain that first time Mavis got Alan. It cured her enough in one week to get her on a plane to England, so the ten days I'm on the camp should be enough to see if we can cu . . . improve Mave.'

'And if it doesn't, you go home and we're worse off than we were,' Lori says.

'As I see it, if she's no better, then you're no worse off, and if she is better, then I might stay for a while – but I'm not staying if she's sitting in this kitchen, stuffing her face, smelling like a sweat factory and ruining my lungs with smoke.'

'It's just another joke to him, Lori. She's something to laugh about – '

'Dying of lung cancer is no joke. Think of the little kids,' Jamesy says.

'Shut up, you. You're as mad as he is,' Lori says, and suddenly realises what she has said, realises it's true. Jamesy is a bit like Eddy. Not in looks, but in other ways.

He's talking again, or still. He's a big talker. 'We move a bed in for her. Put her couch in there, and the television. We feed her three normal meals a day. What's wrong with that? All she does is smoke, eat, watch television, and go to the toilet. If she's got it all in one room she won't have to walk up and down that step and end up falling

203

over. And if we put enough furniture in there, there won't be room enough for her to fall over.'

'How do we fit her bed and couch in?' Lori is still thinking of the custard powder, and thinking the only difference between her and Eddy is, he had the nerve to do what he was thinking; she was too chicken to try it.

So now it is done and it's scary – like some accident, where people are just driving along a road looking at the view, then suddenly, without any warning, they're all dead. She's standing in the kitchen and her stomach is jumping and she's thinking of how things went from Henry's good to something so bad that it couldn't get worse. For weeks she planned to mix the Valium in condensed milk and pour six packets of pills down Mavis's throat while she was asleep – murder her. That's what she was planning to do back then. All Eddy is planning to do is to get her out of the kitchen, make her take her pills, put her to sleep at night instead of letting her eat. And maybe save her life.

Lori only stopped planning murder when she got control of the bankcard and things got a bit better. She began to think life was almost okay when there was money for food and shoes and stuff. But it isn't okay. It's surviving, not living, it's keeping things going from one pension day to the next and waiting for Mavis to commit suicide with food. It's waiting until the house falls down.

And it's going to fall, this week, this month or this year.

Then they'll all be split up and they won't be a family any more. Having families split up isn't okay. Having Alan – and even Eddy – back in the family is. And that's the truth, though she wouldn't ever tell Eddy.

Maybe he's right. The doctor wants Mavis to take those tablets. Maybe they should give them to her the best way they can. Would it really matter if they had to lock her up to do it? Who's to know, anyway? No one sees her, except the kids – and Nelly.

They'd have to tell Nelly. She'd be okay with it. She's not like a grown-up.

Jamesy has decided to go with it. He's trying to drag the couch out of the wall. Mick is measuring how many heaped tablespoons of custard powder are left in the packet and he can only make six and the last one isn't really a heaped tablespoon, either.

'She's probably made two or three lots, Lori.'

'If she'd taken five in the first lot of custard, then she wouldn't have been able to make the second lot, Mick, so she's probably made a big serve, that's all, and even if she made two lots, it would take a heap more than ten Valium to do much harm. There's a lot of her.'

They walk out again, stand beside the green door and stare at Mavis. She doesn't look blue like she did that night she fell. Lori looks at the door, at the bolt on the door, knowing that for some reason she is the one who has to say yes – or no.

She has to say no. Of course she does. Now. She has to say it now. She can't just stand here looking at that door all night.

If she says no, Eddy will go back to St Kilda in the morning.

She turns to him. She's missed the laughing since he left. Ten days of laughter, ten days of his mad cleaning lady routines. Ten days without Mavis in the kitchen. They could look on it as a sort of holiday. None of the kids has ever had a holiday.

She shrugs, closes the green door and her hand reaches for the slide bolt Martin fixed high. It probably won't slide. It hasn't been slid for over a year. It's probably gone rusty and jammed.

But it slides eagerly into its keeper. So easy.

Like it was meant to be.

brick walls

In the kitchen Jamesy has been waiting for that signal. He drags the old couch free. Eddy is up on a chair pulling down dusty packets of pills. There are eight packets of Valium, some ancient, the packets faded, but the pills are still sealed up tight inside the bubble packs. There are two packets of Aropax, which are antidepressants, two lots of fluid pills, a container of Slow K, just potassium, and three other types of pills, which Lori knows nothing about and Eddy hasn't got his Internet to find out what they're for. Behind those pills and beneath them, like a dusty mess of scrap paper, are the prescriptions, some curled, some faded, some nibbled by silverfish and probably out of date, but some brand new. There is one for Aropax. It's got a heap of repeats and there's a whole mess of Valium scripts – not that they'll need any more of those.

'At eight Valium a day and one Aropax, we've got enough pills here to keep her going for about sixty days,' Eddy says.

'So we give her a two-month sentence for child abuse,' Jamesy says.

'She's on remand for ten days,' Judge Eddy says.

Alan is standing back shaking his head. Mick is shaking his head too but he's picked up a packet of Valium and the instructions say one tablet three times a day. Neil is trying to help Jamesy push the couch across the vinyl and the metal legs aren't doing the vinyl any good.

'That packet is out of date, Mick,' Lori says. 'The new packets all say two tablets three times a day and two at night, when necessary.'

Eddy reclaims the packet, dusts it with an old towel. Out of date or not, he's going to use it. Alan moves to stand in front of the couch – to stop its progress. 'Leave it where it is. This is stupid. We're not doing it.'

'We are.' Lori lifts one end, just to save the vinyl, then she and Jamesy are lifting it, dragging, pushing the old couch through the door, where it jams. Eddy climbs over, helps tug it free. And the green door is open and after one hell of a struggle Mavis's couch goes through.

The logical place to set it is against the north wall, the weatherboard wall, but that couch's metal frame starts marking out a new hole through to Mick's room before they even get the thing positioned. Have to look for a brick wall. The loo is in the southeast corner, and they can't sit the couch beside the loo. The hand basin and window are halfway along the south wall; there would be enough room in the southwest corner – except Mavis would be sitting too close to the door, which is dead centre in the west wall.

They've got no choice; it has to be that long north wall, the brick section which Martin joined up to the weatherboards then took out to the edge of the east verandah. It's still close to the loo, but it's a long way from the door.

The room is full of junk. Greg's old mattress is dragged out and tossed onto the backyard junk heap. They haul out the collapsed chest of drawers, which Eddy names kindling. It goes on the wood heap. He loves cutting kindling. Mick finds the long extension cord Henry always kept with his electric drill. They plug it into the kitchen power point, out one door and beneath the other before carrying in the television, which won't work without its cable. They pull it out of its socket then Jamesy goes up through the manhole with Eddy's torch, drags the cable up and across, finds a gap in the brick-room ceiling, and pokes the cable through. It's not neat, but the television picture is clear. Mavis's queen-sized bed is too big to drag through the house so Lori says she'll do a swap. Her bed has got a timber bookshelf bedhead which might do less damage to that weatherboard wall, which it will have to go against. They've got no choice; Lori wants to use that bed as a barricade between the couch and the door.

Then they are done with the furnishings, it's way past two o'clock and Mavis hasn't moved. Maybe she'll never move again.

'She probably needs her stomach pumped,' Mick says.

'She needs it bypassed,' Jamesy says, while Eddy and Lori make up the bed with clean sheets, and Mavis's five big pillows so she can sleep propped up. She's got the old quilt, but they toss in an extra blanket, a clean towel, a face washer, a comb.

Lori picks up the half packet of cigarettes from the floor, the lighter beside them. There's a lot of ash and butts around the loo. She sweeps up, places the lighter in the box and the box on the couch.

'No can do,' Eddy says. 'She'll set fire to her mattress like the crims do in jail.'

'She'll die of withdrawal,' Mick says, but Eddy has got those smokes. He removes the lighter then tosses the cigarettes into the stove. Sacrilege. Those things cost money.

They eat toast, drink cocoa, speak in whispers. It's like, what have they done? You can't go around doing things like that – even if it is for the person's own good. It's illegal. They know that. They've been watching the news on television since they were in the pram.

But they've done it.

'I'm going to bed. I'll take my globe out of my light so we can leave the one on in the brick room. She's not going to know where she is when she wakes up,' Mick says.

'*If* she wakes up,' Alan says.

Lori is awake before eight, and for a moment what happened last night didn't actually happen. She almost says, do you know what I dreamed we did last night? Except Eddy is in the kitchen and he's cleaning it up and it looks big and bare. It sounds bare too, like voices sound loud in it. No couch. No television. No Mavis. She's locked in the brick room, all right, flaked on a bed not wide enough for her. But she's snoring steady and her face isn't blue.

Most of the kids are standing around, feeling jumpy, feeling scared to talk above a whisper. Everything looks different, even the hole in the plaster wall, which they all knew was behind the couch; it's much worse than they thought it was because while Mick is fitting on his brace, Neil pokes a knife through the weakened plaster on the other side of the hole so he can watch how Mick fits that contraption.

An empty cornflakes packet and a big cross of Mick's masking tape almost plugs that couch hole, then they sit, get on with eating the cornflakes. It's so quiet you can hear them chewing. It's so quiet you can hear the old battery clock ticking on the mantelpiece. They didn't know it ticked.

'I'm going to school. I'll walk,' Mick whispers.

'If you're not staying, I'm not staying here. I'll dink you,' Alan whispers back.

'You can't just turn up at the high school. You have to get enrolled or something.'

'I'll enrol myself, Mick.'

'Do it next week,' Lori says. 'You and Eddy stay here and watch her today. And don't let the little ones go anywhere near Nelly – not until I tell her.' And by tonight there mightn't be anything to tell anyway. Mick has got the bread out and the plastic bags, he starts cutting lunches so they form an assembly line, spread, fill, cut and shove sandwiches silently into plastic bags. Alan spreads extra, makes three-layer Vegemite sandwiches.

'You can't just turn up at school, Alan,' Mick whispers.

'Well, I'm not going to be here when she wakes up, either. What if she doesn't wake up?'

Mick rubs his neck, looks out at the brick room as a shudder works its way down his spine. 'We'll see what happens today. Just see. We've got to go, Lori. We're late.'

Alan takes off for the river with his sandwiches, plus Matty and

Timmy and the old pram; Neil and Jamesy head off in the other direction.

That leaves Eddy. He's cool.

He sweeps the kitchen, washes down the benches then makes a small medicinal custard. It's a bit lumpy but it tastes okay. He makes pancakes too, learned how the last time he was up here, and he makes great pancakes. The clock ticks its way past eleven before he hears movement, hears the loo flush. Only then does he spread his pancakes with apricot jam, an Aropax crushed and mixed with it; he rolls each one, sets them in a row on a big plate, scrapes the custard into a bowl, makes a mug of tea, and while Mavis is trying to get out the door, he carries her breakfast tray to the window. 'Good morning,' he says. 'Can you open your window, please, Mave. I've got your breakfast.'

She stares at him, at the plate, says nothing.

'Your pancakes are getting cold.' His words don't appear to be making it through the glass, so he waits until she gives up on the door, squeezes between the foot of her bed and the washbasin and starts belting and yelling at the window instead of opening it. Fast then, Eddy is around the side, slipping the bolt. Plenty of time to run in with the tray and place it on her bed. She's not a fast mover and it's a tight squeeze getting back to that door, which he closes, bolts. Then *he* bolts, spends the day in town, eats McDonald's for lunch, spends an hour in the supermarket buying low-fat ice-cream, two tins of sugar-free pineapple, a bottle of diet chocolate topping, a new broom and a bundle of six cheap tea towels because the ones in that house are germ factories.

Alan's day is productive too. He's been sitting with a fisherman and taking every European carp he pulls in, tossing them flapping into the pram. Matty won't share it with gasping fish, so Alan ends up filling the pram with firewood and sitting Matty on top. The twins are waiting at the gate with their loot when the others arrive home; they don't want to brave the house alone, due to Mavis is awake and she's letting the whole neighbourhood know she's awake.

Eddy and Lori offer her a bowl of ice-cream, pineapple and chocolate topping. She doesn't open the window but her coffee mug cracks the glass. They stand back, wait for her to settle down. She doesn't. The mug smashes through. They run, open the door while she's bellowing through broken glass and they place their offering on her bed.

They get the stove going, get Alan's fish cleaned up and wrapped in supermarket bags and they are trying to peer through that broken window when the empty ice-cream bowl is tossed through, both glass and china flying free. She's more active than she's been in months, panting for her smokes, leaning against the door, hitting at it.

'We've got to get plastic containers and some decent plastic mugs,' Lori says, peering though the break while the air inside turns a brighter shade of blue and Mavis's colour is starting to match it.

'We can't do this, Lori,' Mick says. 'She's giving herself a heart attack.'

'We're not giving up before we start, Mick. Who said it was going to be easy?' Lori comments, and she returns to the kitchen, starts making a small medicated custard, making it smooth, pouring it lovingly over two beaten eggs. She adds vanilla while Mavis gasps out just how she's going to murder the lot of them.

They can't get the custard in. She's onto their trick of getting her to the window before they open that door, so she's not leaving the door, and every minute or so she's heaving her shoulder against it. She hasn't got a lot of power but she's got a lot of weight and the three screws holding the slide bolt are rocking in their holes. It's Jamesy who ransacks Mick's screw collection and comes back with six long ones, the screwdriver and Henry's electric drill.

'We can't do this!' Mick is growing louder with his protest; maybe he has to be louder; there's a lot of noise to compete with. He takes the drill, though, when he sees Jamesy isn't going to give up until he wrecks it, and he takes the fatter, longer screws, puts them in the slide bolt and in its keeper, squeezing a bit of wood glue into the screw holes, using all of the screw holes instead of the half Martin

211

used. He has plenty of worried eyes assisting him. Others glance occasionally through the broken window while Eddy wriggles a bit of the glass free.

'Pour the custard into a container with a lid, and we'll drop it through to the basin,' he says. So that's what they do while Mavis and Mick are working on opposite sides of the door.

They wait. It takes forever, but she finds the custard, eats it. Half an hour later the custard works and Mavis is sitting panting on her couch, watching the television.

'We have the technology,' Eddy says.

'We can rebuild her,' Jamesy grins. They are sweating, and the day isn't even that hot.

'Shut up, you morons. We're going to have to medicate her three or four times a day, like it says on the packets.'

Nine o'clock and the little ones, worn out with fishing and no television, have been in bed for hours; the big ones are still wandering, wondering, peering in that window as they walk by, but not letting her see them. She's quieter when she doesn't see them.

It's Alan who finds a length of chipboard, probably left over from the kitchen floor when it got extended. Like Mick, he's been against this plan from the beginning, but it looks as if he might be coming around. 'If we could get the broken glass out, we could reach through and screw this onto the windowsill to put her meals on.'

It's a pure brilliant idea; they can't keep putting food on her bed or dropping it into the washbasin, but they have to wait until Mavis is sleeping to do it. She's still watching television.

They give her more medicated custard at eleven and a packet of sugar-free mints.

'What time did she wake up this morning?' Mick says.

'Eleven.'

Mick nods, goes to bed. They're all worn out with lack of sleep, and stress and guilt. They sleep like logs, and if Mavis yells for her smokes, they don't hear her.

Eddy's Xanax custard is served four times a day and apricot

jam on toast or pancakes disguises the taste of the Aropax Mavis has with her breakfast, which doesn't seem to be altering her brain waves any, not by Friday, the day Martin comes, and thank God they hear his ute. The kids run out to the fence, talk to him out there. He's got a pile of fruit and vegetables from Karen's farm and he wants to carry the boxes in.

'It might be better if you don't stir her up,' Eddy says.

'How come you're back here?'

'Just visiting for the weekend. It's our birthday.'

He says the same to Nelly when she wanders over the next day – about the stirring up and the visiting, except he says he's visiting for a week. The other kids are still pretty much in shock. They are not looking at Nelly, just hoping Mavis won't start yelling.

Half of Eddy's ten-day camp in Tasmania has been used up, like his Xanax custard powder – more than half of that has been used up. Eight will only go into fifty six times. Eddy is sitting at the table crushing Valium tablets and pouring the powder into a jam jar where eight heaped tablespoons of custard powder await their additive, when Mick suggests that those pills could lose their potency lying around mixed up with other stuff, which could be the reason Mavis is refusing to act tranquil.

Eddy stops crushing. 'So we crush as needed, as with the Aropax?'

'*We* crush? *You're* going home next week.'

'I've been thinking about that. I've been thinking that Mave and her SWAT team have been back to St Kilda in that old furniture van and they got me again. She really wants to keep me this time,' Eddy says as he caps what he's crushed, places the jam jar with the tablets on top of the cupboard.

'Did she get you before you went on the camp or after?' Lori says.

'Before. Otherwise Mum will sue the school for losing me. She likes suing people.' He's looking around the room and not much liking what he's seeing, but his eyes are taking in everything, absorbing it, accepting or rejecting it. He shrugs, draws his eyes back to the faces watching him. He raises his eyebrows, shrugs again. 'You know, don't you, that Mum can't legally take either of us back, not if our natural mother wants us?'

'She doesn't want any of us – except to murder us. You heard her.'

'Whatever.' He's looking at the walls, at the ceiling, one hand rubbing his mouth. 'I heard Watts telling Mum and Alice one day that they wouldn't have a leg to stand on if they took Mave to court. Judges always give children to their natural mothers. He also said, as the other siblings were with the natural mother, and she owns her own house, the courts wouldn't take Eva's claim seriously. Also, he said that Eva and Alice's relationship would probably go against them – if the hearing came up before some homophobic judge.'

'Does he know about them?'

'Of course he does. He knows everything, and even if he didn't know before, he knew when he made the new will after we came home from England and Mave still had Alan. Mum was going through one of her dying periods so she made a new will leaving everything to her partner of twenty years.'

'Old Alice, her *partner*?'

'They are sort of married, you know. And old Alice wouldn't care if the whole world knew she was a lesbian. I think she'd like it. It's Mum who tries to cover it up, and if she's dead, she's not going to care much, is she? Watts said that by using that terminology it makes the will legal, otherwise Mave, being Mum's next of kin, could probably try to break Eva's will like she tried to break Grandmother's.'

'How come she couldn't . . . couldn't break it?'

Eddy shrugs.

'Do you know anything about Mavis's father?' Lori asks. 'Was he going to leave all of his money to Mavis or something?'

'I don't know that either. All I know is he died about seven years before our grandmother. Mum never mentions her father. I've never even seen a photo of him. Don't know what he looked like.'

'The image of Vinnie. We've got a photo. So, Mavis being the baby of the family could have been his pet and he could have planned to leave her the lot and we would have been rich.' Lori walks off to find the photograph.

'She would have eaten it all,' Jamesy says.

Alan's not interested in Grandfather or his money, only freedom. 'So . . . so, what you were saying is, Eva can't make us go back.'

'Not if Mavis wants to keep us.' Eddy looks at the photograph Lori has tossed onto the table. Not much to see, only a big hand-painted face, too blue eyes, a grey suit and a lot of wavy red hair. He shrugs. 'Watts told Mum, when she was trying to get you back that time, that the only hope she had was to prove Mave an unfit mother.' Lori and Jamesy laugh. Those two saw the worst of Mavis. Mick doesn't laugh, he takes the photograph, thinks of Vinnie, wonders where he is.

'So, you can live here with us if you want to?' Lori says.

'Go feral.' Eddy starts playing the monkey, like, scratching at his armpits.

They make the phone call that night from Nelly's – which is a mistake. Lori tries to keep her talking so Eddy can speak in private but Nelly is too smart. She knows something odd is going on over the road. Lori hasn't told her about the lock-down, due to that lock-down isn't going to last. Mavis is going totally out of her brain.

Eddy is talking fast as Nelly starts dusting the doorframes beside that phone. He doesn't say much, just about the furniture van and the off-duty policeman who was leading the team who specialise in kidnapping kids. He's holding that phone pressed close against his ear so Eva's words are trapped.

'I've got the gear I packed for the camp and Alan's clothes fit me. I'm okay. Yes. She's knitting me a school jumper at the moment. Yes.'

Alice starts her barking; she must be on a second phone. Lori can hear her two metres away. Eddy is not into inventing fiction for her. 'Got to go. Tell Mum I'll call her later.' He hangs up.

'What's going on?' Nelly asks. 'What furniture van? What off-duty policeman?' Eddy shrugs. He's agitated, wants to leave. 'Who is knitting you a school jumper? And what's your aunty doing, letting you two miss so much school?'

'We're gifted. We don't need much school,' Eddy says and he's out the door, Nelly behind him.

'I want to know what's happening over there, Smithy. Half the town can hear her yelling.'

'She's . . . she's trying to give up smoking,' Lori says. 'Since last Tuesday. If she's still having withdrawals by ten days then . . . then she said she'd stop trying. Thanks for the phone, Nelly.'

Nelly doesn't believe her, so Lori runs.

They talk about school that night. 'You two missing so much school is sort of child neglect,' Lori says. 'It would probably be an excuse for Eva to prove Mavis is an unfit mother.'

'I'm staying here and I'm going to school on Monday,' Alan says.

'So, you get enrolled and we'll take it turn-about to go. That way we won't be missing school and we tell Nelly that I've gone home.'

'Like one in, one out at all times,' Alan says.

'At all times.'

It sort of sounds silly, but as sensible as anything is sounding these days. They are all scared of what they've done, scared the police will drive up one night, scared of the space in the kitchen, scared of no television, of no Mavis sitting on that couch. It's like they don't recognise this room when it's not full of smoke and lolly papers and Mavis. Eddy might have thought they had freedom before, but this much freedom is threatening, due to it's not freedom. It's like they are all locked in now.

On Monday Alan goes to school and Mavis gets four letters, from Eva, Mr Watts, a bill, and some bank wanting to give her another credit card. The kids don't give her the mail, just keep on with the two Valium four times a day. They don't try to clean her room, though they supply her with clean towels, clean tent and sheets. She leaves them sitting on the chipboard window shelf, which was Alan's idea, and which sure made life easier. They can creep up, drop off what they're carrying and disappear fast. It's better that way. Seeing them just riles Mavis up, then they end up making her custard.

The high school teachers could probably use a bit of medicated custard too, because on Eddy's days at school, he's giving those teachers ulcers. He's a maniac without a conscience; the computer teacher is getting to think Alan Smyth-Owen is a genius with a bad memory, or a schizoid. Most of the teachers are a bit suspicious, especially Lori's, due to she has totally stopped wagging it and stopped smartarsing everyone. She's sitting quiet in her classes these days, keeping her head down, and actually handing in incredible homework.

'Your presentation has undergone a vast improvement', one of her teachers says. 'Keep up the good work, Lorraine'. Not old Crank Tank, though. 'This is not your work. Write it again'. That's what she wrote across the middle of a perfectly good assignment – too perfectly good. Eddy did it. He does all her homework. He'd do Mick's too, if he'd let him; it's something to do on the days he has to stay locked in with the little kids, which makes him stir-crazy, but he's plain straight out crazy anyway and worth his weight in gold. Lori is getting to the stage where she'd almost pay him to stay. She might have to soon; he spends money like it's water and he's running out of the stuff, talking about going home to get some more – that or trying to pay the cheque for the school camp into Mavis's account. He's already changed the name on it and it doesn't look too bad.

But no way. That's exactly the sort of thing that would bring the police knocking at the door. 'No way, Eddy. You burn that thing or you'll blow everything.'

He doesn't burn it, but he puts it back in his wallet.

Since Mavis stopped smoking they don't need to get the shopping home delivered, because they sure as hell don't want anyone coming near the house. They sort of shop now when necessary, or Lori and Eddy shop. He's spending mad – even if he can only do it at the supermarket. He's a pain, actually, like he piles expensive stuff into the trolley which Lori has to keep putting back. And he prefers real butter – only because it costs more.

She didn't put enough things back on the Friday and she's five dollars short. It's so embarrassing.

'Mum told you to use the card,' Eddy says.

'Shut up,' she hisses. People are staring. Lori hates people staring. She's handing back two packets of biscuits and some lamb chops, which she didn't put in the trolley, when Eddy takes her purse and hands the card to the check-out lady, who swipes it through the machine like she doesn't care whose card it is, just wants the pin number, and fast. Lori prods it in.

'Want any cash out?' the lady says.

'No thanks.' And it's done and paid for and they are out loading the bags onto bike handles. 'You total bloody moron! Why do you think I always get the money out at night?'

'So you look like a thief?' Eddy says.

'Because I am. Mavis didn't give me the card. I took it.'

'To buy food with. Of course she gave it to you. She's house-bound. Someone has to do the shopping for her.'

They have lamb chops for dinner, roasted in the oven with potatoes. Mavis gets one and one quarter of a roast potato, but she gets a large bottle of Diet Coke, which was on special. She always used to tell Henry that Coke got rid of her fluid and they haven't been giving Mavis any fluid tablets due to Eddy didn't know what they were for. He does now; he's been on the Internet at the library. He drops two small pills into the Coke bottle, waits for them to melt, then tastes it. It's okay, so they leave it on the window shelf when they leave Mavis's dinner.

As they're walking away they see Bert Matthews's head peering over his side fence. How long he has been standing there, Lori doesn't know. He's probably seen them putting stuff on that window ledge, the brick room window is in full view of Bert's house and he sees everything – but he's a bit deaf.

'We'll have to be more careful,' Lori says. She's looking at the bank statement and there is a pile of money left over from last week and that's mainly because they are not buying cartons of cigarettes. 'You can pay extra off the rates this week, Mick.'

Mick is nodding, sort of smiling for the first time in like days and days. He's a pure Henry, he is; he just loves paying bills.

The brick room loo gets flushed about ten times in two hours and though the television is still blaring, Mavis is quiet, so quiet that the little kids are standing close to the green door, listening to the show. They miss their television.

'Maybe in a month or two, when we get the rates paid, I'll start saving Mavis's ex cigarette money in a special jar and we might be able to save enough for another television,' Lori tells them. 'But I'll only put the money in the jar if you are very good, and you don't tell anyone, not Nelly, or Bert, or Spud, about Mavis sleeping in the brick room. And if Neil behaves himself at school and doesn't tell anyone there.' Neil hasn't been going to school lately. None of the kids trust him as far as they could kick him.

The three little ones nod. They won't tell – not if it means getting a television and chops for dinner, and a big bucket of ice-cream living permanently in the freezer, and ice-cream cones always in the cupboard.

They won't tell.

in the pen

Time must have slipped into fast-forward mode or something – like only yesterday Martin's wedding was still a month away, and when he didn't turn up for his usual Friday night visit, they thought his ute must have broken down and sort of said, thank God! They had an extra bad night with Mavis. She's going through that stockpiled Valium like the packets grow on trees so they tried cutting her down to one tablet four times a day. It wasn't enough. It was two a.m. before they got her settled.

Then it's barely ten o'clock, Saturday morning, and they hear the ute rattle into the drive. It's Eddy's day inside but the rest of the kids head for doors, using the old divide and conquer routine, half out the back and around the west verandah and the rest out the front.

They head Martin off before he gets to the verandah, then they step back, stand back because Donny is with him. He looks different, not quite as skinny as he used to be, and his hair is longer. He looks guilty, and not a lot like the old Donny.

'G'day,' he says, handing Mick a piece of paper with his super-market phone number on it and also his mobile number. 'Long time, no see, eh?' He's too well dressed, like maybe he's been told to clean himself up for today.

No one is saying much. Lori isn't saying anything; she's leaning against a verandah post, giving Martin a slit-eyed, sliding stare, like, who did you think you were fooling? We knew all along that you'd ask Donny to be your best man.

'Put that number somewhere safe, Mick – just for emergencies. I'll be away for three weeks. Karen's parents are shouting us a honeymoon in New Zealand, so if anything goes wrong while I'm gone, you'll have to ring Donny,' Martin says.

Mick nods, wishing Martin was already in New Zealand, and Donny with him.

'How's she been?'

'Wonderful,' Lori says. 'Really looking forward to the wedding. Nelly made her a bright red tent and a hat to match.'

'We booked the furniture van for five – and one of those fork-lift things to load her in,' Jamesy says.

Mick gives them a look, like, stop your stirring. He wants his driveway cleared. Wants to get inside. Hopes the last one out closed that front door, due to Mavis spending a lot of time nodding off during the day, she's not sleeping so long at night. 'We haven't had to call the doctor recently,' he says.

'How are you for money, Mick? Have you got plenty of food?'

'Oh, we'll eat well at the wedding tonight,' Lori says.

'If Mavis leaves us anything,' Jamesy adds.

Poor Martin, he's not looking happy. He's wondering what he's done, but knows full well what he's done. He's lied, that's what he's done. He's been saying for months how it was only going to be a small wedding and that he wasn't inviting any of his family. He's invited Donny, hasn't he? It's like a whacking great slap in the face, like Donny can be cleaned up and made acceptable but Lori can't. She bets Martin has invited his workmates too – but not his own sister. He could at least have asked her to be a bridesmaid or some-thing. Not that Lori would want to be rotten Karen's bridesmaid and wear a stupid dress, but . . . but not even being asked so she could say no, and knowing that Donny got asked, well, it's making her as mad as hell.

'Have you heard from Eva?' he says.

221

'What time were you expecting her? Did you invite Alice too?' Lori says.

'Cut it out, Splint – ' Then his mobile rings and it's Karen, probably making sure he's not going to leave her standing at the altar. 'Okay,' he says. 'We're off now. Yeah. We'll pick them up. I've got it. Yeah. Yeah. He's with me. See you tonight. Me too, darl.' And he disconnects, gives Lori a sick look, then turns to Mick. 'We've got to keep moving, Mick. Ring Donny if you need anything. Don't lose those phone numbers.'

'As if Mick ever loses anything,' Lori scoffs. She turns on her heel and walks inside. Minutes later the ute rattles away.

It's a relief to see it go, really. It's not that she wanted to go to his stupid wedding . . . just . . . just wanted to be invited. All the kids wanted to be invited. They've never been to a wedding. Anyway, at least now they've got three whole weeks of not watching for him on Friday nights.

It's funny, really; like, to Lori, Martin was everything when she was little. She's losing him a bit at a time now, and it doesn't even hurt. And Donny – it was like seeing a stranger. Maybe you've only got a certain amount of room in your life for brothers and since Eddy came home she's had to push the big ones aside. Anyway, who needs grown-ups around, always telling you the right thing to do whether it's right or not? Those two would sure as hell tell them to let Mavis out. And Lori is not letting her out. Okay, it's stressful being scared someone will hear her, and it's not nice having to keep heading Nelly off at the pass, but the stress of owing money and running out of money was much worse.

They go back to the kitchen, where Eddy is sort of niggly; he wanted to get a look at Donny, who he's never seen. He'll get over it, he always does. Anyway, he was the one who came up with the mad idea of one twin in and one twin out at all times, which really isn't working very well, not at home and not at school either, the teachers are not total idiots.

The next day, Sunday, Alan is in and Eddy's free, so he's planning to make the most of it. He drags Mick and Lori out of the house before eighty-thirty and their first stop is the phone booths outside the post office. The phone wakes Eva; it's a while before Eddy can get much sense out of her. He'll go back to Melbourne one day for sure because he still keeps all of his stuff in the case, keeps it folded and separate. He sleeps in the bunk room with Alan and Jamesy, but doesn't spend much time in there – the room is a total pigpen, he's been saying lately. He says it to Eva on the phone this morning. Lori can't hear what Eva is saying but she can get the gist of it, and it's sickening. Eddy's voice gets posher – if that's possible, until she probably says something about picking him and Alan up from the school.

'I wouldn't do that,' Eddy says fast – so maybe he's not planning on going yet. 'No, Mum. No. Mave has warned the teachers about the likelihood of that sort of thing happening. They've been told to call the cops if you or Alice are sighted anywhere near the school.' Eva talks for a while and Eddy nods, then he says, 'She's got a bad heart. I feel a bit sorry for her. It's like she's relying on me to help out. No, I don't mind. No one has relied on me before.' Half of that is true. 'If I were you, Mum, I'd let her get us out of her system. I mean, well, you were always stressing out about her coming to Melbourne and taking us one day, so . . . yes, I know. But what's the use of you taking us home now and her and her team snatching us again – or worse still, going to court and charging you with kidnap? That's what she said she'd do after your last letter.'

Lori presses her ear against the receiver, wishing she could hear what is being said on the other end; something is being said because Eddy is standing, listening for a long time.

'I don't know where she got the money. The town probably took up a collection. She's got heaps of friends. Yes, it's true. It could. Yes, it's a total pigpen and it should be condemned.' Lori knows what he's referring to. She thumps him. 'Quit it,' he says, then listens again for minutes. 'No, Mave has this neighbour who is prepared to swear in court that she saw Alice drag me into the back seat of the car that

223

day, then go roaring off. They spend a lot of time going over the evidence to give in court – if it comes to that. And Lori says that . . . Yes, Lorraine, my sister. Well, she told Mavis's solicitor that Alice came into the bedroom in the middle of the night and tried to take her too. I mean, we haven't got a leg to stand on.' He's sorting through the change in his pocket because the red light is blinking. Lori finds a dollar, drops it in the slot. 'Mave is expecting that. Yes. Her boyfriend is advising her. Yes. He's a policeman. No, she's got legal aid. It's not looking good, Mum, I mean, we could end up stuck here forever.'

'She can't do this to me,' Eva wails. Lori hears that one loud and clear.

'Alan and I have been very worried about what this is doing to your nerves, Mum, and we thought, why don't you and Alice go for a trip somewhere for the winter and get your mind off us?'

Lori hears the phone clicking, or a greyhound's teeth clicking, then she feels another presence on the line. Eddy winks, shares the phone with her. 'We could ring Mr Watts if we need anything. Yes. And we could board at school until you get back.' Alice doesn't argue about that.

'We're going to get cut off soon. Mavis only gave me three dollars. Money is a bit short this week, what with the wedding. Yes. Martin. The oldest one. Yesterday. Alan and I needed new suits and shoes. We were groomsmen.'

'Call your mother back and reverse the charges,' Alice barks.

'I will next time. Mum, are you still there? Yes. I don't suppose you'd like to post us up a few dollars. We need a heap of books for school and I don't want to fall behind.'

'Let her buy his books!' Alice barks, and Eddy swaps the phone to his other ear.

'The Commonwealth,' he says. 'Yes, Mum. It's in the middle of town. That would be great. We'll go tomorrow. No, no. She won't touch a cent of it, I promise you. Yes. She seems happy – had a great time at Martin's wedding. She was up dancing all night with her boyfriend. No. She never brings him to the house. He takes her to a motel twice a week, just to give her a break from the kids. No. We're not left home alone; her best friend comes in to sleep over.'

Eva must have started asking about Alan because Eddy says he's home with Mavis, that she likes one of the boys to be around to look after the little ones. 'We're more reliable than the other kids.' Lori thumps him again. 'Yes, he's . . . he's not pining too much.'

The money eventually runs out and the kids head over the bridge to Willama West. It's a long bridge, the low land beside the river on the west bank is flood-prone, so the bridge just keeps going and going. It's worth making the trip, though, because of the Trash and Treasure market.

Mick is on Lori's bike, his good foot sort of scooting it along. You're not supposed to ride bikes on the footpath and it's too dangerous with Mick on the back of Lori's to dodge mad drivers on the narrow road part, so the other two are walking, pushing Jamesy's bike. Mick hasn't made one for the twins yet. He's probably got enough parts but not enough time. He's getting away from the house a lot more since the twins came home, and he's looking so fit and happy lately. Also, he's stopped talking about letting Mavis out.

Eddy, who is accustomed to trams and cars, decides he's had enough walking. He climbs onto Lori's carry-seat then the idiot pedals off, poor Mick balancing up front, trying to steer. They disappear in a tangle of legs, Lori yelling, scared sick they'll come off and dislocate Mick's bad leg, or break it, but they come racing back, Mick half laughing, half scared. They are racing down the footpath, doing ninety k's an hour, and by the look on Mick's face he's feeling stuff he's never felt before. He's feeling a bit wild, and he's feeling the wind through his hair and the gentle April sun burning down. Life seems pretty good. He's never had much of a chance to feel wild, and Lori can see that he's loving it, loving Eddy. They nearly run over her, but Eddy slams his legs down like steel pistons, burns rubber on his expensive treads.

Willama West is what people call the poor side of town. Land is cheap there, due to it being so far from the town. They've got an old hotel and a few rough-looking shops and old buildings close to the bridge, but the new estate is about five kilometres further out and well away from the river. Anyway, that's where the market is. A heap of young families have built new houses in the west, and every Sunday now they have a market where you can buy fruit and vegetables almost half price. People sell old car parts and old shoes and second-hand clothes. Anything. Everything.

The kids are looking through a stall full of used books when they find a how-to-diet book. It's a bit moth-eaten, but it's only twenty cents. They buy it, and Eddy buys one of Stephen King's. They get some picture books for the little kids then walk on. At one stall they find two second-hand school tracksuits for Neil and a pair of almost new leather boots that will fit Timmy. They buy potatoes and Eddy wants cobs of corn and celery; they buy cheap disposable nappies for Matty, who still needs them at night, then they load all the stuff on the bikes and start back over the bridge a lot slower than they came across, their bikes loaded up like packhorses, so Mick is walking. He's reading from that diet book too.

They learn a lot. Like Mavis needs vitamin pills and sugar substitutes. They've been giving her the medication and they've cut her down to three meals a day, plus supper, but they've been feeding her far too much fat and sugar. Even low-fat ice-cream is not allowed. Also those stews, and all the oil Lori uses when she bakes potatoes, are definite no-nos.

'No more baked potatoes. We have to start boiling them, and no more chips. If we're going to do it, then we might as well do it properly,' Mick says.

They buy a heap of diet stuff that week, including skinny milk; the book says women of Mavis's age need a lot of calcium. They look at the sugar-free mints Eddy has been feeding her by the packet; each mint has got about twelve calories in it. And choc-mint biscuits! They usually give her two with her night-time cocoa. She's not getting any more, even if they are on special. They buy strawberries, apples, sugar-free chewing gum and diet crackers. The book says she can eat strawberries and chew chewing gum until it comes out of her ears.

In the next days that diet book takes over their lives. They become experts on what's good and what's not. Like grapes, even though they are fruit and good for her, a dieter can't eat them by the bunch. They are full of sugar. And bread – a dieter can have only four slices per day, and if she has a potato or rice, then she only gets three slices of bread. There's new stuff to cook in the book too; it's got a heap of diet recipes in it with coloured pictures of how they are supposed to look, like a pink pudding made of low-calorie jelly beat up in half frozen low-fat yoghurt. Eddy makes it one day while he's on duty. And there's chicken pieces that you take all the skin and fat off, then boil up with zucchini and celery, carrots, onions, curry and stuff, and it tastes like the best food, and there's hardly a calorie in it. They all diet on chicken stew night.

No one has ever eaten celery before, except Eddy and Alan, but you get a heap for two dollars and it's got almost no calories. Lori starts putting it in all of her stews, and if you can make stews out of chicken and minced steak, then you can make them out of anything, fat sausages, baked beans, pasta. Tomato and Worcestershire sauce were Henry's favourite flavourings for his stews, and curry, so all that stuff goes in with a bit of ground ginger, because Eddy found the jar of ground ginger when he was cleaning out a cupboard and Lori didn't know what else to use it for. The pasta stews turn out excellent, but the pink sausages that swell up to twice their size get to be the most popular stew. Everyone loves it. Mavis only gets one sausage, because of the fat, but they give her a ton of raw celery, cut up with apples and cucumber and sprinkled with Weight Watchers dressing. She eats the apple and throws the cucumber and celery at them, usually while it's still on her plate, but they keep giving it to her, because it makes her plate look full and also, the diet book says, dieters have to learn new eating habits whether they like it or not.

They're now giving her the Valium in her cocoa, the Aropax in apricot jam, the fluid pill in Coke. She only gets one fluid pill every second day, due to the last time Eddy gave her two she was up all night, and also due to the fact that they can't get the potassium pills into her because they are hard as marbles, and if they crush them with Henry's hammer, they taste like yuck. The book says bananas are full of potassium, so she gets a banana on her fluid pill day. They still need to make her a medicinal custard if she's throwing one of her rages, and that adds the calories up. So do bananas. They are all experts on calories. That diet book has got every single bit of food listed on six pages at the back, like a whole slice of bread has only got seventy calories and a little chocolate biscuit has got about ninety-nine. Also butter – one tiny teaspoon of it has got thirty calories. Mavis is going to have to learn to eat her toast without butter.

There's no regular attack on the door any more, and the abuse is probably halved at certain times. Like when the quiz shows are on, she turns her abuse on the intellect of the contestants.

The kids used to love watching the quiz shows. They stand outside the window listening one night and Mavis would have beat the lot of the contestants. She's not dumb and she's not mad, just sick in the head about something. God knows what.

It's weird, though, how she has taken over their thinking. For months Lori and the kids stayed out of her way, tried to pretend she wasn't there. Now it's Mavis this and Mavis that; everyone is doing it. Like, the nights are starting to get cold, so on the Saturday, when they see one of those sealed oil heater things at a garage sale, they buy it for Mavis, then Mick finds an old extension cord with four power plugs and he takes off the skirting board in his room, drills out a square in the bottom of the outside weatherboard, from his side, not Mavis's, and after a lot of wriggling, they manage to poke the power plug through to the brick room, then plug its end into Mick's power point, which will give Mavis a power point for her television and her heater with two left over. They are actually getting organised.

It's late on the Friday evening, just past dusk but not quite dark, when they see the top of Nelly's head trying to creep past the west window. Lori races out back, heads her off before she gets around the corner. And she just hates doing it too, because Nelly has been so good to them.

'What's going on over here, Smithy? Something is going on.' Her voice is loud, it's always loud, and Lori wishes she'd learn to whisper.

'It's better if you don't come in, Nelly.'

'Yeah, I've latched on to the idea that you don't want me coming in, all right, but what I want to know is, why you suddenly don't want me coming in.'

'It's just . . . just better if you don't. For Mavis. I was going to come over and visit you and ask you if I can please sew up the bum of Jamesy's tracksuit.'

'There is nothing going on in my house that I don't want you to see, Smithy.'

'There's nothing going on here either. Not really . . . or not much different to what's always been going on.'

'You could have fooled me.'

She goes after a bit and she's not happy. The kids talk a long time about if they should tell her what they've done, and what else can they do but tell her?

'Fix the gate,' Mick says.

'What good is that going to do?'

Not much. Most of the picket fence has been used for firewood, though the rails are still there and the gate itself is okay.

'We have to tell her.'

'And she'll tell Bert Matthews and he'll tell his wife and she'll tell Australia.'

'We'll do something. Tomorrow we'll do something.'

They start early by removing the gate from the corner post. It's one of those big old-fashioned gates, made of pipe and wire, and wide enough to get a car through. It's also heavy as lead, but they haul it down to the second-last verandah post on the west side. The hinges are rusty and useless but they've got no gatepost to hinge it to, anyway, so they find some wire in the potting shed, choose a fence-post almost opposite the verandah post and they wire the gate between them; it's not as if they ever want to open that gate, just close a gap. And it's done in an hour and when it's done, the old gate stands up strong, but it's not going to stop people from walking down the verandah, so they start on the fallen lattice, which isn't as easy.

Wood is funny stuff. It might look rotten but most of that lattice isn't too rotten and in the places where it is, Mick strengthens it with wood glue, front fence pickets and a few screws from his collection, then he wires it to the same verandah post, wires it to the old support against the west wall and, just for good measure, wires it to a verandah rafter. And there is no one not equipped with wire cutters or an axe who is going to get down that side of the house.

The two-foot gap between the brick room and vacant block fence won't be so easy to close off, so they eat an easy lunch, feed Mavis a boiled egg, which she hates, and a pile of greens, which she hates more, but that's okay; the electric drill is noisy and it's complaining louder than her about having to chew a hole into a brick wall. It's not a big drill, probably only meant to drill wood, but Mick gets three holes in the mortar joints, then he hammers in blue plastic plugs and screws on a length of four-by-two, which used to be part of the rail that held the pickets. He screws up a frame between the vacant block fence and the wall, then screws on overlapped sheets of corrugated iron which totally seal that space. It's so successful, Lori suggests they extend the vacant block fence the same way, at least the bit between the brick room corner and the old laundry, which might stop Bert Matthews and his wife from seeing the kids passing food through to Mavis.

There is still a pile of corrugated iron on the junk heap, which used to be the walls of Henry's potting shed before he got the fibreglass. It's hard, noisy work, and it takes the rest of the day, but they extend the length of two fence-posts, screw and wire a rail along the top of them, supporting it with any bits of old timber they can find on the junk heap, then they fix corrugated iron to posts, rails and fence palings and it's done. The wind probably won't blow it down, and as long as it doesn't, no sticky-nosed neighbour under nine foot tall is going to be looking over that fence again.

It's funny, though. They worked all day just to keep people out, but when it's done, they see what they have achieved. They've made themselves an escape-proof back yard where the little kids will be able to play safely. The big ones are all getting sick of rounding up those wandering little buggers.

It's better. It's so much better. Everything is better.

Except Mavis. She's getting worse – like, she doesn't want her steamed European carp and the two tablespoons of peas and rice, so she throws it at them, and half of it doesn't make it through the window.

'That was your dinner, Mavis, and you're not getting anything else. And if you don't pick that fish up off that floor, then it's going to stink as bad as you do. Have a wash,' Lori yells, which doesn't help matters.

At nine they have to give her a double medicated cocoa, due to they gave her an apple but no sharp knife to peel it.

As if they'd give her a sharp knife! She's dangerous enough with a fork.

one thousand calories

Due to Eddy's reduced circumstances he's fallen in love with the Willama West market. Most of his allowance is spent there; he absolutely refuses to step inside the op shop, which is Lori and Mick's favourite place. They saw a sewing machine in there the other day and thought about buying it too. A ton of stuff needs sewing up and Mavis's tents are falling off her, and they can't ask Nelly to make new ones. Like, you can't dodge people, build a fence to keep them out, then go over the road and say, please, Nelly, can you sew this for me? You just can't do it – or Lori can't. Won't.

They don't plan to go to the market on the Sunday, but when the rain starts falling, Eddy starts nagging, so Lori rides off with him around two. The best time to get bargains at that market is at the end of the day when the stallholders want to pack up and go home, and if you add rain to that, then boy, do you get some bargains.

And it's fate, because at that first stall, Lori finds two dress lengths, one bright blue, navy and green floral and one orange and pink striped floral. They're dirt cheap and they've got *dress length* pinned onto them. She grabs both and pays fast.

At the same stall, Eddy, who won't go pure feral, finds three second-hand sheets, two pillowslips, an almost brand-new feather doona and its cover, then he stands bargaining in the rain until the lady says he can have the lot for twelve dollars. And for someone accustomed to being so rich, he sure likes to get a bargain.

232

'All of that stuff probably belonged to some old dead person,' Lori says. 'She might have died in bed, and you're going to sleep in her sheets and under her doona.'

'As long as she's not under there with me,' Eddy says, piling his stuff on the handlebars of Jamesy's bike.

They get some cheap vegies and fruit, get four second-hand mugs and two dozen pairs of socks. They find a second-hand sweater for Lori and Eddy gets it for fifty cents. He mightn't be much good to shop with at the supermarket, but he's super brilliant to shop with at this market. They save a fortune.

It's not that night or even the next that Lori raises nerve enough to go over to Nelly and ask if she'll sew up two new tents for Mavis. Eventually she has to go, due to the buttonholes on both shoulders of Mavis's last petticoat tent now being ripped. Most of the time she's wearing a blanket cape, which is lucky, and no one looks at her much, they just sort of drop the food and run.

Twice Lori gets as far as the road, turns around and comes back. Eddy says he'll do it, but she can't let him go over the road because he's too confident and too posh talking and Nelly will know he's not Alan and she'll know they are trying to fool her.

Finally she heads off, knocks at Nelly's door. It was always a good place to knock, always a safe place, but tonight Lori feels like a criminal.

'What are you doing here, Smithy?' Nelly says, flicking her outside light on but not opening her fly-wire door. 'I thought I was number one enemy.'

'You know you're not and you never will be.'

'Yeah? So what's with your gate and barricades?'

'It's just . . . just we have to keep the kids off the street.' It comes out in a rush and sounds like a lie and Lori can't look at Nelly's eyes. She's standing there, the floral material still folded stiff in her hands, like it's been folded in a trunk for thirty years.

'And what's with young Alan? I seen him out front with the kids the other day, then I seen him again walking out the front door.

Am I seeing double, Smithy, or are you trying to fool a crafty old dog?'

Lorry shakes her head. 'I wondered if you could please make Mavis some tents, please, Nelly.'

'So, she's still alive then. Bert Matthews thought you'd buried her. He reckons that's why you built your barricades.'

'Of course she's alive.'

Nelly opens her door, takes the material. Lori stands back, looks at her feet. 'What have you done with her, Smithy? You've done something.' Just a shake of her head, a step away, a quick glance across the road. 'You know I'm not as silly as I look, don't you?' Nelly says.

'I know you're not.'

'That's a back-handed insult if ever I heard one.'

'I didn't mean . . . it's like . . . I mean, you know what she's been like, and you know I'm not as silly as I look either, Nelly, and things over the road aren't as mad as they look either, and not as bad as they were either, and it's sort of . . . sort of better for us . . . and for you . . . if you don't know what we're doing over there.'

'I don't know, and that's the bloody trouble. But I'd like to know. She's still alive, though – if I'm making new tents for her. At least I can tell Bert that much.'

They stare at each other for a few seconds, but Lori is saying no more. 'What are you standing out here for?' Nelly says and she walks into her sewing room, Lori tailing her.

'You don't have to do them now.'

'It only takes me five minutes.' She sets up her ironing board, presses the creases out, almost, then she's cutting one bit in half. She cuts a bit of a U for the front neck, then sits Lori at her sewing machine. She can use that machine, has been using it for yonks and she doesn't break the needles any more. She sews up the sides of both tents then gives the chair to Nelly so she can do the tricky bits.

It takes more than five minutes, but not too much more. Nelly is starting to make buttonholes across the shoulders when Lori reminds her that Mavis won't be doing any more breast-feeding. Nelly looks at her, nods, stitches up one shoulder, and halfway across the other one, makes two buttonholes at the edge of the neck, then sews a hem around the neck, sleeves and skirt, finds some buttons in her button tin, sews them on with a special machine foot, stitches a square onto the front for a pocket and in less than an hour, Mavis has got two new tents.

'Ta for that, Nelly. Seriously, ta.'

'Seriously, what's with the gate and the fences? You're locking me out, I know that much, but who are you locking in, Smithy?'

'We're all right. True. We're better than all right, better than for ages. The chooks are laying like crazy and you know the money we owed the council for last year? Well, Mick has paid it all. And we haven't had to get you to call the doctor for ages. So whatever we're . . . whatever we've done over there has got to be better.'

Nelly stares hard at her, like, trying to read behind her eyes. 'It depends on what you've done, doesn't it? But I'll accept that, Smithy – just as long as we both know that we're not as silly as we look, eh?' Nelly says. 'Just as long as we both know that.'

Lori is halfway out the door. 'Ta for everything. For every single thing. For before . . . for feeding us, for looking after the little ones, and for now, for the tents. And one day maybe I'll tell you all about it. Okay?'

'I'll settle for that.'

'Tomorrow we'll bring you over some eggs, and Mick's got onions and carrots too.'

'You don't have to, Smithy.'

'I didn't ask if I had to, Nelly.'

That night Lori puts a new tent and clean sheets on the windowsill, with soap and a towel, deodorant, a bottle of disinfectant, some air-freshener, and a loo brush. She tosses in the old jacket, which might be better as a cape than that mouldy blanket. The air coming out of that room smells mouldy, worse than when Greg slept in there. They've talked about cleaning it up while she's asleep but it would be too dangerous.

'You're the mother, Mavis. You're the one who is supposed to be clean,' Lori says. It does no good, but when Eddy delivers the breakfast and medication the next morning, he actually gets the dirty tent flung in his face. It goes straight in the green bin. Then a blast of air-freshener hits Lori when she takes Mavis a salad lunch and two diet crackers – no butter. Her eyes sting for hours, but that night two filthy sheets come out.

That's good. That's very good. They go in the laundry, get soaked in bleach until washday.

No one can see any change in Mavis's brain or her shape. In her new tent she looks twice as big and six times as visible as she looked in her stretchy petticoat tents, but at least the new one is loose and clean and bright.

'It's got to be glandular,' Alan says. 'She always said it was glandular. And fluid. She always said that.'

Then, on Friday night, Martin turns up. He's back from his honeymoon and surely it's not three weeks yet? Maybe he got a brain and left Karen in New Zealand. No one heard his ute, no one saw him walk past the window, heard him climb their gate. He walks in through the back door while they're eating home brand apple pie and ice-cream.

'Where is she?' he says. 'What did you do with her?' He's been talking to Nelly! Or maybe Bert Matthews, like, he thinks she's dead and they haven't told anyone. The television is missing. Her couch is missing. 'What have you done with her, I said?!' Like what could they have done with her if she'd carked it? Carried her out? Buried her? Hired a forklift and a bobcat digger?

Neil tells him she's playing grizzly bears, that Eddy is Davy Crockett. He sings the song and dances around the kitchen, and the stupid little coot can sing in tune too. Matty dances with him, tries to sing, his dummy in his mouth, but Martin isn't waiting around to applaud.

He's in the front bedroom, he's checking the bathroom, all the bedrooms, then he comes back, sees the bolt has been slid on the green door and he knows. 'Oh, Christ,' he moans, runs to open it, knowing now where they've hidden the corpse.

They cower in the kitchen until they hear that bolt slide. Then they hear Mavis, hear that green door slam shut. Eddy pushes by Martin and slides the bolt home.

'You can't do that! You stupid pack of half-witted bloody kids. You can't do that!' They sort of shrink into themselves, except for Eddy. He's mentally packing. Martin doesn't open the door, though. He comes back to the kitchen, walks in circles for a bit then sits down, shakes his head, keeps shaking it. 'You can't do it, I tell you. It's illegal.'

'You sound like Henry doing his illegal. You didn't take any notice of his illegal when you were building that room,' Lori says.

'You can't do it!'

'Shut up saying that. And we've already done it and we are not undoing it, and who else came up with a better idea?'

'Shit,' he says, then he's quiet for a long, long time. Mavis isn't. She's thumping that door again, turning the air blue again. 'Are you feeding her?'

'Of course we're feeding her. What do you think we are? She usually gets a thousand calories, most days,' Lori says. She's not familiar with kilojoules; the diet book is old, printed in the calorie days.

'She looks as if she's dropped a ton,' Martin says, sort of quiet, sort of head-shaking quiet.

'She's got rid of some of her fluid, that's all.'

'She's dropped a ton. You can see it on her neck. On her chin. She's got one. You can see it on her arms, her feet. See it all over.'

'We can't see anything.'

'What are you feeding her?'

'We've got a diet book, and we go by what it says to do each day. It's for two weeks, so when we get to the end, we start back at the beginning again,' Alan says.

'And they make her have celery, and she don't like it, and I don't like it too,' Neil says.

'It's good for you. It's full of roughage, and you eat it every night in stews and you don't know it, and get away from that cornflakes packet or we'll put you through Mavis's window the next time we feed her,' Lori says.

Martin is leaning, elbows on the table, head shaking, while he stares at the green door. Alan gets out the new family bible they've stuck together with sticky tape and tries to show him the fortnight diet plan.

'We give her everything that's on it, mostly, so if it's in the book, it can't do her any harm, can it?'

'Harm? She's dropped a ton. She looked like death warmed up the last night I saw her. Her feet were footballs. She could hardly move the last time I saw her, but when she saw me just now, she moved all right.' His head is still shaking from side to side and he's still staring at that door. 'She got up from that couch like I haven't seen her get up from that couch in months. Shit!'

'She looks the same to us – except her feet – except the way she gets up.'

'You're looking at her every day. I haven't seen her in weeks. How come she hasn't knocked that door off?' Mavis is still thumping it.

'She's not this bad all the time. She's due for her pills.'

'She's taking her pills?' Martin has been around this place when Henry tried to get Mavis to take her pills. He's not understanding.

'We give them to her in her food,' Lori says. 'And we're going to run out – '

'What?'

'We're going to run out of Aropax soon and we ought to get some of the Valium prescriptions filled too. We're going through an awful lot of it.'

'You crazy little shits. You can't go around locking people up, drugging people's food with Valium.'

'Don't you start that again, Martin. Anyway, the doctor said she had to take – '

'He didn't say to lock her up and feed her the bloody pills in her bloody food, you mob of stupid little buggers!'

'Eddy done it,' Neil says.

'We *all* did it. And keep your voice down.' Lori climbs up on a chair, drags down the pile of dusty scripts. 'The doctor didn't write out all this stuff for the flies to use as loo paper. He's a doctor and he's supposed to know what he's doing. And we know what we're doing and we're doing it the only way we can because nobody else is doing any bloody thing at all, are they? Except talk about putting us in homes and letting her die.'

'I bet he doesn't bloody well know how you're doing it.'

'Someone had to do something. You just ran off and married stuck-up Karen, who we're not good enough for.' Lori has got the scripts on the table and Mick is sorting through them, finding Valium that might not be out of date, placing the silverfish-nibbled ones to the side. He finds an Aropax with a heap of repeats and he hands one of each to Martin, who sort of looks at Mick, looks at Lori, runs his fingers through his hair.

'You can't do this, Splinter.'

'You said she looks better. We're trying to save her life, and we're not asking you to do anything except get some prescriptions filled. What's illegal about that?'

'I'm not getting involved, that's what.'

'You can get pills for your own housebound mother!' She's not going to listen to him ever again. He left everyone for bloody Karen, and now he's got a wife who is too good to even bring around to this dump for a visit – not that Lori wants her to visit, not that she wants anyone to visit, not right now, but she could have before. The prescriptions are on the table, she pushes them at him. 'Get the Aropax. And this one is her fluid pills. This one is the Valium. Her pension number is already on . . . on the Aropax. That one. See?'

'How long have you had her in there?'

'Since I came home the second time,' Eddy says.

'And she's staying in there until she's small enough to get out the window,' Jamesy adds.

'Or until someone makes us let her out – and it's not going to be you.' Lori's eyes have got that brick wall look. Martin can't hold them. He looks back to the green door, shakes his head.

'She was killing herself with cigarettes and food. Everyone could see it,' Mick says. 'The last time the men came to get her on her feet, the doctor said she'd probably had a heart attack and the next one would kill her.'

'And what were you planning to do with us when she was dead?' Lori adds. 'As if we don't know.'

Martin looks from Mick's quiet eyes to the brick wall eyes of this sister, that half wild little skin-headed bugger who has gone and turned into something else while he wasn't watching. He shakes his head, takes the scripts and puts them in his pocket. He takes out a fifty. Offers it to Lori, or Mick.

'We don't need your money.'

'Since we stopped her smoking, we've got pots of it,' Jamesy says.

'Shii-iit!' Martin sounds just like Eddy. 'Shiiiiit.' He's still offering the fifty, so Eddy takes it.

'So, how much weight do you think she's lost?'

'Christ knows.'

'What did she used to weigh?' Eddy is folding the note, long and slim. Lori thinks he's going to put it in his pocket but he reaches for the ex cigarette money jar and slides it in with the other fifties.

Martin is watching him, staring at the jar. 'She reckoned she was close to thirty stone once, I know that much. I think that was before Timmy was born – or Neil. It was probably Neil. God knows what she was that last time I saw her. God knows. Thirty-five – forty.'

'What's that in kilograms?'

'Multiply it by seven then take away a bit,' Alan says.

'Shiiiiit,' Martin says.

'If a person who is, say, eighty kilograms can expect to lose half a kilo a week on a thousand calories a day, like it says in the book, then a person who weighs three times as much is going to lose three times as much each week, isn't she?' Alan says.

'Shii-iit.' Martin shakes his head.

'Stop saying that. We're trying to teach Neil not to swear. He's getting into awful strife with his swearing and pulling faces at everybody at school. We got a letter for Mavis again this week.' Lori takes the cornflakes packet from Neil, pushes it back into the hole in the wall, sticky-tapes it in so the little ones can't make that hole through to Mick's room any bigger than they've already made it. All the little kids do it. They miss their television.

'Christ!' Martin says.

'Is Christ good to say at my teacher?' Neil asks.

emotional blackmail

Mavis

*Your cruelty knows no boundaries. From the day of your birth
you have caused nothing but grief. And after all the pain, the
sorrow, you now choose to use those boys as weapons against
me. If you think I will respond to this emotional blackmail with
offers of money, then you are wrong. This time I intend taking it
to the courts, and there is not a court in the land that will force
those boys to share your squalor.*

Sincerely,
Eva

For once in her life Mavis is innocent, but she doesn't get to read
Eva's letter. She's been in lock-down mode since mid March and
now it's late May, when the seasons do their annual swap-over.

It's raining cats and dogs the night Donny calls in. He wouldn't
believe it when Martin told him what they'd done so he's got to see
it for himself. He comes to the front door, finds it locked, knocks,
yells at the lounge-room window, so they let him in and he looks a
bit out of place. He's grown thicker around the shoulders, his hair
is longer and he's wearing a pigskin suede black jacket. Also, he
drove up in a near new car.

'Look what the cat dragged in,' Lori says.

'You're thinner than her, Splint, but you're still a chip off the old block.' And he's still pretty much the same even if he does look different. He sits with them in the kitchen and tells them about Martin's wedding, but mainly about a bridesmaid called Jackie, and maybe they know why he's looking so pleased with himself. He doesn't talk about Mavis, but he has a quick peep through the window when they give her the medicated cocoa and a diet cracker for supper. She doesn't see him, and he doesn't tell the kids that what they're doing is illegal either. It's a while since he's seen her but he doesn't say she's dropped a ton, which is a bit disappointing.

Then he's leaving and he asks if they need anything, offers money. Eddy exchanges the money for a Valium prescription.

Donny isn't too sure about this kid who looks like Alan but isn't Alan. 'Better if you get them done in town, Splint. Use that money to pay for them.'

'We've already got Martin to get a heap filled here. They are getting out of date.'

'They mightn't do them in Albury.'

'Tell them your mother is staying with you for a week and she forgot her pills and she found these old scripts in her purse,' Eddy says, putting the fifty in the cigarette money jar. He's money hungry and he's got an answer for everything; he'd make a good politician, Lori thinks. Edward Smyth-Owen, MP.

'They'll think I'm a druggie, that I pinched her prescription.'

'Not if you dress like that, they won't. Druggies can't afford two-hundred-dollar jackets,' Eddy says, quick as a wink.

Donny looks at his jacket, looks guilty, then leaves the way he came. But he comes back a week later, still wearing his jacket and loaded down with supermarket bags, as well as a packet of Valium. He also brings a set of dusty bathroom scales – and what the hell does he think they're going to do with them? Ask Mavis to hop on, please?

'She's not talking to us. We don't go near her. What are they supposed to be for?'

'My mate's mother was chucking them out – '

'So you thought we could give them to Mavis so she could chuck them at us,' Jamesy says while Lori unpacks tins of food, which were probably also being chucked out. Mick is playing with the scales, turning the button on the end. 'They only go up to a hundred and forty kilograms,' he says.

'Scales go around twice, don't they?' Donny claims them, steps on, almost gets to seventy. Eddy stands on Donny's feet, and they clinch, Alan climbs on Donny's back while Eddy hangs in there, and maybe it skips over the '140' before the boys fall in a heap.

'You'll end up as tall as her,' Donny says. 'You're getting to look like her too, Splint, now that you've got a bit of hair.'

'Go ahead, make my day, Quack-quack.'

They laugh. Even Donny laughs. He was always Quack-quack, like Mick was Pullit, and Jamesy was Gnome Face. They can remember. Martin . . . well, it started with an F and it rhymed with Martin. Vinnie was Moron. Greg? No one ever bothered to give Greg a nickname – other than 'mummy's boy', which he was.

They sit then, eat popcorn – Eddy is a whiz at making popcorn – and they talk about the old days, get to talking about Henry and his potting shed, his nightly songs.

'Could he really sing?' Eddy asks. They look at him with disdain, like he's got the stinking audacity to question some precious God-given fact.

'Of course he could sing. He was better than those three tenors put together,' Lori says, and Eddy nods, goes quiet for a bit then gets up and goes to the shower. He stays in there until Donny has to leave.

Dear Mavis,

A long time ago I gave up expecting any form of common decency from a slut who spread her legs for anything in pants. I gave up expecting that you may still have an ounce of humanity in your

244

heart, however I did expect a reply to my letter and a figure I can work with.

How much longer do you intend disrupting my life and the lives of those boys? Have you any comprehension of the emotional damage you are causing me? As if you care. As if for one moment you ever considered the damage your actions caused this family.

You have not previously been backward in coming forward with your demands for money. How much do you want, Mavis? Put a price on the lives of those boys and let me buy them out of purgatory.

Please reply.

Eva

Mavis doesn't reply, doesn't know she's supposed to reply, though if she saw that letter she might like to reply and name her own price.

So life goes on and it's so good, it's frightening.

Donny pops in some Sunday nights and he always brings his supermarket bags full of food, and most Fridays they meet Martin at McDonald's. He won't come near the house now, won't set foot in Dawson Street, probably won't even drive over the railway line, due to he's petrified that someone is going to find out about Mavis and he'll end up in jail, and his father-in-law, who is a hard-headed, silly old bugger, so Martin says, will have his guts for gaiters. He buys them dinner on Friday nights and always gives them fifty for their jar. He's making piles of money and he's got nothing to spend it on, except a new ute, but he pure refuses to get rid of his old one, due to his father-in-law keeps on nagging him to get rid of it.

It's good talking to him out of that house, like they learn heaps more about Karen, who is an only child. She's got her own hair-dressing salon and a posh new car, and she and Martin live for free at her parents' farm. That's how Martin got to know her; he and his boss built their new mansion and it took them six months to build it too, because Karen's father kept changing his mind about stuff.

'Imagine being an only child with rich parents,' Lori says.

'It has its fringe benefits,' Eddy says with a sort of yearning in his voice.

One day he'll go back, be an only child with fringe benefits. One day. Every time Mavis gets a letter from Eva, the kids watch him. They know he's thinking about going. But he doesn't go, though he's calling their house purgatory now instead of pigpen.

They're so careful. Neil has been warned to behave at school because if the teachers smell a rat, they'll send more than letters for Mavis; they'll send the cops around to let her out and things will go back to the bad old days, and nobody wants the bad old days back, do they?

Neil makes a face, Timmy shakes his head and Matty says, 'Dow,' shakes his head too, and sucks hard.

The nights are too cold or wet to do much walking, but Mavis's ex cigarette money is crowding the jam jar. They count it one night and discover they've got more than enough for a little television advertised in the wet junk mail, so they buy it, wheel it home in Matty's pram and plug the old video player into it, then Jamesy goes up the manhole to connect a new cable. And the television works and, God, it's good to have the shows back again. The little kids would sit in front of that box all day if the twin on house duty let them. They do one wet Thursday.

Mick and Lori come home from school and find them still sitting in their pyjamas. Eddy has been repairing the wall, mutilated by Mavis's couch. He's sealed it with the cornflakes packet and pasted over the lot with newspaper. It looks solid enough and Eddy reckons he's going to paint it if it ever dries.

They cut Mavis down to five Valium, then to four per day, which she takes in coffee now. Donny bought them a huge tin-full and no one else wants to drink the stuff. It's, like, months out of date.

246

Anyway, things have settled into a routine; Mavis still yells, yells double when they give her salads, but only things like, you wait, you little bastards. Those sorts of things. She doesn't yell as much as she used to and she hardly ever yells for cigarettes.

The kitchen door is still off its hinges but the kitchen is warm enough. Mick had tons of wood delivered before the rains came, and they've hung an old blanket over the doorframe and another one as an outside door for the little passage between the kitchen and the brick room. Those blankets keep the cold out almost as well as two doors, except when the wind is blowing in from the south, but the stove never goes out, so warmth has crept through the house.

Mavis

I have just returned from speaking with my psychiatrist and he suggested that I write out what is in my heart. Loathsome, depraved, obese slut born of corruption, born with the mark of the demon on her brow. I cursed you then, and wished you dead, so die, you obese cow, and give me back my sons.

You made a mockery of my childhood. You alone were responsible for Mother's illness. And when I chose to live the life Mother dreamed for me, you turned the man of my choice from me with your gaping legs. Fat, filthy, fecund freak.

Do you know the best day of my life was the day Mother's will was read. The joy, the pure pleasure I felt seeing your face when you learned the truth. And his face too, watching him run, his filthy little tail between his legs. She placed a barb in your depraved heart that day, didn't she? and I laughed.

You won't beat me, you repulsive whore. They are my sons. Mine. One way or the other, I will get them back.

Eva

Dear Mavis

A brief line to advise you of the seriousness of Eva's present situation. If she is to get over this final disappointment, her doctor has advised me to get her away from the house for a few months. We fly out on Sunday for a tour of Europe. If you decide you've had enough of the boys, contact Watts. He'll make the necessary arrangements.

Sincerely,
Alice Blunt

Wow! Phew! Relief! They're going. Eddy claims the two letters, reads them over and over then tosses them onto the table. The decision to go or to stay now taken out of his hands, he's looking more than a bit stunned.

'I hope she doesn't stop paying the money into my bank account,' he says.

She doesn't. When the fifty arrives on Friday, he relaxes, stops looking towards Melbourne and starts talking a bit more like a human being – like he even stops calling the loo a toilet.

So there are no more letters for Mavis; now there are weekly postcards coming addressed to Masters E and A Smyth-Owen. Some of them even contain weird money, and the ten pounds from England turns into almost thirty Australian dollars! Eddy is rich again. Alan won't touch Eva's money.

Lori has claimed that last letter and she spends a lot of time attempting to decipher its contents, coming to the conclusion that Mavis probably led a wild life before she pinched Henry, and maybe, if Grandmother's illness was caused by Mavis, she might have been old when Mavis was born and probably never got over having her – either that or she wanted her to be a boy and she turned out a girl. The 'born of corruption' could mean Mavis's father was a mongrel. But it's all supposition. There's nothing concrete.

She learns heaps about Europe from Eva's cards, like she finds out where some of the countries actually are because Eddy buys a huge map and sticks it on the kitchen wall with Blu-tack so the kids can track Eva and Alice from Greece to Egypt to Germany. They stick the postcards up with Blu-tack, and Neil wants to stick up the pictures he draws at school. He's excellent at drawing, though one of his pictures looks suspiciously like a giant locked in a brick box.

'What's that one about, Neil?' Lori asks.

'That's a grizzly bear with a sore head in . . . in a cage,' Neil says.

'With red frizzy hair! Grizzly bears don't have red frizzy hair. And cages have got bars, not bricks. Don't you draw any more of those grizzly bears at school.'

'I drawed one at school and my teacher put it on the wall.'

He was always a troublemaking little bugger. Right from day one, the kids knew that if anyone was going to throw a spanner in the works, it would be Neil. And he's done it! The stupid little twit pinches a full packet of Valium, which Donny dropped in late on Sunday night, and which got left on the kitchen table. Anyway, Neil takes it to school for 'show and tell' and all hell breaks loose.

Jamesy gets called to the office. Neil has had a great 'show and tell' time. He's told how Mavis is locked in the loo, and she can't get out, and Eddy puts her to sleep with these magic pills so she can't yell at everyone and kill them.

'Who is Eddy?' Jamesy asks.

There must have been some phoning between schools because the high school Smyth-Owens get called to the office. It's on the intercom, and the last time that happened it was for a family who had to go home, due to their grandfather died. Everyone looks at Lori as she leaves the classroom, like they are thinking her mother is dead. Lori is thinking something worse than that. She's thinking her mother is out.

No police around the office, no strangers – it's almost a relief to see the principal, who asks about Eddy.

Eddy, who is supposed to be Alan today, shrugs. 'Eddy who?'

Mick just shrugs, goes red, looks guilty, but Lori, who is learning a lot from Eddy, and not just about the school's computers, says, 'Neil has got a sort of pretend friend who makes him do all the bad things. He probably calls him Eddy. I don't really know.'

The Valium subject is raised and Lori can't think fast enough, but Eddy can.

'Neil must have taken those pills last night, Lori.' He turns to the principal. 'Our mother was looking for them everywhere and when she couldn't find them she had a setback – which is probably what Neil is talking about. She got so stressed out she had a panic attack and locked herself in the bathroom for an hour, just to get away from the little kids.'

'She had a . . . a complete nervous collapse when our father died and she's taking antidepressants, Aropax, and Valium for her nerves, and other stuff,' Lori says, swallows, looks at her shoes.

The principal talks at them for fifteen minutes about small children and poisoning and drugs, but he's got bigger drug problems in this school than a packet of Valium. After a bit he calls the state school and tells them that Michael, the oldest boy, will call in at lunchtime to pick up the tablets, as the mother is waiting for them.

Lori dinks Mick around to get the pills, sealed in an envelope that contains a letter for Mavis and some literature about keeping dangerous drugs in a locked cupboard. It's not the drugs that need to be locked away in their house; they've had the dangerous stuff locked away for a while and it's becoming a bit less visibly dangerous. They can all see the weight coming off Mavis now.

That night they have one of Henry's kitchen table lectures. They sit Neil down at the head of the table and threaten to lock him in with Mavis if he ever does anything like that again. Feed him on celery and broccoli and nothing else. Keep feeding it to him until his hair turns green. Then they go to the window and ask Mavis if she would please write one of her letters to Neil's principal, because he wants to hear from her regarding Neil's uncontrollable behaviour, and he'd also like to know that she received the enclosed item.

She won't play ball but she belts into Mick's timber wall and his floor is rocking.

They medicate, wait forever for the custard to calm her down. It doesn't, so they start writing drafts of their own letter – which isn't going to work because that school has received years of Mavis's mad letters. They pass a packet of chocolate biscuits through the window with a sheet of paper and a biro, and they say, 'Please.' It's their first mistake. Those biscuits bring back memories.

Eddy heads for Henry's typewriter. He's super fast on the library computer, but he's breaking the no-swearing rule trying to get a letter out of the typewriter. They spend two hours over it, five heads together. They make three drafts before it sounds right, sounds like a tame Mavis, full of howevers, then they spend an hour practising her signature, which is on the cigarette note and the withdrawal form Lori still carries in her purse. That signature doesn't look hard to do, but no one can do it.

They've ruined her diet with those biscuits so Eddy makes a pile of pancakes, and they try a bit of bribery. They'll give her half the pancakes before she signs and the other half after. It's seriously the wrong thing to do. She's over her thousand calories, maybe over three thousand with those biscuits and half of the pancakes, and they've gone and let her know there are more. She throws a screamer, stabs the back of Eddy's wrist with the biro when he tries to reclaim his night's work, which she won't sign anyway. He doesn't get the letter. She rips it up, so he stands at the window eating the rest of her pancakes. Which is the third totally wrong thing to do. She starts belting at the door with her shoulder and she's got the energy now to keep it up.

They get out, head up the street, listening for how bad she sounds. On a scale of one to ten, she's bellowing at fifteen. Lori and Mick go to Nelly's and give Martin a call – not that he's going to do anything.

'You can at least phone the school for us tomorrow, explain about how she's had a nervous collapse.'

Nelly is standing close, sort of cleaning, tidying her already tidy kitchen bench, sort of pretending she's not listening while her ears vibrate.

'I've explained why I can't get involved, Mick. If I do that, then later on, when she gets out, she's got proof that I knew about her being locked up. I'm an adult and she hates my guts. She'll have me in jail for forced incarceration,' Martin says.

'What about us?'

'You're juveniles. You're too young to know any better.'

Lori grabs the phone. 'So let a pack of juveniles who don't know any better forge her bloody signature.'

Nelly is wiping closer to the phone now and her ears are almost beeping like radar scanners. Lori hangs up while Martin is still talking, and serve him right for running off and getting married.

'What's going on?' Nelly asks.

'Thanks for the phone,' Mick says. 'I'll bring you over some eggs tomorrow.'

'What the bloody hell is going on over there? I can hear her banging and yelling from my verandah.'

'Neil did something wrong, that's all. We've got to go.'

'Is Martin coming across?'

Lori shakes her head.

'Do you want me to call the doctor to quieten her down?'

Lori shakes her head and she runs.

It's after midnight before they get Mavis quiet with a big, hot, highly medicated custard. She finally flakes.

Eddy's final, final draft reads:

Dear sir,

Neil is a difficult child, as you well know, and a problem to his mother, who is not well and on Valium for her nerves and medication for depression. She is too upset about the trouble he has caused you tonight to write back. Being housebound and not having the telephone connected, she is unable to contact you. Please telephone her doctor if you have any more questions on this matter. His name and phone number are listed below.

Yours faithfully,
M J Smyth-Owen

Mick signs it. The M J Smyth-Owen sounds good, sounds grown up, and no one will recognise Mick's writing – no one can usually understand it to recognise it.

'They'll probably think Martin signed it,' Lori says. He's an M J too.

Bloody Martin. Bloody Karen. Bloody Bungala. Lori has never been to Bungala, but she hates the tinpot little dump. She's never met Karen either, and she hates her too. Doesn't try to work out why she hates her, just does. Hates her like rat poison.

She used to do a lot of thinking, attempt to work out the world, used to like being on her own to live a while alone inside her head. There is no time to think these days, no getting off on her own to do any serious thinking, no sitting beside Henry's grave either. She hasn't been out to the cemetery since Eddy came home. Just too much to do. Always something. Too much happening. Too much being scared. Too much to learn. Too much being happy too. Just too much of everything.

Like buying that old sewing machine from the op shop, which the lady let them have for two dollars. It's ancient and heavy as lead, and they had to borrow a supermarket trolley so they could wheel it home, but it works perfectly. Lori has been practising on it by sewing up ripped sheets, and they are all ripped so she's got plenty to practise on. There is cooking to get done, and learning how to cook new things. That diet book has been a pure godsend. It's teaching her heaps about cooking – even if what she serves on the plates doesn't look a lot like the pictures.

Since Donny started calling in, the cupboards are tiptop full. A lot of the stuff he brings is weird, like he probably picked it up out of the supermarket's garbage. The last time he brought two packets of seasoned breadcrumbs and twelve tins of sausage and vegetable stew, which tastes nowhere near as good as Lori's sausage and vegetable stew. They give it to Mavis. It's got the total fat content and calories it contains written on the side. They use the breadcrumbs with egg and flour to make a batter for the slices of European carp, then they fry it in boiling oil, like at the fish-'n-chip shop. It's delicious. They tip Donny's tins of sweet curry stew in with their minced steak stews and create new taste treats. He also brought a pile of slimmer's jelly. Mavis gets to eat a heap of jelly.

They still stockpile baked beans when they are on special, and condensed milk, not that they use much condensed milk, except on rice with sultanas. Baked beans and condensed milk are hangovers from the old days of emergency rations, or even from the old days of Henry. Most of what is in the cupboards and freezer has been bought on special, which is better than being forced to buy it when it's not on special.

Mick is a great list maker. He bought a magnetic list-thing to stick on the fridge and Eddy keeps writing stupid stuff down, like 'computer', like any fool thing he thinks of, but his letter has fixed up the school. They don't hear another word, not for weeks, not for a month. Neil even comes home one night with a stamp on the back of his hand for being good. That's a first!

Winter is on its last legs when Eva and Alice come back from their trip and start getting legal. Mr Watts is sending his letters again, which are mostly about departments of community services and stuff. All Eva sends is loving letters to her boys. They sort of stir Eddy up more than her killer letters to Mavis, like they get him looking towards Melbourne a lot, get him calling the house ratshit instead of purgatory.

'Go back to her if you want to and I'll write and tell her that I'm not going back,' Alan says.

'What if we went back for a week?' Eddy says. 'They can't lock us up.'

'Can't they?' Alan says, looking out at the green door.

Eddy sighs, gets out the typewriter and writes another letter for M J Smyth-Owen to sign.

Dear Aunt Eva

I hope you had a good holiday and thank you for your solicitor's letter. Mavis is still too upset to reply, however, she says to tell you that she has been in contact with the television station and they are interested in paying her for her story. She has also been in contact with legal aid again.

I am very sorry that these new arrangements have upset your nerves so much. So is Mavis. She said to tell you that if you agree to send them back, she would be happy to allow Eddy and some of the younger children to have a week's holiday with you during the September school holidays, which would allow them to see how the other half live and may help to civilise them, as you did such an excellent job of civilising Eddy, who is a perfect gem to live with.

Yours faithfully
M J Smyth-Owen

'And that's the last one,' Eddy says. 'That typewriter is ratshit.' Everything is ratshit now; he's picking up a lot of Willama expressions and finding a few new ones of his own.

He starts looking in the local papers for second-hand computers, focusing his frustration on computers. Like, he says, if they can afford to buy a television and a truckload of mill-ends, then they can afford to buy a second-hand computer. He could do everybody's homework twice as fast if he had a computer. They could all learn to use it and move into the twenty-first century, for Christ's sake. What's wrong with them, for Christ's sake? Do they want to stay Sticksville hillbillies all their lives?

After a week of it, Lori has had enough. 'Go back to your fucking computer then, and to mad fucking Eva. After what she wrote in that letter about her own sister, she's sicker than Mavis, and if you want to go back to her, you're fucking sicker than her. We didn't ask you to come up here anyway, and we're getting pure fucking sick of you always slinging muck at our place as if you think you're better than us.'

'Slinging muck? There's so much muck around that there's nowhere to sling any more of it.'

'Go then. Get out and fuck off and see if we care.'

No one likes to see those two arguing and they've been doing a bit of it lately. The rest of the kids go quiet. They've seen too much arguing. They know where arguments can lead.

Maybe Eddy knows he's gone too far. Lori only uses that F word when she's really riled up. 'Go?' he says. 'Just when I'm starting to fit in?' And he gets down on all fours and pig squeals, grunts around her feet, and when she kicks him, he crawls to the fridge and writes 'computer' on the magnetic list, adds 'pig food'.

They chase him and get him down and write 'computer' all over him with Mick's pen from the magnetic list thing. They cover him with 'computer' and waste half the pen, but they're laughing and he's still pig squealing and snorting.

The rotten stuff washes off him. They should have used biro.

the visitors

Something had to give, and it gave. The school, some sticky-nosed neighbour or Eva must have dobbed, because the department of child services writes to Mavis, like, will Mrs Smyth-Owen please call them at this number? She doesn't call, so she gets another letter. If they do not hear from Mrs Smyth-Owen in the next week, she will be receiving a house call.

Of course they don't hear from her, though at times the neighbours are still hearing plenty because the Valium is getting low. And why the hell didn't the doctor write repeats on his Valium prescriptions like he did on his Aropax and fluid pills?

Eddy calls Donny at the supermarket one Friday and asks him to go to the doctor and say he's got bad nerves. Donny comes up for a flying visit. He's got plenty of weird food and some supermarket executive stress pills, but Mavis is not acting like a stressed executive and the pills taste like poison when crushed, anyway.

They pack the food away and give him a script the silverfish have been nibbling on. It's not out of date, though, and the all-night chemist near the high school gives him the pills. Four Valium a day slows down Mavis's cursing.

There's controlled panic in the house now. Every car that drives down the street is suspect. Even the new Jehovah's Witness couple are eyed with suspicion when they turn up at the front door on Saturday. Eddy opens the door a crack and tells them that his mother is out and that he's not allowed to open the door. They push a God book through the crack and Eddy takes it back to the kitchen, tosses it onto the table with everything else. 'You're dead in the water if anyone walks in on *this*,' he says.

'You always say *you're* dead, as if it doesn't even concern you,' Alan says, and keeps on looking for Matty's mislaid dummy, which might stop him whingeing around Lori's knees while she's trying to make Mavis's breakfast. Timmy finds the dummy, which was on the floor with everything else. He plugs that whinge. The kids turn to him, see him, know that he's been finding that dummy and plugging that whinge for years now. He's such a no-trouble, good little kid – too good for his own good. He even looks good – someone would adopt him fast.

Mick is walking the kitchen looking at the benches, at the newspapered patch where the couch hole used to be. He walks slow through the house, the others tailing him. They are all seeing stuff they don't want to see today. Like the beds are just mounds of blankets, except Eddy's, which is a top bunk. It's made up with sheets and a quilt and it looks so alien. They pick up stuff as they walk, then put it down again, kick it to another place. It's impossible to undo this mess. Like, where do they start?

Back in the kitchen Eddy has got the last bank statement, which was Blu-tacked to the wall. He's got the ex cigarette money jar down from the top of the cupboard. It's stuffed.

Lori claims it. She hasn't counted it in weeks, just pokes each new fifty in and screws down the lid. She digs the notes out now, tosses them onto the table where they lie curled a while. All of that money and what use is it? Money is for food and bills, but they've got plenty of food and Mick has paid the bills. What else could that money buy? A bulldozer? A team of cleaning ladies? She's sorting though the notes, tossing them one by one at Mick, who sits smoothing, flattening, counting while the others stand around.

'Maybe we could spend a bit, try to fix things up a bit,' Mick says.

'How?' It's a communal wail.

Mick shakes his head, looks at the back door, still propped against the wall for Mavis emergencies, looks at the old woollen blanket he hung in place of that door; it wasn't clean when he nailed it up before winter, now it's filthy. Then he's on his feet and he's ripping that blanket down. He gets his tools, his screws and wood glue, and in fifteen minutes the blanket nails are out and the door hinges have been moved up half a centimetre, new holes drilled, extra long screws screwed in and the door grinds shut. He doesn't know why he didn't do it before.

'So what looks the next worst?' he asks. Eddy falls on the floor, kicks his feet and laughs while he points in six directions at once. They look at the dusty brown curtain doorway to the passage, look at the broken west window, the broken louvres, the broken window in the bunk room, which Henry covered with plastic, which keeps peeling off.

'Glass is pretty cheap, ' Mick says.

'Cheap or not, we can't bring anyone around here to put in new glass and you can't do it. You'll cut your hands off.'

'Those social worker people are going to come whether we like it or not, Lori, and if they get a look at this place the least they'll do is take the little kids away,' Mick says, and he goes for Henry's old tape measure while Lori swears, says four f words in a row, then adds, 'And don't you little kids ever dare say that word. I'm just showing you how bad swearing sounds.'

They measure the broken windows, except Mavis's, then Lori, Alan and Mick go out to the glass place, where the glazier tells them he'll have to do the measuring up himself. Mick gives the address. The outside world is coming in to get them and there is not a thing he can do to stop it.

'Oh, you're Mavis's kids,' the glazier says. He knows the house, Bert Matthews is his uncle. 'I'll come around tonight, around five.'

When they get home, Eddy and Jamesy are painting the kitchen wall which has got the newspaper repairs, and they're using a bucket of blue acrylic paint Eddy found in the laundry. It's fourteen-year-old exterior paint, which Henry must have bought when he planned to paint the house.

'It looked pale blue when we opened it,' Eddy says.

'But as we dip deeper, it gets brighter,' Jamesy adds.

And it's totally bubbled that newspaper. It's a typical example of kids trying to fix one thing and making two things twice as bad. Most of the east wall is a bubbly bright blue botched-up blotch and the floor is blue spotted.

'It looks fucking ridiculous,' Lori wails.

'Lori sayed dat bad word,' Timmy says.

'Well, it does look bloody ridiculous. We should have known better than to leave you two here by yourselves! You've ruined the kitchen and it was the best room we had.'

'Then we're up crap creek in a barbedwire canoe, aren't we?' Eddy counters, and he keeps on painting.

They are feeling hopeless. It's over. Mavis is ranting, throwing stuff and doing her own swearing. At four they make her a highly medicated cocoa, which zaps her while the glazier does his measuring. His quote is high, but there's tons of money in the jar.

'How much for cash?' Eddy asks. That's what Eva used to do.

'I'll knock twenty off,' the glazier says.

'We've got a deal,' Eddy says, not looking up from his paint job.

The glazier is standing at the back door, eyeing that blue paint – it's pretty hard not to look at – but they can't let him keep standing there so they get him into the kitchen and close the door. 'Where is your mother?' he says.

'Out visiting the neighbour. She said to find out when you can do it.'

'Friday, and I'll need her say-so.'

'She left the money to pay you – in advance. Cash. She needs you to do it tomorrow morning. Early,' Eddy says.

'I could, I suppose. For cash.'

'Early?'

'Eight-thirty.'

He comes at ten, when Mavis is due to wake. Mick and Alan watchdog the glazier while Lori watchdogs Mavis, and Eddy goes to Kmart and buys two rollers, a packet of cheap paintbrushes and four litres of cheap white paint to tone down the blue. He mixes a batch in the laundry bucket, two jam tins of each. It tones it down a bit so he rolls the new mix over the old, gets a few more bubbles, but as it dries, that east wall is actually looking solid.

'It makes the other walls look filthy,' Lori says, not yet ready to admit it's better.

So the maniac starts on the other walls. Then, as soon as the glazier leaves, they all grab a brush or roller and they are into it, painting walls, and themselves, blue, and as soon as it dries it gets another coat.

The ceiling is splattered and smeared by blue, so they paint it too. It only takes about an hour with everyone at it, standing on the table and falling off the table, and it only takes about an hour to dry because with the stove burning and the door back on its hinges, glass again in the windows, the kitchen is stinking hot. They slosh on another coat before dinner and wonder what happened to the day, which sort of disappeared beneath the stink of paint and a bright blue haze. No one went to school, no one cooked a stew for dinner. They eat baked beans late; they smell and taste of blue paint. Mavis gets beans too and hates them, hates her kids, threatens murder, but too bad. She's going to live for two more years whether she likes it or not.

Eddy is no sleeper. He's into it already when the rest of the kids start wandering out at eight the next morning. He's scrubbed all the benches, scraped blue paint off the table, stuck the map back on the wall and made a full border of postcards below it. The eastern wall is the only continuous wall in the kitchen and it looks really excellent.

'Wow.' The room still stinks of paint but it doesn't look like the same room. They can't believe how clean and bright it looks, the blue water of the map sort of blending in with the blue wall, and covering a bit of it too, and that border of postcards. It looks sort of . . . sort of modern, like it might have been planned. Except the ceiling. They wish they hadn't painted it, but it's too late now.

After a fast breakfast they get rid of Neil to school and the rest wag it. Mick and Alan put new screws in the hinges of a couple of cupboard doors, then paint them blue while Lori heads off to buy some white lacy curtain stuff like Nelly's to cover up the messy window frames. The cheapest she can find is six dollars a metre, but it's long enough to cut in half. She gets the machine out and stitches a hem on the cut bit and a bit of a heading on the other, and when those curtains are hung on elastic they actually look almost posh, so she rides off to the reject shop to buy a posh white plastic lace cloth for the table.

And it's perfect. It matches the curtains and ties the room together and looks so good it makes her eyes water, though it might be the fumes coming off the plastic tablecloth, which, as long as you don't smell or touch it, looks like a proper crocheted cloth, like Nelly has got on her dining room table.

The floor is a mess of spilled blue paint. Eddy wants to rip up the vinyl but Lori won't let him, due to half the wood underneath it is the old kitchen floor and the other bit is chipboard from when the kitchen stole part of the back verandah. They find Henry's mop on the vacant block. Neil has been using it for a horse. Lori mops while, ahead of the mop, the boys scrape off blue paint with kitchen knives. The vinyl is a bit worn in places, and it's got a few rips in it where Mavis's couch used to live, but it comes clean after three buckets of water. And this room sure makes the others look bad.

The dusty brown curtain over the passage doorway goes next. Eddy tosses it into the hall, then starts work on the bunk room, shooting junk out from beneath the lower bunks with a broom. He finds stuff no one has seen in months. Alan finds *Jurassic Park*, a book lost a week after Henry died. He wants to read it again, but they

262

won't let him sit down. Then they are all into shooting stuff out from beneath the beds. Mick finds Vinnie's long-lost boot and one of Martin's sweaters, unsighted since he left home. It's a classy sweater. Mick claims it.

Alan is walking around with the wet mop in one hand and *Jurassic Park* in the other, so Lori grabs the mop and after a bit she actually finds a decent looking vinyl floor under the dirt in Mick's room. This is like a haphazard treasure hunt; they do a bit here and a bit there, but stay clear of the lounge–bedroom.

'So, when they come, we keep the lounge-room door shut and leave Mick's door open and tell them she's gone out visiting the neighbours.'

'Can't. She'll hear them.'

They forget lunch, forget Mavis, forget Neil. He finds his own way home from school at four and the kids suddenly realise what Mavis is yelling about. She hasn't been fed.

It's a bit like when they had a pet budgie. For a while everyone wanted to feed it, then after a while, everyone forgot to feed it and one day it escaped and magpies got it.

They eat scrambled eggs that night, because the eggs are piling up in the fridge and they have to get rid of them. Mavis didn't get any lunch so she gets a heap of scrambled eggs, two pieces of dry toast and a pile of sliced tomatoes. She likes the look of that heaped plate and forgets to yell, so they forget to medicate her.

'Bed. Everyone. We're going to school tomorrow,' Mick says.

'It's only eight o'clock.'

'Bed,' Lori says. She's asleep on her feet.

It's Friday, Eddy's home-duty day, but he's not staying in. He wraps the little ones in their parkas, disguises himself with Henry's scarf and hat and reading glasses, lifts the kids over the side fence, and they go to Kmart, where he buys umpteen dozen cheap wire coat hangers. They return home the way they came, over the fence.

The midday movie isn't suitable for general exhibition but the little kids are too young to know it. He sits them in front of it and starts unpacking his case, hanging his clothes in the wardrobe. By the time the movie is finished, he's hung his own, plus most of the semi-clean stuff previously chucked, stuffed or kicked into corners.

Lori gets in at four and climbs over a mountain of old clothes he's marked for the green bin. 'Shit,' she says. 'The kids will have nothing to wear.'

'Lowie's swearing again,' Timmy says. That kid is not only good, he's a goody-goody. She's the main swearing offender, and she has been trying to teach Neil not to swear so she has to stop doing it. Next week she'll stop – if she's still alive next week.

Saturday. Social workers probably don't work weekends. The washing machine does. Alan hits the supermarket, buys a million pegs, more washing powder, floor-cleaning detergent and a new mop head. The old one has died of the mange. Lori and Eddy hit the market early on Sunday looking for second-hand sheets and don't find one.

'Bugger.'

Come Monday, they dress for school, but no one, other than Neil, is going, unless the department people come. If they do, the plan is, slide the bolt on the green door and everyone take off over the side fence. They've got Henry's old ladder leaning on one side and a metal garbage bin on the other – so they can get Mick over fast.

Eddy's got the porridge boiling; the kids love his porridge and this morning Mavis gets some, due to she's awake early. They forgot to medicate her last night.

She's never eaten porridge. 'What's this shit?' she yells, and there is almost a wail in her voice. 'You don't expect me to eat this shit!' They ignore her. They've got bigger problems than Mavis's taste buds.

The beds are stripped before Neil is delivered to school, and the extra beds and mattresses carried out to the potting shed. Everything gets a wash, sheets and blankets; the washing machine just keeps going and going, but the sun is warm by ten, and there's a bit of a wind, so stuff from the weekend is finally drying and being brought in to be ironed dry, or hung in front of the stove. At lunchtime they're eating baked beans with one hand while sorting the washing with the other, making piles of whose is what, and who can use that, and that bloody thing wasn't worth wasting detergent on.

'Pitch it,' Eddy says.

A lot of stuff is getting pitched. The mound of rejects keeps getting higher. They are all saying it now. 'What about this?'

'Pitch it,' voices chorus. The green bin is going to be full this week. So are the neighbours' bins, at this rate.

Eddy hasn't run out of hangers yet so Mick fixes up the rail in his wardrobe and Eddy hangs stuff where nothing has ever hung before. The door hinge being broken for years, that door had to be kept locked so it didn't fall off. Mick cuts a bit of leather from Vinnie's old boot; one boot isn't a whole heap of use and it still stinks anyway. He makes a leather hinge, tacks it to wardrobe and wardrobe door. And it works. He's so inventive.

There aren't enough intact sheets to go around. Lori raids what the glass man left in the ex cigarette jam jar and she rides up to Kmart, buys a few cheap sheets, while Alan takes over the mop. He's mopping the bunk room walls now, spraying them with Mr Muscle then slopping water everywhere, but the vinyl wallpaper is coming clean. The blankets, that also came clean, are not drying.

Eddy has got his almost brand-new feather doona, Lori has been using Mavis and Henry's new doona – she's been using their bed since Mavis moved out back, though she's never washed that doona cover before. It sort of changes colour. Dirt is funny stuff. You forget about the colour of it when life revolves around finding enough food, but the house isn't dirty now and it's starting to smell different; wet, but different. It looks more than different, like Lori's room actually looks good; it's got decent curtains and carpet. Kids were not allowed to play in this room in the old days, so it survived. The lower half of the walls are brown panelling and above the panelling there's a textured pinkish beige wallpaper. Once the bed is made and the dust swept off the dressing table, the room looks like a real bedroom.

'It makes our room look like crap,' Eddy says. 'We need doonas and covers. Blue ones.'

'We need a million dollars too.'

'They've got doonas at Kmart for twenty-something dollars each. I saw them in the junk mail. Pitch those blankets in the green bin, and the pillows.'

Lori is out at the clothesline, wringing water out of the ends of the blankets, and she's still doing it when it's time to pick Neil up from school, but no matter how much she wrings out, the blankets look wetter. No one is going to be using those blankets for, like, days. Alan collects Neil and Lori grabs the bankcard; she and Eddy go to Kmart, toss five single-bed doonas into a trolley, then Eddy tosses in four navy blue sheets to use for bedspreads, and he's not putting them back.

'Mick can have my doona and cover.'

Mean gets to be a habit but Lori is breaking that habit today. She picks up two green sheets for Timmy and Neil's beds, tosses them in. They are working in fast motion, thinking fast, paying fast with the card, but riding home slow like a pair of pack mules.

Matty still sleeps in the cot. Because cot blankets are smaller, no one used his spares. They dig out two clean ones from the linen cupboard and that's about all it's got in it. Everything else is on the clothesline.

'Tomorrow we go to school because those sticky-nosed buggers will probably check out the schools before they come to check us out here.'

doing an eva

It's Wednesday, and Eddy has disappeared. He was there for breakfast and now he's gone. It's Alan's turn to go to school, and as sure as hell, Eddy hasn't decided to do a swap. Then Lori looks for the bankcard that lives in her purse, which she left on the kitchen table. It's not there, nor is the old withdrawal form for two hundred dollars.

'He's taken off with my card and licence.'

'He's doing an Eva – gone spending mad,' Alan adds. 'That's what she does sometimes, and once she starts, she can't stop. Alice has to hide her cards until she gets over it. Eddy used to be as bad as her in Melbourne . . . sort of spending addicts.'

They wait for Eddy to come back, they stand out front and watch for him, and for strange cars that might be the department people, then Alan gets on Jamesy's bike and rides off to find his twin, who has probably cashed that withdrawal slip so he can buy a computer – or he's paid in Eva's cheque for that Tasmanian school camp.

'Kill him if you find him,' Lori says. 'Murder the moron.'

Minutes later they both turn up, one bike looking like a loaded camel. Eddy has bought a dozen pillowslips and six pillows and they are strapped onto the carry seat of Lori's bike. She's relieved it's not a computer, but he's not going to see that she's relieved. 'We didn't need them,' she yells.

'Of course we needed them.'

Nelly is out at her front gate, staring hard, both twins are out and

Eddy's not wearing his disguise. Lori waves, runs inside, Eddy behind her. He tosses the card onto the table, and the bank withdrawal licence. 'It's only a loan. I'll pay you back when I get my money.'

'We've got a million pillows, you moron.'

'They died of old age a hundred years ago. They're hard as bricks and they stink. The pension is due again and you're too mean to spit, Lori.'

'Yeah, well you're a bloody spending addict like Eva, and we don't need her in this house. We've spent too much money already. And you give me that cheque that you're still carrying around, you money-hungry moron. You give it to me now!'

'I won't, you bossy bitch. You think you're God come back as a female. If you were two hundred kilograms heavier, you'd be as bad as Mavis.'

Stress. They are all stressed. They're all standing there wide eyed and worried. This is their first real killer argument. Lori and Eddy are yelling true and not so true stuff, but it's the true bits that hurt most.

Lori stops yelling first. Someone has to stop first and Mick wants her to stop. She walks over to the mound of new plastic-wrapped pillows now tossed onto the kitchen floor and she picks one up, belts Eddy over the head with it. He falls down, pretends he's dead.

Then it's all right again, because he's only dead until Lori turns her back, then he's up and he's grabbed a pillow. He belts her with it. Then everyone has got a pillow and everyone is belting everyone else and Neil has got the old pillow from his bed. He tries to belt Timmy with it and all the stuffing falls out.

Of course the old pillows are dead. Everyone knew it, it was just that Eddy saw it. They are laughing, ripping off plastic and chucking it. There's plastic everywhere, and a mound of pillows and pillowslips that the little kids start rolling on.

'Grab that plastic before one of them suffocates himself,' Lori says.

No one goes to school. It's far too late. They put the television on and sit the little ones in front of it, and there's stereo kids' shows, one from the brick room, the other from the kitchen where Eddy is belting out two notes for the schools on Henry's typewriter.

Everyone has got the flu, except Alan and Neil, who had to do some shopping for their mother this morning, the note says. Those two are going to school at lunchtime and they'll take the notes. Mick signs them. M J Smyth-Owen.

That night they're too tired to lift their baked beans to their mouths. They've been washing walls and doors and the bathroom. They feed Mavis half a tin of baked beans and six diet crackers, which is what she had for dinner last night. She screams at them and keeps it up until Eddy makes her a Valium custard.

So tired. Legs tired, arms tired, backs that want to hit their clean new beds.

But who will dare to crawl into these beds? The new pillows, new pillowslips, the sheet bedcovers all tucked in tight, even on the bottom bunk bed which no one uses. That room looks like it's never looked in its entire life. Its walls were covered with blue striped vinyl wallpaper the same year Henry bought the second set of bunks, and it must have been tough as nails because it's only ripped a bit behind the bunks. The floor is bare boards, and with all the water and Mr Muscle Alan has been sloshing around, they came clean. And the fireplace has got a nice mantelpiece, which Alan also cleaned with the mop. They wish they had curtains now, but they've spent too much. The window only looks out onto the verandah and fence, and to the bush over the road; no one can see in, and they wouldn't see much if they did climb on the fence because the bottom window hasn't been washed in umpteen years and the new one up top is still smeary with putty from the glass man.

'Woe betides anyone who doesn't hang their stuff in that wardrobe,' Eddy warns. 'Woe betides anyone who doesn't use the drawers, who knocks my stuff on the floor, who pinches my socks, leaves one pair of underdaks on the floor. Woe betides anyone who doesn't make his bed properly every morning.'

Jamesy names him *Woebetides*.

Everyone is falling down tired, so pure proud of themselves, laughing tired. They've got this house looking as good as when Henry was alive. They've got it looking better!

But it's going to end. Those sticky-nosed buggers will walk into this place and let Mavis out and it will probably make the newspapers, like DEMON CHILDREN LOCK UP MOTHER. GO ON SPENDING SPREE WITH HER BANKCARD.

No one will see that it was the locking up, and the feeding her pills, and that diet book, that kept her alive. No one will know that she's maybe a bit more sane than she was, due to the locking up. They'll open that green door, Eddy will go home and Mavis will continue her self-destruction party. The first thing she'll do is get herself another chequebook and a new mobile phone, then she'll start stuffing and the kids will start starving. She's more agile now. She'll be more dangerous.

'We just have to sweat it out, Lori,' Eddy says, like he's reading her mind.

Maybe that's why she doesn't think too much these days, because that crazy idiot always seems to read her mind. It has got to be something about life force, like all family heads being wired into some central core.

'Thursday tomorrow. They'll be here for sure.'

'So you lot go to school and when they get here, I'll tell them I had to lock her in because she told us to lock her in when she's having a panic attack, and that she's only been in there an hour. They can't do anything to me. I'll just go back to St Kilda for a while.'

He didn't say go home. He didn't say, I'll go home to Mum.

He won't go. He's hung all his clothes in the wardrobe and shoved the case under the bottom bunk. He won't leave now – or not until they all have to leave.

the final day

No sign of the enemy on Thursday and now it's Friday, and maybe the department mob have forgotten about their house call, or they've got the flu. Please, God, let them all have pneumonia.

It's Eva's money-in-the-bank day and Eddy wants it. The kids are over their pretend flu and gone to school when Eddy locks the front door, dons his disguise and lifts the two little ones over the side fence. If anyone comes while he's gone, if they climb the gate and slide the bolt on the green door, then too bad; there are things he needs to buy.

They don't get around the back, but Mick finds their card in the letterbox that afternoon, and later on they find Matty sucking on another one that must have been poked under the locked front door.

'Back Saturday morning' they both say. So they *do* work at weekends.

One more night to scare the little ones into silence. One more night to scrape down cobwebs and wash windows, clean the bath and basin, wash the floors again.

'Wipe your feet on Eddy's new mat before you come inside, I said. Do you want that emergency care lady to get you again?'

'Dow,' Matty replies, but Neil is not too sure. He's into new experiences.

'Brush that soot off the stove, Mick.'

'Whose underdaks are these? Who left them on the bathroom floor? What do you think my new laundry basket is for? Decoration?'

They are the army of the little people, digging in for battle, determined to survive the adult attack. While a pasta stew is cooking, half of the kids are inside hitting the windows with Windex and old rags while the other half work outside with hose, broom, bucket of water and dishwashing detergent, and by six o'clock you can see through the windows for the first time in fourteen years, so they hang the two navy blue sheets Eddy bought for curtains, and the bunk room smells like a material shop.

Mavis's room smells like a cross between a public loo, a budgie cage and a mouldy sweat factory. It's disgusting and Mavis looks disgusting. The kids stand at her window when they deliver her dinner – a pile of cabbage, carrot and broccoli, with a taste of pasta stew poured over it. She hates cabbage and broccoli, but that's all she's getting. Just looking at her, listening to her tonight, makes them know their work has all been in vain.

'Your mouth is as disgusting as this room, Mavis. Clean it up and we'll give you a packet of chewing gum to clean your mouth,' Lori tries.

Mavis has never been into cleaning, and her language isn't fit for general exhibition, so they take the little kids inside and put them in the bath because they sure aren't getting into those clean beds with dirty feet.

They are studying Mavis again at eight and she hasn't had any Valium since midday so she doesn't like being studied. They gave her a loo brush, months back, which has never been used for its intended purpose. They've given her deodorant soap and roll-on deodorant and deodorant powder and cans of air-freshener, which are her favourite weapons.

'So we open the door tomorrow and we all take off and leave her to it.'

'And where do we sleep tomorrow night?'

'What if we don't give her any Valium tonight, then give her a double dose in the morning before they come?' Eddy says.

'Like, wear her out, then zap her hard,' Jamesy says.

It might work. When she sleeps, she sleeps heavy.

She's sitting on the couch when they pass her coffee through the window, strong coffee, which is supposed to keep people awake. The couch looks putrid and so does she, like her hair hasn't been washed in weeks, and probably not combed in days. She's got combs, she's got her hairbrush. They bought a baby's bath at the market three weeks back, and maybe it's about big enough for her to get her feet in, though her feet don't look as if they've ever been in it. They gave her the hand shower attachment Henry used when he showered her and she hasn't used that either, except as a whip which she aims at heads through the window. She could have connected it to the taps, could have had a fast shower if she'd wanted to. The walls are brick and the floor only cement. It would dry. She's got towels, got a bottle of shampoo.

'We'll give her another coffee before we go to bed and something to eat, like biscuits.'

'Popcorn has got less calories.'

'Who cares about calories? She won't when she gets out tomorrow. Give her a packet of chocolate biscuits.'

Lori makes the second strong coffee at midnight. She gives her four chocolate biscuits – and a brand-new tent with long sleeves. She made it, and it took more than an hour to make, too – it took from half-past eight to half-past eleven, but she had to do something to keep herself awake so she could make that coffee to keep Mavis awake.

Mavis sure looks tired. She's sitting on the couch yawning, but she comes for the coffee and stares at the biscuits. 'What's going on?' she says, and it's the first normal sentence she's said since she's been in there.

'I've been making you a winter dress,' Lori yawns.

It's floral windcheater material, bought at the market weeks back,

273

brownish with big orange flowers and green leaves all over it, but it was cheap and extra wide, so tonight Lori experimented, tried to make long sleeves by curving the sides a bit beneath the armholes. She couldn't make buttonholes on the shoulder, so she recycled a long zip fastener from an old windcheater, stitched it in from neck to navel, and broke two needles doing it too.

Mavis doesn't even look at the dress. She's too busy chomping on her biscuits. Lori stands at the window, watching her chomp.

'Open that bloody door,' Mavis says.

'Have a wash, why don't you? You look filthy,' Lori says. 'And wash your hair too. You've probably got nits.' Shouldn't have said that, but what's the use anyway? What was the use of nearly killing her neck to make that dress? No use.

So tired. Everything is aching and everyone else has been in bed for hours. That's where she's going too. Mick removed the globe from his light before he went to bed; they intend leaving Mavis's light turned on all night. It might help to keep her awake.

The morning actually comes before Lori closes her eyes, and that might sound stupid but it seems true. And . . . and Mavis is wearing her new tent!

It looks like a second skin, stretched to fit. It looks seriously atrocious. Like it shapes all of her bulges instead of skimming them and it reaches down to the floor so it's tight at her ankles too; it hobbles her. But it sure makes you see that she's thinner! And how the hell she wriggled into it, God only knows. And how she didn't pinch her stomach to death doing up that zipper, who knows? She's sort of sitting like a trussed-up giant turkey on the couch, sort of nodding, the television playing some slam-bang-whiz kids' cartoon show. She sees the kids at the window and wakes up enough to do the usual.

They wait, clock-watching and keeping an eye on that window, refusing to let her go to sleep.

Then it's nine o'clock.

'All systems go,' Eddy says and they pass in a highly medicated cocoa, two slices of toast with butter, apricot jam and Aropax. She's tired, but she sort of hobbles over to claim her breakfast and eats the lot standing up, which is probably easier than sitting down. Then fifteen minutes after the last slurp of cocoa, she's flaked on her bed doing her chain-saw imitation.

Fast then, they are in the brick room, sweeping, washing, tacking a scrap of leftover white lace curtain at the window, tacking shade cloth on the outside, tacking the old brown curtain to the brick room ceiling so it hangs in front of the illegal loo, working fast, working quiet, while Jamesy stands guard at the door, ready to shoot the bolt and lock the kids in with her if she moves. They'll go out the window. They'll get Mick out somehow.

All that tacking makes Mavis's eyes flutter, otherwise she's not moving, and as soon as they stop with their tacking, she starts her chain-sawing snore, sounding just like when Bert Matthews prunes his apple trees.

'Maybe four Valium was too many. There isn't so much of her now,' Alan says.

They glance at the sheet and the pillowslips. They are dirty, but they can't do much about that; she's lying on them.

The clock ticks its way to eleven. The kitchen has been swept again, the bathroom checked for underdaks, and they are waiting, sweating. Then the car stops out front and Jamesy runs through the house spraying air-freshener while Eddy unlocks the brick-room door, opens it slow, prepared for the charge.

No charge. Mavis is still flat out on her back. Jamesy gives her feet a spray with air-freshener and her feet don't even flinch. He and Eddy place the quilt over her, pull it up to her chin, then down again, due to it's exposing her filthy feet. They sidle by the end of the bed, spray the couch with air-freshener, toss the tartan blanket over it and sidle back to the door. Jamesy waits there, on door duty, while Eddy disappears down to the chook-pen. That's their latest plan, made ten minutes ago. They don't really know if it was Eva who dobbed on them or just one of the neighbours; they've made so many plans and discarded as many, but there's no more time to wonder if they discarded the right ones or not. The department people are knocking at their door and Mick is turning the key.

'Good morning. Is your mother in?' the man says, his nostrils flaring as he sniffs the scent of Forest Glen. He's poked his nose through this door many times before and the scent and greeting were not so sweet.

'She's asleep,' Mick replies.

'She's on a strict diet now and it makes her tired,' Lori adds. But the buggers are coming in anyhow and not waiting to be invited.

People have learned to come to this address in pairs. The man is familiar, the woman a stranger. She looks around, sees age, sees dilapidation, holds her jacket closer to her shoulders as she walks the dark passage; the male's eyebrows rise, become lost beneath a sparse sandy fringe, when he's hit in the eye by the blue kitchen. It's so tidy, it's almost painful to behold. He sees the curtains and the clean cloth on the table and a bunch of red geraniums in a posh vase bought from the reject shop. He looks up, sees the blue ceiling, but no Mrs Smyth-Owen, or her couch and lolly papers.

She is the reason he is in this place.

'Can you tell your mother we're here,' he says. Lori shrugs, opens the back door then walks out to the brick room. The two follow her and the little ones follow them.

Mavis is snoring, smelling of Forest Glen. Her hair is very red, daggy and greasy. She didn't wash it, but she looks sort of peaceful, sort of vulnerable lying there on her back, rattling the rafters.

'The doctor said she needs her rest,' Lori whispers. 'Her heart is weak, due to her . . . her morbid obesity.' She got that one from the television. 'She's taking a pile of tablets every day since she had her last heart attack.'

'Mmm,' the woman murmurs, and the man raises his eyebrows to the woman. They turn, return to the kitchen, and maybe they are pleased there is no adult around, which gives them the freedom to stick their noses into the fridge, the freezer, the cupboards. They're packed with food. The woman looks in a pot on the stove. One of Lori's pink-sausage stews is bubbling there and it smells good.

The male walks through to the lounge, checks out the two beds and Matty's cot. The carpet is rotten, and the curtains, and pretty much everything in that room, except the new doonas and the green sheet bedcovers. Then they go to the west bedroom, Lori tailing them, Mick bringing up the rear, the little ones behind Mick. The four bunks are made up hospital-tight, by Eddy, their navy blue sheet bedcovers tucked in.

The duo 'mmm' at each other and Lori knows why – because this room looks like a room. They walk into Mick's room, which until a week ago was a dog's breakfast of a wrecked bed and chucked stuff. Now it houses only one bed, covered by Eddy's ex quilt and cover. There is an old desk complete with typewriter, a bookshelf full of books; it looks like a study–bedroom. It's also the most dangerous room because it backs onto Mavis's pen and it's got that hole drilled through for the extension cord. A lot of noise comes through that little hole.

Please, God, let her stay asleep. She usually wakes at eleven and it's after eleven, but maybe it's her empty stomach that wakes her, and this morning her stomach isn't empty.

Mick has got the bookcase against his shared wall, and his wardrobe. He's pushed his old desk against the west wall. He's got a swivel office chair too, which he picked up at a garage sale for two dollars, and a desk light, found long ago at the dump. The light only needed a wire connected up and a new screw in the swivel bit of the chair.

The visitors ask Mick a lot of questions, and he answers in his quiet voice. They look at Henry's typewriter, which Eddy might think is ratshit but Mick is learning to love, because his writing is worse ratshit and always will be. They start acting a bit different then, not so condescending. Mick is fifteen now, and he looks fifteen and sounds it, and he sounds serious about finishing high school and going to university, so serious they almost believe him. Lori almost believes him. She leads the visitors out of his room, leads them hopefully towards the front door. They sidetrack into her bedroom.

This furniture isn't old junk; it's a proper bedroom suite. They open the wardrobe, which is still full of Henry's clothes, still full of the smell of Henry. He always hung stuff, had a fetish for hanging stuff, which Eddy must have inherited.

'Our mother can't bring herself to throw his clothes away yet,' Lori says. 'She had a complete nervous collapse, from grief. It's been a . . . an extremely challenging time for her but she's getting better – as long as she's got no stress.'

'Mmm,' the woman says, nods, smiles benignly at small beings who have crept closer, who now stare up at her with wide, trusting eyes. Lori backs out to the passage, opens the front door. They don't take the hint. They want Mavis.

Some prime minister in the olden days once said that life wasn't meant to be easy, and oh boy, was he right.

Back in the kitchen, the man is looking at his watch, the woman studying the border of postcards Blu-tacked along the eastern kitchen wall, little kids surrounding her. Maybe they know her from that time they were in emergency care.

Timmy pulls at her skirt, and Lori hopes his hand is clean. 'Dat is a pitcher of da Colosim from Eba,' he says.

'Colosseum,' Lori corrects, draws him away, checks his hand. It's clean enough. She offers tea. The visitors accept stale coffee, sit, then the woman asks about the twins.

So it was Eva who dobbed on them. Lori makes the coffee in new mugs, opens a packet of biscuits and decides it's no use trying to hide Eddy. She sends Alan to find him, and Eddy comes from the chook-house with an ice-cream container full of eggs.

'Pleased to meet you guys,' he says, offers his hand. The man takes Eddy's hand, shakes it. The woman just stares from one twin to the other. They are still the same person to strangers, though to Lori and the kids, they are not even a bit the same.

'Your aunt was previously married to your father, Edward?

I believe your father wished you to remain with your aunt, who you have lived with since nineteen – '

'Since we were around two. We both had operations at two and again at five. Want to see my scar? Mine's bigger than Alan's.' He doesn't wait, but flashes it.

'Mmm. And you lived with your aunt until last February?'

'Eddy did. Alan didn't. Our mother never wanted the twins to stay with Eva and Alice, but once those two got hold of them, they wouldn't give them back,' Lori says.

'We want to live here now,' Alan says.

''Cause Eva pinched all Mavis's dollars, 'cause Eva is called a lebsian,' Neil says. The woman's mouth drops four inches. They see her tonsils. And Jesus, how does that little twit remember that word? Nobody has said that word in months. He could have a brain in his head if he'd stop pulling faces long enough to find it.

'You shouldn't say that,' Lori chastises.

'Mavis says that,' Neil defends, but he's looking out back, looking into the brick room, looking right at what is snoring in the brick room. He doesn't like Mavis and celery and broccoli, so he says no more. Matty crawls up on Lori's knee, cuddles his face against her, sucks hard on his dummy.

The visitors toss each other a few meaningful glances, then the man stands, walks to the brick room. Mavis has rolled over and her quilt has fallen to the floor; she's showing all her humps and bumps through the colourful material, showing two very dirty bare feet, but there's not a lot of light in there and the visitors are standing back.

'What time does your mother usually wake?'

'It depends on . . . on things. She wanted to get the house looking nice so she was up at dawn and she exhausted herself,' Lori says. It's after twelve and Mavis is starting to lick her lips between snores. It's a sure sign she's dreaming of food and thinking of waking. 'At weekends, when we're home to look after the little ones, she occasionally sleeps all afternoon.'

'She panics if she gets woken out of a deep sleep, thinks something is wrong with one of us kids,' Eddy adds.

'The last time she had a heart attack we had to get the doctor and about six men to get her up off the floor. We can give you his phone number if you like.'

The woman looks at the man. She's not here to make things worse, and she's got a bad back, can't lift a thing, and she's not going to attempt to –

The man raises his eyebrows. It's Saturday, after all. He's got a wife and his own kids and he wants to watch the football this afternoon.

Mick is not doing much, not saying much either, but he wants those visitors away from that green door. 'Would you like to see our vegetable garden?' he says.

They follow him to his onion patch. He's proud of those onions, which the bugs leave alone. He pulls two, offers them to the woman. She takes them, can't do much else; doesn't want them – they give her wind. 'Goodness me. That's wonderful. Wonderful.' She turns away before he can pull any more and she walks back to the kitchen, glancing at the sleeping mound as she passes, and at Jamesy, who hasn't left his post beside the green door. The man walks back, the kids at his heels. He's holding a bunch of silverbeet, probably full of bugs.

'Perhaps your mother could arrange another time . . .?' He speaks to Lori, who seems to be in charge. She nods, tries not to do it too emphatically. He juggles the silverbeet, offers a card. 'School, Edward.' He's looking from one twin to the other. 'You haven't been attending school.'

'I've got an IQ of a hundred and seventy. Alan makes sure I keep up – or I make sure he keeps up,' Eddy says, takes the offered card, puts it in his wallet beside a twenty. The man notices the twenty, loses his eyebrows. Twelve-year-old boys with mothers on supporting pensions shouldn't be carrying twenty-dollar notes around.

Eddy knows it too. He's like ten steps ahead of the rest of the world. 'Mum said I'd be going to school on Monday. I've got to go to the shops to buy some books today.'

'And why were you not enrolled before?' the woman asks.

'It's a long story.'

'Mmm?' the woman says. She's got time to listen. And she puts Mick's bloody onions down – on the clean tablecloth, and they are covered in dirt. Then she sits down again. Bugger. The man doesn't sit.

'Mum probably wouldn't want me to tell you,' Eddy says.

'Mmm?'

'Well, it's because of Alice, Eva's partner.'

'Mmm?'

'She's been putting the fear of God into Mum for months.'

'Mmm?'

Eddy is inventive, but he's working hard on this one. 'Well, with a heart condition and social phobia and her obesity, she's got enough problems without having to worry about me being kidnapped every time I leave the house.'

'Kidnapped?'

'Yes. They've kidnapped me before and threatened to get me if I go to school. We blame anxiety for Mum's last heart attack, don't we, Lori?' He's running out of steam. He needs help. Mick isn't saying a word. He's leaning against the kitchen door looking pale. Alan is standing beside the fridge, looking paler.

'Aunty Eva has been . . . sort of appalling to Mum,' Lori says. 'Like writing terrible letters all the time and getting her solicitor to send legal letters and stuff.' She hunts through a drawer full of junk, finds that last mad letter from Eva, which is perfect evidence, like the *loathsome, depraved, obese slut* bit, and the *born of corruption* bit, and the bit about cursing and wishing her dead. It sounds totally mad. Neil has drawn a picture on the rear of it but it's only a fire-breathing dragon picture with red hair and probably celery and broccoli growing around its feet. She shrugs, offers the letter, right side up. The woman reads it, passes it to the man. And does it make his eyebrows disappear. She hands them another, this one from Mr Watts. It's sort of threatening.

They tut-tut for a bit, shut up for a bit while the kids stand around, waiting for the buggers to go.

'You have more – '

'Our mother usually burns them. They . . . they upset her, make her scared stiff to let Eddy out of her sight.'

'I was always their favourite – after Alice decided I was a borderline genius. Alan's IQ is only about a hundred and fifty, and he gave Eva a hard time when he found out our father had left her because he was a bit old-fashioned about her and Alice having a lesbian relationship.'

'Eddy said lebsian.' Neil pulls at Lori's T-shirt. 'Lori, Eddy said – '

'Anyway . . . anyway, Mum knew that if I left the house Alice would probably snatch me like she did the last time.'

'The last time, Edward?' the man says.

'I thought she would have told you about that.' The visitors shake their heads. 'That's Mum for you. She likes to keep family things in the family and that's the main trouble with her. If she'd just talk to people, just let it out, she'd get better.'

'Not that talking to her psychiatrist does Eva much good,' Lori says.

'You were saying, Edward, that your aunt's partner . . . grabbed you.'

'Yes. When I was just a kid, about nine. I was playing in the drive one day and Alice picked me up and threw me into the back seat of the car and the next thing I knew, I was in England for twelve months. I think they drugged me with Eva's pills. She's hooked on pills. She's got an eating disorder too. Like, she's scared to eat in case she gets fat like Mavis and her father, so she's always sick.'

It's twelve-thirty. Mavis's eating disorder will be waking her any minute. Lori wants Eddy to shut up now. And saying about pills – he'll get Neil doing his Valium show-and-tell bit in a minute. But the visitors are both watching Eddy and shaking their heads, understanding so much more now. That poor woman. Saint Mavis, the martyr.

Lori picks up the onions, looks at the patch of dirt on her new tablecloth, which is keeping her eyes away from the visitors.

'Mum knew once you got here, and saw things were okay, that you'd throw a spanner in their works. She said this morning. "Get your books today, Eddy. When the department people get here, they will see that you're so much better off with your family. We mightn't have much, but we've got love in this family".'

Big-mouth actor, moron. Lori wants these people out. She walks, with the onions, toward the passage. 'I'll tell Mum what you said about making another appointment.'

The man looks at his watch, looks at the front door. Eddy is still talking. 'She'll be disappointed she didn't get to talk to you, because she also wanted to speak about getting me and Alan back on her dependants list for the pension.'

'We'll see that she gets the forms,' the woman says. 'If she has any further threats from your aunt or her partner, she can, of course, take out a restraining order.'

'That's a last resort.'

And finally the woman is standing. She takes a last look at Mavis then walks. They're on the front verandah, Lori straddling the worst broken floorboard. She pushes the onions at the woman, who takes them, looks at the broken board, at the house, and God it looks bad, sort of grey and tumbledown, guttering hanging, weatherboards hanging half off.

They walk to the car. But the buggers don't get in. They walk over the road to Nelly's. 'She'll give them an earful about Mavis.'

'She mightn't be home,' Eddy says. 'Someone picked her up about half-past ten.'

'That's over two hours ago.'

They watch at the lounge-room window, wait. Then the two are back at their car. They're driving away.

And they hear the green door slam and for five minutes the door quakes and the ceiling shakes and the neighbours are probably out watering their gardens. Nelly isn't. She wasn't home. Sometimes you can almost believe there is a God.

They make a coffee and a slice of toast and Aropax jam, then remember Mavis has already had one tablet – too bad. Upping the dose of Aropax might alter her brain waves faster.

'The welfare people said you were doing an excellent job, Mave,' Eddy says.

'They said they're going to send up some forms for you to fill in, to get Alan and Eddy on your dependants list,' Lori adds.

Getting money out of the government always made Mavis happy before; it doesn't work today. 'I'll fill in some bloody forms. I'll fill in your bloody death certificates before you're all much older. You open that bloody door now, or by Jesus, when you do, you're going to be very sorry.'

'That's why we won't open the door. You start acting like a normal sane person and then we'll open it,' Lori says.

This is communication. Maybe not the sort they'd hoped for, but at least there is a backward and forwarding of words! The toast and coffee are tempting. She claims them and walks to her television, turns it on and sits down. She's still yelling but not so loud, just that she wants more toast. 'And put some bloody butter on it!'

wally johnson

The market will be crowded today, due to the sun is out. The kids don't need anything, except potatoes, but they're in a celebratory mood so they take off early, all of them. Those social workers might have been pains in the bum, but they've made the twins free, and free together for once. People are staring at them too when they meet head on, on the bridge. Mick is scooting along on Lori's bike, the two little ones are in the pram and the rest take turns at pushing it.

And typical, what happens when you go to the market when you're not looking for anything? You find everything, that's what happens.

At the first stall Mick pounces on a little bike with training wheels and it's exactly what he wants for some experiment. It only costs five dollars. About two stalls up from the bike, Lori finds a roll of patterned curtain material with birds on it, which they can use for the little kids' room; their curtains are pretty much rags. They'll have to do something about that room eventually because it looks like crap beside those other rooms.

'Cheep-cheep,' Eddy says.

It's cheap all right, and sort of water damaged, but the lady gives them the whole roll for twelve dollars. They have an early lunch, a burned sausage on bread, and they walk again, head for the vegetable stalls, get their potatoes and Mavis's celery.

Then Eddy goes and finds a stall with boxes and boxes of old wallpaper. He digs around there for half an hour until he digs out five rolls that actually match. Twelve dollars the lot, the lady says. Eddy offers her ten and she takes it; the sun has gone, black clouds are blowing in, and rain and wallpaper stalls just don't mix, due to the glue on the back of the rolls.

They're in the last row and heading home to feed Mavis when they see the lounge suite. It's on a trailer and it looks almost new with its bright grass green knobbly material. The guy has got '$150' on it so nobody wants it – except Eddy. He's got his ivy and bamboo wallpaper in that pram, which he's going to stick around the top bit of the little kids' room above the panelling – so he says.

'That green suite will match the ivy. We'll turn it back into a lounge room.'

'And what do we do with the little kids' beds?'

'Get rid of them,' Jamesy says. 'And the kids.'

'You and Mick have got your own rooms, and we've got three in ours. That's discrimination. You take one little kid each and we'll put Neil in with Mavis,' Eddy says.

Neil nicks off, gets lost and they have to separate, spend the next half hour looking for the little bugger. And they haven't fed Mavis. She'll be yelling her lungs out.

'We've got to go. Come on. It's going to rain.'

But that lounge suite is still sitting on that trailer, so bright that it keeps drawing the eye. Maybe it's one of those fate things. Maybe the kids are still on a high from yesterday, but they start walking around it, talking around it and watching for other buyers. Not one person even looks at it.

'If I can get it for a hundred, can I have it?' Eddy says.

'Don't be stupid. And he won't let you have it for a hundred.'

'Want to bet?'

Like a school of sharks rounding up a diver, they circle that trailer, their circle growing smaller, like the price tag on the green suite has grown smaller. It's down to $120.

'How much?' Eddy asks as soon as rain starts spitting down.

'What's it to you?'

'My mother needs a new couch.'

'I'm giving it away at a hundred and twenty and I'm not splitting it up.' They can see his price tag, they can also see he's wanting to toss a tarp over the suite. Eddy pokes at the couch, then the bloke says: 'She can have it for a hundred and ten and that's as low as I'm prepared to go. It was my mother-in-law's and it's hardly been used.'

Eddy shrugs. 'She said not to get green. She reckons green is unlucky. How long did your mother-in-law have it before she died?' Eddy asks.

'I told you. It's damn near brand new. If your mother is interested, you'd better get her because I'm packing it in for today.'

'We'll take it off your hands for fifty and we'll dye it.'

'Stop wasting my time, you cheeky little bugger,' the guy says.

Eddy walks away, but the spits of rain are getting bigger. The weather is bargaining for him. The guy gets the tarp over half of his trailer then the wind whips it back, flips it. Mick holds one end, but Neil has climbed up to one of the chairs. He jumps on it, and they discover its wobbly leg.

'Get off, Neil. It's broken. You'll break your neck,' Lori yells.

'It only needs screwing in,' the trader says. 'Where is your mother?'

'Sick, and she's pretty weighty.' Eddy is on the trailer, upending the chair with the wobbly leg. Lori has claimed Neil, and she's threatening to put him in the pram with the celery.

'She can have it for ninety-five.'

'How much extra to deliver it?'

'Ninety-five and I'll deliver it when I finish up here,' the trader says.

'Sixty-five and you've got a deal,' Eddy bargains. That's what Eva would have done.

'Piss off. You're keeping the serious buyers away.'

'Okay. We'll go to seventy-five and that's our top offer. Take it or leave it.'

'You cheapskate little bugger.' He's looking at the couch, looking at the junk set out on a second tarp, looking at the sky. The kids are not moving. 'Show me the colour of your money and I might start taking you seriously,' the guy says.

Eddy pulls out a five and some change. Lori digs deep for two fives and a handful of coins. They pool it, count it. 'We can make almost twenty dollars deposit to hold it and my sister will go home and get the rest.'

'Where do you live?'

'Down the end of Dawson Street. Out the East.'

'Oh, you'd be Mavis's tribe,' he says. 'Why didn't you say so? She can pay me the rest when I get there.'

It's funny the way he sort of changes his tune. Like, everyone seems to know Mavis, but they don't hate her. Maybe it's pity. Lori doesn't like pity. She eyes the guy up and down, watches him pocket the notes, count the coins.

'Do you want me to bring your other stuff over for you?'

Jamesy is pushing the new bike, Alan has got the roll of bird material on his shoulder. Matty and Timmy are sharing the pram with vegetables and wallpaper. Where's Neil?

'Neil. Get back here!'

'Thanks,' Eddy says and he starts unloading the pram. Jamesy's not too sure about giving up the bike, but it gets tossed on the trailer, which the guy has now stopped trying to cover with his tarp. That's their lounge suite and too bad if it gets wet.

'How's Mavis doing these days?' he says.

'She's sick. Got a bad heart. We have to do all the shopping.'

'Yeah? I've heard a bit of talk about her being crook. I'm real sorry to hear that. You give her my regards and tell her Wally Johnson said they miss the laughs at the pub.'

Miss the laughs? Five sets of eyes stare at him, but he's loading his other junk now, and on top of their shopping. They walk off.

'Is he talking about the same Mavis?' Jamesy asks.

'Seventy-five dollars. It's a steal,' Eddy says. 'So, what are we going to use for the rest of the money?'

'What are we going to do with a lounge suite, more like it?'

'What if Wally gets there before we do? What if Mavis hears him – or if he hears her?'

'What if he nicks off with our twenty dollars as well as our other stuff?' They are circling that trailer again, watching their new lounge suite get wet, Jamesy giving voice to what a few of them are thinking. They haven't had much of a chance to learn trust.

Lori shakes her head. 'He's okay,' she says. 'And if he's not, then I think I know one of his daughters from school.' She turns the pram for home. 'I'm pretty sure he's Wendy Johnson's father and I know where she lives. I chased her home from school one day when we were about seven.'

The spitting rain has turned to a gusty shower, which looks as if it might last for a while. No one is dressed for wet weather. 'Someone take this pram. I'll dink Mick home and we'll call in at the ATM and get out the rest of the money.'

'Make Mave a medicated coffee before Wally gets there,' Eddy suggests.

The suite is dripping on the front verandah, but it will dry; they've moved the little kids' beds and cot into the middle of the room, due to Eddy wants to start wallpapering, like, yesterday. He hasn't got a clue how to do it, wants to run the paper around, horizontal, not bother cutting it. Mick and Lori have seen it done before. Henry and Martin were good at wallpapering.

Mick's bad leg being no good for climbing ladders, he gets the job of measuring and cutting the paper on the kitchen table, then Lori rolls it, wets it in the bath, runs with it to Alan, who is halfway up the ladder. He hands it to Eddy and the two of them flatten it on the wall, which isn't easy. There is a picture rail halfway up and brown wooden panelling below it, so it's only the bit above the rail they have to paper. They rip the first bit, wreck the second, get the hang of it with the third and by the time they hang the fifth, they even start cutting the top and bottom bits off almost straight.

It's faster than painting; it's magical stuff, because when it's done, which isn't until after school the next day, it looks truly excellent – once the bubbles and wrinkles dry out. They wish they'd painted the ceiling, which probably hasn't been painted in fifty years. It's a dirty brown.

Pension day, and white paint is on special at Kmart. It takes two coats to cover up most of the dirt, but it doesn't take long to paint it with all the mobile big kids taking turns up Henry's ladder. They've got paint left over too, so they paint the passage ceiling, only one coat, which doesn't cover up all of the dirt, but the passage is dark unless they put a new globe in the light; they don't put in a new globe.

But that lounge room! They can't stop looking at it. Every morning when they get out of bed, they look at it; every night when they come home from school, they look at it. The wallpaper has got a green ivy pattern with brown bamboo on white and with the white ceiling, it looks like a proper room.

So the little kids get evicted the next Saturday.

Matty, who has grown heaps, has been rattling the bars of his worn-out cot for a year, so they toss it and move him and Timmy into Mavis's bed, then squeeze a single bed in beside it for Lori. Mick cops Neil. Having Mavis only one wall away might scare some sense into him.

It's a bit like the old Henry days, playing musical beds. They get to talking about him, like how, in the old days, Henry used to cook rotten stews and cook bugs in the silverbeet and how Martin always called it bug stew. They talk about Vinnie and Greg, just memory stuff, and for an hour Eddy sits listening; he can't join in, due to he didn't know Henry, Vinnie or Greg.

Then Alan starts on about Henry's flowers, Henry's songs, and Eddy gets up and walks to the bathroom, has a shower, like for half an hour.

He's a hard one to work out, so quick-witted that it's like living with an out-of-control computer sometimes; he's not scared to hit buttons just to see what happens, but he goes quiet too, and he disappears into the shower or to the shops, just takes off to be by himself sometimes.

'You'll wash yourself down the plughole one day,' Alan yells.

our own faces

The old wardrobe that has lived forever in front of the lounge-room fireplace almost flattens Lori when they're trying to turn it on its side so they can get it out the door. It's huge and heavy and it takes them half of Sunday morning to rehouse it in Mick's room – against the dangerous wall, beside the other wardrobe, so he's now got almost matching wall-to-wall wardrobes, which he glues and screws to the floor, wall and each other, which might slow Mavis down if she ever comes through those weatherboards. This means they have to move Mick's bookshelves into the passage, which also means that they'll have to put a globe in the passage light so people can see what book they're looking for, which means another coat of paint for that passage ceiling. It's never-ending once you start on cleaning up a house, and that's why people don't start doing it.

The lounge room is big once all the junk has been cleared out, but the carpet looks terrible, stained and faded into odd rectangles and blotches, white paint spills and bits of stuck-on wallpaper. Eddy won't have a bar of it, or of trying to scrub it clean.

'Pitch it,' he says, and he and Jamesy start ripping it up before anyone can stop them. They find wide, dark-stained boards beneath it, like the floor in the bunk room, and like the bunk room floor, it washes clean after about ten buckets of water.

They start on the fireplace then, start wiping away years of dust, picking dust off in furry clumps. They find a few dusty books and

Henry's old wallet with his driver's licence and seven dollars in it, which he lost, like, years ago, then had to get a new licence. They find a hired video that got lost one year, an old dummy melted into the wood. They find a really nice glass or crystal vase and two dollars twenty in coins, and also Martin's old swimming trophy, but best of all, beneath the dust and junk and cobwebs, they find the mantelpiece and a long oval mirror which hasn't got a crack in it.

It's a true lost treasure. It's something grand and it belongs to them.

'It's an antique,' Eddy says, up on a chair, reaching high to drag down an old shirt someone must have pitched up there; he uses it to dust the carved bits of wood, right at the top. 'How come no one ever noticed this room, never knew about this fireplace?'

'We knew it was there. Henry put the wardrobe in front to stop the wind blowing down the chimney,' Mick says. 'The top was always there. You papered around it. You saw it.'

'I didn't know it was there,' Jamesy says. He's climbing too, wiping at it. 'Look at those fancy carved bits around the frame.'

'If we had a bit of furniture polish we could get those scratch marks off. Mum got a really bad mark out of the dining room table with a bottle of furniture oil.' Eddy's hand is running over the timber, sort of loving it, then he heads for the laundry to find an old bottle of O-Cedar oil he's seen in there someplace, and he finds it – probably left there by the last person who owned this place. They spend the next hour sloshing it on panelled walls and fireplace, spilling it on the floor, then taking turns at sitting on an old pillow while someone drags it around and around the lounge room, rubbing the oil in. They use so much of the stuff that they have to go out on the verandah to dodge the smell.

Their suite is still a bit damp and one chair leg still wobbly. Mick fixes it by screwing it in and it's solid as a rock, which they discover in the hour it takes to haul that suite inside and move it around until it looks just right. The couch is against disintegrating curtains, hiding the worst of the bottom bits. The two chairs are in the corners, one each side of the fireplace. It looks seriously excellent – except for the curtains.

'We need new curtains, a classy picture for over the mantel-piece and a shade for the light globe,' Eddy says.

'I'll order a chandelier tomorrow,' Lori says. 'And a Rembrandt.' She's been studying famous artists at school this term.

It's when she's cooking Mavis scrambled eggs that she thinks of Henry's potting shed and remembers an oval picture frame the last owner left in there, and she's over the fence, running through the rain to retrieve it, wiping off a hundred years of dust and spiders. Lori always liked that old oval frame, which is still intact, even the glass is intact, and the hanging wire. Even the photograph is intact.

'That's an antique, or the old dame in it is,' she says, presenting it to Eddy.

They hang that hard-faced old dame high over their mantel-piece and she glowers down at the group now testing their lounge suite, and maybe they know why whoever dumped her in the shed dumped her there. She's making this room feel freezing cold, or that damp suite is.

Eddy wants to light a fire. Lori and Mick tell him he'll set the chimney alight and he'll burn their new lounge room and them too.

'We've got to dry out the couch. My bum's wet,' he says and he goes out back and gets a huge block of wood that's always been too hard to cut. It's soaking wet and so is he, but he gets some dry kindling and a pile of newspaper and he's setting light to the lot. That block sputters itself dry then the flames catch on and the fire starts tossing out heat. It doesn't even smoke.

Late now, bedtime late; no one wants to leave that fire, but they get rid of the little ones, tuck them in tight, tell them an old fairy tale that ends with 'and they lived happily ever after, now go to sleep'. When Lori returns to her place on the couch she's got the box of photographs from the top of Henry's wardrobe. They sit close, shuffling photographs like cards, just looking at them.

There's one of a beautiful girl with a mop of long, fluffy hair. She's holding a rose.

'Who's that?' Jamesy says.

'I don't know. Probably from Henry's England. She might be an old girlfriend or something,' Lori says.

'It's Mavis,' Alan says.

'Crap.'

'It is. When she was seventeen,' Eddy says. 'We've got a big one of that same photo in St Kilda. It's coloured. The rose is orange. It matches her hair.

They all hush as they pass the photograph around and stare at it. Martin would have known Mavis when she looked like this, Lori thinks. Martin would have remembered her like this. That's why he used to get so mad about her being fat. He could remember what was lost.

It is her. Lori can see it now she knows. She can see it in the eyes and the hand holding the rose. 'My God!'

Mick finds a photograph of Henry, the one Lori has always loved. He doesn't look much older than Martin, and he looks a bit like Martin – except he's dressed old-fashioned posh. 'That was taken before he left England.'

'When he was happy,' Lori adds. He looks happy, looks so young and . . . and like the whole world belongs to him.

'If we want pictures on the walls, we should get these copied,' Alan says. 'They can make copies of old photographs. I saw some before and afters in that photo shop window.'

'It would cost a fortune.'

'Probably no more than a carton of cigarettes used to cost. We can afford to have our own face looking down at us instead of that hard old dame's. She spoils the frame,' Alan says. 'What's the use of hanging up other people's ancestors?'

Our own face? He can't mean Mavis's face, he must mean Henry's, Lori thinks. He's looking at both.

They sit on, and decide which one they'll have – if it doesn't cost too much. Lori says she wants Henry – though she'd like to give her vote to Mavis; it's a gorgeous photo. She always thought it was one of Henry's old girlfriends, always used to wish that he'd married her. And he did – sort of.

'They must have looked good together when they were young,' Eddy says. 'If I had my computer and scanner I could make those two photos into one.'

'You haven't got your computer and Mavis probably wasn't even born when that photo of Henry was taken. Eva is fourteen years older than her and Henry was twenty years older.'

'What was she doing nicking off with him for? He was old enough to be her father.'

'Maybe she had a father fixation,' Lori says.

They talk frame costs, and Mick, who is on day-watch duty tomorrow and Tuesday, says he'll go and check out how much two photos and one frame would cost, and see if the shop can put one of the photos in the old dame's frame. With Eddy starting full-time school, they plan to each take two sick days per fortnight to do day-watch, but not the same days each fortnight, just in case the school starts to smell a rat.

Jamesy makes cocoa all round and he drops off a mug at Mavis's window, plus two diet crackers with Vegemite. No Valium. They are going to have to cut her off Valium or ring up Martin, get him to phone the doctor and see if he'll give them another prescription – or try to get Donny to go to the doctor and cry nerves.

'We'll have to move the television in here,' Jamesy says.

'If the little kids are watching television in here the suite will get wrecked.' This room sort of belongs to Eddy. He created it, so they agree that the television can stay in the kitchen. 'Next time those social workers come, we'll sit them down in here and give them a cup of tea,' he says.

They laugh, picture it. Picture a coffee table. They'll have to get a coffee table like Nelly's, and a small plastic lacy cloth to hang diagonally over it.

Eddy starts playing the welfare dame, Henry's old reading glasses perched on his nose, then Jamesy takes off the man, keeps lifting his eyebrows. The two of them get a real act going. 'Mmm. We're here for another visit, Mrs Smyth-Owen. I've brought along the "Mother of the Year" medal for you. Mmm. Oh my, but haven't you got the lounge room looking just lov-er-ly. Oh, what a lov-er-ly warm fire, and what's that stink?'

'Mmm. What stink? Oh, you mean the O-Cedar oil.'

'Mmm. Marvellous stuff. Have you tried bathing the children in it, Mrs Smyth-Owen? Wonderful stuff. It kills head lice and foot odour with one application.' Eddy warms his hands, then dusts a chair with a tea towel before he sits down, the towel over his shoulders, his arms folded and holding that tea towel close, like the lady was wearing her jacket over her shoulders that day and sort of hugging it close. They are great actors. They ape the duo's expressions, and the audience love it. They are laughing fit to choke, which only makes Eddy and Jamesy go at it harder. It's better than television.

They want Alan to play Mavis, accept the medal, but Alan is sitting back, content to be entertained. He's quieter than his twin and it's plain obvious that he still believes in miracles. 'We can have our own face on the wall,' he said. He was looking at the photo of Mavis, all right. It's like he looks on her as their own now.

Eddy tries to make Lori play Mavis, but her mind has been away, sort of saying over and over, our own face, our own face.

'Nick off, moron,' she says.

Eddy weaves it into his act, so that all Lori has to say is some insult and Eddy makes it sound as if she's doing a Mavis. They are choking with laughter, and Lori is getting more inventive, getting caught up in his game.

'Shush,' Alan says. 'I think I heard her laugh.'

'You're dreaming,' Lori says, but they shush for a long time; they hear the wind and the old house creaking and groaning, like it knows it's lost its chance to fall down, like it knows it's going to have to stand up for maybe a few years more. They hear Spud Murphy's dogs barking and the television in the brick room blaring.

Then that laugh again.

They haven't heard Mavis laugh since she laughed at Henry that Christmas Day. They listen, hope it was her. Probably only the television. They wish she was thin, and back to beautiful like she was in the photograph – which would be twice as gorgeous as Wendy Johnson's mother. They wish Mavis was sitting in the new lounge room, laughing with them. The room is silent and all eyes stare at the fire or at the hard-faced dame above the fire and Lori's mind wanders far away.

She's looking at the photographs of her English grandparents. They are just people, strangers. There is nothing of them in her, not her eyes, not her mouth, not her hair, or her body. There is no more of her in them than in that old dame on the wall, but she could see there was a bit of seventeen-year-old Mavis in her – the curly hair, the hands, the eyes, a bit of the chin.

You can't borrow ancestors. You can't make yourself look like them. Okay, you can learn new ways from borrowed ancestors, maybe better ways, you can learn to speak like them, but you can't be *of* them. She thinks of Henry. He was like a shadow that came out of nowhere, came out of Lily and a boy called Henry. Just a shape of life, floating on air. His borrowed family caught that shadow, tied it down and kept it safe; they gave Henry their name, left him their money and their photographs when they died, but it was like they'd taken his . . . his moorings with them when they died, like he had nothing to hold on to except a borrowed name, so he just floated away again.

She springs upright in her chair and stares at the dame on the wall, suddenly understanding why Aborigines, raised by white people, need to go back and find their own. It doesn't matter if they were actually stolen from their mother's breasts or just given away by their mothers, and it doesn't matter if the white people who looked after them were good, bad or indifferent, because it's not about that.

It's about the life-force elastic connecting people back to someone they know they belong to. Someone of their own. So some of them had more European ancestors than Aboriginal, but like poor little *child Henry*, most of those European ancestors didn't hang around long enough to even see the babies they left behind. Everyone needs someone of their own to cling to, even if it's only one of your own people's faces looking down at you from a wall. If Henry had had a photo of Mary or old Woden the Indian, or fourteen-year-old Lily or even the boy called Henry, he would have known there was some life-force thing that went back, and back, and back forever. He wouldn't have given up and killed himself, because if elastic stretches back then it has to go forward too, right?

She looks at Eddy. He's holding the photo of Henry, sort of staring at it, like he doesn't like it, or maybe he likes it too much. Yeah, for sure he likes it too much because his eyes haven't got that smartarse look in them. They look sort of big and sad.

Family. That's all there is.

Lori hasn't done a whole heap of thinking lately – hasn't been game to think much further than the next day, the next week – due to Mavis. Sooner or later someone will make them open that door and let her out. Then this room and everything else will all go to hell.

Big always rules small, like, size is power. Small countries get taken over by the army of big countries, who kill the people, wreck everything then set up that country the way they want it. The little people lose their houses and half of them starve until the aid workers come in to feed them and give them tents. How do you control big countries if you are a small country? How do you make a world change when you can't make people change their socks? How do you stop Mavis's eating unless you lock her away from food?

You can't.

So why is Martin so paranoid-crazy about her being locked in?

Because it's illegal, and why it is illegal is because everyone in this world today is supposed to be equal and, like, have equal rights, prisoners who murder people, even, and crazy people, everyone is equal. And how can kids believe that crap, when the whole world is in-your-face unequal? Like all of those parliament guys getting to fly overseas every week or two and not paying one cent of their own money to do it, and poor Henry, always dreaming of flying home to his England and never getting to do it. That's not equal. And it's not fair.

And allowing a person to kill themselves with food if they want to, due to equal rights, is also crap. That's like a country attacking itself, like civil war, and no one sending in their army to stop them.

Getting away to the river by herself to do some hard thinking used to make Lori happy, but her thinking tonight is making her feel sort of sad, sort of hopeless sad, like how can anyone ever hope to fix up this stupid world? Probably, each person just has to try to fix up the bit of it that belongs to him and let the rest go to hell if it wants to.

She shrugs, sniffs in a big whiff of O-Cedar oil and wet couch and woodsmoke. They are good smells. Eddy sure fixed up this part of his world. And he fixed up the boys' feet – as soon as Lori starts to even think she smells dead socks, she mixes up a brew of Condy's crystals and makes the one with the diseased feet soak them, makes them spray the insides of their shoes with vinegar. She takes control before the bacteria get control.

Henry knew pretty much everything. He must have bought those Condy's crystals, yet he didn't use them. Why? Because he was only a shadow and a shadow just floats where it is taken, sort of stuck to the feet of the one who is taking it. Lori is not a shadow. Vinnie was; he went wherever he was taken, just clinging, becoming the shape of the one he was with.

Mavis is not a shadow.

Lori looks at the window. Dark out tonight. Late now. Who is Vinnie clinging to tonight? She takes a deep breath, doesn't really want to think about that. Her eyes wander the rotting curtains, seeking a safe place for her mind to go. Those old curtains will have to stay up for a while because the roll of curtain material bought for this room is no longer good enough for it. Mick's room needs curtains. He won't mind having the birds and Neil will love them. And Mavis, she'll need a new summer tent soon. She'll get birds whether she loves them or not.

Lori's last attempt at tent making wasn't a success, but the next time she'll do better. Maybe if she cut the tents in four bits, like two big oblongs for the body, and two small ones for sleeves, then sort of shaped the top bits in like raglan sleeves, stitched those top bits together and threaded elastic through the neck and cuffs. It might work out better than a zipper – or leaving one shoulder seam open.

She yawns and her mind wanders to *if* land, like *if* two years have passed and she's left school and Mavis is slim and beautiful and wearing jeans and dangling earrings, and her face is looking like that photograph, and *if* she's looking like that she'd never want to eat again. The mind picture is coming and it's coming strong. Lori can see her in the kitchen and she's making her custard and –

Cut that picture. Cut it fast. *If* and pretend stuff is for little kids. Once Mavis is out, the couch will be back digging a hole in the wall and the kitchen will be Mavis's kitchen, not Lori's. That's reality. That's looking the future in the eye. And Mavis will never be slim and beautiful again because she won't ever be seventeen again. That's fact and it's no use thinking *ifs* and pretending that things are different to what they are.

Still, they can at least have a picture of how she was when she was beautiful. And they can have a picture of Henry too, of before he got lost. They can bring him back into this house and make him stay, make him put down new roots, so that she and the brothers have got something to hang on to, and maybe, wherever Henry is, he'll be able to grab on to them too and stop his floating around.

'We'd better put that fire out and go to bed,' Mick says.

Eddy prods the log back with his foot. 'It's safe. If the chimney was going to catch, it would have done it by now.'

'What if a spark flies out?'

'What if the roof falls in, more likely,' Eddy says.

'What if Mavis escapes and axes us in our beds?' Jamesy says.

The what *ifs* keep getting sillier and the laughing starts again.

'What if we don't wake up in the morning and get to school?' Lori says. 'Go on. Go to bed. Everyone.'

'Yo, boss,' Eddy says, but they go.

It's funny the way they let her be boss – probably because she's the one who carries the bankcard. She also gets to make the decisions about spending the extra money. Like Eddy asked her if he could have the lounge suite, as if she was the boss of the money. Probably she got born bossy, like a chip off the old block. She sighs, thinks maybe she'd prefer to be like Mavis than Henry.

Wow! What a thought. Put that one to bed!

Matty and Timmy are sound asleep, snuggled up together in the central sag. The poor old mattress has had to stand a lot of pressure and it's just about caved in. Lori is pleased to creep into her narrow bed, but tonight she lies on her back, thinking, watching the new patterns on the walls made by the flickering fire. It's warmer in her room tonight. Fire warmth is beautiful.

She rolls over. This sure is a hard bed, which is due to having wooden slats beneath it instead of a normal base. She'll get used to it. After a bit, people get used to most things – like celery and cucumber. Mavis eats them now. Mostly.

The glow from the lounge room fades as the fire slowly dies and she sleeps.

decisions, decisions

Life isn't fair. Things start to get a bit easier in one direction and they explode in another direction. It's Saturday and it's late; the kids are eating a pile of fried sandwiches, and Mavis, who they left starving for her lunch until three o'clock, due to they've been doing the rounds of the garage sales, can smell their fried sandwiches. She's cursing the lot of them – and her plate full of salad and boiled egg – when the kids hear footsteps on the verandah.

No one heard a car drive up. No time for medicinal coffee or custard. The first they know of their visitors are footsteps on the verandah. It's a nice day, both front and back doors have been left open to let some fresh air through. Mick's door is open, and his window. Everything is open – except Mavis's door.

They think it's the social workers but it's not, because the footsteps don't stop at the door. Social workers at least have the good manners to knock.

Lori runs, tries to head the intruders off mid passage, but a rangy greyhound brushes by her, an anorexic poodle not far behind. Eva and Alice have tried threats, bribery and corruption, and probably the legal way, so now they turn criminal. They've got kidnap on their minds, like, if Mavis and her team can snatch those twins from St Kilda in a furniture van, Eva and Alice can do it too.

Eddy pales, shrinks two sizes, places his sandwich down as Alice enters the kitchen, snorting and snarling like she's been forced to chase a lure she's got no interest in catching. She's blowing smoke from her pinched nostrils and it looks like steam; her lips drawn back in a snarl aren't holding her teeth in today; the teeth are fighting to get out, to bite off rats' heads, or kids' heads.

'Out to the car. Move it, boys,' she says.

'Please, darlings, hurry,' Eva whimpers, looking seasick beneath that blue ceiling, looking washed out against that blue wall. 'Where is she?'

'In the loo.' Lori is standing behind them, looking at that green door and wondering what has happened to Mavis, who has stopped her cursing. 'Close the door. Close that door!' she mouths, signalling to Eddy.

He's sitting in front of it and he hasn't said a word. Eva mock-kisses him – she doesn't get a chance to kiss Alan.

'I'm not going with you,' he says, dodging around her, leaving his half-eaten sandwich for whoever gets to it first, and he's out the back door and over the side fence. Gone bush.

Eddy watches him go, wants to go with him. But this is his mother, isn't it? This is who he still thinks of as Mother. While he didn't see her, he could put her on hold, knowing if he wanted to go back, he could. He just hasn't felt the want yet, or not often. Not a lot to want back there, really – except his computer and the money. That's what he thought. But seeing her here now, in the kitchen, strange wanting stuff is grabbing at his insides. It's like he's come face-on to his own green door. He can go through it, get rid of this wanting feeling, or he can slam that door shut and shove the bolt, but once he's locked that door, he could be stuck here forever.

Does he want to be stuck here forever? Probably not. He doesn't know. This place is like a game he's been playing. Maybe he ought to go home. He can't make up his mind. Doesn't want the decision. Not today. This is a real-life decision, not computer stuff, not funny fiction for the telephone. He has to take off, go after Alan and leave the decision for another day, and if he doesn't go over that fence soon, he's going to go back, crawl into his computer for the rest of his life.

It's a brilliant computer, better than the library's; Eva always bought the best. He's got his own room in St Kilda, he gets pots of money to spend and he sure misses that money. Doesn't miss the school. Misses the city. Doesn't miss old Alice. Misses the traffic and the buzz and the crowds and the ocean. Up here there is nothing. Everything is dry and looks like crap. Nothing to do – except being with the kids and living free.

These kids? Alice? No contest.

And Eva?

He's on his feet now and holding the back door wide, looking out at freedom, but he can't go over the fence, leave the decision for another day. There might not be another day. Won't be for Lori and Mick if Eva opens that green door. He's looking at that in-your-face door. Mavis is going to yell out any minute now, then Eva will let her out.

Or will she? Maybe not. Probably not. But even if she doesn't open the door, she'll call the cops on her mobile and they'll open it. Kids can't lock their mothers up and feed them on rabbit food, even if it is for their own good. Okay, so he did it, but he wasn't so involved with this place back then. It was just a game, like, can I beat the odds? A longer game – a more interesting game.

It's not a game now. It has become his glorious quest and he has to shut that back door. Eva isn't dumb, and old Alice is whippet smart. But if he shuts the door he's locked in with both of them and he'll cave in and go. He always did around these two. It was easier. Just give them what they wanted and he got what he wanted. Got anything he wanted.

But does he want to go back to being who he was before? Empty. Lonely.

No. No, he doesn't want that. Okay, that's one definite.

There is a lot of stuff he wants in St Kilda. Plenty that he doesn't want. Here he's accepted – needed, even – and he wants to get this house painted on the outside – paint it white, paint its roof red – wants to do a lot of stuff. But more than that, he wants this mob. They are the only ones who ever filled up that empty, lonely place inside him. They need him too. They like him – most of the time. And they like him for who he is, not for who he's pretending to be.

But what about his computer?

He can use the ones at the library when he's desperate, and he's been looking at second-hand computers; they get some real cheap deals at the computer shop, and the guy who runs it says he'll have some good ones in a month, the whole works for four and a half hundred – which would be better than nothing.

Still, if he doesn't go back, Alice will probably make sure that account at the bank is closed. She's the boss and she uses money like a weapon.

He really wants his computer. He had so much stuff on it.

But does he want it enough to go back to being chained up like a stray pup and retrained into rolling over, playing dead on cue, and never even getting a pat on the head for doing it? Eva might be big on words and external stuff, but that's pretty much all she is big on. Alan used to say she was plastic coated, strong plastic coated, so you break your fingernails trying to get at what is inside. Up here no one can afford plastic. Up here their skin is exposed. You can touch them, cuddle the little kids, tickle them and make them laugh.

And Mavis. What is actually inside her skin? There is so much of it no one could ever get in. Not now. But he's going to get her skinny. Yeah, and beautiful again. That's his glorious quest. He didn't know Henry, can't ever know Henry now, but he can get to know his natural mother – when she's thin and beautiful. He wants that, needs that more than needing his computer. It would be like his coming home had made her beautiful again, like he was something special for once.

Old Alice is still nagging. He's not listening, but God, he loathes that nagging mouth. It's all teeth. He can't stand to look at it, but he's looking now, watching those teeth. His stomach is turning over, and his brain is like lightning flitting from one side of the argument to the other while the fried sandwich he's eaten is trying to come up and choke him. He keeps swallowing it back down, looking at Alice's stained carnivore teeth, working up some aversion therapy as he closes the back door. Slowly.

Lori is standing, hands on her hips, wondering what took him so long. The little kids have stopped eating. Matty fishes for his dummy string, places his sucking tool in his mouth, stares big eyed at Alice's teeth.

'If he wants to stay with us, he can,' Lori says, and Mick nods, eggs her on. 'He's our brother, and we didn't know him till February. And he doesn't legally belong to you anyway. He legally belongs to Mavis and to us.'

'Go out to that car, boy. Your mother has been upset long enough by this business.' Eddy turns to his mother. 'After all your mother has done for you. If not for your mother's care you would have died. You wouldn't be here now to defy her.'

'Mavis is his mother,' Lori says, and she wonders what's come over Mavis, like why isn't she yelling, belting the door down now? And Eddy, he's dumb. Those buggers have got out their old lobotomy scalpel and they are cutting him again.

'I have been a mother to you, darling. The best mother that I knew how to be.'

Maybe she was too. Maybe she just didn't know how.

'You're breaking your mother's heart, boy.'

They are throwing that 'mother' word around as if it's expendable. They are throwing it so hard it starts to sound like it's something else. It's sounding like a word no one knows the meaning of.

Mother?

Sister and brother. That sounds real. That sounds good.

Eddy is staring at Lori, he's shaking his head, and she's worried. She steps closer because he looks as if he's going to start bawling . . . or . . . maybe just head for the shower for an hour. His back is to the closed door. His eyes are sort of pleading – help me, someone, convince me – so she tries.

'Why can't we all be one family? Why can't you just come here and sit down and visit like other aunties do? Why do we have to be like . . . enemies?'

'Hold your tongue, miss,' Alice snaps, but Eva accepts the invitation and she sits, puts her head down on the plastic tablecloth and turns on plastic tears.

'No one understands what she did to me. No one will ever understand what I went through for her. She stole my childhood,' Eva sobs.

Eddy walks towards Eva, and Alice sees that those tears are winning the day. She grasps his arm.

And he's going. He's looking at Eva, looking like he always does before he has one of his showers. He's looking at Lori, sort of hopeless now, sad and shaking his head, like, what else can I do?

Until Neil runs at Alice and kicks her ankle. 'You leave our brother alone, you bully duck,' he yells.

That sure breaks the spell, and breaks Alice's concentration. She hasn't heard that one before, and she's never been attacked by a face-pulling six year old before either. She releases Eddy's arm.

He's stepping back, and back, his eyes that never leak are leaking bad. Neil isn't retreating. He's standing in front of Alice, his legs spread wide, his face belligerent, and he's never looked more like Mavis.

Eddy wipes his nose with his wrist, then with the same hand points to the enlarged photograph of a young Henry, which now hangs on the kitchen wall. 'That's my father,' he says, his voice breaking, and near breaking Lori's heart. 'That's my own father and he's dead. Alan knew him, and all these kids knew him, and I didn't. And I can't ever know my own father because of you, Mum.'

'You know it is what he wanted, darling. He planned so much more for you than . . . than *this*.'

'Well, it's not what I wanted!' he yells. 'Did anyone ever ask me if I wanted to know my own father?' Eva is dabbing at her eyes, but Eddy is crying for real now. 'You lied to me. All my life you lied to me, and all the time my own father was only a few hundred kilometres away and I could have known him like Alan did. And now he's dead and it's not bloody fair.' He's bawling hard, and it looks weird on him. Lori didn't know he could bawl.

'Watch your tongue, boy,' Alice snaps. It's the wrong attitude because it makes Eddy upgrade his language.

'This is none of your fucking business. You're nothing to me, you're a nagging old bitch. I hate the sight of you, and I always did.' He's breaking the no-swearing rule, but that's okay, and he's almost as loud as Mavis, his nose is red and he's sloshing tears everywhere, and that's okay too, because those tears are fighting tears.

'Yeah. And if you tell lies, then you get put in the lock-up with Mavis, and you have to eat fucky celery,' Neil yells.

Eddy's head damn near rotates a full circle and his tear taps turn off fast. He wipes his nose with his wrist, grabs hold of Neil, muffling his blabbing little mouth before it says more. Lori is heading for the back door.

'You know that Henry placed both of you in my care,' Eva says. 'You know he had plans for his darling boys.'

Lori is beside Eddy and Neil, ready to stifle the little twit, throttle him if necessary. 'Yes, well our mother never wanted either of them to be with you, did she? She said she wouldn't trust you to raise rabid Rottweilers. And our father is dead now, so Mavis is the boss of this house and she wants the twins to stay here. She's even got the papers to put them back on her dependants list,' Lori says. 'And if you cause any more trouble, she's going to take out a restraining order, because that's what the department of . . . of welfare for children and supporting mothers said to do. And they said that they'd give her any help she needs to do it too.'

Eva is on her feet. She doesn't like the sound of that.

'You'll be sorry, boy. There will be no more money paid into that account,' Alice says.

Eddy, still holding on tight to Neil, lifts his chin. 'I'm not your boy, and this isn't about fucking money, and you keep out of this – '

'Yeah, 'cause we got plenty of fucky money,' Neil yells. 'We got a jar full of fucky money, so there.'

Eddy is shaking, but he's holding Neil against him like a vice. Lori doesn't know if he's trying to shut him up or just trying to soak some fight from the feisty little coot. Mick is standing silent, scared. Jamesy and Timmy are sitting at the table, sharing Alan's sandwich because it doesn't look as if he's coming back to get it.

'One day Mavis may be sorry for the harm she has done to those who loved her.'

'Loved her? You lying bitch.' They hear that bawl from the brick room and from Mick's room up the hall. Alice steps back. Eva steps forward. They look from door to door. 'Get out of my house or I'll come in there and throw you out, or call the cops to do it for me, you apology for a bloody mother, you lying, child-abusing, queer bitch.'

They hear the toilet flush. Alice walks fast to the passage door. There is thumping coming from the room beside the kitchen. An ogre stomping in high heels. The kids know what it is. It's Mavis belting into Mick's timber wall with the loo brush.

'Get out to that car, Edward,' Alice's teeth snarl.

'Get yourself a chihuahua. It will stay small enough to kick around,' Eddy says.

Alice leaves, via the front door. Eva stands on, watching the back door. The noise is coming from behind the back door, but when she moves to follow Alice, the footsteps seem to be heading for the passage.

'How can you tolerate . . . *this*, my darling boy? How can you tolerate her? After what you have been *accustomed* to.'

'How can you stand kissing those teeth?' Eddy says. He's getting mean now, and he's looking mean, and Eva doesn't like it. She flinches and her high-heeled sandals trip-trip-trip down the passage.

'I'm taking out a restraining order against you tomorrow,' Mavis screeches, and it's too clear. Maybe she's broken through Mick's wall.

The kidnappers move out to the verandah. They don't know which floorboards to watch out for and Eva goes through one. And she's down, sprawled flat, one leg knee-deep in the verandah. Even the old house is fighting for Eddy. Maybe it heard him thinking about white paint.

Lori isn't far behind them. She closes the front door, except for a crack. You can see a lot through a crack in a door, hear a lot. She's listening as Alice lifts Eva's leg out. Her pantihose is ripped to shreds, her shin bleeding and she's bawling for real now.

'Look at the hovel. It should be condemned, and she's in there laughing at me. She's not going to beat me, Alice. Let her take out her restraining order. Let her take it to the courts. No court in the land would fail to see that those boys would be better off with me.'

'It's immaterial to me, lass. If that's what you want to do, then we'll do it together, but she knows too much. The media will tear you to shreds.' Eva is sitting on the edge of the verandah, already torn to shreds. Alice is lifting her skirt, tying a man's handkerchief around her shredded shin.

'Hop in the car, lass.'

'That stinking, filthy hovel. Do I need stitches?'

'It's just a scratch. Hop in the car, lass.'

'I want them. I am their mother.' She's a bawling banshee! Alice sits beside her, puts her arms around her, hold her while she bawls.

Henry never put his arms around Mavis, comforted her when she bawled. Henry never touched anyone, except when he cut their hair. He never really said nice things – never said much at all, when you come to think of it, and when he did talk, like he did at Christmas, it wasn't conversation, just sort of . . . sort of self-indulgent.

Growing up is too hard. It makes you see things, understand things that you don't really want to understand. Like those two women. They look like a loving couple sitting there.

You get pictures in your head about things when you are a kid,

Lori used to think all lesbians had short hair, muscles and were all about thirty. These women are old and they've been together since forever, so Mavis says. They were together when Mavis was a little kid, back in the seventies. Mavis used to say Eva only married Henry because her mother was starting to wake up to what was going on with Alice in the bungalow and Eva got scared Grandmother Hilda would leave all her money to a lost dogs home.

These days it doesn't matter much if you're gay or straight, but those two are still playing it like it's 1970. Maybe they started a lie and now they are trapped in it and Eva has to have those twins so she can keep that trap locked fast.

Why didn't Henry get those twins back? What was wrong with him? He of all people should have known that kids need to know their own families or they get lost. She thinks of Eddy, the way he was clinging to Neil, as if he was trying to soak up some of Neil's life force to make himself strong. She thinks about wild little bugger Neil too, fighting hard for Eddy. That's what a family is, it's caring about each other and fighting for each other, being there for each other. And maybe holding people close when they cry, making them feel better.

Eva is feeling a bit better. She's looking at the house and wanting to kill the sister who ruined her childhood then stole her husband with her gaping legs.

Mavis used to tell a different story – like, she told Martin one night that Henry had been too dumb to see what was going on with Eva and Alice until the night he came home from the club where he used to sing, due to it catching on fire, and he caught Eva and Alice together in the bungalow. Mavis found him trying to hang himself from a tree branch that wouldn't hold his weight. It snapped and Henry snapped and that's the night Martin got started. Mavis was seventeen and still at school. Henry was thirty-seven. She was probably one of those wild free-love kids. She used to talk a lot a few years back, talk about the city and parties and sleeping on the beach all night.

Alice lights a cigarette. 'We certainly have more freedom without them, Eva. There's no denying that.'

'What sort of mother would send her sons to England to live with relatives? What will people think of me?'

'You worry too much about what people think, lass. We're old enough to let them think what they like.'

'We could . . . go to . . . England. We always intended to travel when you retired, didn't we? Go to Paris, remember, darling?'

'Live like the natives for a year, lass.'

'When we were young. God, I must look a sight.'

'Never to me, lass. Never to me.'

'If she takes out a restraining order, the media will get on to it. Lord knows how much she'll tell them.'

'She'll make certain that we have the television hounds baying at the door.'

'I couldn't live with it. Not after all these years. I *couldn't*, darling.'

'It's up to you, always up to you, but I'll tell you now, I'm getting too damn old for this.' She puffs smoke, blows it fast through her nostrils. 'How's that leg feeling now?'

'Throbbing. We'll have to go somewhere, buy a bandage and disinfectant. That filthy hovel! I should get a tetanus injection.'

'Get the doctor to look at it when we're home.'

'You're so good to me.' Eva is wriggling out of her pantihose, trying not to lift her dress too high, then they are off, and she tosses them at the front door, gives the house one more murderous look and, leaning heavily on Alice, limps to the car. 'We *will* go to Paris, darling. We *will*. We'll rent the house, and by the time we get back, the boys will be more than ready to come home. You see if I'm wrong.'

Mick comes to stand behind Lori as the car moves away. They watch it turn, watch it to the corner, watch it until Timmy comes to pull at Lori's shirt.

'Eddy's wun off cwying,' he says.

yowies and songs

They find Alan down at the river, three decapitated, de-tailed carp strung on a stick he's propped between two tree branches. Eddy is down there too. No court jester now, he's sitting on a high clay bank, his head on his knees, Alan standing off, watching his fish, watching Eddy and looking relieved, like, phew. So that's over.

He glances at Lori. 'Phew,' he says, then he wanders off and she takes his place leaning against the tree, looking at the fish. They are small. The small ones are best.

She's looking at Eddy too and he won't lift his head. Maybe he's sorry already that he's stuck here with them. She doesn't want him to be sorry so she walks to his side, thinks she'd like to say something nice to him, make him feel better. Cuddling and touching people were pretty much alien in Henry's time, but she's learned how to cuddle the little kids and make them feel better when they cry. She can't cuddle Eddy, but she could probably find something nice to say, if she tried. She sits beside him on the clay, not too close, sits for a long time, tossing pebbles and small clods into the river and trying hard to think of something nice to say.

'Alan can remember Henry from when he used to go down to visit you. I bet you can too.' Eddy shakes his head, wants her to go away. She's not going. 'He used to sing a song about you and Alan, and Alan says he can remember him singing it in Melbourne.'

Eddy shakes his head, sniffs, a fuck-off sniff. His eyes are red and his nose is stuffy and he is feeling like a howling fool. She knows this but she won't go.

'You were like his hidden treasures, you know. I always thought of you as Henry's twins, not Mavis's. Nearly every night when he was watering his flowers he'd sing this song. I can't sing it, but it was something like, "My precious sons, my boys, you are the best of me. My precious sons, my joy, you'll live the rest for me".' She talks the words, surprised she remembers them, and she knows that she keeps turning the son and boy into plural, but she wants Eddy to think that that song was about him and Alan – whether it was or not. He sniffs, lifts his head, looks at the sky but won't look at her. She keeps on talking, just like Nelly kept talking that night she found Lori sitting almost in this exact same place. 'He must have sung that song to you when he went down for visits – if Alan can remember it.'

'I didn't know Henry! Leave me alone, will you?'

'I remember heaps of stuff from when I was five. I remember stuff from when I was three.'

'Cool for you! Now fuck off.'

'I bet you remember him. Anyway, you saw him that day you came here for dinner.'

He turns to her then and his face is hurting, like Henry's face used to hurt, and his mouth is trembling; he's going to start bawling again in a minute. 'That day we came here he looked like a grandfather and he belonged to you kids, not us. And no one told us he was our father, anyway. Eva just told us we were going to visit Aunty Mave and her children. I didn't know who Henry was that day and I can't remember him singing. All I remember of my father is . . . is maybe a shadow of him coming into the bedroom at Eva's then going out, so fuck off, will you, and leave me alone.'

She shrugs, doesn't move. 'Henry, the little shadow, coming and going? That's all he was, really – to all of us. A stooped little shadow, coming and going and never stopping long enough for anyone to touch it. He was always doing things. Every time we saw him he was cooking, cleaning, cutting hair. The only time you could get near him was when he was cutting your hair. He had to touch you, move your head. I used to keep putting my chin down, just so he'd have to keep lifting it up. And I used to make him cut my hair about every three weeks, so I could be close to him. And in the potting shed, sometimes I could creep right up close when he sang, sort of breathe his used-up air.

'My precious sons, my boys, no more I fear the pain, though summer's gone for me, I know you'll warm the rain . . .' She's singing the words now, just singing soft. She can hold a tune, though her voice is thin compared to Henry's, but in her head it's like his powerful voice is singing along with her, leading her on, telling her the words she doesn't think she knows until she gets to them, and then they're there, waiting and ready.

'*Fear the pain*?' Eddy is actually looking at her.

'Yeah. It was about a man who was dying. He used to sing a lot of songs about dying. He probably always had a death wish.'

He looks at the sky for a long time, sniffs. 'I remember someone singing a song about fearing the pain and winter rain. I always had an earache and tonsillitis in the winter and I thought it was about summer being over and the pain starting up again.'

'I told you so, you smartarse. Henry was probably the only person in the whole world who ever sang that song.' She slaps at a non-existent fly on Eddy's back, like she used to swat nonexistent mozzies on Henry, and she does it so the smartarse bit won't hurt; leaves her hand on his back too, rubs it a bit, just for a second. 'None of us wanted you to go back with Eva. We couldn't cope here without you. Two days and we'd be back to living in a pigpen.'

He's not ready yet to talk. He's feeling embarrassed about his tears, and it hurt him to hurt Eva. Maybe life force can trickle over into an aunt – not that Lori has ever felt the trickle, and Eva is always so doused in perfume, there's not a chance of homing in on any family scent. For a long time they sit quiet, watching the others muck around and yahoo through the trees.

'How about Neil, eh?' Eddy says.

'That wild little bugger! I think he must have been born wild, like Greg.'

'I don't know Greg, and I don't know the other one either.'

'Vinnie.'

'I'm not part of this family and I'm not part of Eva and Alice. I'm no one. And I didn't ask to be given away.'

'You weren't given away, it's just that you nearly died up here. Mavis never gave you away – just let Henry rent you out for a while, like Eva rents her house. She knows she can get that house back whenever she wants it and Mavis was always planning how to get you back. She tried all the time – until she got too fat to do anything about anything. And Henry . . . I don't know. Maybe he had too many kids. Maybe he just gave up.'

'You mob were lucky, growing up with your own parents.'

'You didn't miss much, Eddy,' she starts, then bites her tongue. 'Of course you missed knowing Henry, but as far as knowing him and Mavis together, like proper parents, then you were lucky to miss some of that. I never ever saw him hold her or kiss her like husbands do on television. Not once. Alice kissed Eva and she held her when she cried and she petted her, said all the right things.'

'Henry must have thought Mavis was okay. They had enough kids.'

'Henry didn't want the babies – or not the ones I can remember coming. Having babies was Mavis's thing, just a part of her civil war. Every baby she had she got fatter. Or maybe her fat was a war against Henry.' She shrugs. 'Who knows why she had us? We could have been like her private revolution against the government . . . sort of a financial-based takeover. She always got money from the government – even before Henry died, not heaps, like now, but an allowance for each kid she had.'

They are quiet for a long time, thinking their own thoughts, then Eddy says, 'I didn't think much about fathers until we went to London. We rented a flat there and old Alice used to sleep in Mum's bed. Mum said it was because there weren't enough beds and we couldn't find a big flat.' He shrugs, looks at the sky. It's changing colour. Night is coming. 'I missed Alan like crazy, but he wasn't missing me.'

'He was so. He screamed for you for about two months.'

'You're cow-crapping. All he wanted when he came back to us was you lot.'

'Cow-crap nothing! He screamed blue murder for you. "I want my Eddy. I want to go home". It was pure awful. Don't tell him I told you, but he used to wet the bed too, and he wouldn't eat anything, and he spent his first winter here catching every bug invented.' They are quiet then for a long time and Lori doesn't like the quiet. 'What's England like, anyway?' she says.

'Wet.' He smiles a bit, then shrugs. 'I saw a lot of stuff.'

'Like what? Castles and cathedrals and daffodils?'

'Yeah.'

'That's all Henry used to tell me about England. And snow, and green fields and old villages and houses with thatched roofs.'

'I saw that. And I saw Mum kissing Alice one day, sort of taking her shirt off kissing.' He shakes his head. 'And I heard stuff. She had a baby once. I heard her and Alice talking about it and thought for a while she was talking about having me and Alan. It wasn't about us. It was another one.'

'What did she do with it?'

'Adopted it out, I suppose. That's what they did in the old days.'

'So somewhere out there we've got a cousin, floating around like Henry and never knowing his own people?'

'I suppose so. That's what screwed Mum up, I think. She was probably raped or something. She hated that baby's father, went on and on about him hurting her. That's . . . that's when I got obsessed by fathers, started wondering about mine – wondering if she'd hated him too. I started watching kids with their fathers. Mum had always told me and Alan that our father lived in London, and I was in London, so I told her I wanted to see him. Nagged her about it. She wouldn't produce him. Nothing made any sense over there. The stuff I heard . . . you don't know much when you're ten.'

'I know. And no one will tell you the answers you need. Like, when I was about ten, I actually asked Henry what gay meant, and he said happy. I knew that wasn't right so I asked Martin. He was about eighteen, and he said it stood for *get* rid of *all yobbos*, which was a government undercover conspiracy to control overpopulation of the lower classes, and that I shouldn't go around asking anyone else what that word meant or the FBI would come looking for me.' Eddy laughs, and it's so good to hear him laugh, Lori laughs with him.

'Gay women still want kids. That won't stop overpopulation,' he says.

'Yeah, but they sure have a lot more trouble doing it. And just think of China for a minute. Like, for years married couples over there have only been allowed to have one baby and they all want sons so they abort the girls. There won't be enough girls for those sons to marry, so they'll have to go gay. No wife, no baby.'

'They'll clone themselves.'

'They'll still need a woman to incubate it.'

They're mucking around now and their theories are becoming more absurd, until Lori yells out to Matty, 'Stay away from the water, Matty. You do as you're told, or next time we'll leave you at home with Mavis.'

Matty is going on three, a redhead, but he's a brownish red, closer to Mick's colour. He needs a haircut, too; he's starting to look like a girl with his mop of curls, but he looks cute. His blue-grey eyes wide above his dummy, he walks to her side, looks towards home. Mavis makes a good bogyman. She sure scared Eva away.

Lori brushes the curls from his eyes, lifts him onto her lap. 'He's going to be another Mick. He's not as smart as Timmy was at the same age – ' She stops short, didn't mean to say that out loud, but she knows in her heart that Mick is better with his hands and his nuts and screws than with his books, even if he does wear them out with studying.

'You've got a brain in your head. You could do a lot better at school if you studied a bit,' Eddy says.

'Who wants to? Anyway, I'm dumb, ask old Crank Tank. She hates me.'

'She thinks you're a big-mouthed smartarse.'

Lori is seeing something new in Eddy tonight. It's like he's ten years older, almost as old as her. It's been a hard day, and on such days she ends up feeling about thirty. It's been interesting, though, talking to him alone, learning more about him, but the talk is over because Mick crawls up the bank and flops down beside them.

Alan wanders up. 'Burned your bridges now,' he says. 'I hope I didn't sort of . . . make you do it . . . if you didn't want to do it, that is.'

'I'm a Sticksville convert, Sticksville.'

A speedboat races by. They watch it, read the name on the boat. *Flighty*. It's sure flying. The brothers wave while Lori scratches her name in the clay with a twig. *Lori Smyth-Owen*.

It's a borrowed name. Henry didn't have his proper name to give her. Maybe he was Henry Woden, but Lori Woden sounds ridiculous – so does Lori Smyth-Owen. It's plastic-coated tourist stuff, something to take home from your holiday and shove in a drawer. She scrubs out the hyphen and the Owen with her twig.

Lori Smyth. Martin calls himself Smyth. She likes it. It sounds more like her – no bullshit, and maybe not so dumb, just a big-mouthed smartarse. She liked what Eddy said, and she likes it that he likes her and the kids better than Eva's money. She feels older somehow, and more proud tonight than she's ever felt before. In part it's because of what Eddy said, and also part of it is knowing she was able to care about him, sit with him and find the right words to start making him feel better.

'I suppose we should get back and cook Mavis a nice dinner – for helping us out.'

'Have to keep her metabolism running, the book says. Regular food.'

But they sit on, looking at the sun sinking down behind the trees, sinking down in the west. Henry's west.

'What got into her today? Why didn't she yell for help?'

'She hates Eva more than she hates us, that's all. It doesn't mean anything.'

'She'll love us when we get her down to a normal size,' Eddy says. 'I wonder if she'll look a bit like that photo when she's thin?'

'Come off the grass! She's nearly forty, and what's going to happen to all her spare skin? She'll deflate like a balloon, go all wrinkly,' Jamesy says, offering another fish. A big one.

Spring is here and the fishermen are at it again. More carp for dinner. It's good for Mavis. Fish is low in fat and high in protein and fish fat never turns into people fat. That's what they said on television the other night – if you can believe anything on television.

'We've got enough fish. Alan's already got three,' Eddy says.

'So now we've got four. We'll fillet it before we put it in the freezer so we can fry it in breadcrumb batter like we did that last one. There was nothing wrong with it.'

'Skin is like elastic,' Mick says, looking at the fish. 'It stretches and shrinks to fit. And it's a living thing. Cells keep changing.'

'So, you reckon that maybe Mavis's new cells will get the message as they keep replacing themselves, and she'll sort of start pulling into shape?' Alan says.

'She needs exercise. It says in the book that she should increase her exercise gradually.'

'How do you make her get exercise?'

'Give her some dumbbells to throw at us,' Jamesy says, throwing the fish head at Eddy. Eddy takes the mark and the fish head is tossed back hard.

They sit a while and talk about the diet book that says walking is the best exercise.

'We could get her one of those treadmills we saw in that junk mail,' Mick says.

'Too big to throw.' Jamesy tosses the fish's tail at Eddy, follows it with the head.

'Not for her! And quit pitching that. I stink of fish. I'm sick of fish. I want roast lamb and mint sauce.'

'And caviar. And a computer.'

'A decent treadmill would cost a fortune,' Eddy says.

'It doesn't have to be a decent one.'

'She'd break the back of a cheap one. You'd be better off buying a computer for me.'

'We've got to pay the electricity bill this week.'

'And get the sawmill to deliver a couple of truckloads of mill-ends so they've got all summer to dry out.'

'I wonder if Eva would pack up my computer and send it up on the bus.'

'You've got a nerve,' Alan says.

'Alice has got her laptop and Eva can't use a computer. Anyway, if they are going to rent the house then they'll have to put the furniture in storage, so what's the difference in storing the computer up here?'

'You've still got a nerve asking her.'

They stand then, and together brush the dust and sand from the seats of their pants while Neil paddles in the last of the speedboat's waves and the tourists' lights start glowing from across the river.

'Shush, everyone,' Lori says. 'Stay low for a minute.' She gathers a handful of clods, then scrambles down the steep clay bank to hide amid the exposed roots of a giant gum while the speedboat docks and two men get out. A third is backing a 4WD down to the water.

The light is almost gone. They won't see her. Her hands cupping her mouth, she lets rip a bloodcurdling yodel and follows it with a hail of clods.

And the two guys stop connecting *Flighty* to the boat trailer. They turn to the river and, God, Lori wishes she could hear what they're saying. She can't. The river is too wide here, but they sure are looking for her, so she lets loose another yowie challenge.

It's been a long time since she's done that, but she hasn't forgotten how. Martin taught her that call. He used to do it all the time when he was about fourteen, and some tourist wrote to the newspaper once, saying he'd heard a strange animal, and had actually seen it, racing through the trees.

Mick remembers. 'Come on, you stirrer,' he says. 'We have to feed Mavis.'

Just one more, one super special one, because those men are still looking across the river, and the third man is out of his 4WD and he's got binoculars. She's crouching low in her yowie nest, collecting clods, and she's giggling. Maybe this is the last time she'll play the yowie. You can't do this sort of thing when you're grown up, and tonight she's got this powerful grown-up feeling growing in her heart. Maybe it's just relief, but it's sort of like the weight of the world has suddenly lifted itself off her shoulders. Maybe she's just happy.

And the cry goes out across the river, long and threatening. That one will make the newspaper for sure.

Mick is straddling his five-dollar bike with the training wheels, bought at the market the day of the lounge suite. He's added some pipe to the seat and to the handlebars so he can sit in comfort; he put two motor mower wheels on where the trainer wheels used to be, and a prop on the front wheel for his bad leg. He made it a fixed-wheel, only one pedal due to he only uses one foot, though half the time he just scoots it along using his good foot and wearing out his boot. It used to take ages for him to walk home from the bend but now he leads the way. If he doesn't make it to university, he'll probably become a famous inventor.

They feed Mavis more eggs, but in an omelette this time, and with two slices of toast, then she gets tinned pineapple and a dot of low-fat ice-cream.

'That ice-cream is sort of thanks for getting rid of Eva and Alice for us,' Lori says.

'I hate their guts,' Mavis replies. 'And yours too, you little bitch. And if you call that ice-cream, then I don't. Give me a decent dollop I can at least taste, and open that bloody door.'

'Not till you stop hating everyone's guts – and hating your own.' Lori says.

halfwit hulk

They are down to their last eight Valium tablets and their last Aropax repeat. They are out of fluid pills, have been for three weeks. Mavis doesn't seem to be missing them, so they take her off Valium too. The weight is falling off her and she must know it. She's wearing her new bird material tent and it looks almost like a dress, even if the birds are upside down at the front, and the sleeves are too long and the skirt dips down to the floor at the sides. Maybe she'll be okay without her Valium now. She'll have to be okay because they need those last few for emergencies.

She's not okay. She starts doing her block, and it keeps getting worse. She's yelling for her cigarettes, yelling out for Bert Matthews to open the door. They get Henry's old transistor radio, hook it on the fence between Mavis and Bert – he might be half deaf but his wife isn't. The radio runs out of power before Mavis. Alan heads off to get new batteries while they crush two of Donny's executive pills and mix them with jam. It tastes rotten. They live with her yelling for two days and it's not getting any better, so it's back to Valium coffee, two a day, and two will only go into eight four times.

It never rains but it pours. They get a letter from Mr Watts saying that Eddy's computer will be arriving by rail, but when they go to collect it they find it's all packed up in a huge box with *fragile* and *this way up* written all over it. It's too big to go in the pram so they have to ring Martin to pick it up. He turns up the next night, the computer box in the rear of the ute, which has been painted and has got new bucket seats.

And stuck-up Karen is sitting in one of them!

She's blonde and little and she's got one of those pug noses that give you a view halfway up her nostrils. She wrinkles it at Martin when she sees the house, and sneers down it at the mess of kids swarming around Martin's ute that almost looks brand new – which he's parked out on the street instead of in the drive.

'Nice to finally meet all of my new brother-in-laws,' she says – and she's not so smart. 'I hope you don't expect me to remember all of your names.'

Stuck-up bitch. 'Ya only got one sister-in-law, luv. If ya try really, really hard, ya might be able ta remember her name,' Lori says, putting on a good dose of Bert Matthews's yobbo drawl. Which probably isn't a very nice thing to do, or to say, but Lori feels like being mean tonight. The Valium packet is empty.

They get the box out of the ute and carry it to the verandah, then Lori walks inside. Martin starts coming after her. She turns fast, can't get out, he's blocking the door.

'You're getting to be a sarcastic, smart-mouthed little bugger, Splint, and it doesn't suit you,' he says.

'Well, stiff bickies.'

'She's my wife – '

'Yeah, well, now I know why I wasn't good enough to go to her wedding, don't I? She looked at us as if we were a mob of deadbeat yobbos with AIDS. And I saw the way she looked at you when she saw the house. And you wouldn't even be here in this street if we hadn't begged you to pick up Eddy's computer. You're ashamed of us too, now that you've got Miss Piggy.'

'If I didn't care about you, you snitchy, mean-mouthed little bitch, then Mavis would be out and running amok, and you kids would be split up. I'm caring about you by staying away, by keeping my mouth shut about what you've done in there – and you know it, too.'

326

'I don't know it. And she is running amok. We're out of bloody Valium.'

'Then why didn't you ring me?'

'What are you going to do about it? Take her out to the farm and give us a break for a week or two?'

'I can ring the bloody doctor. Get a new prescription, you smart-mouthed little bitch.'

'And he'll come around and give her a check-up. Cool.'

'Would you want to come around if you were him?' Lori shrugs, hears Eddy ripping open that box on the verandah. She's just dying to get a look at the computer. 'You'd better get control of that tongue, Splint, before it starts controlling you. Don't turn into her. One of her is more than enough.'

The doctor is willing to prescribe, sight unseen. He writes the prescriptions for Valium and Aropax and fluid pills, plus repeats, so it's back to apricot jam and Aropax, three Valium coffees a day and a fluid pill twice a week. They'll never be able to let her out of that room. They'll be stuck here feeding her Valium till they're sixty-five.

But life gets back to near normal, except for Eddy. He's in another time zone. No one can talk to him for days, and no one can eat at the kitchen table either. They've got to buy a computer desk and Eddy wants a good one, a new one. He's been saving for a computer so he goes out and spends the lot on a desk so posh they allow it to live in the lounge room. And woe betides any kid not in high school who goes within a metre of it without supervision.

If Eddy is in computer heaven, so are the high school teachers. All the Smyth-Owen homework is now printed out on a laser printer. 'Presentation excellent', one teacher writes on Mick's essay, and he gets a B+.

Time is creeping up towards October when they lay-by a cheap treadmill and a heap of other Christmas presents at Kmart. The lady in the lay-by office looks at them as if they are kids, because their stuff is costing a pile of money. Lori flashes Mavis's supermarket note for cigarettes, which says she's housebound, and they've got a hundred dollars in cash for the deposit, so after a bit it turns out okay.

Lori is cooking two chickens, bought on special at the supermarket. They were near their use-by date, but didn't look or smell off. She made onion and mixed herb sandwiches, then poked them inside the chickens, as practice for Christmas, which is going to be a really good Christmas this year. She's putting a great pile of frozen chips in the oven and the smell that comes out is so good she can hardly wait for the chips to get hot because it smells just like Henry's roast chicken.

Alan is sitting at the table, reading, Eddy is down the town, trying to find out how much it would cost to get the phone reconnected so he can get up on the Internet, Mick is on the computer finishing off an assignment which has to be in tomorrow and he wants another B+, when Vinnie walks in the front door. He's either drunk or stoned out of his brain because he doesn't even notice their lounge room!

Lori runs in from the kitchen, leaving her chickens sizzling.

'Greg's done a bunk with the cops on his heels,' Vinnie giggles. 'He's into heroin for real now and he's been nicking stuff from houses. Got caught trying to flog a DVD player so he had to piss off to some place.'

He's unpacking his stuff on the couch. He's got the DVD player – or another one. He's got two classy cameras, a man's gold watch and two lady's watches all tangled up with one T-shirt, three stiff and stinking socks, the remote control for the DVD and half a six-pack of beer. And he's not even old enough to buy it.

The kids stand and stare at him. He was always a bit rotten, but never totally rotten. He sure looks rotten now. He's only a year older than Mick – like, sixteen – but he's huge and he's probably still wearing the jeans he left home in, probably hasn't washed them since he left home, either. They don't reach his socks, and the bum is worn through and flashing flesh – he's too much flesh to contain. And he's had his head shaved. And he's rolling a smoke and it's not tobacco, which isn't going to help a brain that needed all the help it could ever get.

And he's in the house for two bloody minutes and already Lori can smell his stinking feet. Nothing she can do about him or his feet. He's too much. Too big. His head is damn near level with the top of the doorframe. She might think she's grown up but she knows her limitations so she leaves the boys to it, heads for the kitchen and the jar of Vicks, smears two worthy dabs up her nose then returns to the passage, leans near the lounge-room door, breathing that old familiar air and not liking it.

She puts his beer in the fridge when he tells her, too, doesn't nag him about the stolen junk he's tossed onto their couch; it's a no-no leaving junk on the couch. She's silent, listening to news of Greg and cops and court, listening to tales of smashed-up cars, until she smells hot chips, and Mick, wanting to get on with his assignment, turns back to his keyboard.

'Greg nicked one of those briefcase ones from a car. It had games on it,' Vinnie says, leaning over Mick, poking at keys. And five pages of Mick's assignment, which took him five hours to type in, is lost in cyberspace.

Mick is computer illiterate; he doesn't have a clue, just panics, yells for Lori because Eddy isn't around. The computer has cried 'barley' and the screen is flashing blue with black stripes. Lori turns it off at the power point.

'He said not to do that, Lori!'

'It's all we can do. It will keep it in there somewhere, Mick,' she says. 'Did you name it?'

'I was just going to save it when he did something that disappeared it.'

'You were supposed to give it a name.'

'It wasn't finished!'

Then Eddy comes home, sees the hulk before he sees his computer, hears Mick's lament. 'She's cool,' he says. He glances at the culprit, doesn't say, 'Who are you? How are you? Your feet stink,'

329

though he probably recognises him as another family member by that stink. 'We've got rules in this place. What you don't understand, you don't touch, moron.'

Eddy doesn't know it, but Vinnie has already had too much of that 'moron' thrown at him. He shoves Eddy towards the fireplace and, not expecting things to get physical, Eddy's feet sort of tangle as they connect with the hearth. He falls forward, slams face first into the antique mantelpiece which he loves so much. And he's down.

Lori backs off, backs out of the lounge room. Big country dropping bombs again, wiping the little country out, and just when it was starting to get up on its feet.

She stands at the door, again planning murder by Valium, watching Eddy get up slow. She's seen him playing the clown, seen him all closed up and hurting when Eva was here, but she's never seen him knocked down before. There is something new playing behind those blue eyes. They are cold, like chill-out freezer cold, so cold they're almost glowing hot. Vinnie might be half a metre taller and half a ton heavier, but he could have bitten off more than he can chew by touching that precious computer. Eddy is wiping at his eyebrow, at his bloody nose, but his eyes above his bloody nose are saying, Vinnie, you're a goner.

Maybe Vinnie sees it. He sniggers and backs off. Eddy sits down, sits quiet, dripping blood onto his keyboard, Mick looking over his shoulder. 'Don't worry about it now,' Mick's saying, 'someone grab him some toilet paper,' he's saying, but he's looking at his notes, leafing through his notes, sweating, praying, wanting Eddy to worry, to drip blood onto the keyboard, sweat blood out of that keyboard, only find that missing file.

Vinnie looks bigger in the narrow passage than he did in the lounge room. He sort of swaggers into the kitchen, Lori behind him, certain he's going to grab a chicken, hot from the oven. He sniffs at the chicken and chips smell, looks at the blue walls, the ceiling, then goes to the fridge while Lori closes the back door, stands with her back against it. Alan's book is on the table, but he's taken off some place.

'That's it, you've got it,' Mick yells from the lounge room.

'Of course I got it, and it's now called *Halfwit Hulk*.' Eddy yells those words, then he's up and out the front door. Mick walks through the kitchen and out the back door. He doesn't even look at Vinnie.

Lori starts hacking up the chickens, digging out stuffing that smells like Henry's chicken stuffing but looks like oily herb and onion sandwiches. She hears noise from out the back which she recognises as Mick's drill. He knows it's time to eat. They all know, and they're usually inside helping out when it's time to eat, not fixing stuff.

Vinnie is sitting watching her dish food out onto assorted plates. He's drinking beer and smoking his stuff and she can't take the plastic lace tablecloth off to set the table. He's all over it and dropping his ash all over it and the floor. She always takes her cloth off when they eat, but she gives up trying today. It's going to be ruined. Everything is going to be ruined. She cuts a few slices of breast meat for Mavis, removes the skin, counts out ten chips for her, fills the plate with broccoli, carrots and beans, all boiled up together in one saucepan. She adds a squeeze of lemon juice and a spoonful of cottage cheese, then shares the remaining chips between the rest of the plates while Vinnie helps himself to a chip or ten.

The little kids can smell chips from a kilometre away. They are in and sitting, waiting, but the big ones, from Jamesy up, are still sawing and drilling.

Lori is passing out the plates when she gets the giggles, because she knows what they are doing. She bets she knows, and when they finally come in and shut that door, she's dead certain she knows; they are giggling too, but on the inside.

No one has fed Mavis. Vinnie hasn't even asked about her but he's going to be asking soon. She's smelling the food, yelling for her food. God, don't let her give the game away. Not yet.

Vinnie sinks what's on his plate then pinches two chips from Neil, pinches chicken from Timmy, tries to get Jamesy's drumstick but misses out, and he doesn't like missing out, so he grabs a handful of Matty's chips on his way to the fridge for more beer.

Mick goes to his room, turns his light on, nods to Eddy, who picks up Mavis's plate, then they both disappear out back, close the door behind them.

'What the bloody hell is going on?' Mavis yells. It's muffled but Vinnie hears her, flinches. Maybe he's not so big, after all.

'Where is she?' he says.

'Doing the washing,' Lori replies, quick as a wink.

There is the sound of metal being nailed now and more muffled yelling from Mavis. Alan gets up, Jamesy follows him out. They close the back door.

Vinnie is watching that door, staring at it, sort of expecting Mavis to come through; he's still drinking his beer, though, and the little ones are watching him drink, watching him roll a smoke.

'Go outside and play,' Lori says. They don't move, just stare at Vinnie as if he's flown in from Mars. His eyes are glassy and he's rubbing at his bald head. Lori wipes her tablecloth. She'll have to take it outside, spray it with Mr Muscle then hose it clean. Or buy another one.

Then Henry's radio starts playing on the fence and Mick and Eddy come back to the kitchen. This time they leave the door open.

It's going to happen. It's going to happen soon the way Vinnie is putting away the beer. It's going to happen and they can't wait for it to happen. Mick's eyes are smiling but he's whistling softly, stopping his mouth from smiling. Eddy is just leaning on the sink, wiping at the taps with the dishrag.

Vinnie gets up, flicks Eddy's ear, calls him moron, calls him Sadie, the Cleaning Lady. Eddy doesn't say a word, just keeps wiping at the taps until Vinnie swaggers by him and out to the brick room. Alan and Jamesy are leaning, one on either side of that bolted door. They watch Vinnie pull the bolt, step inside to use the loo, then Alan pushes him in the small of the back, Jamesy slams the door, and Alan rams the bolt home.

'How about that, you great, ugly, bald-headed, computer-crashing moron mongrel?' Eddy yells. And he's sure getting to sound more like Willama.

'How about that, shit-for-brains?' Jamesy adds.

'You're dead. You're stone dead. You just don't know it yet. Shit!' Vinnie screams. He's found Mavis and she's not doing the washing, but Mick's drill is drilling again. He's got three lengths of four-by-two front fence railing which he's already cut to length and drilled. Now he's screwing them to the doorframe, and no one is forcing him to screw them either. He's screwing them fast, using long screws, strong screws, barricading that door which Vinnie is throwing himself at.

He's not going to get through, but it's probably better for the little ones if they don't hear what is going on behind that door, so they leave the dishes in the sink and go over the railway line to town, eat ice-cream at McDonald's.

black slime

The kids come home late – but not late enough. Mavis is vomiting, and moaning. They hear Vinnie. 'I told you. I warned you, you mad bitch.'

'You've killed me, you bastard.'

'Shiii-eeet,' Eddy says. 'He's bigger than I thought he was.'

'You took it. I didn't make you smoke it.'

'She's got into his stuff,' Lori says. She tosses the little ones in the bath, closes all the doors because Mavis is punctuating her bouts of vomiting now with calls on God to save her. It's sort of funny – from the other side of the door – sort of non-Mavis.

'How long will it last? How long?' Mavis is begging Vinnie to say five minutes, but he doesn't; he never could tell a lie.

'I dunno, I told you. A few hours, that's all. And don't you thump me again, or I'll thump you back. I didn't make you do it. You lay off of me, you mad bitch.'

There's more vomiting, and more calling out for God's help. They have to get the little kids out of hearing range because the bathroom isn't out of hearing range.

'Get into bed. All of you. Quick.'

'Vinnie was bad, so he got put in with Mavis,' Neil says, his eyes staring at that door.

'That's what happens, see. I told you. Now you get into bed with the little ones and tell them a story, then go to sleep. All of you.'

In the brick room the noise goes on for hours. Mavis is losing it – she's lost it. She's talking crazy stuff, screaming at Vinnie like he's someone else, like she's somewhere else.

'We'll have to get the doctor,' Mick says. 'I'm going over to Nelly's.'

'We can't get the doctor. Wait.'

It doesn't get any better. Mavis is bawling and talking and Lori is finally learning some stuff about Mavis's father. She's crowding that door, learning a lot and wishing Vinnie would stop his bawling so she could learn more.

It sounds terrible. There is stuff coming out of Mavis that no one knew she had in her, like she's a tap blocked up with gunk and it's turned on and pouring out black slime. 'I loved you, you perverted bastard. You were all I had to love. They didn't tell me. Nobody told me what you'd done.'

There is stuff about her mother trying to kill her too, but Lori can't make head nor tail of that bit. Like, 'Why didn't you let the crazy old bitch drown me at birth instead of slicing my life away, bit by bit?'

They set the radio volume louder and it pretty much cancels what Mavis is screaming. Mick walks out to the street, looks at Nelly's house, now in darkness. Jamesy and Alan head for the potting shed to sample the noise level there while Lori and Eddy remain at the green door. They are getting a word or two when the music stops and the announcer cuts in; they are looking at each other, sort of wide eyed, when Mick comes back.

'Someone is going to call the cops in a minute. You can hear the noise up at the corner. We're going to have to turn the radio off. It's just making it worse, Lori; it sounds like a mob of druggies brawling at a party, and half the neighbours are out at their gates looking down this way.'

They turn the music down, wait, pray for silence – and don't get what they pray for. Mavis is going on about combing her father's hair. There's no sound at all from Vinnie. Maybe she's killed him. They turn the light off, hoping the lack of light might shut her up.

It doesn't. It gets her screaming. 'Help me. Somebody open the door.' They think she's back in the present until she starts screaming for Daddy. Like, 'Help me, Daddy. It's dark, Daddy. I want Daddy.'

They run, turn the light on fast. 'I was only a baby,' she's sobbing, and it's plain cruel awful. 'I didn't know why they hated me. They lived with you, you perverted bastard. They covered up for you and let me love you.' She's a demented thing, howling like they've never heard her howl before. She's raw inside, chewed up and raw and her guts are full of black slimy gore that keeps spilling out. Lori is getting scared. She's never heard of plain grass doing that to people. Maybe it was spiked and she's overdosed. Maybe Vinnie had some of Greg's heroin or something mixed in with it.

They check on the little ones and they're out cold, all three curled together in Mavis's ex central sag. It looks like a whole bundle of little heads, close and safe. Their door is closed tonight. The bunk room boys give up and go to bed, close their door too. Mick and Lori walk a while, but they're tired. They go to Mick's room, close his door, just to keep the noise in, then they sit on the beds, listening through the wall, through the open wardrobe doors, through the hole Mick drilled for the power board and extension cord. They learn a lot. Maybe they learn enough.

At three they know that Vinnie is still alive. 'Lie down and sleep it off, for Christ's sake,' he moans.

Lori takes his advice, lies down on Neil's bed. Maybe she dozes, but it's dawn before Mavis stops bawling and flakes, which allows them to turn Mick's light off and grab a few hours of sleep.

All quiet on the southeastern front come morning, apart from Mavis's raucous, flat on her back, chain-saw snore. They get out of the house early. It's Jamesy's day on house-watch duty, and it's not safe to let Neil go to school today. He's sure to dob. It's not safe to stay in the house today either, so Jamesy and the little ones head for town with the high school kids. They've got money for lunch at McDonald's.

'Everybody will meet up at the little park beside the post office at four, so no dawdling,' Lori says. 'Don't go home. Don't go anywhere near the house. If we open that door now, then that's the end. We've just got to ride it out. Nothing else we can do.'

There is no way to get food into the brick room because Mick has also barricaded the window with his four-by-two's and he's hammered a sheet of corrugated iron over the barricade, hung the shade cloth over the iron to disguise it. The prisoners are in lock-down mode. With the light off, maybe they'll sleep all day. They've got tap water, so they won't dehydrate. Mick is going to work out some way to feed them tonight – anyway, a day of fasting can cleanse the system, the old diet book says, and by the sound of the slime coming out of Mavis last night, she sure needs some deep cleansing.

It gets to four o'clock, but it's a slow day. Jamesy and the little kids are tired out with looking for something to look at. They're waiting at the park, and together the kids walk home, creep to the barricaded window. The brick room is silent, its occupants either dead or sleeping.

They wait until five. Dead silence. Mick drills two holes between the central boards of the green door. It's pitch dark in there, the occupants wouldn't know night from day. He gets Eddy's torch, shines its beam through one hole while peering through the other. And he sees Mavis's leg move. He gets a better angle and sees Vinnie on the couch. He's intact.

'His chest seems to be rising and falling,' Mick says, drilling more holes, to a pattern, then an ancient keyhole saw, which might have belonged to Jesus before Mick bought it at the market, works hard to cut out an eight by twenty centimetre slot. A terrible stink pours out.

'Nothing we can do about it. Mavis has got soap and stuff. Let them clean up their own mess.'

By six-thirty there are sounds of movement behind that door,

337

sounds of the loo flushing, so they turn the light on. Lori has made two medicated custards; there is no way they can get a mug of cocoa through. She knocks on the door, offers a slim, sealed circular bowl through the slot. The cellmates are slow to move. Mavis comes, takes the bowl, tries to take the slim, square bowl as well.

'Is that you, Vinnie?'

'Bloody no, you rotten little mongrels. Let me out,' Vinnie yells back.

'Let him take his custard, Mavis, or you don't get your drink.'

Then Vinnie is at the door and he's not interested in the custard or the extra spoon. He's throwing himself at the door, threatening murder.

An eye to the slot, Lori watches Mavis slurp her custard, clean the bowl with the edge of her finger. Then she does something very interesting. She grabs Vinnie's arm and sort of throws him away from the door so he slams against her bed. And boy, she looks about as sprightly as old George Foreman! She looks as if she could go a round or two without dropping dead!

'Last night didn't do her any physical harm,' she says to Eddy, who is waiting with a plastic cordial bottle, soft enough to dent. 'But how she can eat in there, I don't know. It stinks like something's dead.'

'Throw out your dead. Throw out your dead,' Eddy keens, his hands cupping his mouth to the slot. He gets Mavis's custard container, no lid, shoved in his face. He tries to force the bottle through but it won't go, so Mick has to cut out a bit more wood in the middle of the slot. Mavis snatches the bottle neck the next try, and she tugs, fractures the plastic and wastes half the slimmer's cordial but, more important, wastes the dissolving orange flavoured vitamin in it. They cost a fortune.

'Share what's left, Mavis,' Lori yells. 'And give us back the lid of your custard dish or you won't get any dinner tonight. And both of you, you clean up that mess in there. I can smell sweat and sick and stinking feet from out here so it must be ten times as bad in there.'

They leave them to share or not to share and Lori puts the unused medicated custard into the fridge. Vinnie might eat it later, and if he won't, Mavis will. It's obvious that he's losing the war. He's big, but Mavis has got a psychological advantage.

That night the fence radio is playing and the neighbours are out watering their gardens. They've missed their entertainment. The language coming from the pen is more normal today, though Vinnie is doing a bit of pleading to be let out. It sounds so okay out on the street that Lori takes the opportunity to walk over and catch up with Nelly, who is weeding her front lawn and getting an earful.

'Vinnie came home drunk and smoking marijuana. Mavis is keeping him in the house,' she says. It's true enough. She stands looking towards the house that used to look about as bad on the inside as the outside. For some reason it now looks really terrible from across the road. No wonder Karen turned up her pig-nose at it.

'How is she?' Nelly asks, sort of fishing for details.

'She was okay until Vinnie came home. He's stirred her up again – the only thing that settles her down a bit is music.'

'Well, it's not settling me down, I can tell you that much. I can't stand that thump-thump-thump jungle beat crap.'

'We'll change the station.'

They have a good talk later, and Nelly tells Lori how to make syrup dumplings, which are easy. The kids have them for dinner. Mavis and Vinnie get a container of Donny's tinned sausages and vegetables, and toast, or maybe Mavis gets the two meals. And who cares if she's over her thousand calories?

Three days later and their new selection of slot-sized containers with lids are coming out of the brick room with the lids on. Vinnie is tame. There is no more calling Mavis a mad fat bitch – he's promising to leave the house and never to set foot in Willama again. He's promising to take Greg's stolen DVD player and the other stuff to the cops and give evidence against him; he's promising he won't touch Eddy's computer and he's slurping his medicated custard like a lamb. They are giving them one Valium each, twice a day, and they're counting the rest at night, and it's so much trouble medicating the two of them and making sure the right one gets the toast with the Aropax that they give up, take Mavis off her antidepressants. She doesn't sound a bit depressed. Maybe she's enjoying the company. Maybe they should have got her a dog or something months back.

Eddy reckons Vinnie had speed pills, and Mavis is having a go at them. She's, like, on a high. She's Speedy Gonzales with a foul mouth.

'Bringing bloody drugs into my house, feeding me bloody drugs, you skin-head little bastard.' She's got the adjective wrong. 'Sit down and shut up or I'll finish you off now and save the bloody hangman the trouble in a few years time. I should have drowned you at birth.'

'You tell him, Mave,' Eddy eggs her on. 'You tell him.'

'He's exactly what she needed, a bit of exercise to tighten up the flab,' Jamesy says. 'He couldn't have come home at a better time. I mean, if we'd given her that treadmill for Christmas, she probably would have broken her neck the first time she used it, but a few weeks of this, and by Christmas she'll be ready for it.'

They squirt air-freshener in through the slot, push in a clean tent for Mavis and one of Henry's singlets and a pair of his under-pants for Vinnie. They poke in the thinnest towels and try poking a worn blanket through, but even with Mavis pulling, it won't go. Vinnie has got the tartan one from the couch, and Mavis's winter blanket cape, and she must have donated one of her pillows to him. The kids know they should have thought about blankets and pillows – they should have thought to toss a mattress in before they barri-caded the door – even built a feeding hatch. Nothing much they can do about it now. If they make the slot any bigger, it will weaken those central boards, Mick says.

They spend a lot of time away from the house and when they're home, turn the television volume up a notch. They serve the pris-oners three slim meals a day and life goes on.

paint and forgery

Vinnie has been in the pen for almost two weeks, his hair is spiky and he's looking a bit more like the boy who left home, though he's not taking as well to forced incarceration as Mavis. He's wearing her blanket cape, complaining of the cold on a day that reads thirty degrees on the verandah, so it must be forty in their windowless cell.

'He's got some bloody virus,' Mavis yells.

They make her a triple dose of medicated cocoa, served in a long, slim slot-sized plastic container with a screw-on lid which they bought from Kmart, specifically for hot drinks, and through the slot they watch her drink it, and watch Vinnie, on her bed, looking half dead. The coffee doesn't zap her, but they wait until she's nodding off on her couch, looking relaxed and staring at the television before they unscrew the four-by-two barricades and pull the bolt. She thinks about getting up, then sighs, decides against it, as Lori and the three mobile boys race in and half carry the eager Vinnie out and into the bathroom. He's pale and he's shaking and he's hardly got the strength to walk, let alone threaten, or thump.

The twins and Jamesy strip him, get him into the water where they soak him for an hour, pour buckets of water over his head, and disinfectant over his feet. It's not so easy getting him out. They pull the plug, wipe him off where he sits, get him into Henry's singlet and underpants, then spray his feet with vinegar. He falls out of the bath in the end, but they get him up, walk him to Neil's bed. And he's in it – no help required. Neil can move into the bunk room and stop being one of the little ones.

'We don't have thieves, liars, drunks and druggies, or any fighting in our house nowadays. Can you get that into your thick head?' Lori says, standing over Vinnie, soluble aspirin jumping and fizzing in a glass.

The bed is clean and soft. Vinnie sinks down into heaven.

'We don't have stinking feet, or clothes chucked on the floor. If you stay, you soak your feet in Condy's crystals every night for a week and you change your socks every single day and spray the inside of your shoes with vinegar.' He nods, wants to die, but he nods. He's ready to drink vinegar, eat his socks boiled up with European carp and Condy's crystals. 'As soon as you're fit again, you mow the lawn, chop wood and help us paint the house.'

'White,' Eddy adds.

'Right,' Vinnie whispers.

'And you look after the little kids for us while we go to school. They're the rules. Spit your death and hope to die and I'll give you some aspro.'

He sneezes, sprays the room, which is as close as they're going to get to a spit; she gives him his soluble aspirin which zap him for twelve hours solid.

The barricade comes off the cell window and the air coming out of that room is murder. Mavis isn't complaining, she's looking pleased to be able to spread herself, so they try her on two soluble aspirin in orange juice with her breakfast – just in case she's got Vinnie's virus, and also to see if aspirin might actually work as a substitute for Valium.

But she's acting different, sort of tame – tame for Mavis, that is.

'Have you got any bloody newspapers in this place?' she yells.

They tell her they'll get her some, but in the meantime, would she like to read the forms the pension people sent a while back? Maybe she'd like to fill them in and put the twins on her dependants list.

342

She doesn't say yes, but she doesn't say no either. They leave a packet of chewing gum, the pension papers and a biro when they leave her lunchtime salad and boiled egg. She yells out later, asks them when those redheaded little buggers came back, so they tell her February. She yells out again: 'What bloody month is it, you crazy little shits?' They tell her, and when they pick up her salad plate the papers are under it, filled in and signed, and she's got Vincent Andrew on it too. She's forgotten what year it is – or maybe she can get an allowance for a sixteen year old. She'd probably know. She used to know all the pension stuff better than Centrelink.

In appreciation, they give her pink sausage stew for dinner with a decent-sized boiled potato and a pile of carrots and cabbage. She looks pleased with it, looks sort of pleased with herself. It's probably only about the pension papers; she always did like getting money out of the government. And so what? It's a bit less for them to waste on Canberra and overseas trips.

Vinnie is on aspirin, slimmer's cordial and executive stress vitamin pills for five days and when he's finally out of bed he's pale and quiet, and he looks as if he's shrunk a bit. Henry's singlets almost fit him but his trousers just about reach Vinnie's shins. Lori lops the legs off two pairs, turns them into long shorts, which don't do a lot for his freckled tree-stump legs; he's not going to want to step outside the house, and hasn't got any shoes to step out in. Eddy pitched his stinking sneakers, and all the other stuff he wore home, in the green bin. They probably stank up the whole dump when the garbage was emptied.

'Good hash. Better than Henry's,' Vinnie says, eating Lori's minced steak stew like it is nectar of the gods, forking up the mashed potatoes and silverbeet, wiping his plate clean with bread, his eyes looking peaceful, sort of tame, as if they know they've come home. It's probably a long time since Vinnie has felt safe.

'So, do you want to stay here or not? Make up your mind now,' Lori says, like, hit him while he's weak, before he gets big again.

'Yeah. All right. I'll stay.'

'No stirring Mavis up, no pinching the little kids' food and no nicking off and coming home again when you feel like it, because we won't take you back a second time.'

'Yeah. Okay.'

'What size shoes do you wear?'

'Twelves, I think. I used to.'

'I'll see if I can get you a pair from the op shop.'

He nods, eats syrup dumplings and ice-cream, looks at Timmy's plate when his own is empty, but he shakes his head, places his spoon down.

He shakes his head a lot in the next few days, especially when Mavis bellows from her pen. But she's not bellowing much at all and she's only getting half a Valium twice a day. She's doing the crosswords in the *Herald Sun* and she doesn't even look much like Mavis, except for her daggy red hair. Her features are sagging something awful, like her bulging tyre cheeks have long gone and her multiple chins have sagged into a neck which disappears beneath her faded curtain material dress. That dress sort of floats over the humps and bumps now, and at some angles, when she turns her head fast, she's even got a jaw. Maybe Lori knows why she never totally lost her nubby little chin; it was always attached to a very determined jaw.

They give her boiled chicken breast on Saturday, with a huge serve of green beans, cabbage and celery, onion and potato all boiled up together with the chicken breast. She never liked vegetables but she eats every scrap now. They give her a small half of a roast potato and two thin slices of roast lamb on Sunday, with just a dribble of gravy and a pile of salad, which is mainly cucumber and lettuce and celery, because the diet book says that these three have pretty much no calories. She gets fish on Monday, European carp, stuffed with Mick's onions and Nelly's lemons. She eats it and seems . . . seems sort of satisfied.

It's November before they introduce Vinnie to a paintbrush. He's more than willing to help slap a bit of paint on the kitchen ceiling, he's been going on about feeling seasick since the first day he was able to lift his head up and look at that blue. He reckons it brings back memories of the day Greg pinched a boat and they ran out of petrol in the bay, got picked up by two fishermen four hours later.

The pension money has sort of mushroomed since they posted off Mavis's pension form, and the paint was on special at Kmart, proper ceiling paint, which doesn't drip as much; either that, or Vinnie knows how to put it on without dripping it. It takes three coats of white to cover that blue, and he sure paints slow; he also finds the last packet of Valium and Lori's ex cigarette fund in the jar on top of the cupboard.

'The thieving mongrel.' Five pills are missing. When she counts the money, she knows a fifty has gone.

They don't say anything to Vinnie, because they want him to paint the kitchen walls before he takes off; the postcard border is falling down and when you get a scratch on a bright blue wall, the white shows through so it looks even more scratched. Also, they haven't spent a penny on clothes for him, except for his Kmart shoes. He's still wearing Henry's lopped-off trousers and underwear, which look so bad he's got no desire to leave the house, so he couldn't have spent their fifty yet.

He's not one of them. He ran while Mick and Lori had to stay, and he's been with Greg too long, that's the main trouble.

They call a meeting in Henry's potting shed, decide to open a bank account in Lori's name for the ex cigarette money and for what is left over in Mavis's account each fortnight, sort of put it away safe for emergencies.

Banks. They've got thieves' hearts and computer brains. Because she's only a kid, Mavis has to sign the forms before she can open an account. Bloody forms, bloody notes to teachers. They are the bane of Lori's life.

Knowing Mavis's attitude to money, they can't tell her about putting her pension money into Lori's name, so everyone has a go at the signature. Vinnie is keeping quiet. Maybe he knows that they know he knocked off their fifty. He's on his knees painting the kitchen cupboards black and he's keeping his head down, painting slow, painting careful.

Jamesy does the signature best. It's only a squiggle, a big M that sort of runs into Sm O and a tail. They are going to get him to do it, and if any questions get asked, they'll say Mavis had a fall and sprained her right wrist. Then Vinnie stands up, looks sort of guilty. He puts his brush on a sheet of newspaper and comes to sneeze over Lori's shoulder, then he picks up the pen and make the M Sm O squiggle.

Perfect.

The forging mongrel! He can barely write his own name! They turn on him, accuse him, and he gets back down on his knees, starts painting again, slow, careful.

'Greg used to make me do it. I never done it in Melbourne because the banks wouldn't give it to me,' he says.

'So you learned to pinch money instead. We know you knocked off our fifty, and Mavis's Valium – which are more precious than money. And you'd better not try forging that signature again,' Lori says, '. . . unless we ask you to.'

They let him off his knees to sign the bank forms, then he gives them the fifty.

'I only wanted some jeans. Every time I bend over in these bloody things they nearly cut off my b – '

'We don't have swearing in our house,' Neil says.

the hope chest

It's not all easy. Vinnie has his moments and so does Mavis, but it's pretty easy. Lori is feeling hopeful when she and Mick go to the op shop to get Vinnie's jeans. They find a pair that are half okay, and a blue tracksuit that should fit him. Then Lori finds another one, a giant's tracksuit, bottle green, but barely used. She takes it too, for the future, for Mavis, maybe next winter.

A big lady is looking at a maroon dress, and when she puts it down, Lori picks it up fast, holds it high. It looks a lot smaller than Mavis's tents, but she tosses it over her arm and searches on. There's a bra in a box that looks as if it might fit an elephant. She grabs it, then buys two perfectly good T-shirts for Vinnie.

'I don't suppose you'd have any really huge knickers, would you?'

The op shop lady digs deep, finds another giant bra but no knickers. Then she goes to the men's side and offers three brand-new, still in their packets, men's boxer short underpants, stretchy grey ones with elastic waistbands. Lori holds a pair high, measures them with her eye. Mick gets embarrassed, walks out and leaves Lori to it.

The saleswoman doesn't even charge for the two bras. Maybe she thinks they won't fit. 'They've been here since Adam was a boy,' she says. 'Glad to find a use for them, love. How is your mum going these days?'

'Still housebound.' Lori gives her ten dollars and won't accept the change. If that woman can be charitable, so can she. She's got a pile of money in her account and Mick is getting worried that the bank people will start wondering where it's coming from – he still thinks people run banks.

Eddy keeps telling them that they have to stop being so mean with money. They got a heap of back pay, which he wants to use on painting the roof and the weatherboards. Which is ridiculous. That would be a huge job. Anyway, Lori and Mick are too scared to spend that bonus, just in case the pension people have made a mistake and they ask for it back.

They are walking by the curtain shop when Lori sees some material that would be perfect for lounge-room curtains. It's shiny greeny-brown stuff and it's reduced from nineteen dollars a metre to twelve. She wants it, like, six metres of it. The window is long but not wide. They buy it and buy cotton to match, and some wooden ring things to put on the top. And a rod, a gorgeous thing with plastic antique knobs at each end.

Eddy stirs her about spending money, tells her that it probably cost as much as roof paint, red roof paint, and how come she can have curtain material without asking anyone and he can't have roof paint?'

'You don't know your limitation, that's why,' she says.

'And neither do you. You should have bought those ready-made ones from Kmart.'

'They were the wrong colour. Anyway, Nelly said before that she'd help me.'

She does too – she does the brainwork and Lori does the stitching. For two days those curtains get carried backwards and forwards over the road, but when they are done and hung, they look just brilliant. That room looks pure brilliant – as long as you don't look too closely at the wallpapering, which is not actually brilliant. One day they'll have to replace it because one bit along the verandah wall is always rolling down and half falling off and they have to keep gluing it back.

'So, we'll paint the outside next. White,' Eddy says.

'It's not worth it.' Mick is sick of the stink of paint. 'Those boards are so rotten they'd drink paint by the bucketful.'

'Paint is like glue,' Eddy says. 'It will glue the boards together.' No one takes him seriously. Painting those old boards would be a huge job.

Except Vinnie. He takes him a bit seriously, like he argues with him about having a red roof. He wants a green roof. Vinnie has gone paint happy since they gave him his first brush. He and Eddy have just finished the bathroom, which looks truly awesome, or would look awesome if they could afford some vinyl for the floor.

Anyway, a couple of nights later, Eddy takes to Mavis's brick wall with the leftover bathroom paint and he paints swastikas all over the multicoloured bricks, paints 'Lori, the dictator' across at the back, 'Lorraine the pain' on the side.

'It improves it,' Vinnie says. 'The bloody thing has always looked like a diseased boil on an old dame's bum.'

November is almost over when Eddy goes off one Friday afternoon and spends Eva's fifty on ten litres of white outdoor acrylic. She's still paying that weekly fifty into his account at the Commonwealth Bank – probably forgot to tell her accountant to cancel it before she left for Paris.

She writes every week or two, or sends postcards, the message always the same, like: 'To my darling sons. We miss you so much'. That sort of thing. Alan hardly looks at the cards, like he won't look at her money, though the account is in both names. Eddy writes to her and he still calls her Mum. They are so different. They are not even like brothers, let alone twins.

Anyway, that same night Eddy gets the ladder out and he and Vinnie start painting the bricks. Vinnie, who still catches every bug that's going around, sneezes between careful brushstrokes, saying amid sneezes that Eddy should have bought roof paint first, due to they'll splatter the white walls with the green roofing paint, and, anyway, they need new guttering more than a painted roof or walls.

It's true. The guttering is mainly rusted out, and the downpipes are all down. Not that they can do anything about that. That's work for a plumber.

'I wonder where that Jeff bloke is.' He sneezes. 'You remember, Mick? That bloke that connected up the pipes and stuff when me and Martin built this bloody abortion.'

'I dunno,' Mick says. He's not much into talking to Vinnie.

'I could probably put a bit up myself,' Vinnie says, looking at that roof, sort of rubbing his head, which has now gone back to a mess of carrot-coloured curls.

'It could hurt,' Lori says. She's not happy about those painted bricks.

Vinnie doesn't get it, he's still sneezing and talking guttering to Eddy, who is still sloshing the paint on.

Those two started out wrong but they've pretty much got over it. Maybe they both feel a bit on the outer. Eddy gives way as Vinnie climbs up the ladder and walks around on the roof for half an hour. And he finds out why the wallpaper keeps coming unstuck over the lounge-room window. The roof is leaking. One bit of iron is bent up and rusty. He fixes it too, or him and Mick work out how to fix it. They get another sheet of corrugated iron from the junk heap down the back and swap it over, then the next time Lori sees them, they are looking for her new measuring tape so they can measure the house for new guttering.

Nelly, who is working in her garden, sees them and she comes over to where the fence used to be. She never comes any closer. It's like she knows what's going on now, like maybe Martin told her. Anyway, she tells them they'll need new bargeboard on the west wall.

'Bargeboard?' Mick says.

'The wood bit the guttering sits on, Smithy.'

'We'll have to pay someone.'

'Jesus!' Lori moans.

'He was a carpenter,' Eddy says, sloshing a swastika on the front weatherboards, sloshing beneath it, 'Lorraine Louise, give me a squeeze' – due to something that happened at school the other day, the eavesdropping moron.

Anyway, Nelly heads for home and rings up the bloke who did her new guttering ten years or so back. He'll come around and give Mavis a quote. Eddy is in the shower, trying to wash paint out of his hair, which Lori put there, while she was sloshing paint over Eddy's bloody graffiti. Anyway, it wasn't her that he should have been writing about. It was Leonie Perkins.

As it turns out, the plumber is five foot nothing, wears a hearing aid and looks about eighty, but he says he'll do the job if Vinnie can do the wrecking work and lend a bit of a hand with the lifting; he'll order the stuff and the bargeboard and he'll come around on Saturday and do it for cash in hand, which is illegal with the GST, but he's on the pension, so it's got to be cash in hand.

'We don't have a problem with that,' Vinnie says.

Lori and Mick ride over to the bank to withdraw the deposit money. It's going to cost a fortune but the old bloke says if Mavis is stuck for cash, she can pay him off a bit at a time. They're not stuck for cash, it's just that they don't want to use the back pay. 'We'll live off the land, Mick, eat what's in the cupboards and freezer. Live on eggs and baked beans, get the kids down to the river for some fish, get home brand porridge instead of cornflakes. It will be all right.'

Vinnie is good at wrecking. He and the mobile boys are on the roof pulling the old stuff down when they find another sheet of roofing iron gone warped, which Henry had weighted down with bricks. Vinnie tosses the bricks overboard and nearly kills Neil, who dodges in the nick of time and only gets half a brick on his big toe. He'll probably lose the nail. While Neil goes bellowing off to nurse his wound in front of the television, the rest of them head for the junk heap looking for another bit of corrugated iron.

Spud Murphy has been leaning on his fence, watching and yelling out stuff. He yells out that he's got some roofing nails so Mick limps over the road to get them, and ends up falling in love with Spud's oil drum full of nails and bolts and nuts and junk. He doesn't come back for an hour. It looks as if Mick has found a new friend.

Anyway, for two days there's banging and tearing tin and Mavis yelling at everyone to shut the bloody noise up because she can't hear the television. Lori tells her that the guttering is so bad they've got to get it fixed. She also tells her there is a bloke coming around to do the spouting at the weekend. She offers Mavis a packet of chewing gum and Alan's *Jurassic Park*. Mavis takes them, makes no comment. Maybe she's plotting her freedom.

They've got a two-Valium custard ready to go, but the plumber bloke comes near dawn and they can't wake her up just to zap her again, and maybe she won't wake up for a while, or the plumber won't hear her above the noise he's making. He's turned his hearing aid off and he's deaf as a post without it.

By the second day, the kids have all got stiff necks from looking up, following Vinnie and the old bloke's progress. His name is Mr Wilson and he looks half dead this morning, doesn't even comment on the illegal brick room, which is now painted white, which improves it – like, it's not so in-your-face when you step out the back door.

Lori is leaning against those white bricks guarding the window and nursing yesterday's Valium custard, which they didn't need to use, while Vinnie and the old bloke work their way to the corner, and around the corner. No custard required this morning, either. It goes back in the fridge. Vinnie helps himself to it for morning tea, the bloody idiot. He's half zonked for the rest of the day, like falling off the ladder while he's holding stuff, like almost dropping the barge-board when he's lifting it for the old bloke – and almost dropping him too. And by late afternoon, Mavis could have used that custard. She's screeching about the noise again, and the old bloke, who has worked his way right around and back to the front verandah, and is now sitting on it, his hearing aid turned on while he's having tea and a smoko, lifts his head.

'She can't get you, 'cause she can't get out the door,' Neil assures him.

'Grown herself in, eh?' the old bloke says, nods, almost nods off. 'I heard about that happening once to a feller.' He looks at the house, shakes his head, feeling guilty about the new guttering. 'They had to knock the wall down to git him out.' He sighs, thinks about standing but changes his mind. 'I seen your mother once, you know. She was no lightweight back then. Life's a real bitch, sonny,' he says, 'and then you croak.' And he's up, feet under him, and he looks about ready to croak.

They watch his every step, and at six-thirty he's still moving, though the later it gets the slower he moves – and how he keeps on moving they don't know, but he gets it done before it's pitch dark; he even gets the new downpipes in. Then he won't take all the money, just what it cost him for materials. They keep pushing it at him, wanting him to take it and go while he still can, but he's standing there, sucking on another smoke.

'You're a good kid,' he says to Vinnie. 'You too, lad,' he says to Mick, who is still shoving the money at him. 'You're all good kids. And you tell your mother I said so, too.' And he shuffles off to his truck, the kids following close at his side, wanting to take an arm, help heave him up. Then he's in and the old motor's roaring. Mick drops a bag holding a dozen eggs and the rest of the money onto the passenger seat and hopes he or his wife notices the money. 'Thanks,' the kids chorus. 'Thanks very much, Mr Wilson.'

He drives off into the night but they stand on just staring at their new guttering. Not a lot of light left to see by, but the house seems to be standing taller, as if that old bloke has given it back a bit of pride. Eddy is not pleased the guttering turned out green. He didn't know it would be coloured and no one knew it was going to be green. Except maybe Vinnie. He's standing with them, yawning instead of sneezing, and maybe it's not the Valium; he looks as tired as the old bloke.

'You told him to order green,' Eddy accuses. Vinnie yawns again, doesn't deny it. 'I wanted red guttering, a red roof.'

'I want me dinner,' Vinnie says. They walk back to the verandah.

'A green roof will look good,' Alan says. 'It will look cooler than red.'

'Be real,' Lori yawns. 'How could we possibly paint a roof red, green or purple?'

'We're painting it – even if it has to be green.' Eddy is prepared to give up on red but he's not giving up on his painted roof.

'I don't like anythink what's green,' Neil says. 'And I don't like celery.'

'Fish and chips,' Vinnie says, looking in the fridge. Eggs, eggs and more eggs.

'No. And you're all mad,' Lori says. She takes out her favourite baking pan, sloshes in some oil and starts cracking eggs, tossing in leftover boiled rice, shaking in pepper, salt, a dash of tomato sauce, a can of the mixed vegetables Donny brought up months back. A bit of a stir, a bit of milk, a handful of cheese to cover the mess and she slides the pan into the oven. 'As if we could paint a whole roof! It's not even worth discussing. Someone do something useful. Toast. Chuck a bit of salad on a plate for Mavis and get those little kids bathed. Food will be ready in half an hour.'

They eat a lot of eggs in the next week, they eat them fried, baked, boiled and scrambled, eat them in stale-bread puddings, eat them cold with salad while the boys talk paint. Lori just ignores them – until Mick gets converted and goes up to the paint shop, starts talking roof paint. By the weekend Vinnie is sick of eggs; he wants meat, so he commits murder, and it's tough chook for Sunday dinner. Two tough chooks. They've got too many chooks, anyway. The poor buggers are as crowded as battery hens in that pen.

'You should have boiled the bloody things,' Mavis yells when they feed her a chewy old boiler's breast. 'You can't roast old chooks, you boil them, you silly little buggers.'

Vinnie has a second go at murder, and this time two young roosters lose their heads. The kids are living high off the land.

Lori still won't agree to talk roof paint, and Mick won't agree to doing it unless they do it properly, use the paint recommended by the paint shop man, which must be made out of crushed-up emeralds because it costs a fortune.

It's funny, really, how you talk so long about the *if, if, if,* until that *if* sort of starts to turn into a *how* and even *when.* They buy the paint next pension day and wheel it home in a shopping trolley.

Spud Murphy sees them on the roof that evening, trying to hang on with their toenails while they clean it down, due to the man at the paint shop told Mick they'd have to clean it before any paint goes on. Spud offers his roof ladders. 'And don't break the bloody things,' he says.

Mick gives him a dozen eggs; the chooks have gone egg-laying crazy, probably because they've got a bit more room to lay in. Anyway, the roof ladders get hauled up and hooked over the roof's peaks; they make washing that roof dead easy, no more sliding down as they work with hose and broom.

Henry always used to say that many hands made light work. On Saturday they rise with the sun, aware that by midday the roof will fry the lot of them like eggs in a pan. Ten hands start slopping, brushing and rolling their precious emerald-studded paint on the west side while Mick waits below, filling up jam tins with more paint and passing them to Neil, who's standing halfway up the ladder, which doesn't give the painters an excuse to stop. Vinnie is playing boss, walking that roof like a circus performer and pointing out the missed spots; maybe he's found something he can do better than them.

Mavis becomes a secondary consideration that weekend. They give her a fried sandwich for tea on the Saturday, though she doesn't get fed until nine-thirty. They started on the east roof as soon as the sun skipped over to the west, and they kept on painting until there was no light left to see where they were putting it. The sandwich is loaded with oil, but all the cooks are too damn tired and sore to cook anything, and they've got to get up at dawn again tomorrow, and the only thing Mick can cook is fried sandwiches, and who's counting calories?

Mavis's eyes sort of light up, almost like in the photograph on the lounge-room wall. It's months since she had anything that might qualify as junk food, and she always loved bread and grease. She could eat a loaf of sliced bread and a tub of margarine in one sitting in the old days, and she loved fried sandwiches. This one is cheese and tomato and she eats it like a lady, then licks her fingers, like it was so good. So good. Her eyes are looking right at Lori when she hands the plate back. She's got big eyes. They don't look old. She's got eyelashes too, darkish brown and long like the twins, not sandy stubby ones like Donny's.

'Make me another one,' she says.

'You get diet yoghurt tonight,' Lori yawns. 'Then you can have an apple.'

'Peel the bloody thing then,' Mavis says.

The kids are painted green and burnt scarlet by the time they get a second coat on, but the roof looks as if it's laughing down at the tired old weatherboards, which are crying out now for their share of love. They've got to do it. They've got to paint those boards even if they're not worth painting.

'Youse have done a real good job on the roof,' Bert Matthews says. 'I might hire youse to do mine.' He's joking, though Vinnie doesn't know it.

'We've got to do the walls, then you're on.'

'Could we get them done by Christmas? Then invite Martin and Donny to dinner,' Lori yawns.

'Christmas. We forgot to pay something off our lay-by this week,' Mick says.

'Pay them next week and we'll pick it up. I'm going to bed.'

paint

Eddy adds Eva's money to the cigarette jar on Friday; bills still have to be paid. They pick up their lay-by on Saturday, hire a disabled taxi and get the Kmart guys to load the treadmill in. The taxi driver is not too happy having to help Vinnie get it out, but he does. Eddy gives him a dollar tip. Lori gives him two more.

They eat old boiler soup, full of Mick's carrots, onions and zucchini on Sunday, and it's all right, too.

Nails, Mick writes on his list. A lot of the old boards are loose. Fill-A-Gap. A lot more boards have got splits. Sandpaper. No one writes down that other word. No one mentions that unmentionable stuff. There is a new dirty word in this house.

Paint.

One of the kids only has to whisper it, and it makes them all flinch. They look at hands where old blisters have dried. Lori cut her finger on one of the brushes when she was painting the roof and it still hasn't healed. Maybe she's willing it not to heal, but Alan gets her a bowl of hot salty water. Henry used to say salt killed germs better than antibiotics. It fixed his tonsils. He hasn't had one cold this year. She sighs and sits soaking her hand, then sticks on a bandaid.

The window frames have to be scraped down, Nelly says, due to there is a bit of flaky paint left on some of them. The twins and Jamesy get stuck into them with kitchen knives and sandpaper while

Mick hammers nails and screws screws into sagging weatherboards. Vinnie is working behind him, filling cracks with Fill-A-Gap.

Christmas is breathing down their necks when they buy a ton of cheap outdoor acrylic and two more tubes of Fill-A-Gap then shout themselves a taxi ride home.

'How's Mavis going?' the driver asks.

'Good,' Mick says, which is true – when she gets fed on time and they don't give her baked beans – even if it does sound like a lie.

Every taxi driver in Willama knew Mavis's address and they are probably missing her more than most. 'She's not getting out these days, eh?'

'She can't get out – ' Neil starts.

'Neil! Remember Vinnie?' Lori says. It's enough to silence the blabbing little bugger, who has already said enough to convince the taxi driver that the new talk going around town is fact. Mavis Smyth-Owen has grown herself in.

The kids have decided to do the verandah posts, bargeboard, doors and window frames lemon. They've all been looking at houses, trying to decide what colour to put with the white and green. They settle for lemon. There is an old house down near the high school which is white, green and lemon and looks sort of sedate, serene. It's got a similar roof to their house, a similar verandah too, similar sort of lacy woodwork between the verandah posts, which is going to be a pure pain in the bum to paint. They'll let Vinnie paint that, and the fancy woodwork around the little roof gable.

Nelly offers her trestle ladders with the board you can put between them to stand on, then she stands on it herself one day while the kids are at school. She's an excellent painter, so is Vinnie. The kids get home and those two have already got a coat of paint on the front of the house and it's like, wow!

Nothing is happening at school except a couple of excursions that no one, other than Neil, is going on. They cost money. The rest of them wag it, but even with Nelly helping it still takes over a week to get two coats of paint on, and get those boards looking okay, and okay is good enough to look perfect from Nelly's side of the road. They are sick of the stink and the brushes and blisters, sick of climbing up and down ladders, and they are never touching another paintbrush if they live to be a hundred, and that's all there is to it. Until they come home from school on that final day and find Vinnie has been around the house filling up previously unsighted cracks with Fill-A-Gap, marring the near perfection of their paint job.

'What did you have to go and do that for?' It's like the joint cry of the damned.

He's spent too much time with Mick lately; he's starting to sound like him. 'If a job's not worth doing right, then don't bloody do it at all, I say.' They attack Vinnie, four on one, and they get his Fill-A-Gap gun, get him down and sit on him, try to shove its nozzle up his nostrils, fill up a few of his brain gaps.

But he's probably right. One more coat. Mick thinks he's right, so it's more *effing paint* first thing in the morning. They'll get it done before Christmas Day or bust. And oh boy, when the third coat is on, it looks better than okay, and that wooden lacework looks so posh. Even the trellis looks better.

The neighbours are hanging around in droves. Even the ones they don't know are going for walks at sundown so they can stare at the Smyth-Owen place. It's like, Christ, what's happened down here? You can read it in their eyes.

'That old girl is looking bloody good,' Bert Matthews says. He's on the front verandah, wriggling a loose board – not the one that attacked Eva's shin; she broke it. He starts nosing around the windows then, pretending he's checking the paintwork, but he's actually trying to get a look inside. 'Do youse want a hand putting a few boards on your v'randah? I used to do a bit of chippie work in me day.'

'Not yet, thanks,' Mick says. 'That's for after Christmas.'

'How's your tomatoes going this year?' Bert asks, heading towards the back yard, wanting to get a look through the kitchen window, get a look at Mavis.

The wire hinges are off the gate. It's leaning back against the fence, due to the inconvenience of lifting ladders over it, or carrying them through the house, so Bert continues his constitutional down to the back yard.

'Got any ripe yet?'

'A few.' Mick follows him.

'How you doing in there, Mavis?' Bert yells at the kitchen louvres.

'None the better for your asking, Bert Matthews,' she yells back, and she almost sounds like her old self, sort of cheeky.

Whether it's right or wrong, what they are doing to her is working. She's as tame as a lamb lately, and shrinking every day. It's sort of scary – the hoping is. And the watching and the waiting is scary too, like, will she go off her head again, start yelling again? And when will she go off her head again?

She shrank heaps while they were working on the house and didn't have time to feed her regularly, or look at her too often. There was so much of her that, for a while, the bit that came off wasn't obvious, but she's getting down to people size now, and it's so obvious, it's sort of almost too wonderful, almost like an *if* that came true.

Martin nearly drops dead when he comes around late on Christmas Eve. Donny comes too. Lori wanted the boys home for Christmas dinner to eat home-grown chook, which tastes heaps better than bought chook. She wanted those boys to drive up Dawson Street by daylight, really see the house. Of course, they couldn't come; Donny is going to Jackie's place and Martin and Karen are having dinner with her parents. But they're here now, and they have brought a ton of presents and drinks and lollies, so it's like a party.

Anyway, Martin is just plain flabbergasted, even by what he can see in the half dark. 'I'm flabbergasted. I'm bloody speechless. Who did it?'

'We did.'

Donny is so impressed he doesn't believe they did it, like maybe the town people did it for them, or the Salvation Army.

'We did it all – except the guttering. Except the front, which Nelly did for us. Ask Spud Murphy, ask Nelly. Ask anyone.'

The boys can't stop looking at stuff long enough to sit down and have the party. They look at the outside by torchlight, they look at the lounge room, at the Christmas tree, then they go back outside to shine the torch all over. They get to Mavis's window and Donny returns to the kitchen.

Martin doesn't. He's standing there, staring at her. And he's totally floored. He says that too, says it to Mavis, like, 'I'm floored. I am wipe-out stupefied, Mavis. You're a shadow of your former self.' Lori hasn't had time to make new tents, and the upside-down bird one Mavis is wearing hangs on her like a sack.

'I'm flabbergasted,' Martin says. His head is inside the window and Lori is standing with him, as proud of the transformation of Mavis as she is of the house. 'They've given you a new lease on life,' he says, as if he wants her to talk to him, to say something that's not, 'Get out, you bastard.'

She doesn't say a word, just turns her back and lifts her skirt to him, gives him a good view of her rear, but she's got her op-shop grey boxer shorts on which flap around her knees, so it's not too gross.

'That's looking pretty good too,' he says. And she still doesn't scream.

Then he's back in the kitchen and shaking his head. 'You bloody kids. How did you do it?' Vinnie starts sort of big-noting himself, but Martin is not taking much notice. He's looking at Mick, he's looking at Lori.

'Eddy nagged us into doing the painting,' Lori says, and Donny looks at Alan.

'Him,' Alan points a thumb.

'I'm floored,' Martin says for the umpteenth time, and finally they have their party because Donny has to leave soon.

'Got any prescriptions you want filled?'

They shake their heads, look at the presents he's left in supermarket bags on the floor. Look at the food he brought. Two huge frozen chickens, which is coal to Newcastle, but he's also brought a pile of other stuff.

'Ta for everything,' Lori says. She gives Donny three pairs of socks from beneath the Christmas tree. She's had an ongoing affair with new socks since Eddy came home and burned the stiff ones. Martin gets his socks too, but he stays on, stays for hours after the little ones have been put to bed.

They get to talk Valium. 'I suppose I can ring the doctor again, but sooner or later he'll want to come round. What do I say to him if he wants to come around?'

'Tell him she's much better, that she's off the Aropax and she doesn't want to see anyone until she's lost some more weight,' Eddy says.

'No. Don't tell him she's lost weight or he'll really want to come around. Just say to him that she's well, but she still needs Valium, in case of emergencies.'

That old doctor is no masochist; he writes another two scripts.

mick's mate

'You know what you can do with bloody Christmas,' Mavis says when the bolt is drawn on Christmas morning. She's sitting, reading *The Tommy Knockers*. They've already ascertained that much via the window. She looks up from her book when the door opens and the kids shove in a second-hand electric fan on a stand, then the tread-mill – which they've all tested, and it does work – then a tiny laminex kitchen table and one matching chair, which they picked up at a garage sale for five dollars. Mavis doesn't show any interest in her presents or the open door, so they close it again and slide the bolt, go to the window.

She gets up, her thumb keeping her place in the book, and she walks between the basin and the end of her bed, no strain getting by, either, and she claims the fan. They watch her bend over, easy, pull out the heater plug and replace it with the fan's. She looks at the watchers at the window, shows them her thumb, then sets about making herself comfortable. The bed gets shoved lengthwise against Mick's wall. What's she up to? Clearing a passage so she can make a charge the next time they open that door?

Matty wants to be lifted up to see, so Lori lifts him. They watch Mavis drag the table, place it close to her couch, go back for the chair and fan, position them, then she sits at the table, finds her place in the book and reads, the fan blowing on her hair. The only barricade between her couch and the door is the treadmill. She hasn't looked at that.

'That other thing is a treadmill,' Lori says. 'The instructions are with it, and they tell you to take it slow at first.'

'Get lost, you crazy mob of little buggers.'

'Ik's Mewwy Kissmak,' Matty says. 'Wowi gog a puggy ana cusgag.'

'He's nearly three bloody years old. Is he retarded?'

'We gone hab fwheary nour hout,' Matty lectures around his dummy. It's unintelligible, which is lucky.

'Get that bloody dummy out of his mouth and he might learn to talk,' Mavis says.

They walk away, but when Lori returns to the window with Mavis's Christmas dinner, she can see the treadmill has been swung around to point east and west – and it's no lightweight, either. She's clearing a pathway. But it's pretty remarkable that she can clear a pathway! She's moving so well these days. It's amazing just to watch her stand up, walk to the window, take the plate Lori has placed on the shelf.

'Ta,' she says, and that's amazing too. It's like she's tame – or is she just doing a tame act because she's realised that abuse isn't going to make them open the door? Probably. Probably waiting her chance to get out and start stuffing again. A leopard can't change its spots.

Or maybe it can.

Lori is changing – or some of her attitudes are changing. Right from when she was about seven, she's always been ready with a nasty reply when she thought the kids at school were having a go at her; and with Karen that night, she was pure nasty, which sort of still comes natural, but she's trying now to force herself to stop being naturally nasty – and bossy, because . . . well, maybe because of what Martin said that night, but more because . . . well, actually, because of Paul Perkins.

He's nearly sixteen, and a few months back he decided that Mick was his best friend. And also, he's got a sister, Leonie, who is sort of trying to make Lori a best friend, due, probably, to the fact that she hasn't got any friends, not in Willama. They've only been in town since late October and they live in the East, not close, like neighbours, but in the next street back from the town. There are just the two of them in the family, and they've probably never had anything to do with big families and little kids. Not that they ever come inside the house, though they used to call by on school mornings and all ride to school together, and some evenings now they knock at the door and they all go down to the swimming bend together.

They play with the little kids, help watch them, and Paul, well, he sort of mucks around with Lori, treats her as if she's a girl, the moron. She's got new black bathers she bought for the swimming sports – which she won, the one hundred metres, the four hundred and the relay. Anyway, those bathers sure make her look like a long-legged, long-necked girl. A lot of boys stare at her now and sort of hang around her and Leonie, which is the reason Eddy wrote what he did on the wall that day.

She tells them to *eff* off and she should tell Paul to *eff* off too. She would, except for Leonie. Lori likes the idea that she's got a friend – seeing as she hasn't really had one since first grade. She should tell him to *eff* off, though. But . . . but if you like people then you like them and that's all there is to it . . . and he's . . . he's likeable.

He's almost good looking, no pimples, and he doesn't laugh at Mick's crazy bike, and lately Mick has got game enough to take his brace off in front of him and hop down to the river for a swim; he's a good swimmer, due to that rubber leg doesn't bother him too much in the water, but he's never taken his brace off before, not in front of anyone except family. That's another reason Lori doesn't tell Paul to *eff* off; she doesn't want to spoil things for Mick.

That's what she tells herself, but it's not really true. Like the other night, he grabbed her around the waist when she was trying to race him across the river and she got this stupid yucky weird feeling in her stomach and started wondering what she'd do if he ever tried to kiss her and what it would be like if he did kiss her and . . . and other stuff.

What a moron, she thinks, watching Mavis dip her finger into the gravy, taste it. A lot of the flavour came out of a packet of Gravox, but it tastes heaps better than Henry's gravy.

'What are you waiting for?' Mavis says, licking her finger.

'Nothing.'

'At least it tastes like food for a change. Where's me rabbit food?' She almost makes a joke.

'I'll get you some if you'd prefer it.'

'Stop standing there, staring at me like I'm a bloody monkey in the zoo.'

'You've lost a ton of weight, you know.'

Mavis makes no reply, just picks up her knife and fork, starts eating, but she sure has lost a ton. She's thinner than that time they went to Melbourne, thinner than Lori can ever remember her.

'There's pudding and custard later.'

'Enough to fill my back tooth, I suppose?' Mavis says.

After New Year they buy a good solid lounge chair at a garage sale and they have to wheel it six blocks home. Lucky it's got castors. People look at them as if they are crazy, and a mob of kids starts poking fun, so Eddy says it's for Mick to sit on when he gets tired of pedalling his bike, then Mick gets off his bike and says, 'I'm tired already,' and he sits on the chair. They all kill themselves laughing as they push him along for a block or two.

They make a medicated custard for Mavis that night for supper, because they want her sleeping on her bed. Also, it was such a struggle getting that mouldy old couch in, it's not going to be fun getting it out. They wait until she's in bed, then they creep in, leave Mick at the door, to bolt it if he has to. They'll go out the window.

Maybe they are all stronger than they were a year ago, but mainly, they didn't have Vinnie then. His muscle makes the difference, makes it easy. He's up one end, Alan and Lori at the other. They lift that couch, tilt it so it goes through the door, then stand it on end to get it through the narrow walkway between kitchen and brick room. Easy. It's out. They all yell, 'Pitch it,' and it gets run down to the junk heap, gets pitched.

Vinnie picks up the new chair as if it's nothing, carries it above his head and sets it down in the northeast corner, and suddenly that brick room looks a whole heap better. He's getting to be worth having home; maybe they'll raise his pocket money – if they need to.

Something very funny happened to Vinnie on Boxing Day. Something no one expected would ever happen to Vinnie. Because he's the biggest, it's natural for the neighbours to think he's responsible for the paint job, which, to a large degree, he is. Anyway, this guy came knocking at the door, and he asked Vinnie if he was interested in a job. He's a painter, married to the daughter of the old plumber bloke who did the guttering, and his offsider is in the Albury hospital, being treated for something. He said to Vinnie that he was looking for a young bloke who's proved he isn't scared of a bit of hard work and who is handy with a paintbrush. He can't offer full-time work at the moment, but it might work out full-time in a couple of months. Then he started talking money.

Vinnie got all embarrassed and he went bright red. 'Yeah, I like painting better than plumbing. Right. You're on,' he said. So it looks as if he might get a bit of work, which will mean he won't need pocket money. And also, he won't be able to look after Matty when the kids go back to school. You win some, you lose some. It's good that it happened, though, good for Vinnie's self-esteem or whatever, and good for Henry too – wherever he is. He'd be so proud to think that some guy had sought out one of his sons, when heaps of kids in town haven't got jobs. Lori even feels a bit proud.

The painter told Vinnie he'd need white overalls, so they bought him a brand-new pair. The op shop had no white overalls. He hasn't taken them off since he got them, except when they are on the clothesline; he's trying to wear that brand-new look out of them. He's plastered up the cracks again in some of the worst window frames, and he's given them another coat of paint. He's the best window-frame painter, due to working on the theory that it's easier not to paint the glass in the first place than it is to scrape the paint off.

Eddy might have eventually made the kids do the house even if Vinnie hadn't come home, but Lori knows they wouldn't have done it so well – probably would have slapped on one coat and said that's good enough. You have to give credit where credit is due.

And you have to give credit to Mavis too. She still has a few choice words to say about her meals, but she eats what they give her, and they are pretty certain that she's trying to use that treadmill at night. They haven't actually caught her walking it yet, but Mick says he heard it once and heard her cursing it.

She was supposed to be dead months ago – probably would have been if Eddy hadn't come home – but there she is tonight, sleeping on a single bed and not using all of it. She doesn't look much bigger than a lot of other women who are walking around town.

They are still admiring Mavis's new chair, still watching her sleep, when Vinnie says, 'How long was she in the pen before I come home?' He's leaning against the doorframe, his curls brushing the top. They are all leaning someplace.

'It will be a year in March,' Lori says.

'I'd like to know how much she's dropped. She is metamorphosing before my eyes,' Eddy says. 'I am God. I am the creator.'

'Give her another couple of months and she'll be crawling out that bloody window,' Vinnie says. 'There's still a lot of her, but it's soft. If she got determined, she'd squeeze it through.'

'Yeah,' they murmur. Then Mavis licks her lips, rolls over, looks at her new chair as half of the kids skedaddle to the window and Lori prepares to close the door.

'Get me a set of scales, you mob of crazy little buggers, and we'll find out how much I've dropped.'

Eddy is gone and back again in seconds with Donny's old scales. He slides them across the cement floor and they don't go far enough. She comes close to collect them, and she carries them back to the new space near her chair. The door is wide open and they crowd at the door, and just inside the door.

'Nick off,' she says.

'I've got a vested interest in this.' Eddy edges down to the basin. He wants to see. He's got to see this.

She eyes him, then steps on the scales, pushes them to the limit and then some. 'They're bloody mad,' she says. 'They're sitting on the twenty. Twenty what?'

'That's a hundred and forty, plus twenty. One hundred and sixty kilos.'

'What's that in stones?'

'Divide by seven then take away a bit,' Alan says. 'It's around twenty-three stone.'

'It's not.' She's shocked, but her face looks alive. 'You're mad,' she says. 'It can't be.' She stands on the scales again. 'It's not on the twenty, it's on the seventeen.'

'A hundred and fifty-seven. You're a bit under twenty-three stone,' the mathematician says.

'Jesus! I must have gone close to forty at my peak!' She's got this wide-eyed, mouth-drooping look of sheer amazement on her face as she gets on the scales again, and stands there, holding her sack-dress close while looking down at her feet. 'Christ. I was twenty-eight stone when I got pregnant with Neil and the doctor didn't know how I did it – or how Henry did it.' She's still looking at the scales. As she gets off, they sort of gasp, shudder back to zero. She moves them with her foot, moves them against the wall, sort of claims them, lovingly, then she goes to her new second-hand chair, sits down, tests it. Claims it too.

'You should be up riding your treadmill instead of sitting all day. You'd burn the fat off twice as fast and it would help tighten up your saggy skin,' Lori adds.

'I'll give you bloody saggy skin, and I'll get all the exercise I need on you, you lanky little bitch. What are you feeding yourself on? Long soup?'

the countdown

The department of community services lady arrives in town early one Monday morning in March while the kids are at school, and she didn't have the decency to let anyone know she was coming. Vinnie's job is haphazard. Last week he worked five days, this week nothing. It suits him, though, and suits the kids, saves them missing too much school. Anyway, he's supposed to be looking after Matty, but he's watching a DVD on Greg's stolen player and Matty is not watching it with him when the kids get home from school.

'Where is he? You've let him wander off again!' Lori yells.

'I didn't.' He starts to tells his tale of woe. 'A woman came from the department of something – '

'And you let her take him – '

'No, no. I had to let her in, though.' The kids are staring at him. 'I took her in the lounge room, like you said I had to if they come, and I tried to make her sit down but she wouldn't, then while I was sliding the bolt – like you said I had to if they come – well, Matty come running to me, and she followed him.

'Anyway, Mavis is walking her treadmill and she sort of gives the nosy bugger one of her looks. "Haven't you got anything better to do all day than chase me around?", she says. "There's people with problems out there, you know." Doesn't get off the treadmill. Just keeps walking to no place. Walking slow, and watching *Play School* on television. "You're looking well, Mrs Smyth-Owen," the dame says. Mavis gives her a look, then walks a bit faster, like she's showing off. Then the dame says, "The house is a credit to you." Mavis just keeps walking.'

'What did they do with Matty?'

'I couldn't lock the door before I got rid of the nosy bugger, could I? I couldn't, so I let her out, then run back, and the silly little bugger is in there with Mavis, sitting on her bed and watching *Play School*.'

'She could have got out.'

'She didn't seem to want to. She was walking. She must have walked for fifteen minutes – twenty minutes. Or more.'

'Shit.'

'Shit, all right. Anyway, I tried to make Matty come out, then Mavis gets off her treadmill, so I slammed the bolt home and left him in with her. Nothing else I could do.'

Lori runs to the window. They all run out behind her. Matty is all right, but he starts bawling when he sees Lori, like he knows he's done something wrong.

'Stop your bawling, Matty. We'll get you out,' Lori says. Matty isn't stopping, he's bellowing. They think about a medicated custard, but Mavis was never much interested in bawling little Matty. She swaps him through the window for a bowl of popcorn and her Diet Coke.

'Her did put my dum-dum down da loo,' Matty bawls, his eyes accusing the dummy thief. 'Her did make it go away. Whoosh.'

'You're too big to have dum-dums now,' Lori says.

'I want my dum-dum. I want my dum-dum.'

'What do you want me to do? Stick my arm down the loo and get it out for you?'

'I wanna nuvver one. Not dat yucky one.'

'What would you like best? One new dummy or three lollipops?'

'One-two-free ollypops.'

It's hard to believe that a whole year has gone since Eddy came home. Time has moved so fast. Lori turned fourteen on the twelfth of February, but the distance travelled between thirteen and fourteen is huge. She's done so much, learned so much. She's in year nine.

Timmy started school this year, though he won't be five until June. He looks too small, but he's a good little kid and not giving the teachers any trouble. The worst is over. Matty is three and he's dry most nights. Two more years and he'll be at school. In less than one year Lori will be fifteen. That has always been her aim, just to get to fifteen.

Who will Mavis be in one more year? She won't be in that brick room. She shouldn't be in there now. They have to stop bolting that door, but how do they stop? When do they stop? Lori used to joke about it, say Mavis was serving a twelve-month sentence for self-abuse, like March to March, but March has come and they are still locking that door.

If she'd just yell at them, tell them to open that bloody door, they probably would now, or maybe they'd have a good reason not to open it, but she doesn't yell about it. She seems content with her scales and diet food, her books and her television. It's as if she wants to be in there. Maybe they've given her social phobia.

She's reading, reading anything they give her, and she's a fast reader, like, she's gone through all of their Stephen Kings, now they're getting books for her from the library. She's washing her hair more often and having showers over the baby bath. It's like she's re-discovered independence.

By the end of March the scales won't reach one hundred and forty kilos. Mavis tells Mick when he drops off her dinner at the window. 'They're stopping at one thirty-nine,' she says. 'That's over two less than last week. What is it in stones?'

'It's dropping off you,' Mick replies, and checks his conversions with Alan. They all go out and praise her, like they praise Matty when he has a dry nappy in the mornings, which works better than looking disappointed when he doesn't.

'Thousands of people are bigger than you. Mrs Daws from over the back of Nelly's has got to be over twenty stone and she's not as tall as you,' Alan says.

'If you were really close to forty stone, then you must have been dropping two kilos a week, Mavis,' Lori says.

'I ought to strip the hide from your bloody bones.'

I ought to, not I will.

The fact that she's talking to them, sharing her weight loss with them, is more than they ever expected. They took her cigarettes away, fed her on rabbit food, called her the enemy and declared war on a rampaging dictator. Now the enemy is communicating. Negotiations, though, don't always lead to peace treaties.

They put a few new boards down on the front verandah and tack up a sheet of clear plastic so it falls over the brick room window, lets in the light but blocks the wind, and they look at Mavis's dwindling proportions in context with that window, look at the summer tents, made in October, sacks by March.

Lori washes the maroon dress she bought at the op shop. She irons it, hangs it in Henry's wardrobe and finds an old woollen cardigan there. It's maroon, with a pattern on it. She can remember it, remember it tickling her face. She washes and presses it, then offers it through the window. Mavis puts it on over her flowing tent. And it fits – fits easy.

That cardigan brings back a heap of memories. Mick remembers it. 'We can't do this any more, Lori,' he says.

'She's not complaining,' Eddy says. 'I want to get her down to normal size.'

'Like, Lori's weight?' Jamesy says.

They laugh, look at Lori. She's five foot eight, which is almost as tall as Mavis, but she's all hair, legs, arms, neck, and enough breast. She washed her hair tonight and it's gone frizzy, so she looks even more like that photograph of Mavis at seventeen. Her eyes are different, but her chin is the same, and her nose, and she's definitely got Mavis's hands.

Paul Perkins told Leonie that Lori was a real babe and Leonie told Lori. It was sort of embarrassing, but nice too, though she made a joke of it.

'Like, as in Babe the pig?' she said. 'Gee, tell him thanks, like, heaps.'

She still hates girly clothes, won't wear them, wears jeans or shorts and faded T-shirts, still dresses like a boy. She can paint, she can use Mick's drill to put up curtain rails, she's the best cook, and more inventive – though Eddy does his share. She can sew a bit, chop wood. She's one of the boys, yet not one of them, doesn't want to be a boy any more.

She always hated school, right from first grade, and hated everyone at school, but this year with Leonie it's been different, and she's really excellent at computer studies, actually gets decent reports, due to Eddy, who is more than half computer.

What's going to happen to the computer when Mavis gets out? What's going to happen to Eddy? Will he pack up his computer and go? Not that he talks much about St Kilda now, except when he needs money. He wants to get the telephone connected so he can get on the Internet, which would be good, but expensive. Lori is still a mean-arse with money though they've got tons of the stuff. Mick has opened his own account and all of that stored money is making Lori feel safer, though she'll probably never feel truly safe about money again. That's the main reason she can't make herself open the green door. If she and Mick had a thousand dollars each in their accounts she might open it – but that wouldn't be enough to buy food for a month and pay the rates, and what about the other bills? Getting the phone connected would be one more bill.

Vinnie wants to get it connected and says he'll pay for it so his boss doesn't have to drive around to tell him if there is work or no work. And it would be great to be able to get up on the Internet.

But if they let Mavis out and they've got the phone on –

'God!'

To Lori, that computer has been like some benevolent God that moved in and did its bit in helping to sort her out. It's got a spell check, which frees her mind, allows it to go beyond spelling and into the inside of what goes on in her mind. There has always been a heap of stuff going on in there, but a sort of confused heap that never would come out right, and she's never worried much if it came out right or not. The only time she ever gets good marks for assignments is when Eddy or Alan do most of them, when they look up all the stuff she is supposed to look up.

What goes into her head during class sort of gets added to the mess already in there – if it's interesting enough. Sometimes it is, and sometimes it's just bullshit, and she gets mad, and opens her big mouth again, says what she thinks, which people shouldn't do these days – it's like the truth has to be gagged, and everyone's mouths stuffed full with politically correct talk, which drivels out on cue. Deep inside, most people don't *feel* politically correct; they are too worried about money and surviving, except when they get dressed up to go out. Then they put it on and it's like they are putting on pointy-toe stiletto shoes which half cripple the wearer, but they are the fashion so the people have to grin and bear the pain until they get home again and kick the buggers off.

Lori prefers sneakers and bare feet – at home and when she goes out.

the accidental metaphor

Mavis keeps on walking and the treadmill keeps on working. It wasn't expensive; things don't have to cost a fortune to be worth owning – like the house. It's old and the floors shake a bit and a grown-up probably would have replaced a heap of the boards before they painted it, but it's a good old house and it looks so dignified, so peaceful, like an old lady who has lived a hundred years, like she's seen so much that nothing is going to surprise her now. She just sits there at the end of the street, looking out at the world, sort of accepting of all things, and not even worrying about what is going to happen next week or next year. She's been there, done that, now she's just enjoying her old age.

So Easter comes and so do the tourists, and school breaks up for two weeks, which will be the last of the good-weather holidays for a while – and the teachers know it. They hate kids enjoying holidays so they give out heaps of assignments. A lot of kids complain, not just Lori, but the rotten teachers are all clones, all taught to justify big assignments by saying they are preparation for the hard years of eleven and twelve. As if Lori is even thinking of doing years eleven and twelve.

Eddy does most of two assignments; Lori adds a bit, just to make Eddy's words sound less like his words and more like her own, but the third assignment is on multiculturalism, and she just refuses to go along with what Eddy is writing. Pure refuses.

'Give old Crank Tank what she wants and you'll get what you want,' he says.

'That might be how you got around Eva and Alice, but it's not what I do. I'm not putting my name to that cow-crap.'

'Do it yourself then,' Eddy says and he walks off to spend a bit of time doing his stencilling on the bathroom tiles. Lori closes the computer and goes out to Henry's potting shed to water his plants. Some of the plants are still alive and looking well. She's been doing a no-no, hitting them with soapy water – God's creatures or not, they are getting a bath and they don't like it. Henry's exotic flowers are thanking her for it, though.

Holidays go too fast. They always did and they always will, and on the final night she still hasn't written one single word of that bloody multicultural assignment. It's late, after midnight, and she can't sleep; she keeps thinking about Henry and Mavis and the house and what they hadn't done to the house, and why Mavis and Henry hadn't done it. And she's thinking about how she sort of loves that dear old house now; even though it had been neglected for so long, all it needed to bring it back to life was a little bit of love. She loves what they've done, and she's so proud of it, and she wishes she could invite Leonie home sometimes – or Mick could invite Paul.

Can't.

They've got to let Mavis out. It's like locking her in is locking them in too, locking the kids away from living like normal people. But if they let her out, what's going to happen to the house? What's going to happen to the bankcard? What's going to happen to the kids and to Mavis's diet?

They'll have to do it, though.

'God.' If only she was sixteen, and if she had ten thousand dollars in the bank. 'If,' she says. 'Big *eff*.' She rolls onto her back, listens to the house sounds. A window rattling, the roof creaking, the fridge humming. She knows this house, knows all of its sounds – hasn't slept one night of her life under any roof except this roof. Doesn't want to, either. Doesn't want to go to Western Australia, doesn't want to go to England, just wants this dear old green roof, though there is no way she is going to sleep under this roof tonight; her head is working overtime.

And she still has to do that bloody assignment. She has to write something or old Crank Tank will do her block. What if she uses the bit Eddy wrote and just tones it down? What did he write, anyway?

She gets out of bed, starts up the computer and finds the file. And she's not handing that in! So she won't hand anything in, and old Crank Tank can do what she likes, and too bad. She had Lori in year seven and she hated her then, spent most of her life sending her to the principal, and she hasn't undergone radical brain-altering surgery in the years since, so too bad. When a teacher starts out hating you, they hate you forever and that's all there is to it.

The decision made, Lori creeps out to the kitchen, pours a glass of milk, drinks it while she walks out back to the brick room window to see what Mavis is up to. She's not up to much. The light is off, the television off and she's snoring.

Strange night sounds. Sound of breathing, sound of Matty's little cough. Sound of a bed squeaking as someone rolls over in the bunk room. It's like a whole house full of sleep. She tiptoes from room to room, listening at doors. Dark in and dark out tonight, except for the glow from the computer. She creeps into the lounge room to turn it off, but instead sits down and selects what Eddy wrote and deletes it. Just a blank screen now. Nothing. She stares at the screen, then her fingers take off. She can touch-type – actually, she can type faster than Eddy, who can't touch-type.

Maybe what she ends up writing is brought on by some lack of sleep induced semi-coma, but when all the words are out of her head and on the screen it's after two o'clock and she sort of likes what she's written and isn't quite sure why she likes it, but she runs the spell check then prints it out – without letting Eddy add even one comma; she adds a few with a black pen, probably puts them all in the wrong places, but at least those commas are her own, as the words are her own, and at least it's done and she's got something to give old Crank Tank tomorrow. Now maybe she'll be able to sleep.

So school goes back and the tourists go home and it's nice when they've all gone back where they belong and the town starts settling down to normal. There's a different feel about Willama after Easter, like it's snuggling down quiet for the winter, drawing the fog blankets close around its ears.

Teachers might demand that assignments are handed in on a certain day, but that doesn't mean they have to hand them back on a certain day. Probably too busy making red lines all over Lori's.

She shouldn't have done it. Shouldn't have handed it in. Should have done it the way Eddy said. Just give the people what they want, he said. And that's bullshit. People aren't clones yet, so why should they all think like clones, write like clones?

But she shouldn't have handed it in. She hadn't mentioned multiculturalism, not once. She'd written about families and houses, and of taking care of your own house and the people who live in your house, and how, if all of the brothers and sisters live by the same rules, and everyone does their share and they don't try to take more than their fair share, then there are no family wars.

But some family members are greedy. They want to rule the world. Some like red t-shirts and they demand that everyone in the family wear red t-shirts. Some like baggy green shorts and some like heavy black boots, each dominant one trying to force his will on the others.

Individual family members have to be allowed to make small decisions, but individual choice has to be put aside when it comes to caring for the family home, otherwise that house may end up with green spouting, red roof, multicoloured brickwork and striped weatherboards, so it gets to look ridiculous beside its neighbours.

No one has got any pride in a ridiculous house and that's when the fighting begins and the poor old house begins to fall around their ears but everyone is too busy half killing each other to notice the leaking roof.

Eventually the roof falls in and strangers come to feed the children and find that family another house to live in.

However, unless that warring family has learned from their mistake then they'll do the same stupid things to their new house while they spend their lives looking west to the sunset, pretending that their old multicoloured house was a palace which they were forced to leave.

This is living a lie. This is not facing facts. Like, if that house was so much better, then why did they leave? Why hadn't they slept in the rubble until they'd all learned to work together to rebuild it, to paint the boards white and the roof and spouting green, because all it takes is many hands working together to make a tumbledown old house stand tall and proud beside its neighbours.

She had ended up going back to the beginning, like Eddy always does. She'd written how many brothers and sisters can sleep safe at night in a proud house, and how some of them may be big and some may be small, some dark, and some redheads, but when the lights are out at night then you can't tell which heads are red and which ones are dark because all you can hear is their breathing.

That's about all she wrote. And the whole thing will probably be red lined, and too bloody bad.

Finally the Crank Tank hands it back and she sort of looks at Lori, like, what are you? She's pretty old, pretty fat and pure cranky, so Lori ducks her head, shrugs, looks first for the red lines; she always looks first for those red lines. And there are a few and a few red question marks and commas too, but written right on the bottom of the last page, also in red, is 'An excellent metaphor. Well thought out, Lori'. And in a little red circle, A–.

Old Crank Tank gave it an A–.

She gave it an A–!

Lori can't stop looking at that A–, and it looks heaps better than the A she got for the assignment Eddy did for her. She's never before got an A–, not in the whole of her life, not for work she's done herself. Maybe if she really tried, she could scrape through this year. Nobody gives out medals for being dumb. And school is not so bad, it's not really rotten bad like it used to be. And some of the teachers don't hate her. The sports teacher actually likes her, due to Lori always wins the swimming, and the high jump, only because she's got long legs. She's fast at running too – though she doesn't run so fast now when Paul is chasing her. It's nice having a sort of boyfriend.

She's got two girlfriends, real, true friends she can say anything to, Leonie and a new one, Shana, who originally came from India. Her family moving to Willama was like . . . like fate, and the way she and Lori sort of clicked from that very first day – even if her father is a doctor. It was like maybe Henry, wherever he is, or his ancestors, sent Shana to Willama as some sort of sign.

She's really dark, darker than most tribal Aborigines. Anyhow, she and Lori and Leonie are pretty much inseparable these days.

They are sitting, eating lunch and talking about Crank Tank and their marks for the assignment, which gets them onto talking about where their ancestors came from originally. Leonie's came from England centuries ago. She even had a convict relative who got sent out here in chains in the early eighteen hundreds, and just for stealing one lousy rabbit. All of Shana's people came from parts of India.

Then it gets to Lori's turn and she goes quiet, sort of considers giving up Henry's BIG secret. But how would they react? It would probably sound as if she was trying to do a Kelly Waters, go black, just so Mick could go to university for free – though Henry would prefer to see him sitting on a drum digging sewerage ditches.

But deep in some place inside, her liver or her kidneys, or maybe in her heart, there's this need to claim that lost part of who she is – not just the Aboriginal part, but the Indian part too, and the white boy part, that *boy Henry* who worked for Mr Howie. And one day she's going to do it. When she's old enough. She's going to find Lily, or find some of her other kids, not necessarily to claim them, just to know that they are out there.

'Where did your people come from, Lori?'

Lori looks up, looks at Leonie. 'Australia? Where else is there?'

'I mean before. Everyone came from some place.'

'Just call me the united nations, the end result of non multi-culturalism, which happens when you're too busy surviving to worry about culture and all that other religious cow-crap.'

'Get off your soapbox.'

'Yeah.' The wind is blowing, tossing her hair, but the sun is hot on her legs, turning them brown, turning Leonie's red. 'I'm German mainly, on my mother's side, plus Scottish, a bit of Irish, English. I've got a good dose of Indian on my father's side, plus Aboriginal and only God knows what else – my father was adopted when he was a year old so nobody knows much about him.'

'So you're an Aborigine?'

'If a few tablespoons of black blood turns you black. I've probably got a whole litre of Indian blood but I haven't noticed it turning me into a Hindu yet.' She looks Leonie in the eye. 'Why didn't you say, oh, so you're a German? I've got a double dose of that – probably at least three litres.'

'Yeah, well, it didn't turn you into a blue-eyed blonde, did it?'

'Heil Hitler,' Lori says and she clicks her heels.

They laugh, and so much for Henry's BIG secret.

two women

It's late May and the nights are cold. Last year's winter tent is miles too big for Mavis so Lori attacks it, turns it into a dressing gown and replaces it with the huge green tracksuit she bought from the op shop. And Mavis gets it on too. She looks a sight, because the top isn't long enough, but she also looks proud of herself, sort of struts as she gets off the treadmill and comes to the window for her dinner.

They're going to have to let her out. Every day now Lori knows that what they are doing is so wrong. What if Paul or Leonie came around one day and no one was home and they climbed over that gate and found Mavis locked in? Lori was only a stupid kid when she bolted that door, but she's not a kid any more

Paul kissed her the other night, on the front verandah, in the dark, like a proper television-boyfriend kiss. And it was like the night Alan nearly drowned her, like she needed air but couldn't get any, which might have been due to his nose getting in the way of her nose, or maybe she just held her breath when she shouldn't have, but her legs felt like jelly snakes afterwards. Anyway, that's another story.

Mavis is the one Lori is worrying about today; she's metamorphosing before everyone's eyes, like Eddy is always saying. And . . . and she actually called Lori 'Lorraine' for the first time in yonks instead of smartarsed little bitch or worse. She stuck her head out of the window and called out, 'Lorraine. Come over here a minute.'

And when Lori went over, Mavis said really quiet, 'I've started again. Have you got any . . .?' It was just about women's business, but it was like they were the only two women in a whole world of men.

'Don't need 'em,' Lori said, then she went to the supermarket by herself and got what Mavis wanted.

'You should need them by now. What's wrong with you?' Mavis said, taking the two small packets.

'Who cares?'

Today Lori is standing watching Mavis wash her hair in the hand basin. She's stripped down to her op shop tracksuit pants and a too tight T-shirt, and she's no pretty sight. All of the spare skin around her waist and back and upper arms is saggy. Her stomach is the worst bit, and her hair, which is long and terrible. She used to have really nice hair. Her face has never been ugly and it's not wrinkling up, except maybe around the eyes and a bit around the neck, but if she had eye make-up and lipstick –

Eddy comes out the back and Lori moves away from the window. 'She's washing her hair,' she whispers, wanting to protect Mavis. Last year she wouldn't have cared who looked in that window and saw that saggy skin. 'We have to open that door, Eddy. We've become the new tyrants. Power to the masses. It's a replay of the French Revolution.'

'Cut off her head,' Eddy says, and mimes knitting. Lori elbows him, walks into the kitchen.

Then Alan buys in. 'She's the colour of bread dough. She needs sun. She'll get sick soon, then what are we going to do? People need sun.'

'Redheads don't,' Eddy says.

Alan is all for letting her out. He's softer than Eddy, who is still full of cheek and this sort of frenetic energy. If he's not working, he's at his computer, like his brain can't turn the power off. Mick, who is raking ash out of the fire, isn't buying into the conversation.

'She'll be okay now,' Alan says. 'I bet she'll want to stay on her diet.'

'She'll want the bankcard,' Jamesy says. He's also got a thing about money.

'And as soon as she gets her hands on money, she'll start stuffing. As long as she's got no, like, temptation, she's not tempted.' Vinnie speaks from experience. They listen to him too. He was tempted a couple of times by Mavis's Valium, so Lori keeps the new packet hidden in her room. What he doesn't see, he doesn't want.

'Let her climb out the window if she wants to get out,' Jamesy says. His memory is long; he saw too much of the bad Mavis and can't remember enough of the good. But there was good. There was the comedian and, earlier than that, there was the woolly maroon cardigan and delicious stews and apple pies and – there was good. 'She'll be able to walk anywhere she wants to walk when she's out. She'll go walking up to the pub for counter meals and she'll be laughing with Wally Johnson and the other blokes and she'll probably end up having more babies.'

Five sets of eyes turn to Jamesy. Why hadn't anyone else thought about that? He's grown up this year, and he's grown even older in the head. He's eleven, going on sixty, but he's got them all thinking of more babies and maybe understanding a bit why Henry hanged himself.

Lori looks for Matty, the last of them. And God Almighty, he's got to be the last. Can't take any more shitty napkins, any more kids on her back. 'Where is he? Matty? Where did he go?' she says.

'He was under the table a minute ago.'

They check under the table. 'Matty,' Vinnie calls out back. 'Matty! Where are you? That little bugger is turning into an escape artist.' Vinnie heads for the front door, calling through the house. 'Matty? Are you in here? Matty!'

'Matty! Will you answer when you're called?' Lori is in the back yard, adding her bellow to Vinnie's, and she reminds herself of Mavis.

He's climbed the gate again but Vinnie has got him, so Lori walks back to the kitchen. 'What do you really reckon, Mick? Like, this isn't living like normal people, is it?' she says, harking back to her previous subject.

Mick shrugs, looks at the kitchen floor where he lay helpless on the day of the dislocated leg. There is brand-new black and white checked vinyl on the floor and it still smells new. The kitchen walls and ceiling are white, the cupboards black. It has been changed and they did it. He pulls out the stove's ashtray, empties it into Henry's metal bucket to sprinkle around his garden. Snails and slugs hate ash. He read that in a gardening book, bought new the other day. And he had the money to buy that book. He can remember what it was like when they didn't have money. He can remember life in this house before he dislocated his leg.

'I know what I want to do, but I dunno what we ought to do. I know she likes what's happening with the scales. She looks excited now when she tells us what she weighs. I dunno, Lori. Maybe Vinnie is right; she knows herself better than we do.'

Around the table there is a joint relieved exhalation. This house is run on democratic lines; the subject has been raised, the decision reached, life, as they prefer it, will continue a while longer.

Then Vinnie is back, Matty under his arm and sucking on an envelope, which is addressed to Mavis. It's from Eva's solicitor because his name is on the front.

'They're into it again. I didn't think they were coming back until September.' Eddy rips off the wet end, opens the well-sucked contents, but as he reads, the blood drains from his face and his hand moves to his mouth. 'They're dead,' he says, sort of quiet, breathless. 'They're both dead.'

'Don't muck around, you moron.'

'They're both dead. A bus smash. In Argentina. They're dead.' He's standing, shaking, looking around him like he wants to run and he has no place to run to.

'They're in Paris.' Alan takes the letter, reads, shakes his head and reads it again, then he shudders, turns to Eddy. 'What were they doing in Argentina? What – '

And the kids know it's true and many eyes grow wide and they all stare at Eddy.

'They're flying their . . . they are bringing them home tomorrow, it says.' Alan is beside his twin, a smidgen taller than his twin, and heavier. They still look the same to strangers but they are not the same, not their eyes, not their expressions, not their responses to this news, either. Alan doesn't know what he should feel, what he should do. He's jumpy, shrugging his shoulders, looking out towards the river. Eddy is ghost white and shaking. His power has been turned off.

'We get everything plus Watts as trustee,' Alan says, ready to head for the bush. 'It says he's coming up here to get us.'

'You own that house!' Lori breathes and she reaches for the letter, scans it. Alice and Eva are dead, all right, but all Lori can think about is houses. She's got a house fetish. But her own brothers, her own two brothers, own that posh house she once saw. Cool, calm, green. Ocean waves in the distance. She's not a very nice person; a nice person would be saying something different, but she's not saying it. 'You own that posh house? The letter says you two are joint beneficiaries. You're rich!'

The twins don't look like joint beneficiaries. They don't look joined. Eddy looks as if he's coming unjoined fast.

'Get him a drink of water, someone,' Mick says. 'Sit him down before he falls down.'

Alan gets the water and he drinks it, then he remembers what he's supposed to be doing and fills the glass again, offers it to his twin. Eddy sits, drinks, shakes. This news has hurt him but it hasn't hurt Lori. She didn't like those two dead women and she knows a lot more about Eva since Mavis's pot-smoking night, so she actually hates her now, and her mother. They were two rotten heartless people – and old Alice? Well, she was just a rangy, mangy old stranger. Thousands of strangers get killed and you might feel a bit sorry for the families, but you can't get heartbroken about the dead one.

'What does Mavis get?' Jamesy asks.

'Her mother hated her, left her nothing. She used to put her in this big pantry they had, and lock the door,' Vinnie says. 'And Mavis used to sit there in the dark and eat all the sugar and stuff. She was going on about all sorts of muck the night she got into my grass.'

Mick has stopped scraping ash out of the stove. He's standing, rubbing at his frown, rubbing ash on his face. Some tribe somewhere does that when someone dies, Lori thinks.

Alan claims the letter. 'Watts says that he'll be up here on Wednesday. He's expecting us to go back there!'

'We'll have to go back. For the funeral. That's all.' Eddy is sitting statue stiff, his eyes sort of red, shaky – not crying, but his mouth is, and it's working hard at making those words try to come out near normal.

'So we don't have to stay there, with Watts, as our guardian?' Alan is at the door, looking out at freedom. He'll give up his inheritance if it means giving up his freedom.

Eddy's hand shakes as it reaches again for the letter. He licks his lips, gets a few deep breaths in, then reads it again, reads it slow, Mick leaning over his shoulder. They're all grouped around Eddy, stuck for something to say. Dumb.

'If I hadn't left, they would have still been alive,' Eddy says.

'Crap. When your time is up, it's up, even if lightning has to come in that bloody window to get you,' Vinnie says with conviction. He's been there, done that. He's tried most stuff but he couldn't afford heroin. He's been at Greg's side when they crashed a stolen car with the cops right on their tail, and he got out, jumped a fence and ran. He got hit by a baseball bat one night when he went into a takeaway to buy a pie and chips and Greg decided on the spot to rob it. Vinnie didn't get his pie, but he got away, lived to run another day. And he didn't lose the sight in his eye, either, when Mavis tried to scratch it out that night. Close shaves have made him a fatalist, made him good up ladders too, and at walking around roofs like a circus performer.

They watch him open the fridge, take out the milk, think of drinking it from the bottle, watch him change his mind, pour a spurt into a mug, drink it. He even puts the lid back on, puts the milk away, puts the mug in the sink. They're house-training him. Slow.

Then everyone is doing things. Picking up things, looking for something to say. Nothing much anyone can say except, 'Poor old Eva.'

'Poor ole Eba,' Matty says. It raises a few smiles, though they are wiped away fast. This is no time for smiling.

It's time to start cooking a stew, but somehow it doesn't seem the right thing to do. Nothing is the way it was. It's weird. Like, what do we do now? Like, this isn't what was supposed to happen. Where do we go to from here? It's like when you read one of those books where for five hundred pages the author has been setting you up to expect the story will end with the hero getting murdered, then suddenly, on the second-last page, the whole plot changes. The murderer goes off to the jungle and gets eaten by a giant python and the hero wins the lottery. It's not that you aren't pleased for the hero, it's just that it doesn't feel real so you don't believe it, and you pitch the book at the wall.

'We've got to tell Mavis,' Mick says.

People to tell, like when Henry hanged himself. But it's not a bit like when Henry hanged himself because none of this is happening to Lori.

It's happening to Eddy, though. He's got that scared, lonely, empty feeling, like she had when Henry died, and she knows it. And he's got all the guilt too, and that chewed-up hurting inside that won't go away. He's sitting at the table, playing with his empty glass, turning it around and around in circles. A few tears are wetting his eyes, but they're not leaking out.

Alan isn't hurting. He's stalking the room, backwards and forwards, from the window to the door, from the door to the window. Maybe he cried all of his tears for Eva when he first came home, so he's walking, stalking, thinking, like, God, when does life settle down to fishing and reading? Like, God, what's going to happen to me next?

'We've got to tell Mavis,' Mick says again.

'We've got to let her out,' Lori adds.

'Shit,' Vinnie says and he looks up at the cupboard, to where the Valium used to live. 'Shit,' he says again and he heads for the front door.

Lori goes to the green door. She slides the bolt.

It's happening. It's happening.

life force

Mavis knows something is wrong. She jerks out of her chair, looks from face to face, her eyes wide, startled. 'Is he all right?' she says. Maybe she heard them calling for Matty. Mick tells her that Eva is dead.

She shakes her head, stares at the faces, then follows everyone through to the kitchen. Fast. Easy.

Lori makes a cup of tea. It's something to do when there isn't anything else you can do. Jamesy snatches the sugar, replaces it with the sugar substitute granules while Mavis sits down at her old place at the table. She's silent, and they're silent. Eddy is pale. He hasn't moved from his chair. They are watching him, watching her, watching Vinnie creep back, stand in the passage doorway.

Mavis's eyes are roving the walls. Clean. White. They are finding the curtains, the new vinyl floor. It's like she's not sure if she's dreaming this, dreaming she's out. She's sort of disorientated – Rip Van Winkle, slept for thirty years. She can't recognise the new world, and the kids can't recognise her shape at the end of the table, either. It's not the same world and she's not the same shape. She's around nineteen stone now. That's big, sure, but she's tall, so it's not as big as it sounds.

She moves forward on her chair. It's the same chair, but it feels strange beneath her; they know it by the way she moves it forward, moves it back. Then she opens her mouth. 'Dead? Eva?'

'You got a letter from Mr Watts. We opened it.'

'How? Where? When?' She wants information fast, doesn't look at the letter.

Alan does the talking, does it quiet, matter-of-fact. He tells her Alice is dead too.

'Alice? What the hell happened to them?'

'A bus smash,' Lori says and they all nod, watch Mavis, half afraid of what they've done to her, half proud. She's back in their kitchen and she's wearing her tracksuit pants but not the top; she's changed it for a man's tartan shirt. Lori offers a mug of tea, offers a choc-mint biscuit. Mavis accepts the mug, looks at the biscuit long but doesn't take it.

'She's only fifty-three. She's . . . I don't believe it.'

'The funeral is on Friday. Watts is coming up to get us on Wednesday,' Alan says.

'We'll have to go, Mave. She had no one else.' Eddy slides the letter towards her, and she stares at this son she's barely known since he was two years old. She turns to Alan, stares at him, and back to Eddy. Then the mug is down and she's reading.

It's a short typewritten letter. She reads it twice to make it go in. She looks at the blank back. Looks for more. No more, so she places it on the table. Looks at the walls again, then at her op shop shirt, at the leg of her op shop tracksuit pants.

'What were they doing in bloody Argentina?' she says.

Eddy shakes his head. 'The last we heard, they were in Paris. They must have gone for a holiday.'

'She's only fifty-three.'

'Fifty-four next month,' Eddy says.

'June,' she says. 'In June. They named her Eva June.' She stares at Eddy. 'Same date as Timmy. She was twenty-eight when she married Henry. I was a crazy mixed-up fourteen. He taught me to play chess. My father was dead. I had no one.' She's looking around her now, her big frightened eyes staring at faces and finding Vinnie, who is still leaning against the doorjamb. 'You're the bloody living, spitting, breathing image of him – the perverted bastard,' she says.

Everyone looks at Vinnie. 'Not my fault, is it?' he says. 'And I don't go around raping kids, anyway.' There was no wall between him and Mavis on that crazy pot-smoking night; he heard most of her ravings up close and very personal.

Mavis rubs her eyes, sighs in a breath and pushes her long, daggy hair back. She's got Eddy's eyes, or Eddy has got hers. They're identical today, scared, can't find a place to look where it's safe from other eyes. Maybe they want to tell everyone to fuck off so they can cry in peace.

She sure looks as if she wants to cry. So she didn't like Eva, but losing her is like one too many changes in a whole world of change. Maybe she doesn't know what to do with freedom either. She's sitting on that chair, afraid to move from it. She's been dieting hard, walking her treadmill hard these last weeks, but now she's out and the world is pressing on her so she's sitting, staring at that choc-mint biscuit.

She lifts her hand, and they all think she's going for that biscuit, but she just stares a while at that hand, then pushes her sleeve up, studies her arm.

The hand looks good again and it's exactly like Lori's, even the long, strong nails. The wrist looks good, even the elbow, then the sag starts. She checks out her leg, her foot. She kicks off her slipper, looks at her toes as if she hasn't seen them for years, then she puts the slipper on. It's too big and worn flat, worn out and filthy.

She doesn't know where she should look, or who she should look at. It's like she's thinking, who am I? Half of my hard built layers of protection have gone missing and I can almost see myself, and I'm too scared of what I'm going to see.

Her couch is on the junk heap. There's an enlarged photo of a young Henry hanging on a clean white wall where her couch used to be. Her eyes find it, lock onto something safe. 'He was too good for this world. She should have left him in his England. I thought he was so bloody old when she brought him home. A gentle, decent man, your father.'

Matty starts giving the no-swearing lecture, but Lori cuts him off. 'That one was taken before he came to Australia,' she says.

'I know when it was taken.' The voice sounds like Mavis, but the mouth it comes out of doesn't look right any more. It's trembling with wanting to cry, but wanting to talk more than cry. 'I didn't know it then. Didn't know until after Donny was born that I'd been sleeping with my stepfather. Eva was your grandmother – my bloody mother. She had me two weeks before her fourteenth birthday.'

Her mouth is losing the battle. She tries to hold it steady with her fingers but tears are flooding down, wetting those fingers. 'Christ!' she says. And her palms swipe at those tears. 'Why should I cry for her? She hated me, and for half my life I didn't know why she hated me. I didn't find out until the old bitch died, and she hadn't left me one cent in her will.'

She sniffs, sucks a breath. 'I went to Watts . . . planning to break the will.' Her nose is running. Alan passes her a wad of toilet roll, which is cheaper than tissues. She blows her nose, wipes her eyes. 'I found out I was the old bitch's grandchild, and that redheaded bastard I'd loved had fathered me with his own daughter.'

She blows her nose again, sucks air. 'It was probably true. I don't know if it was true or not but it was in the will, written in black and white. That crazy old bitch had been determined to get in one last punch from the grave.'

The kids are standing quiet. Nothing they can say to that. Can't say it's probably not true, so can't say anything.

'Eva told me and Henry the details that night, and she laughed while she was telling us. Her mother tried to drown me in the kitchen sink the day I was born. She'd dug a hole for me in the garden, but my father came home and caught her. He made that pair of mad bitches raise me. Bought the house in St Kilda, moved them down from Brisbane, moved his business.'

She shakes her head, lifts her chin, looks at Vinnie and laughs,

laughs and drips tears. 'As big as a god, he was. I thought he was God when I was a kid.' She bites at her trembling lip, swipes at her tears, then that chin lifts again. 'I had to take what love I could get in that bloody house, and I loved a perverted, child-raping bastard.'

'You weren't to know,' Vinnie says. 'He didn't do nothing to you, did he? So how were you to know?'

'I should have known. They hated him. There had to be some reason. But they couldn't make a move without him, the pair of whingeing, clinging, dependent bitches. They swallowed their pills, gave their parties, and greeted their guests with him at their side.'

She's drowning in tears now, they're running down her face, the wads of toilet paper building on the table. 'I didn't know I shouldn't love him. Nobody told me.'

'Because it probably wasn't true. That's why they didn't tell you,' Lori says. 'They couldn't lie about him while he was alive to defend himself, could they?'

'I've got his red hair. I've got his height.'

'So has Vinnie, and his father was a quarter Indian and a six-teenth Aboriginal. You're out of your brain, Mavis, believing one word that Eva said. She was a total nutcase.'

Mavis puts her head down then, bawls all over the new plastic tablecloth, bawls so hard she's shaking everyone up with her tears. The little kids get scared and start howling in sympathy. Mick nods to Jamesy, a sort of get-rid-of-them nod. This stuff isn't G-rated.

He, Lori and Vinnie have heard most of this tale before and they know there's worse stuff to come. Like how Mavis slept with anything in pants, how she'd had two abortions by the time she was seventeen. They know that Eva and her mother accused her of sleeping with Henry too, when all they were doing was playing chess. And if they lied about that then they'd lie about anything, like Eva lied in that letter – which Lori has still got; she had it laminated, and stuck it on the wall in Mavis's bedroom, and she'd better get rid of it before Mavis reclaims that room.

Lori steps back, glances at Henry's photograph. That's probably pretty much how he looked when he first slept with Mavis, how he looked when he came home early from the club and found out about Eva and Alice. He left the house that night and so did Mavis, but not together. She was living on the street until she was three months' pregnant with Martin, then she went to Henry's office, wanting him to help her get another abortion. He wouldn't let her do it. All life was precious to Henry – except his own.

There is a lot of R-rated material in Mavis's past and maybe it all has to come out sooner or later too, but this isn't the time or the place to release it. Lori walks fast from the room and the little ones follow her, and follow her back to the kitchen when she returns with the maroon dress. They don't know what is going on here, but the bogyman is out of that brick room and she's crying and it's scary. They don't want to be too far from Lori's knee; even Neil is tailing her.

She's got the op shop bra and some brand-new stretchy knickers from Kmart. She's got a clean towel. 'Do you reckon you might feel better after a hot shower, Mavis?' she asks.

Mavis lifts her head, bawls some more, but she's not moving. Lori takes her arm, tenses for that well-remembered elbow jab.

No jab. Mavis stands, allows herself to be led.

They walk to the passage door and Vinnie makes way, steps into the bunk room. Mavis thinks she still has to sidle through the doorway sideways, but Lori keeps hold of that arm, a soft thing above the elbow. Maybe the cells are still young enough to find a new shape. Maybe the skin is elastic enough to get a new memory. Maybe Mavis is young enough to –

Together they walk into the lemon bathroom with its stencilled black and gold pattern around the top of the white tiles. Eddy did it; he said the white tiles were boring. It's a big bathroom and it looks surface posh, even if the black and white checked vinyl does run downhill and shake a bit underfoot. They bought a new shower curtain and hung part of the old plastic lace tablecloth at the window, which looks like really expensive curtain material – as long as you don't touch it.

Mavis isn't seeing any of it. She's standing looking at the floor she last saw wooden, wet. She's not doing anything. Tears are still running.

Have they broken her, killed the inside of her?

Lori sets the shower. 'Do you reckon you can manage by yourself, Mavis?'

She shakes her head, shakes out more tears, so Lori waits while the shirt comes off. She puts it in the laundry basket. Mavis sits on the edge of the bath to take off her tracksuit pants and boxer shorts. She's not modest, never was, never will be. Lori's face is turned away, but Mavis takes her arm as she steps up and into the bath. Steps up and over. Just like that, like anyone else would do it. Doesn't even use the metal handles the people fixed up for her that time. She's sort of surprised that she's done it too. She looks at the bath then and at the heavy plastic shower curtain that cost heaps but works well – doesn't stick to you while you're trying to wash. She sniffs, lifts her determined chin and looks at the window while the water is running all over her. Lori pulls the curtain across and stands outside, passing in the shampoo, picking up the soap, passing the cloth, passing more shampoo.

Mavis stays in the shower a long time, longer even than Eddy. Maybe she doesn't know how to turn the taps off. In the end Lori reaches in, turns them off, passes a towel, tries not to look at the clean, the pink, the new. She gets a second towel for Mavis's long hair, then offers deodorant, baby powder, offers the bra.

Mavis looks at it. It's big, but she shakes her head. Lori keeps offering it. They are not talking. Perhaps Mavis has forgotten how to put a bra on, but Lori is familiar with them, so they get it on and tighten the straps, lifting up what hasn't been lifted up in years.

The stretch knickers stretch to fit, but they fit. Lori wants everything to fit, prays everything will fit, but when Mavis looks at the offered dress, she frowns. It's got fancy maroon and gold buttons to below the waist, and she stands there undoing them, six of them, like she's scared too that it won't fit. Scared to try it. Lori helps lift it over

397

the wet hair, and she lifts the hair free, she finds a sleeve, guides a soft arm in. It's not so hard to do, like dressing a big Matty. She does up the buttons, scared the second one won't do up across the bra, but the dress is big, it's plenty big and, God, how fine it looks, and how good the shape of Mavis in a bra.

The dress falls straight from the shoulders, hangs straight over Mavis's stomach. It's longish and the material is classy, good enough for a wedding – or a funeral. Lori wishes now that she'd bought shoes for her hope chest, but shoes are harder; shoes have to be walked in, they have to fit. Mavis looks at her flattened filthy slippers, walks away from them, barefoot.

There is only a small mirror in the bathroom, a shaving mirror, but it's fogged up. Mavis catches a glimpse of face and dripping hair, of the maroon collar. Stares.

'Want to have a look in the bedroom mirror? You look good.'

No. A shake of her head, and they walk back to the kitchen where Mavis sits again at the table. Mick makes more tea, he makes Mavis three diet crackers with Vegemite. Mavis eats one while Lori towels and combs the long red hair.

'I could cut a bit off for you. I cut the little ones' hair. Only if you like.'

'Ta.' Mavis nods, eats another cracker. Slowly. She never used to like Vegemite but she seems to like it okay now.

A dry towel around her shoulders and Henry's haircutting scissors snip-snip. Twenty centimetres of red hair fall to the tiles, then Lori combs the hair, combing it up instead of down. It wants to lift, to stand tall again; it's trying to come alive. It's looking hard for a life. There is some new grey at the temples, but not much. She cuts a fringe clump to hide the new grey, cuts it like she cuts her own fringe clump. Mavis's curls up, like her own curls up.

It's vibrant hair. It wants to curl, to stand tall. Every strand is in there fighting to curl, so Lori cuts a bit more at the top, keeps cutting, keeping each cut level with the last. She cuts it all the way down, layering it like Henry did, cuts a bit more off the length. Maybe it's not as good as Henry's cuts, but curly hair is kind to amateur hair-dressers. The curls spring up, spring back, cover any faults.

They are all watching that hair come alive. They got used to it daggy, draggy, dull and dead, but most of them can remember when Henry used to wash it and cut that red hair, just like Lori is doing. Henry used to get that hair curling and standing tall.

There is a pile of red growing on the floor and still Lori keeps snipping and talking, like the hairdressers on television always talk, just any words so there won't be that awful silence.

'That colour suits you. I bought it a while back at the op shop, but I could buy you a black dress for the funeral – if you like. We've got plenty of money again. Haven't had to buy anything for ages . . . except food. I saw a really nice dress in Kmart the other day. It was black, and it had a white trim on the front and the sleeves. It would be slimming and good for the funeral. I could get it and some new shoes and pantihose. That's if you like.' Then the comb is on the table and her fingers are lifting that hair. And it's bouncing, it's turning into wildfire beneath the light.

'What size shoes did you used to wear?'

'Nine, or nine and a half.'

'Do you reckon you could wear heels? Not big ones. I saw a pair of black sandals in that little shop beside the restaurant – not too strappy. They had heels, not tall ones, just sort of square, a bit blocky.'

'I used to wear four-inch stilettos.'

'They've come back into fashion again, but they look seri-ously excruciating.' She finger-combs, doesn't want to stop. Maybe she should stop, but it's beautiful hair; it feels good and it smells good, and she's trying to get some life force flowing between them, trying to push some of her life force directly into those strands of hair.

It's been a long time. The wall has been up a long time and the life force has been hitting it hard and bouncing back hard for even longer. Still, they've taken a lot of the old Mavis away. Maybe they have to try to replace what they took away.

Everyone is looking at Lori. Looking at those hands playing the comb, the fingers lifting curls, scrunching them. Lori isn't a bit scared of Mavis; it's like she's petting her. Like they put a bear with a sore head in a cage and she's come out a kitten who Lori has got almost purring with each stroke.

Hypnotising, the rhythm of those hands. The kitchen is so quiet. Everyone is too quiet. Then Alan puts the little ones in the bath and Eddy starts unwrapping the meat for the stew. Jamesy goes out for onions.

'Grab a bit of silverbeet, Jamesy,' Mick says. 'Give the bugs a good hose off before you pick it.'

'Yum-yum, bug stew,' Vinnie says.

Mavis watches. Watches everything, her eyes distant things, but not scared and shaky any more. Lori keeps combing while the boys go about the normal business of doing things and looking occasionally at the new presence being cared for, but better than being cared for, being cared about.

Lori cares about her and they know it.

And Mavis knows it. She's just sitting, statue still, having her hair done.

A shudder travels down Mick's spine. He's scared of how he's feeling. He's scared Mavis will scream, 'That's a-bloody-nough,' and Lori's face will get that old hard, hurt look she used to wear, that she doesn't wear any more. But he's feeling hope too, he's feeling the life force working in him and his eyes are stinging.

Lori sees the shudder. She has been away in her dreams, combing her mother's hair. Okay, so her mother isn't wearing tight jeans and dangling earrings like Wendy Johnson's mother, but she . . . she looks like a mother. She's sitting here at the table and she's real, not some photo, not some middle-aged twit trying to look sixteen. She's big but she's real, and she's got beautiful hair and beautiful eyes and that's a fact.

Then the life force starts flowing. It starts jolting Lori's stomach. It jolts so hard that she steps away.

Mavis's shoulders shiver. She turns her head, as if something wonderful has been taken from her. Then a powerful thump of Mavis's life force hits Lori like a wave from the speedboats hits the bank. It nearly swallows her, sort of draws her back to the red hair. She touches it, lifts it up from the collar of the maroon dress, runs her fingers through it again, lifting it high.

'It's just gorgeous hair. It always was.'

'Everything has changed,' Mavis says. 'Everything has changed, Lorraine. Everything.'

'You just wait till you see our posh lounge room. Just wait till you see what we did to the outside. We look as good as Nelly, over the road. You just wait, Mum.'

Mavis stands up, so easily, so fast. Alan thinks she's going to head for the chook-house and hang herself like Henry did when he called him Dad. He jumps up too, his heart racing like their new second-hand lawn mower. 'Do you want to see the lounge room, Mum?' he says. 'We've got the classiest fireplace in Willama.'

Hit her with it solid. Hit her with it hard. Make the real go in. Make her accept change. Mavis was a total failure, so make her be Mum.

Mavis looks at him, looks around her, then she shakes her head and howls. 'You mob of silly little buggers. You're just like your father.' And she walks out to her brick room bawling, and she closes the green door.

Mick's worried. 'What made her suddenly do that?'

'She'll be better tomorrow. We have to let her do it slow,' Alan says. 'We hit her with too much, all at once. She's in shock. She'll be better tomorrow.' Eddy is saying nothing; he's standing quiet, stirring the spitting meat.

'Did you see how she didn't even want that sweet biscuit? She wants to be on a diet. I bet we can get her down to fourteen,' Jamesy says.

'If she goes to the funeral, we could all go,' Alan says.

'All of us? You mean we'll go too?' Jamesy says, looks from one twin to the other. He can't remember ever being further than Willama West.

'If Mave goes,' Eddy says. He adds curry, stirs. 'It would let her get used to seeing strangers before she has to front all the neighbours. Take her to her father's grave and let her work her way through it slow.'

Lori nods. She knows what it's like to have family trust broken. Like with Greg that night. Okay, she knew he was pretty rotten, but she hadn't known he was pure depraved rotten. Like, what might have happened to her if she hadn't had Martin and Donny to run to? Poor little Mavis – and maybe poor little Eva too. She had no one to run to, whether she was running from her father or someone else.

'I'm not staying at that house,' Alan says. 'We'll stay at a motel.'

'It's probably rented out, anyway,' Eddy says.

'I suppose Mr Watts will sell it.'

Eddy looks off into space, stirs the meat. 'One day we might . . . some of us might feel like living in Melbourne.'

'Like, if Mavis chucks a killing, eating fit,' Vinnie says. They stare at him, like, don't you dare even think that.

'I don't think she will. She's stir-crazy, that's all. I was too when I first came home. Didn't know who I was, what I was supposed to be.' Eddy shrugs. 'I found out, and if she doesn't, then we've got a place to go – if we don't sell the house.'

'All of us? All of us would go to live there?' Jamesy asks. He wouldn't mind leaving on the morning bus.

'You mean you'd give up on her,' Alan asks, 'just like that?'

'If she starts stuffing again,' Jamesy says.

'She won't,' Alan says. 'Her eyes look different. She'll be better tomorrow. We won't take any more meals in so she'll have to come out and – '

'Mmm,' Jamesy says, just like the social worker says 'mmm' when she doesn't yet believe, but doesn't want to not believe either.

Adrenalin is flooding them, flooding the room. They don't know where they're going, but they're all going somewhere, and they'll all go together, because they are a family. They're heading into something over the horizon, but they're not ready for it yet. Maybe in a year they'll be ready. Maybe it has to grow on them. This last year has been crazy stuff and they've all grown so fast. Growing up is better when it's done slow.

But there is a future out there for them now, even if they can't quite see it. It's out there and they know it and it's something bigger than they have ever known before, and it's something far, far better than they have ever dreamed of.

It's the *more*! It's Henry's *more*!

Lori hasn't said a word. She's thinking of the feel of that hair, and the smell of it, and being close to Mavis. She's thinking of that black dress in Kmart and the nine and a half shoes. And she's thinking of the sandals the op shop lady brought that night in her box. They are too big for Lori. Maybe they'll do Mavis until tomorrow.

Tomorrow.

She's looking at the photograph on the wall and thinking, tomorrow. Now, just maybe it was the way the late afternoon light caught the glass of Henry's photograph, but she knows it wasn't, because she saw Henry sort of turn his head, smile right at her.

'Good girl,' he said in her head. He did.

She gets tears in her eyes as she stands looking hard at the photograph, trying to make it do it again. It doesn't, but she knows he's come home to her. He's here. He's in this kitchen. He's in all of them. Not a lot of root, but a whole heap of healthy cabbage.

She walks to the stove and opens the firebox, prods in wood, giving her eyes an excuse to water. The smoke rushes out, and for a moment she is wrapped in a cocoon of smoke and late sunlight.

She is fourteen and three months and she's got a bit of an ache in her tummy – it's a sort of weighty ache. Different. Probably women's business – and it's probably about time. Maybe fate was waiting until she had a mother – not that Lori hasn't known all about that women's stuff since she was six years old.

'So what?' she says and she wipes at her eyes. 'So what?'

The brothers look at her, don't understand.

A pretty girl, their sister. They know that she made them a family, kept them a family. She is of them, but not one of them, female, unknown, but well known.

She is the air of this room, the life of this room. She is in all of the odours of the room. She is in the woodsmoke and in the onions Jamesy is cutting up to toss into the stew. She is everywhere.

She is woman, Henry's daughter, who makes the world for them a not too bad place.